"Have a taste," Sandy said.

Ethan opened his mouth and she eased the spoon inside. As the batter melted against his tongue, she lifted her other hand and rested it against his cheek. With the pad of her thumb, she swept away a bit of the batter from the corner of his mouth, then teased that thumb gently across his lower lip. And that was when the truth hit him.

Good God. She's seducing you.

That thought triggered an all-out, full-blown, brain-zapping sensation that rattled every nerve in his body. He could spot a woman coming on to him from across a crowded room, and he hadn't spotted this?

She swallowed hard, then parted her lips slightly, her breath coming faster. Women had stripped naked in front of him and it hadn't given him one-tenth the reaction he was having now.

"At what point did this stop being about the cake?" he asked.

She looked at him without blinking. "It never was about the cake."

By Jane Graves
Published by Ivy Books

I GOT YOU, BABE
WILD AT HEART
FLIRTING WITH DISASTER

Light my Fire

Jane Graves

BALLANTINE BOOKS • NEW YORK

An Ivy Book
Published by The Random House Publishing Group

Copyright © 2004 by Jane Graves

www.ballantinebooks.com

ISBN 0-345-45841-9

Manufactured in the United States of America

First Edition: November 2004

OPM 9 8 7 6 5 4 3 2 1

acknowledgments

Thanks to Jason Jacoby for his delightfully devious mind and his brilliant brainstorming, to Charlotte Herscher for her insight into the heart of this book, and to my husband, Brian, and daughter, Charlotte, for being the incredibly supportive family every writer ought to have.

chapter one

Ethan Millner hit the gas and sped his Porsche past the last traffic light in Tolosa, Texas, leaving the city behind. He raced down the deserted two-lane highway, accelerating until he'd blown past the fifty-mile-an-hour speed limit and was heading for sixty.

The faster he went, the faster he wanted to go.

Even though the sun had long since disappeared behind the towering pine trees that lined the road, still the choking heat of the Texas summer made it hard to catch a breath without searing a lung. Any sane man would have put up the top on the convertible and flicked on the air-conditioning, but Ethan didn't want comfort right now. The landscape whizzing past him like a video on fast-forward suited his state of mind.

The blonde in the seat beside him ran her fingertips along the polished walnut of the passenger door, then turned to him with a satisfied smile. "Great car, baby. I do *love* convertibles."

The scorching night air licked around the edges of the windshield, whisking the woman's hair into a wild frenzy. She wore a too-tight dress, too much makeup, and an erotic, heavy-lidded expression that said she was ready to get horizontal as soon as he said the word. Ten minutes ago, as they were leaving Bernie's Bar and Grille, he thought he remembered her saying her name was Sheila.

Almost immediately after the Randall verdict had been read, Ethan had left the courthouse, gone directly to Bernie's, and ordered a scotch straight up. He'd downed it in a few gulps and ordered another one. Then he'd sat back to let the anesthesia take effect as he watched the Rangers game on the television above the bar.

Halfway through scotch number two, he'd answered a congratulatory cell call from his father, the one he always received whenever word got around to the old bastard that his son had put another check mark in the "win" column for Millner, Millner, Monroe, and Dade. Sometimes Ethan preferred the near-lethal dose of silence he got on the rare occasion when he lost.

During the third inning, the blonde slid onto the stool next to him. He knew within seconds what kind of woman she was, and that was fine by him. He was long past messing with young law clerks who gave him million-dollar smiles paid for by their rich daddies. Women with kids to support who had desperation in their eyes and his money on their minds. Forty-somethings who'd gotten dumped by husbands with midlife crises that only twenty-somethings could resolve. Every one of them was drowning in her own sea of problems that sooner or later became his problems.

No more.

At this point in his life, only one kind of woman interested him—the kind who was beyond flowers and promises, who could be bought for a drink or two and a spin in his Porsche, who lit a cigarette after sex and reached for the remote to catch the last of *The Tonight Show* as he made his way out the door.

The woman swiped her windblown hair out of her face and gave Ethan a big smile. "You told me you wanted to do a little celebrating tonight. So what exactly is it we're gonna be celebrating?"

He stared at the road ahead. "Winning."

"Oh, yeah? Tell me I picked the right man and you're talking about the Texas state lottery."

"I'm a lawyer. Just won a case."

"So tell me about it."

"Not much to tell. I won. Saved my client from a prison sentence. That's all that matters."

"That's funny. I thought justice was all that mattered."

"Justice?" Ethan gave her a sly smile. "Interesting concept. Please tell me you're not going to sing 'God Bless America.' "

The woman laughed. Even as Ethan smiled right along with her, his hand tightened against the gearshift. Justice? He wasn't sure he even remembered the meaning of the word. He'd simply done his job as he always did, with a competency that made his clients thank God for the day they'd coughed up the extraordinary amount of money it took to retain his services. Ethan had been taught from his first breath what mattered in this game, and if money was a way of keeping score, he was clearly winning.

The woman leaned across the console and stroked her hand along his thigh. "Well, now. If I ever get into trouble with the law, it looks like you're the man I need to call."

"Sorry, sweetheart. You couldn't afford me."

"Oh, yeah? I'd say that'd depend on what you'd take instead of cash, now, wouldn't it?" She inched her palm higher. "Maybe tonight I could give you a little advance payment against future services. How does that sound?"

The woman started talking trash to him, promising him sexual gymnastics guaranteed to take him straight to heaven. Ethan pictured himself peeling away her skimpy dress, stretching her out on a king-size bed, and sinking inside her to the hilt, letting her body take his mind to another place.

But no matter how much he tried to concentrate on her preview of coming attractions, her voice began to annoy him, like the drone of an insect he couldn't swat away. In spite of the freedom of the road, the wind thrashing past, and the prospect of breathless sex with a woman who undoubtedly knew her way around a man's body, he felt tense and confined.

He rubbed the back of his neck. It was slick with sweat.

Maybe the heat really was irritating him. August in Texas could be a real bitch, particularly when they were into their third week of hundred-degree heat with no end in sight. Or maybe it was the fact that the two scotches he'd tossed back hadn't even begun to blur his senses. Or maybe it was the stranger in the seat next to him, a woman whose name he wouldn't even remember in the morning.

Or maybe it was Thomas Randall.

A big shot at Bryan Industries, Randall had been accused of raping a young Mexican woman after hours who worked there as a cleaning woman. He said it was consensual; she said no way. Because the prosecution had little else, the he-said/she-said testimony had worked in Randall's favor. It had been a slam dunk for Ethan to convince the jury that a man of his stature couldn't possibly have committed an act of rape.

Of course, the fact that Ethan had rummaged through the woman's background and unearthed a significant number of sex partners hadn't hurt things, either. He'd danced around the rape shield laws with a creative interpretation of the Sixth Amendment, then hammered the plaintiff about those liaisons in excruciating detail, making her look more promiscuous than a two-bit hooker. The expressions on the faces of the jury members as they left for deliberation told Ethan he'd hit a home run and the verdict wouldn't be long in coming.

Will the defendant please rise.

Randall had stood up and calmly folded his hands in front of him, wearing an eighty-dollar haircut and a thousand-dollar suit, keeping that poker face he'd honed during all those years as executive vice president of a multinational corporation. Ethan stood beside him, his own ability to keep a poker face stemming from something else entirely: He'd been there hundreds of times before.

In the matter of The State versus Thomas Randall . . .

Out of the corner of his eye, Ethan saw Randall's chest expand as he drew a deep, silent breath.

We, the jury, find the defendant . . .

And then came the pause. Always the pause. Jurors watched too much television and had an overstated sense of the dramatic.

Not guilty.

Randall faltered slightly, that momentary weak-kneed reaction that befell even the strongest man when he got the news that he'd escaped doing twenty years in Huntsville. Then he smiled broadly and hugged his wife, who was dressed as if she'd cut her Junior League meeting short to drop by the courthouse for the verdict.

On the other side of the aisle sat the plaintiff, a fragile-looking woman wearing an ill-fitting rummage sale dress. She began to sob, and Randall turned to look at her. When she stared back at him with a teary-eyed expression of utter despair, his victory smile faded. He swallowed hard and looked away. Body language didn't lie.

Defendants did, though. All the time.

"So was your client really innocent?" the woman asked.

"Innocent?" Ethan said. "Of course he was. They all are."

"All of them?"

"Sure. Just ask them. They'll tell you."

The woman laughed again, but it sounded hollow and unnatural. Dusk had transformed the pine trees along the road into huge, hulking shadows, and as Ethan pressed the accelerator down a few more millimeters, he felt as if he were speeding through a black hole.

The woman's expression wavered. "Hey, you're going a little fast, aren't you?"

Her words seemed muffled and distant, like a radio station he couldn't quite tune in. He took another curve, the Porsche's tires squealing in an attempt to maintain their traction against the blacktop. For a split second Ethan imagined what would happen if he touched the accelerator a little harder and that traction disappeared. Knowing his reputation with the Tolosa PD, when the cops pulled his mangled body from the wreckage, the only thing they'd be lamenting would be the loss of a sixty-thousand-dollar sports car.

"Hey, baby," the woman said, her voice shaky. "It's time to slow down now."

Ethan tightened his fist around the steering wheel, the leather hot beneath his hand. He pictured Randall doing a little celebrating of his own tonight. Friends and family surrounding him, glasses clinking, backslapping all around. He pictured the young Mexican woman, crying herself to sleep, then looking over her shoulder for the rest of her life.

Then, like a monster creeping to just within his line of sight, Ethan caught a glimpse of himself, a bleak mirror image of something he'd never intended to become.

"What the hell are you doing?" the woman shouted, clinging to the armrest. "For God's sake, slow *down!*"

He hit the gas harder, his heart pounding, his mouth dry.

The woman gasped. "Look out!"

Ethan blinked, suddenly aware that a pickup truck had lumbered onto the highway from an intersecting gravel road. He slammed his foot down on the brake and swerved hard to the right, but still he clipped the rear bumper of the truck. The impact sent his Porsche sliding sideways, its tires striking a sheet of sand and loose rocks on the shoulder of the highway. The car skated along, turning ninety degrees before leaving the shoulder entirely, bumping down a low incline and smacking into a pine tree. The impact slung Ethan sideways, the seat belt biting into his neck and shoulder.

Then, silence.

For several bewildering seconds, the only sounds Ethan heard were the heavy chirping of crickets, the woman's labored breathing, and his own pulse hammering in his ears. With a muffled moan, the woman dipped her head and rubbed the back of her neck. When she looked up again, her voice shattered the silence.

"Are you out of your *mind?*"

He recoiled. "I-I'm sorry . . . I didn't see . . ."

"Didn't see? Hell, no, you didn't see! You were going *ninety fucking miles an hour!*"

She ripped off her seat belt and climbed out of the car. Staggering a little, she pushed her hair out of her face with a defiant swipe of her hand, then climbed the low incline and stormed down the road.

Ethan glanced at the truck he'd hit. A young man stepped out wearing a western shirt, Wranglers, and a baseball cap, walking with the reeling gait of a man who'd come within a few feet of being T-boned at ninety miles an hour. Ethan gripped the steering wheel, his breath coming in shallow spurts, feeling as if he were moving through a dream.

Then he saw the red lights.

A black-and-white unit came to a halt on the shoulder of the road, its headlights slicing through the darkness. An officer stepped out. As the woman approached him, Ethan could hear her shouting: "Driving like a maniac . . . wouldn't slow down . . . just about killed everybody . . . "

Every accusation reverberated inside his head like the smash of a hammer through glass. He held up his hands. They were shaking.

What the hell had he just done?

When he saw a flashlight beam moving in his direction, he knew the officer was approaching his car. Ethan made his living talking his way out of situations that the average attorney wouldn't even have attempted.

But he wasn't going to be able to talk his way out of this.

* * *

"Mr. Millner. I see you escaped a DUI charge by the slimmest of margins. How very fortunate for you."

As Judge William Davis flipped through the records presented to him by the bailiff, Ethan stood before him, awaiting the disposition of his case. Davis was a judge with twenty-some years on the bench and possessed every bit of the smug bearing that generally accompanied that tenure, and right now he was pouring as much of that attitude onto Ethan as he possibly could.

As he had with most of the judges in the city of Tolosa, Ethan had clashed with Davis in the courtroom more than once. Davis didn't like it when an attorney with a talent for creative defense made the prosecution look incompetent, and in the cases Ethan defended that happened more often than not.

Ethan maintained a deferential expression, but inside he was smiling. This wasn't going to be nearly the legal problem he'd anticipated that night. As luck would have it, he'd sailed through the roadside sobriety tests, and on the Breathalyzer exam he'd squeaked in beneath the legal intoxication limit. Much to the dismay of the arresting officer, Ethan had emerged from the experience with nothing more than a reckless-driving charge.

"You realize, Mr. Millner," the judge went on, "that if not for some extremely fortunate timing on that state highway that night, we could be discussing a manslaughter charge instead of a misdemeanor."

A miss is as good as a mile.

"Yes, sir. I was traveling far too fast and failed to observe the intersection to the degree I should have."

"That's stating it mildly."

That's stating it factually.

"I'm requesting deferred adjudication," Ethan said. "I'll

pay the two-hundred-dollar fine and take a defensive-driving class."

The judge raised one of his excessively bushy eyebrows. "Oh, you will, will you?"

Ethan held his expression steady. No matter how much Davis was throwing his weight around, there was a limit to the sentence a judge could impose in a case like this, so Ethan knew he had the upper hand.

"Actually," Davis said, "deferred adjudication is the general course of action in a case like this, and that's exactly what you're going to get. Only it's not going to be in the form of probation and a defensive-driving class."

Ethan felt a twinge of foreboding. What else could he possibly—

"I'm sentencing you to forty hours of community service."

Ethan felt as if the judge had shot him. Community service? *Good God.* He'd rather pay ten thousand dollars than mess with something like that.

"I see," he said, fighting to maintain an even expression. "And from which roadway will I be picking up trash?"

"No, Mr. Millner, that would be way too easy for you. Physical activity? You can get that by going to the gym and pumping iron. What I have in mind is something considerably more involved."

"Such as?"

"Crime prevention."

"What?"

"Forty hours of community service on a neighborhood crime-watch patrol."

"What?"

"You heard me. You get into a vehicle and scour a neighborhood for suspicious activity. It's a very worthwhile pursuit." He sat back, an expression of extreme satisfaction on his face. "And I know just the person who can administer your sentence."

Ethan gave him a wary look.

"Sandy DeMarco. Perhaps you've heard the name?"

At the mere mention of the name DeMarco, Ethan's brain went on red alert. Hell, *yes,* he'd heard the name.

He'd never met Sandy DeMarco personally and wouldn't know her if he saw her. But he did know two very important facts about her: She was chairman of the Tolosa Crime-watch Council, and she came from a family full of cops who'd just as soon spit on him as look at him. The chances of her never having been subjected to her three brothers' opinions of him were exactly zero.

"There may be a conflict with that," Ethan said. "Her brother was the investigator on a rape case I just won."

The judge raised his eyebrows with mock surprise. "Oh, was he really?"

Asshole.

"I'm afraid I don't have the time—"

"Make the time."

"Forty hours seems excessive for a first offense."

"You're lucky I'm not making it a hundred and forty."

"For anyone but me, you'd be making it twenty."

Judge Davis rose slowly, skewering Ethan with a fierce glare. "My chambers, Mr. Millner."

Davis stepped down from the bench and disappeared behind a heavy oak door. Ethan had no choice but to follow, feeling like a bad boy being summoned to the principal's office.

Which was precisely what Davis intended.

Ethan entered the judge's chambers and closed the door behind him. Davis settled into his brass-studded leather chair, giving Ethan a stony stare. Ethan stood in front of his desk, meeting that stare with one of his own.

"Do you frequently summon defendants to your chambers?" he asked.

"I have a few things to say to you that neither you nor I

would want the rest of that courtroom to hear. Shall I continue?"

Ethan was silent.

"I've been watching you for a long time now, Millner. In all my years on the bench, I've never seen anyone like you. You bend the law, you skew the law, you twist the law, you tie the law into a goddamned pretzel so it's not even recognizable as the law anymore. Just about every time you go to court, one more scumbag ends up walking the street who should be behind bars. And you know what? I don't like that. And now that I have the opportunity to force you to take a look at the other side, that's exactly what I'm going to do."

Ethan had to practically bite his tongue bloody to keep from lashing out. He did his job, and he did it well. *That* was what was eating this guy.

"Perhaps it's time for me to request a jury trial," Ethan said. "That's my prerogative."

"Yeah, Millner, it is. You can walk out of here and right into a courtroom in a few weeks if you want to. I can't stop you." The judge glared at him. "But let me warn you that I have a very long memory, and you *will* be trying cases in my courtroom again."

"Forgive me for saying so, Your Honor, but that sounds suspiciously like a threat."

"I don't give a shit what it sounds like. Take the deal or pay the price for it."

Ethan had a hundred other things he wished he could say on the subject, but experience told him it wasn't wise to utter a single word, no matter how irritated he was. The judge was within his rights to impose community service, and in spite of the fact that Ethan had threatened a jury trial to get himself off the hook completely, he knew what he had a chance of defending and what he didn't. The woman who'd been in the car with him would be the prosecution's star witness.

He gritted his teeth and relented. They stepped back into

the courtroom and made it official, and Ethan left the court-house knowing that before the day was out, news of Davis's creative sentencing would undoubtedly make its way around the entire criminal justice system of Tolosa, Texas. He could already hear the laughter, and there wasn't a thing he could do about it.

He thought about what lay ahead—long, unbearable stretches of time in a car driving in circles. He'd rather take a beating with a hot poker. And with Sandy DeMarco, of all people. What an excruciating experience that was likely to be.

If she was anywhere near as pushy and overbearing as her brothers, he was in for one hell of a forty hours.

chapter two

Weddings sucked.

As a florist, Sandy DeMarco hadn't reached that conclusion lightly. But after dealing with the wedding from hell all afternoon and growing progressively more frustrated, she found herself thinking how nice it would be if people just did away with all the fanfare and headed straight to the justice of the peace, where a bouquet of silk flowers was all a girl really needed.

Okay, so she didn't really hate weddings. What she hated was being the florist of choice for an out-of-control bride who changed her mind like she changed her shoes and went berserk when things didn't go her way. Bridezilla had called Sandy's shop at least three times that day to turn molehills into mountains, and Sandy had just about reached the end of her rope.

But through it all, she kept reminding herself that her customers were always right, even the demanding, unreasonable ones. Fortunately, Josh was on his way to deliver the last of the flowers to the First Methodist Church, which meant that the wedding would soon be over and she'd never have to deal with the woman again.

With a sigh of relief, Sandy grabbed the bouquet of flowers she was taking home. She turned out the lights in her shop and headed for the back door.

Then the phone rang.

She hurried back. One glance at the caller ID told her that the wedding from hell might not be over with after all.

She yanked up the phone. "Josh? Please tell me we don't have another problem."

Sandy heard the muffled, disjointed sound of an organist warming up in the background, punctuated by a sigh of frustration. "She's freaking out again."

Sandy slumped with disbelief. "What is it now?"

"I delivered the bouquets, but she swears they're supposed to have that baby's breath stuff in them."

Wrong. Sandy distinctly remembered the order. No baby's breath. She shoved a strand of hair out of her face and blew out a weary breath. The wedding was at seven thirty. She checked her watch. Six thirty. The church was only five minutes away. There was time to fix the bouquets. Barely.

"Josh, I know it's getting late, but would you mind bringing them back here so I can add the baby's breath?"

"No problem."

"You'll have to hurry."

"I'm on my way."

Sandy hung up the phone, checking her watch again. She really needed to get home. If only Lyle and Imogene hadn't already left for the day, she could have asked one of them to stay. Now she was stuck.

A few minutes later, Josh came through the back door carrying a box containing the bouquets. Sandy spread them out on the counter and started inserting the baby's breath.

"I'm sorry you're having to stay," Sandy said. "Be sure to put these overtime hours on your time sheet."

"It's no big deal."

"It's late. You're entitled."

Josh grabbed a Coke from the fridge. "I just hope this satisfies her. She's a real maniac."

"You just have to use your imagination with customers like her."

"Yeah? How's that?"

"In your mind, just replace her with a truly nice young woman who happens to flip out under pressure. Ninety-nine percent sweet, one percent sour."

"It's the other way around," Josh muttered.

Sandy smiled. "Now, didn't I say you had to use your imagination?"

"Mine's not that big."

"Sure it is. You're good with my customers, Josh. Even the difficult ones. A lot of them have commented on how polite you are. That helps my business, and I appreciate it."

Josh looked away without responding. She tried to give him compliments as often as he deserved it, which was more frequently all the time, but he still didn't take them well. For a boy who'd spent most of his life without receiving any, that was understandable. But now, maybe for the first time in his life, he was heading in the right direction.

Not that it had been easy.

Sandy knew in the beginning that Josh had felt uncomfortable in the midst of flowers and ribbons and balloons and all the occasions that went along with them. Most seventeen-year-old boys would have, particularly those who showed up for interviews with excessive piercings, ragged jeans, horrific concert T-shirts, and just as much bad attitude as they dared show.

Sandy had laid down the law. Rings in ears were fine. Rings in noses and brows weren't. Jeans were okay, but they had to be intact and pulled up to the vicinity of his waist, and he had to wear a shirt with the shop logo. And if he didn't check his bad attitude at the door, he'd never pass through it again.

She'd shocked him with those pronouncements, and the first few weeks had been tenuous for both of them. But now, six months later, in spite of days like today, he'd settled into the job and seemed to truly enjoy it. And Sandy truly enjoyed having him around.

"Okay, Josh," Sandy said, putting the last bouquet into the box. "That's it. Call me if there are any more problems, okay?"

He tossed his empty Coke can in the trash, picked up the box, and headed for the door. "I wonder if the poor guy she's marrying knows what he's getting himself into."

"Probably not. Love is blind, you know."

"Maybe," he muttered as he opened the door, "but it's not deaf and dumb, too."

Sandy smiled. "Thanks for staying tonight to take care of this."

"It was no big deal."

Josh started to pull the door closed, then stopped and turned back, suddenly looking a little uncomfortable.

"Sandy?"

"Yes?"

He opened his mouth to speak, then closed it again. And still he stood there.

"Josh? Is something wrong?"

"No. It's just that I've been here too long not to have said this already." He exhaled. "I just wanted to thank you. You know. For giving me this job. My probation officer had just about given up on me. But you never did."

Sandy felt tears come to her eyes. "You've thanked me already just by doing a good job."

"No. I needed to say it." He nodded down at the bouquets in the box he held. "I'd better go."

He pulled the door closed behind him, and silence filled the shop again.

Sandy stood there for a moment, feeling a surge of pleasure. Everybody had told her she was crazy to hire a kid with a record, but he'd never given her a single reason to regret that decision. Giving him a second chance had been good for him, good for society, and good for her. Nothing made her feel better than expecting the best from people and having them live up to it.

It was after seven o'clock by the time she cleaned off the counter again and grabbed the bouquet she was taking home. She left the shop, and after a quick run to pick up some groceries, she hurried home to put them away. As she was shoving fruits and veggies into her fridge, Oscar galloped into the kitchen and wrapped himself around her ankles, meowing for his dinner. She fed him, then paused to take a deep breath and check the time. It had been one hell of a day, all right. But it wasn't over yet.

Ethan Millner would be here any minute.

Her heart quickened a little at the thought of that, but she told herself it was nothing but a knee-jerk reaction to all the stories she'd heard about him over the years. Judge Davis had asked her for a favor, so of course she'd said yes. After all, everything her brothers had told her about Millner couldn't possibly be true. Nobody could be as heartless as they said he was. As insensitive. As ruthless.

But either way, it didn't matter. She'd agreed to oversee his restitution, so even if he turned out to be the devil himself, she intended to fulfill that obligation.

She grabbed a vase, then reached for the flowers she'd brought home from the shop. As she was filling the vase with water, the phone rang. She answered it without checking the caller ID. When she heard her brother's voice, she realized what a mistake that had been.

"Sandy? It's Alex."

Oh, Lord. Here we go again.

Dave and John had already called, so apparently now it was Alex's turn. And if she didn't shut him down right away, she was going to have to listen to the same song, third verse.

"To answer your questions, Alex, yes, Judge Davis asked me to administer Ethan Millner's community service. Yes, I agreed to do it. Yes, he's doing his first two hours tonight. And no, I am *not* out of my mind."

"Look, I know John and Dave have already talked to you, but—"

"They phoned hours ago. You're falling behind."

"I was in court most of the day. Listen to me, Sandy. You don't know what that guy is like."

"I don't?" Sandy laughed in disbelief. "As if I haven't heard the three of you talk nonstop for the past umpteen years about what Ethan Millner has done to pervert the legal justice system? What you'd like to do to him for perverting the legal justice system? In excruciating detail?"

"And every bit of it is true. Do you know he put a rapist back out on the street the other day?"

Sandy tucked the phone between her ear and her shoulder as she cut the stems of the flowers. "What are you talking about?"

"The Thomas Randall case. That guy was guilty as sin. He's walking free today because that bastard Millner got him off."

"Maybe he was innocent."

"Innocent, my ass. I investigated that case. I know he was guilty."

"So why couldn't you nail him?"

"Because Millner dredged up background on the victim that made her sound like the cheapest whore ever to walk the street. When she took the stand, he ripped her to shreds. *That's* the guy you've agreed to spend forty hours with."

"Come on, Alex. You act as if he's going to turn me to the dark side just by walking through the door."

"I wouldn't put anything past him."

"You might as well get off it. I've already told Judge Davis I'll do this, and I have no intention of backing out now."

Alex spit out a breath of disgust. "Okay. Fine. But whatever you do, don't get into a car with him unless you're behind the wheel. He damned near killed two people to get that reckless-driving charge."

"Don't worry, Alex. We'll be taking my car."

"And he's cocky as hell. He thinks he's God's gift to women, so make sure you keep your distance from him. I've talked to women who went out with him who swear he has four hands."

"No problem. I have two knees."

"Which are hard to use while you're driving."

"Okay, Alex. How about if I stick some pepper spray under the seat, a Glock in the glove compartment, and have my cell phone ready to dial nine-one-one. Will that make you happy?"

For a moment, there was silence on the line.

"Hell, Sandy," Alex said finally. "Maybe I ought to be warning Millner about you."

Damned right.

Her three brothers always seemed to forget that she'd practically raised them after the death of their mother twenty-three years ago. Even though she'd been only fourteen at the time, she'd filled in that gap in her younger brothers' lives as best she could, and she was crazy about all of them. They'd grown into three big, tough, overprotective, occasionally unreasonable, but always good and loving men, and she liked thinking that maybe she'd had at least a little bit to do with that.

"Thanks for worrying, Alex. I really do appreciate it. But you guys need to shut up about this, okay? Millner can't possibly have three fire-breathing heads."

Just then her doorbell rang.

"He's here," Sandy said. "I've got to go."

"Sandy, wait—"

Over Alex's protests, she clicked the phone off and returned it to its cradle. She figured she'd better answer the door in a hurry or, according to her brothers, the big, bad wolf just might blow her house down.

She went to the entry and opened the door. She froze with astonishment. In spite of her belief that he couldn't be as bad as her brothers had told her, still she'd pictured a man with at least an edge of repulsiveness.

Nothing could have been further from the truth.

He was handsome in the most classic sense, with the kind of face that would stop any woman from eighteen to eighty dead in her tracks. His thick, dark hair just brushed his collar in the back, a tiny step outside the box of conservatism most attorneys lived in. He wore a pair of casual pants and a polo shirt, both fitting his tall, athletic body as if tailor-made specifically for him. And they probably were. He possessed the understated elegance of a man raised with money who was completely comfortable with it.

Sharp. Striking. Sophisticated.

But instantly Sandy sensed something more. Vigilant, penetrating eyes. A chin lifted a millimeter beyond the average man's. A raw sensuality he seemed to exude with every breath. He was the kind of man who made women reach up to smooth their hair or down to straighten their clothes. To keep from doing either of those things, Sandy kept one hand on the doorknob and the other firmly at her side.

"Sandy DeMarco?"

He said her name in a voice as smooth as fifty-year-old scotch and just as intoxicating. Words spoken in that voice could easily sway a jury to his point of view, particularly if that jury were composed predominantly of women.

"Yes. You must be Ethan Millner. I'm running late. Would you mind coming inside for a minute?"

She stepped back and opened the door wide. He strode into the entry, then stopped and glanced around her house as if recording every nuance of her environment and filing it away. For what, she didn't know. But she did know that for all her brothers had told her about him, they were selling him short. His manner went beyond cockiness or arrogance. Instead, he moved with the smooth, seductive grace of a man who *was* the best, not just a man who professed to be.

Sandy went back to her kitchen. He followed her, watching as she clipped the rest of the stems and put them in the vase.

"Unusual flowers," he said.

"They're birds-of-paradise. My favorite. I brought them home from work."

"Work?"

"I own a flower shop."

Without turning his head, he flicked his gaze toward the flowers, then back to her. "Interesting."

"The flowers or the flower shop?"

"Both."

Something about that single word, combined with his blatantly appraising stare, made her feel stark naked.

"So how about you?" she asked, tucking an errant bloom back into place. "What's your favorite flower?"

"I'm not that fond of flowers."

Sandy recoiled. "Oh, come on. Roses, at least. Everybody likes roses."

"Nope. Too sentimental."

"Daisies?"

"Too cheerful."

"Orchids?"

"Too fragile."

Sandy raised an eyebrow. "How about snapdragons?"

His mouth turned up in a faint smile. "I stand corrected."

In that moment, Sandy knew he was completely aware of his reputation and had no interest in defending it. But it still didn't tell her if that reputation bore any resemblance to reality or not—only that he didn't waste a whole lot of time and energy trying to convince people that it didn't.

"So it appears that being chairman of the Tolosa Crime-watch Council isn't all you do," Ethan asked.

"No. That's a volunteer effort. I make my living as a florist."

He followed her back to the front door, where she grabbed her keys and her purse from the entry table. "Shall we go?"

"Yes. Unless I have a choice about this that I'm not aware of."

"Choice? No, according to Judge Davis, I don't believe you have one of those. But don't think of this as punishment. Think of it as education."

"Education?"

"What do you know about crime-watch patrol?"

"I know that a lot of people think it's very effective."

"You don't?"

"Might stop a kid from setting off firecrackers in a mail-box. But it won't stop a pro from cleaning out a house in under five minutes."

"Oh, yeah?" Sandy said. "How do you know that?"

"Because the pros are some of my best clients."

"You sound proud of that."

"Every person accused of a crime is entitled to a defense."

"Well. I can't very well argue with that, now, can I?"

"Sure you can," Ethan said. "I love a good debate."

"A debate? Now, you know I wouldn't stand a chance against you. Not with you being a high-powered attorney and all."

"Don't worry. I'll be gentle." A tiny smile crossed his lips. "I might even let you win. Either way, I think we'd both enjoy the experience."

A warm flush of sexual awareness took Sandy by surprise, and she fought to keep her face impassive. This man clearly excelled at verbal gymnastics. She had a feeling he excelled at a few other things, too.

And why was her mind even going there?

Because it had been ages since she'd felt that warm flush.

This man seemed about as straightforward as a winding mountain road, and that should have irritated her. Instead, she pictured a few breathtaking vistas along that road, with a surprise around every corner, and that warm flush coalesced into a hot little tremor that started somewhere around her breastbone and slid down to her stomach.

Then lower.

"Judge Davis is a fool, you know," Ethan said.

At that comment coming out of nowhere, Sandy looked at him with surprise. "A fool? Now why would you say that?"

"Because somehow he's gotten the idea that forcing me to spend forty hours alone in a car with a beautiful woman is punishment. What the hell was he thinking?"

Lobbing her a compliment was the last thing Sandy had expected him to do, and that hot little tremor escalated to the point that a few Richter scales had to be picking it up. But self-awareness was something she prided herself on, so she didn't bask in the sunlight of his sweet talk for long. She was wearing a pair of jeans and a T-shirt, with her hair in a ponytail and not a smidgen of makeup. Size eight had departed about ten years ago, leaving her firmly in double digits, yet he'd tossed her a compliment as if she were one of the woman he undoubtedly dated—the kind who turned sideways and disappeared.

"Now, Ethan," she said, "with all that phony flattery coming my way, how am I supposed to concentrate on crime-watch patrol?"

He raised his eyebrows with surprise. "Forty hours? Beautiful woman? Where am I not speaking the truth?"

"From what I've heard, truth is something you're not particularly interested in pursuing."

"Ah. It appears you've been talking to your brothers."

"A time or two."

"Maybe they're mistaken about me. Don't tell me you're one of those people who believes everything she hears."

"No. Unfortunately, I'm cursed with an open mind. Forces me to form my own opinions." She sighed dramatically. "It's so much easier just to jump to conclusions."

Okay, now that was a lie. The truth was that she'd already jumped to quite a few conclusions where this man was concerned, but not one of them had anything to do with his morals or ethics. It amazed her sometimes just how incredibly dense her brothers could be. Ethan Millner might be every bit as dangerous as Alex had suggested—the jury was still out on that—but sleazy he wasn't. She couldn't help but wonder if those women who swore he had four hands were protesting too much.

And this was the man whom she had agreed to spend forty hours with in her car. Driving around in the dark. Sitting so close to him that she'd probably be able to hear every breath he took.

No doubt about it. Doing her part to oversee a wayward man's community service had just become far more interesting than she'd ever anticipated.

chapter three

Ethan sure as hell hadn't counted on this.

Sandy's brothers were big, brawny, hardheaded men, so he'd expected their sister to be a little rough around the edges. Instead he'd been greeted by a tall woman with sleek, dark hair, curves where they counted, and the face of an angel. There were two kinds of women in this world: those who were beautiful because they worked at it, and those who shone from the inside out.

Sandy DeMarco shone like a full moon on a clear night.

Not that she was his type. She was too wholesome for his taste, with home and hearth oozing right out of her. Her house was distinctly feminine, with overstuffed sofas, fluffy rugs, cutesy artwork, and the smell of flowers in the air. Any woman who lived in a house like hers expected candlelight, soft music, and the whisper of sweet nothings, with a heavy dose of commitment to go along with the romance. Definitely not his type.

The only thing that made him think twice was *contrast*.

She was head of the Tolosa Crime-watch Council, yet she was a florist by profession. There was a gentle grace about her that suggested a certain naïveté, yet her quick wit kept pace with his at every turn. She lived in that ultratraditional house on Magnolia Street, yet her favorite flower was something so bright and bizarre it would stop an Amazon explorer dead in his tracks.

Contrast.

When he saw that in a professional capacity, it was a warning to stay on his toes. When he saw it in a woman, it drew his attention like nothing else. And clearly she was a woman who wasn't swayed by flattery—no matter how much truth there was at the heart of it—which meant she was sharp and intelligent and self-respecting. He liked that.

He liked it a lot.

The sun was easing toward the horizon as they cruised along Mimosa Lane, which to Ethan's surprise was actually lined with a significant number of mimosa trees. If the residents of this neighborhood took their street signs this literally, he could only imagine what Bonsai Road or Redwood Avenue would look like.

"This is a unique neighborhood," Sandy told him. "We have big lots ranging from half an acre to two or three acres. Houses set back off the street. A creek splits the neighborhood down the middle, with bridges so it can be crossed on foot. It's a beautiful place to live, but a crime-prevention nightmare. There's just too much space between the houses for neighbors to watch out for each other the way they should. That's why we need the crime-watch patrol."

Ethan couldn't help wondering why anyone would want to live in houses like these in the first place. Every one of them was at least eighty years old, with smaller prairie-style houses interspersed among bigger Victorian-era homes. They all had sprawling front porches. Multitudes of windows. Cheery little trim colors. And undoubtedly every one of them was full of creaks and groans and drafty as hell in the winter.

"Rail fences," he said. "That's unusual."

"A lot of people used to keep horses on their property," she went on. "You'll even still see a barn here or there. But now there's an ordinance against livestock."

Ethan thought about his town house. Sleek and functional, with eight feet of cedar fence around the small lawn between him and his neighbors. Throw in a groundskeeper and a twice-a-week maid, and his upkeep was minimal. *That* was the way to live.

Then a house came into sight that surprised him. It was a big, modern two-story with a brick façade, energy-efficient windows, brass fixtures, and young landscaping.

"What's with that house?" he asked.

An expression of distaste came over Sandy's face. "Actually, there are several houses like that in the neighborhood. The lots here are really big, and that attracts new-home builders. They buy an older, smaller house for the lot value, tear it down, and put up one of those."

"You sound disgusted by that."

"I love the character of this neighborhood. That's why I moved here three years ago. Building houses like that one screws it up. But they offer so much money for the houses that a lot of people sell out."

"But not you."

"Not a chance. And if I get one more flyer on my porch or letter in my mailbox from one of those developers, I'm going to scream."

"They just haven't offered you enough money yet."

"It's not a matter of price, Ethan. It's a matter of principle. I've been working toward getting this neighborhood declared a historical preservation area so they can't build in here anymore."

Actually, tearing down these old houses and putting up something more functional seemed like a pretty good plan to Ethan. Leaving ancient structures to gradually deteriorate on excessive amounts of real estate didn't.

"Okay," Sandy said, "what we do on patrol is watch for any suspicious activity, which we then report to the police. Things that seem out of place. People or vehicles that don't fit the profile of the neighborhood."

"And that profile is?"

"Mostly older folks, but we're getting more and more young couples with kids moving in. Stable middle-class people. It's generally retired folks who patrol during the day, and then others take the evening and night shifts. The neighborhood is covered from nine A.M. to four P.M., when most burglaries occur, then eight P.M. to two A.M., when the car thefts and vandalism tend to happen."

"What about the rest of the day?"

"Statistically, there's a low enough risk during the rest of the hours in a day that we don't patrol during those times. Now, where you're concerned, we'll go three nights a week, mutually agreed upon and depending on what part of the schedule is already filled."

Sandy slowed the car, then brought it to a halt. She rolled down the window and smiled at an older couple taking a walk, stopping to chat with them for a moment. Then a few minutes later she did the same with a woman pushing a baby stroller. And as she proceeded through the neighborhood, those she didn't talk to, she waved to. And they all waved back.

Ethan couldn't believe it. He'd landed smack-dab in the middle of Mayberry. "Do you actually know the people you're waving to?"

"Sure."

"All of them?"

"Yes. I'm president of the homeowners' association, so I've gotten to know all kinds of people. Don't you know your neighbors?"

"No."

"Come on. You must know some of them."

"Afraid not. I leave for work early and get home late. No time for that kind of thing."

"You don't know what you're missing."

Sure he did. The minute he got to know his neighbors, it

implied a certain obligation, and the fewer people in this life he was obligated to, the better he liked it.

They made several more slow circuits of the neighborhood, which Ethan discovered was far larger than he had realized. It was a tedious process, but not nearly as boring as he'd anticipated, particularly when they made their way back down Magnolia Street for the umpteenth time and he found himself imagining a bed of big white magnolia blossoms and Sandy lying naked in the middle of them.

Not a bad way to pass the time.

He'd once dated a woman whose face had graced a dozen magazine covers, but she had so many bones sticking out that she looked like a starvation victim. Sandy, on the other hand, had one of those full, curvy figures that told him she wasn't into self-absorbed self-deprivation. She seemed to be a woman who liked people. Who looked forward to getting up in the morning. Who actually ate once in a while. That would be a pleasant change. Most of the women he'd dated in recent memory threw a few spinach leaves on a plate, squirted them with lemon juice, and called it dinner.

"Oh, boy," Sandy said, as they turned onto Mulberry Street. "It's getting late, and Betty Newman's garage door is still up."

She pulled into the driveway of a tidy frame house with a detached garage. "I swear, if I could get everybody to leave their garage doors down, theft in this neighborhood would be cut in half."

"Fewer stolen lawn mowers?"

"And leaf blowers and garden tools and golf clubs. If a garage door is up, you name it and somebody will grab it."

Through the house's living room window, Ethan saw a small, sticklike woman rise from her sofa. She stepped out onto her porch. She wore a green T-shirt tucked into the stretchy waistband of her flowered shorts and a pair of white sandals.

Sandy rolled down the car window. "Hi, Betty!"

The old woman walked stiffly down the porch steps and hobbled toward Sandy's car.

"I noticed it's getting dark and your garage door's up," Sandy called out.

The woman turned and looked at her garage. "Aw, damn it," she muttered. "I forgot again."

"I forget myself sometimes," Sandy said.

"I'm eighty-three years old," Betty said. "What's your excuse?"

Sandy grinned. "Just plain old absentmindedness, I guess."

"Yep. That's how it starts out. Then you end up like me."

"I only hope I end up like you."

"Smart girl. The only people who think it's bad to be eighty-three are those who aren't eighty-two."

"Betty, I've already told Josh this, but will you tell him again how much I appreciate him staying late for me tonight?"

"He stayed late?"

"Yes. He delivered flowers to a wedding."

"I didn't know that. He's not home yet."

"He's not?" Sandy checked her watch. "Don't worry. It's not ten yet. He's still got time."

"He's missed his curfew twice this month."

"Only by a few minutes. He's trying. He really is."

The old woman sighed. "I know. But I still worry."

"Don't. He'll be home soon."

Betty nodded, then craned her head down none too subtly and stared through the window at Ethan.

"I'm sorry, Betty. I should have introduced you. This is Ethan Millner. He's . . ."

When Sandy paused, her brow furrowed, Ethan thought, *This should be good.*

"He's a defense attorney here in Tolosa," she continued brightly. "He's interested in our crime-watch patrol, so he's going to go around with me a few times. Just to see what it's all about."

Ethan leaned toward the window and stared up at Betty. "Actually, what Sandy's being kind enough not to tell you is that I was ticketed for reckless driving and sentenced to forty hours of community service on a neighborhood crime-watch patrol. She agreed to administer my sentence."

The old woman raised an eyebrow. "So you got yourself into a little trouble, did you?"

"Yes, ma'am, I'm afraid I did. But don't you worry. Sandy's going to make sure I pay my debt to society."

"We have to be going," Sandy said quickly. "You be sure to watch that garage door, now."

"I will," she said, then gave Sandy a look that said, *And you be sure to watch that man you're with.*

Sandy backed out of the driveway and headed south on Mulberry Street again. "Now, why in the world did you tell Betty about your community service? I was obviously trying to help you save a little face."

"But your version was a lie. God will get you for that."

"It wasn't a lie! I just . . . omitted some information. That was all."

"And you did it very well. I was impressed. Ever think about becoming an attorney?"

"Are you kidding? My family would disown me. If I were a defense attorney, anyway." She gave him a smile. "Besides, would I really want to deal with all those lawyer jokes?"

Ethan sighed. "I suppose you're going to tell me a few."

"Nah. Lawyer jokes really don't work."

"Oh? Why do you say that?"

"Because lawyers don't think they're funny, and nobody else thinks they're jokes."

Ethan suppressed a smile. "Now, Sandy. You're maligning my profession. I think you've hurt my feelings."

"So tell a florist joke."

"There are no florist jokes."

"Yeah. Wonder why that is?"

"Because you're all about weddings and senior proms and Valentine's Day. Hard to get negative about those things." He gave her a sly look. "So you know a lot of lawyer jokes?"

"Uh-huh."

"What's the difference between God and an attorney?"

"God doesn't think he's an attorney."

Ethan raised an eyebrow. "Do you know how to save a lawyer from drowning?"

"No, and that's a *good* thing."

"Why won't sharks attack lawyers?"

She brought the car to a halt at a stop sign, then turned to face him. "Professional courtesy."

"Okay, Sandy. How do you know all those?"

She grinned. "You're forgetting who my brothers are. And they're in that group who doesn't really think they're jokes."

"How about you? What do you think?"

Her broad smile faded to a softer one. "I told you I make up my own mind."

A strong woman. One who didn't bend whichever way the wind blew.

Yet one more thing to like about her.

For the span of several seconds, Sandy kept her hands on the steering wheel, her foot on the brake, and her eyes locked with his. He stared back without saying a word. As an attorney, he knew how to focus, how to maintain control, how to make sure he never blinked first.

Where she'd learned that skill, he hadn't a clue.

Then a horn honked behind them.

Sandy jumped a little, her gaze flitting to the rearview mirror. She hit the gas and proceeded through the intersection. But even though the spell had been broken, Ethan still felt the aftershocks.

"So who is Josh?" he asked.

"He's Betty's grandson. He works for me delivering flowers."

"He has a curfew? What's the deal with that?"

"None of your business."

"Well, let's see. There are only two kinds of curfews. Family-imposed ones and court-imposed ones."

Sandy was silent.

"Ah," Ethan said. "Court-imposed."

"Oh, all right," Sandy muttered. "He's on probation. He had a burglary conviction a year ago and did six months in juvenile detention. Betty is his grandmother. She took him in when his deadbeat father refused to let him back into the house."

"You have a felon working for you?"

"It was a juvenile offense. He was just hanging out with the wrong crowd. He had a hard time growing up. Somebody needed to give him a break."

"I hope you're keeping an eye on him."

"I don't have to keep an eye on him."

"Why not?"

"Because I trust him."

Ethan shook his head. "A kid like that is probably already stealing you blind and you don't even know it. And if they find out he's violating his curfew, they'll toss him right back in jail."

"He was late by only a few minutes."

"That's all it takes."

"I believe in second chances."

"The day you open your cash drawer to find it cleaned out and the kid nowhere in sight, you'll think again."

"That's not going to happen."

"Actually, Sandy, it happens all the time."

"So you don't believe a kid like Josh can turn himself around?"

"Of course he can. But the odds are against it. You're taking a big gamble when you give a job to a kid on probation."

"Are you always this cynical?"

"Are you always this naïve?"

"Naïveté has nothing to do with it. I just choose to believe the best about people."

"So you think it's something you choose?"

"I take it you don't?"

"Let's just say I take people on a case-by-case basis," Ethan said.

"Let them prove they're worth it?"

"Something like that."

She shook her head. "Boy, you just don't get it, do you?"

"What?"

"Expect the best, Ethan. Watch for it. Wait for it. And you'll get it every time."

Ethan studied Sandy's face, trying to decide if she was crazy or misguided or just one of those extremely rare paragons of virtue. Since he'd never met one of the latter, and since she seemed perfectly sane, he had to go for misguided. A person trying to do good, but in all the wrong ways.

One more reason why she's not your type. . . .

Those words kept trying to wedge themselves into his mind, but they just couldn't seem to get a foothold. The fact that she had a body he wouldn't mind getting his hands on was a consideration, yes, but it was more than that. The world was full of beautiful women, and he'd had his share of them. This one, though, had something more, and he liked the idea of digging deeper to see what it might be.

Then he thought about her family and almost laughed out loud.

He'd never been a fan of irony, and it was hitting him squarely in the face right now. He was going to be spending hours on end with a very interesting woman, yet if he laid one hand on her, he'd be putting himself dead center in the path of three angry, belligerent cops who wouldn't take kindly to any interest he happened to show in their sister. Did he really need a complication like that?

No. He didn't.

There was no need to rock that boat, not when the world was full of women who came without that kind of baggage. Where Sandy was concerned, he could admire her considerable physical assets. He could entertain himself with all the verbal bantering in the world. He could let himself daydream about magnolia blossoms and naked bodies. But that was as far as anything between them was going to go.

Josh sat on a gray-brown bale of hay, his back against the wall of the barn, sipping a warm beer and smoking a cigarette, letting the heat of the August evening wash over him. Aaron had shown him this place a month or so ago. It was way at the back of some lady's property, stuck in the trees that lined the creek. From the way it was almost falling down and the look of the tall grass around it, nobody ever came back here, which made it a pretty good place just to sit and zone out for a while.

Josh wouldn't have called Aaron a friend, exactly. He was just one of those guys he ran into sometimes and hung out with. When they saw each other earlier tonight down by the Pecan Street bridge, Aaron told Josh he had some grass, and like most potheads, he didn't like to smoke alone. Josh had no intention of messing with anything illegal, but the beer Aaron hauled out of his truck to go along with it had sounded pretty good.

Aaron rested his head back against the wall of the barn and took a drag on the joint he held. "So tell me. How's life with the pansies?"

Josh winced. Aaron thought the fact that he worked at a flower shop was pretty damned funny.

"It's a good job."

"Right. Parties and weddings and senior proms and all that crap. Sounds like a real blast."

In the beginning, Josh had thought that a job didn't get much dumber than delivering flowers. But it had worked out better than he had thought it would. Aaron liked to bug him about it, though. He'd even come by once, pretending to be looking at the plants and gift stuff at the front of the shop just so he could give Josh a hard time about it when Sandy's back was turned.

"I get to drive around most of the time," Josh said. "Be by myself. Play my music. As long as I get the stuff delivered my boss doesn't bug me. Sometimes I have to help in the shop, but even that's not bad."

"Ever there by yourself?" Aaron asked.

"Not much. But every once in a while."

"If you need a little help lightening the cash drawer, let me know."

Josh felt a stab of foreboding. "No way. I'm not messing with Sandy. And neither are you."

"Oh, yeah? I'd love to mess with her. In a lot of different ways. I've always had a thing for older women."

"Leave her alone. I mean it, man. You do *not* mess with her."

Aaron smiled. "Oh, yeah? Maybe you're the one who's got a thing for older women."

"Just shut the hell up, will you?"

Aaron chuckled a little, looking at Josh with the weirdly intense but spaced-out eyes of a guy who lived to light up. He took a toke, sucked the smoke in deep, held it. He expelled the breath slowly, the smoke fogging in front of him, then fading away. He tilted his head back against the wall and held out the joint to Josh.

Josh held up his palm. "No, man. I can't."

"Hell you can't. Who's gonna know?"

Josh stared at the joint, thinking about how his grandmother had given him a place to live. How Sandy had given him a job. But man, sometimes life still sucked. That tight-assed bride today had just about made him crazy. And being with his grandmother was tense sometimes, even though he knew she was trying to help him. She was just *there* all the time. Watching. Waiting, he knew, for him to screw up again. He wasn't going to, no matter what, but still it wasn't easy, so it felt good to get out sometimes. Just to relax. It wasn't like he was going to get in trouble again. Not like he had before.

Aaron continued to hold out the joint. When Josh turned away, he pulled it back with a sad shake of his head.

"The chick who lives in the house down the hill," Aaron said. "What's her name again?"

"I don't know. Laura something."

"Now she's *really* a hot one." He glanced out the window. "Suppose there's a show going on again tonight? Maybe we ought to take a trip down there again."

Josh froze. "No, man. No way. They throw guys in jail for that kind of thing."

"That didn't stop you last time."

"It was a dumb thing to do."

"I'd say it was pretty entertaining."

"Shit, man, will you just let it go?"

Aaron shook his head and made one of those huffing noises Josh hated, the one that said, *Could you be a bigger pussy?*

"Anyway, I gotta go," Josh said. "Curfew."

"Aw, hell. Who's gonna know? Your grandmother? What's she gonna do? Call the law on you?"

"I said I've got to go."

"Man, what did that judge do? Chop your balls off same time he told you you had to be in bed by ten o'clock?"

"Kept me out of jail."

"You're still in a fucking jail."

Josh thought about his grandmother. Sandy. The people he worked with. Good people who expected him to do good. And he wished he hadn't even come here tonight. In fact, he decided right then that Aaron was somebody he needed to stay away from.

"No," Josh said. "I'm out of here."

"Suit yourself," Aaron said. He stood up.

"Where are you going?"

"Fun is hard to come by," he said, heading for the door. "I'm going down the hill."

"Aaron!" Josh came to his feet. "Get back here! Damn it, will you—"

Josh reached the door of the barn in time to see Aaron weaving his way through the trees, heading in the direction of the house.

Shit. The last thing Josh wanted was for Aaron to get caught doing something stupid and then saying that he'd been part of it. Where the police were concerned, he sure as hell couldn't afford that.

He tossed the beer bottle aside, left the barn and started down the hill after him.

Sandy checked her watch. It was ten minutes until ten.

The night had grown cloudy. As they drove down Cottonwood Street, only the glow of street lamps and porch lights shone through the darkness. And that darkness made her feel that much more alone with Ethan, sending her mind on a few sexy side trips she hadn't anticipated.

Interesting men didn't walk into her life every day. Hell, *men* didn't walk into her life every day. Men her age, anyway, who were free of encumbrances such as wedding rings. She smiled to herself. If her brothers had any idea she was looking at Ethan with admiration on her mind and lust in her heart, they'd lock her in a closet and throw away the key.

Still, she had to stay on her toes. She'd listened to her brothers talk about his reputation for years, knowing the things they said about him couldn't possibly all be true.

But they couldn't possibly all be false, either.

All at once, something darted across the street in front of her car. She hit the brake, bringing the car to a tire-squealing halt. Ethan whipped forward, then back again.

"What was that?" he asked.

"A cat ran right out in front of me."

Looking to the curb on the opposite side of the street, Sandy could just make out a slender tiger-striped cat crouching in the thick Saint Augustine lawn.

"That's strange," she said.

"What?"

"That looks like Laura Williams's cat."

"Laura Williams?"

"Yes. She lives in that house right there. She doesn't ever let him out."

Sandy pulled into the driveway of one of the houses, killing the engine but leaving her headlights on.

"What are you doing?" Ethan asked.

"He must have gotten loose by accident. He's not used to being outside. He'll get hurt if I don't pick him up. I'll be back in a minute."

Sandy got out of the car, met by sweltering heat even at the late hour. Keeping an eye on the cat near the curb, she approached him slowly, but when she was within a few feet of him, he darted across the lawn. Another approach sent him dashing away again. After a few more standoffs, the cat finally took cover in an azalea bush.

This was going to be tougher than Sandy had anticipated. Just as she thought her only hope was to go get Laura,

Ethan got out of the car and came over to where she was crouched beside the bush.

"Looks like you need some help," he said.

"Yeah. Kneel down and spread out your arms. If he sees you there, maybe he won't run."

She inched closer and just about had her hands on the cat, when he darted out of the bush. As he streaked by, Ethan managed to grab his tail, then put his hand along his back, pinning him to the lawn. The cat let out a howl of anger, but Ethan held on until Sandy could scramble over and scoop him up.

Sandy stood, holding the squirming cat close to her chest. She crossed the yard and walked up the squeaky steps to Laura's front door. She rang the bell. No answer. Lights were on inside the house, though, so Sandy leaned over and glanced through the living room window. Laura was nowhere to be seen, but Sandy could hear music playing. New age instrumental. Soft and serene.

"What's the matter?" Ethan called out. "Isn't she home?"

Sandy held on to the cat with one hand and tried the door with the other. It was unlocked. She glanced back to verify that Laura's car was indeed in the driveway. "She has to be. Her car is here and the front door is unlocked." She swung it open a crack, intending to call out to Laura.

"Wait," Ethan said suddenly.

"What?"

"Don't go in there."

He trotted up the porch steps. He looked at the open door, then rang the bell again. No response. By the worried look on his face, Sandy could tell he suspected that something might be wrong.

"Call out to her," he said.

Sandy pushed the door open. "Laura! It's Sandy! Are you there?"

No answer.

"Does she live alone?" Ethan asked.

"Yes. Maybe she left the door open by mistake when she went to bed."

"And left the lights and stereo on?"

They looked at each other for a few seconds, silent questions humming in the air between them.

Ethan pushed the door open and they stepped inside. The living room was as Sandy remembered it. The house needed a lot of work, with cracked walls, dull hardwood floors, and ancient light fixtures. Still, Laura had managed to make it homey with inexpensive furniture she'd gotten from yard sales and thrift stores. Had it been daylight, the sun catchers at the front windows would have cast rainbows across the floor. And plants were everywhere.

"Keep calling to her," Ethan said.

Sandy did, but there was no answer. "Maybe she's in the shower."

"I don't hear water running." Ethan punched a button on the stereo and the room fell silent. He listened for a moment. "I don't hear anything."

Sandy closed the door so she could put the cat down. The moment she let go of the animal, he raced into the hall leading to the bedrooms.

A gazing globe sat in the middle of a coffee table, reflecting the room around it. Next to it, on a plastic coaster, Sandy saw what looked like a watery soft drink in a glass, as if somebody had poured it and forgotten about it. A copy of *Home & Garden* lay facedown on a sofa cushion. On the coffee table sat an ashtray with a cigarette burned down to the filter.

"Does she smoke?" Ethan asked.

"I don't know. I've never seen her do it." Sandy dropped her voice to a whisper. "Do you think somebody else is in the house?"

"I don't know." Ethan wore a tight-browed expression of uneasiness that filled her with foreboding. "But if they were, I think they'd have heard us by now."

"Maybe she's in the backyard, and that's why she can't hear us."

"If she was going out to the backyard, she wouldn't have left a cigarette burning."

Sandy called out again. Still nothing. She tried to tell herself that everything was fine, but the most ominous feeling crept through her.

Ethan moved tentatively through the living room, and Sandy followed him through the dining room into the kitchen. It was one of the few houses in the neighborhood Sandy had seen that had original early twentieth–century cabinets, which Laura had given a coat of yellow paint. That bit of cheeriness, though, couldn't offset the stained linoleum and faded tile counter. A small dining table for two sat near a cluster of three windows, a basket of ivy cascading across it.

As Ethan headed out to the sunroom, Sandy peeked into the laundry room. She saw a dented washer and dryer. Shelves of cleaning products. Broom. Mop. Nothing out of the ordinary.

"Jesus *Christ*!"

At the sound of Ethan's voice, Sandy spun around, her heart jolting hard. She rushed out of the laundry room and hurried toward the sunroom. As she approached it she saw a clay pot smashed on the floor in a tangle of philodendron leaves. A wrought-iron table overturned beside the hot tub with books and magazines scattered across the floor. The back door was standing open, with glass from a broken window scattered on the floor.

Then she saw the blood.

She froze at the doorway, her mouth dropping open in a silent gasp of horrified disbelief. Blood was smeared on the walls. Spattered on the side of the hot tub. Pooled on the tile floor.

"No, Sandy!" Ethan said. "Don't come in here!"

He strode toward her, trying to block her view, but she'd already looked past him to the corner of the room.

The blood she'd seen so far had only been the beginning.

chapter four

Sandy let out a strangled cry and backed away, her knees buckling. Ethan pulled her into his arms, turning her around so she couldn't see the carnage. But she'd already seen it. She'd already seen Laura lying in the corner, faceup, her limbs twisted at odd angles. Blood streaked her face, matted her hair, soaked her clothes. Her eyes stared blankly ahead, their whites a stark contrast to the crimson-stained skin surrounding them. A few large rocks lay on the floor beside her, and they were covered with blood.

Sandy automatically tried to turn back, but Ethan slid his fingers through her hair and pressed her cheek against his chest.

"Ethan—"

"Don't look."

"I already saw."

"Is it Laura?"

"Yes." She clutched his shirt in her fist, every breath she took filling her nostrils with the acrid scent of blood. "Is . . . is she dead?"

"Yes. Let's get out of here."

Ethan put his arm around Sandy's shoulder and led her out of the room. He walked her through the kitchen. As she stepped into the dining room, her knees weakened again and she stumbled. Ethan caught her, clutching her hand at the same time to guide her into the living room. Her stomach churned with nausea.

Air. She needed air. *Now.*

Ethan yanked open the front door and half led, half dragged her out to the porch and down the steps. The moment they reached the lawn she fell to her hands and knees in the grass, hunched over, nausea twisting her stomach into turmoil. Ethan knelt beside her, his hand against her back.

"Just breathe," he said.

"I can't. I—"

"Breathe."

She took several deep breaths. The hot night air was heavy and stagnant, but it was blessedly free from the odor of blood and death. She held handfuls of the thick-bladed grass in her fists, her shoulders heaving with every breath. Feeling sure she was going to be sick, she stayed bent over, her arms wrapped around her stomach as it tossed and churned, but Ethan was moving his hand up and down her back in long, soothing strokes, murmuring softly to her, and slowly the feeling subsided.

He took out his cell phone and dialed 911. When an operator came on the line, he told her what they'd found. Listening to his voice in the night giving the details of what they'd just seen seemed distant and surreal to Sandy, as if she were watching a bizarre movie where nothing made sense.

"I saw some bloody rocks," Sandy said when Ethan hung up. "From her indoor garden. That's how she was killed."

"That's what it looked like."

"I've never seen so much blood." Sandy squeezed her eyes closed, her face hot, her neck damp with sweat. "How long do you think she'd been there?"

"Not long. The blood was fresh."

"Who could have done that? I just can't imagine . . . " She swallowed clumsily, tears burning behind her eyes, feeling sick all over again.

"Just take it easy," Ethan murmured, his hand warm against her back. He kept stroking it gently, until she rose and sat back on her heels with a final deep, cleansing breath.

"You okay?" he asked.

Nodding weakly, she looked back at the house. The nearby flood lamp seemed overly bright and garish, casting heavy shadows behind the live oak tree that hovered over the house. She imagined evil things moving through those shadows, evil things generally reserved for nightmares.

Tonight they'd stepped into reality.

Thirty minutes later, Ethan stood with Sandy in Laura's front yard, watching the frenzy of activity up and down the block. Red and blue lights swirled in harsh circles as voices crackled over police radios. Patrol cars lined the curb, along with an ambulance and a pair of news vans. Several cops stood between them and the reporters and cameramen, and that was good, because the last thing Ethan wanted right now was a microphone shoved in their faces. A patrol officer had asked them to stay put until the detective who was in the house could come back out to question them.

Unfortunately, the detective inside the house was Ray Henderson. And the moment Ethan had seen him step out of his car ten minutes ago, he knew the odds of this case being solved in a competent and expedient manner had just been cut in half.

The man was balding. Heavyset. He had the classic look of a harried TV police detective, scruffy around the edges, wearing a suit that looked as if he'd pulled it off a thrift-store rack. But his appearance was hardly the worst thing about him. Professionally speaking, he was just about as incompetent as any detective could be and still hold on to his job.

"Ray Henderson's on the case," Sandy said. "I've dealt with him before."

"You have?"

"Yeah. He was forced to fill in for a while as a liaison between the detective branch and the crime-watch council. He was a real pain in the ass. And my brothers don't think too much of him in a professional capacity, either."

"For once, I've got to agree with your brothers."

Sandy sighed. "And I thought this night couldn't get worse."

"How well did you know Laura?" Ethan asked.

"She was a member of our homeowners' association. Came to most of the meetings. We've been to each other's houses a few times for coffee. She seemed very nice."

"What did she do for a living?"

"She worked at a garden center. She told me once that the reason she'd bought the house was because she loved plants and the house had a sunroom with a southern exposure."

"Was she divorced?"

"I have no idea. She never talked about it. She just seemed like a nice, normal person. Are you thinking she might have an ex-husband with a grudge?"

"It's possible. What else do you know about her? Any boyfriends?"

"She never talked about any. She was a bit of a health nut. Loved to jog. She tried to get me to join her a couple of times, but jogging really isn't my thing. The men in the neighborhood certainly didn't mind the view, though. Laura was very pretty."

Several neighbors had ventured from their houses and were standing near the curb, talking among themselves and gazing at the house with the wide-eyed, voyeuristic expressions people always wore when they watched any horrific event unfold.

"I should go talk to the neighbors," Sandy said. "They're out here wondering what happened."

"Let them hear it on the news."

"No. I really should—"

"Talking about it will only upset you again. They don't need to know anything right now. Stay put."

Sandy finally nodded.

The horrors one human being could inflict on another had ceased to astonish Ethan a long time ago. But Sandy wasn't faring as well. Her cheeks were still pale with shock, her eyes drooping wearily. For a cup-half-full, the-world-is-beautiful kind of person, it must have been like a descent into hell. The last thing he wanted her to do was open herself up to questions from the neighbors, which meant she'd relive the whole thing all over again.

She swiped a loose strand of hair behind her ear, sighing softly. Her lips tightened, and for a moment he was sure she was going to cry.

"This isn't supposed to happen," she murmured. "Not in this neighborhood. It's one of the safest in the city. We know each other here. We watch out for each other."

In spite of her incredible naïveté, Ethan just nodded. This was not the time to tell her that this kind of thing happened everywhere. She'd just been lucky so far that it hadn't happened here.

A moment later the front door of the house opened and Ray Henderson walked out. He lumbered down the steps and spoke to a patrol cop, who pointed in Ethan and Sandy's direction.

He came across the yard, eyeing Ethan as he approached.

"Millner," he said, stopping in front of them. "Strange to see you here. A couple of the officers said you and Ms. DeMarco discovered the body."

"Yes," Ethan said. "We were on crime-watch patrol."

Henderson was doing a really poor job of hiding his snide smile. "Oh, yeah. Heard about that."

Sarcasm dripped from his voice, and Ethan knew it was all the guy could do to maintain a semblance of professionalism when he had only a passing acquaintance with the concept.

"Got a hell of a crime scene in there," Henderson said, flipping out a small spiral notebook. "You want to tell me what you saw?"

"We were patrolling the neighborhood," Ethan said. "Sandy saw the victim's cat loose outside when he shouldn't have been. We took the cat to the door. When the victim didn't answer, we discovered that the door was unlocked. It looked as if something might be wrong, so we went inside. In the living room we saw that a cigarette had burned itself out in an ashtray, and a watery drink sat beside it. That seemed odd, so we went through the house looking for her and found her dead in the sunroom."

"Did you see anyone on the premises?"

"No," Ethan said, and Sandy shook her head.

"Hear anything?"

"Her stereo was playing when we went into the house," Sandy said. "Otherwise, we didn't hear a thing."

"What time did you arrive here?"

"It was almost ten o'clock," Sandy said. "We were on our last round of the neighborhood."

"You knew the victim?"

"Yes, but not well. She was more of an acquaintance. She came to neighborhood meetings. We've gotten together a few times for coffee. That's about it."

"Do you know if she was on the outs with anybody?"

"Not that I know of."

Henderson took a few notes.

"What do you think?" Sandy asked. "Do you have any idea who could have done this?"

"There's a broken back window leading into the sunroom. Looks to me as if somebody was robbing the place and didn't know she was in the house, or she came home while the burglary was in progress."

"But the house wasn't ransacked," Ethan said.

Henderson shrugged. "The burglar may not have had an

opportunity to do that before you showed up. The body's barely cold now."

"Pretty gruesome murder for your average burglar."

"He probably wasn't carrying a weapon. She surprised him. He picked up the first weapon he could find. Crime of panic."

Henderson's scenario was possible, but it didn't ring true to Ethan. It looked more like a crime of passion than a crime of panic.

Ethan heard a car engine and turned to see a crime-scene unit pull up to the curb. *Good.* At least there might be somebody competent somewhere inside that vehicle. Some solid forensic evidence could go a long way toward offsetting any investigational ineptitude that Henderson happened to commit.

"You two aren't giving me much here," Henderson said. "Sure you didn't see anything else?"

Ethan shook his head. "Afraid not."

"Okay, then. You're free to go." He flipped his spiral closed. "But I may call you back in if more questions come to mind."

"Laura told me once that she has no family," Sandy said. "But if there's somebody to contact, you'll find them, right?"

"Sure," he said, tucking the notebook inside the breast pocket of his coat. "Eventually."

"Gee, Henderson," Ethan said, "I'd hate for you to go out of your way to make sure that her next of kin were notified."

"Mind your own fucking business, Millner."

"What about Laura's cat?" Sandy asked.

"We'll call the SPCA," Henderson said.

Ethan frowned. "Eventually?"

"You kidding? I get in deep shit if I don't take care of the orphaned animals. You got a dead woman, and people get all worried about a damned cat. Go figure."

"It's a no-kill shelter," Sandy told Ethan. "He'll find a home."

Ethan nodded. "Come on, Sandy. Let's go." They started toward Sandy's car.

"Millner," Henderson said.

Ethan turned back.

"Crime-watch patrol. You're obviously doing a hell of a job. Keep up the good work."

Ethan felt a slow burn of anger, but he kept his face impassive. He merely turned away, taking Sandy by the arm and leading her toward her car. Halfway there, she murmured under her breath. "He is *such* an asshole."

"Yeah, but unfortunately he's the asshole running this investigation."

"With him at the helm, Laura's killer may never be found."

Ethan had to agree. Their best hope of getting this case solved would be if the murderer walked into the police station and threw himself onto Henderson's desk.

Assuming Henderson wasn't on a coffee break.

As they approached her car, Ethan eased Sandy's keys from her hand, then escorted her to the passenger door and opened it for her. She remembered Alex's warnings about getting into a car with Ethan driving, but that seemed silly even to think about now. Instead, all she felt was gratitude. She lived only a few blocks away, but right now it seemed like a thousand.

A minute later Ethan pulled down the alley behind her house and parked in her driveway. He walked with her through the back gate to the patio. When she unlocked her kitchen door and they went inside, she was immediately struck by how quiet her house seemed, with nothing but the low hum of her refrigerator and the faint ticking of the grandfather clock in her living room to break the silence.

She turned to Ethan. "Thank you for driving me home."

"Are you going to be all right?"

"Yes. Of course. I come from a family of cops. It isn't as if I haven't heard about these kinds of things a thousand times before."

"There's a big difference between hearing about it and seeing it. What kinds of locks do you have?"

"Dead bolts front and back." Then she realized why he was asking. "You don't think that just because Laura was killed, it means somebody might still be—"

"I doubt it. But there's no need to take chances."

"Don't worry. I'll lock up once you're gone."

"Sure you're all right?"

"I told you, I'm fine."

But still he stood there, staring at her with that deep, penetrating gaze that caught hers and held it, the same one that undoubtedly would make any witness on the stand think twice about lying.

"I don't think you are," he said.

He spoke softly, his brows drawn together in a worried expression, and for some reason Sandy felt tears come to her eyes. She blinked quickly to ward them off, but that only made a few roll down her face. She wiped them away with her sleeve.

"Damn it, look at me," she said. "It's really not like me to fall apart like this."

"I'm sorry you had to see the body. I tried to stop you—"

"I know. It's okay."

"Anybody would get upset if they'd seen what you saw tonight."

"You held it together just fine."

"I've seen things you wouldn't believe, Sandy. This was just one more."

He eased forward, and she had the sudden feeling that he was going to reach out and touch her. But his hands remained at his sides.

"I'll stay for a while," he said, his voice nearly a whisper. "If you want me to."

He stared at her without blinking, and suddenly she was acutely aware of just how close he was standing to her, so close she swore she could feel the heat of his body mingling with hers. Her brother's words were like warning bells ringing in the back of her mind, but as she searched Ethan's face for some ulterior motive, she didn't see that at all. All she saw was concern.

Still, she didn't know this man. And she felt far too vulnerable to be alone with him now, at this late hour, with her emotions all over the map.

"No. That's not necessary. I told you I'll be okay."

"The moment you close your eyes to sleep, you'll see it."

He spoke matter-of-factly, but his words still gave her a chill. "I'll be okay."

"Do you drink?"

"No."

"Have any sleeping pills?"

"No. Of course not."

"Do you have a TV in your bedroom?"

"No. Why in the world—"

"Then get a blanket and pillow. Sleep on the sofa. Lights on, TV going."

"Why would I do that?"

"Distraction."

When she still stared at him questioningly, he said, "It used to work for me."

"What do you mean?"

His expression turned grim. "Sometimes photos are passed around a courtroom. Gruesome murders. Abused children. Suicide victims. Blood. Violence. Death. You can close the folder, but . . ."

His voice faded into nothingness, but a melancholy expression remained in his eyes that she hadn't seen before.

"I should go." He turned to walk out of her kitchen.

"Ethan?"

He turned back. Sandy took a few steps toward him. "Tonight wasn't a photo. It was the real thing."

"Yes."

"Will you be sleeping on your sofa tonight?"

"No point."

"Why not?"

"I said it used to work for me."

Her brothers had tried to convince her that Ethan's heart was made of stone, but in those few seconds, she heard sadness in his voice and saw sorrow in his eyes and knew there was a whole lot more to this man than met the eye.

He slipped out her front door and clicked it closed. Sandy locked the door behind him, then went up to her bedroom, every step she took on the oak stairs echoing through the silence of her house. She hated this. She hated the horrible feeling of vulnerability it gave her, knowing that if it happened to Laura, it could happen to anyone.

Just go to sleep. The morning sun will make everything look a whole lot better.

She got ready for bed, then pulled back the covers and slid beneath them. Just as she was turning out the light, her phone rang. She picked it up, looked at the caller ID, and hit the button to answer it.

"Alex? Why are you calling so late?"

"Why do you think? I heard what happened tonight. Are you okay?"

The Tolosa PD grapevine. She should have known. "Yes. I'm okay."

"Did you know the woman?"

"She was an acquaintance."

"I heard it was a pretty gruesome murder scene. How are you doing?"

"I told you I'm fine."

"You and Millner found the body?"

"Yes. I was really shaken up afterward, and Ethan was kind enough to take me home and make sure I was all right."

"He didn't get out of line, did he?"

No, he hadn't gotten out of line. All he'd done was give her a strong and sympathetic shoulder to lean on when she needed it the most, but she'd be wasting her breath to try to make her brother understand that.

"Right, Alex. We'd just traipsed through a murder scene. It put both of us in a really sexy mood."

"I wouldn't put it past him."

"Will you get off it? Please? He's not the evil person you make him out to be."

She could tell her brother had plenty left to say on the subject, but for once he kept it to himself.

"Lock your doors," Alex said.

"I always do."

"Call me if you need me."

"I will. Did you know that Ray Henderson's on the case?"

Her brother sighed. "Yeah. That's what I heard."

"Alex? Will you please find out whatever you can about the case and let me know? This was a little too close to home."

"Sure, Sandy. I'll call you the minute I hear something."

Sandy clicked the phone off and returned it to its cradle. She flipped off the lamp and lay down, tucking her arm beneath her pillow with a deep, cleansing breath. She heard a faint squeak, which she knew was Oscar pushing her bedroom door open. He leaped up onto her bed and curled up at the foot as he always did, purring like a motorboat.

But tonight she heard other sounds, too, ones she must have heard a thousand times before but they'd never really registered: The night wind rustling the leaves of the maple tree outside her window. A bigger gust of wind that caused a heavy creaking noise through the rafters. The raspy, metallic sound of her air-conditioning unit as it worked to counteract the August heat.

Then she closed her eyes and discovered that Ethan had been right. It was there. In stunning detail. She saw Laura's lifeless eyes staring through blood-coated lashes, rivulets of crimson crisscrossing her cheeks, her limbs twisted at odd angles like a Raggedy Ann tossed in the corner.

Suddenly the air in Sandy's bedroom felt thick and oppressive. She tried to breathe deeply, but still she felt as if she were choking. When a sick feeling rose in her stomach, she pushed back the covers and sat on the edge of her bed until the sensation passed. She grabbed a blanket and pillow and went downstairs to her living room, where she lay down on the sofa and flipped on the TV.

She ran the channels. An infomercial for a set of cookware. The world poker championship on the Travel Channel. A vintage episode of *Perry Mason*.

Finally the mindless buzz of a late-night talk show sidetracked her thoughts, just as Ethan had told her it would. And as she drifted off to sleep, she silently thanked him, even as she wondered what was left for him to do to chase those same thoughts away.

Ethan came into his town house and locked the door behind him, the snap of the lock echoing through the foyer. The slight smell of disinfectant in the air reminded him that the maid had been there that day. He'd never even met her. Didn't have to. He paid the bill and came home to sparkling chrome fixtures, vacuumed rugs, and kitchen tiles so clean it was a shame to walk on them.

He tossed his keys on the table by the door and headed upstairs to his bedroom. The bed was made, a twice-a-week sight that always startled him. He pulled his wallet and his cell phone from the pockets of his pants, and tossed his spare change in the ceramic jar on his dresser. He took off his clothes and dropped them on the floor of the closet for the maid to get later, then thought about where he'd been tonight. There was something about walking through a gruesome murder scene that moved him to throw them in the hamper instead.

Good God. A murder? Could he ever have imagined that? Then again, why not?

Ethan knew what lurked beneath the surface of the average person, and it wasn't pretty. On the whole, human beings were self-serving, self-indulgent, sometimes violent creatures whose baser instincts were kept at bay only by societal pressure. And when that wasn't enough to keep them in check, that was when he went to work.

Several minutes later he lay in bed, plenty tired enough to sleep. But ten minutes passed, then twenty, and all he seemed to be able to do was stare at the ceiling. He'd seen a lot of grisly murders, but the one tonight had topped them all. Every time he felt as if he was dozing off, he saw the sprays of blood that had doused every wall. Crushed skull bones. Arms thrown up in self-defense that were now caked with blood. Evidence of a rage that knew no bounds, or maybe a psychopath who killed as easily as he dressed himself in the morning.

Then he saw Sandy's face, horrified at the sight.

The man who'd killed Laura Williams was probably somewhere in the city right now. Sooner or later, if the murderer was caught, he'd be looking for representation, for somebody to pull out all the stops to keep him from the capital punishment he deserved.

With the memory of Sandy's stricken face still so fresh in Ethan's mind, he found himself hoping that the murderer wasn't a twisted human being who was guilty as sin but still had deep pockets and insisted on hiring only the best.

* * *

At nine fifteen the next morning, Sandy arrived at the office of Fay Moreno, the crime analyst for the Tolosa Police Department. Fifteen years of experience had given Fay an uncanny ability to bring together seemingly unrelated pieces of information to solve cases. She was the best at what she did, and she had the citations to prove it. Sandy had consulted with her several times in the past few years in her capacity as chairman of the Tolosa Crime-watch Council, but today she had a more personal mission. The murder last night still weighed so heavily on her mind that even the light of day couldn't chase the images away. She hoped that Fay could give her a little good news about the possibility of getting this one solved.

As usual, the woman was glued to her computer screen, checking out overnight crime reports. She'd cut her hair since the last time Sandy had seen her, opting for a fluffy red poof with blond highlights. An unlit cigarette hung from her lips, the filter chewed flat, a habit she'd taken up ever since Black Friday—her label for the day when they'd banned smoking from all public buildings in Tolosa.

"Hey, Sandy," Fay said. "Something told me I'd be seeing you today. Heard it was a pretty nasty crime scene last night. You were patrolling and found the body?"

"Yes," Sandy said, taking a chair next to Fay's desk. "And I hope I never see anything like it again."

"I'm already on it, but so far, nothing. Last murder in this city was three weeks ago, and that was a domestic thing. You know—asshole husband shoots disobedient wife. I went back a few years looking for a direct connection, but I couldn't find anything with last night's MO. And I don't see any murders at all in your neighborhood. Ever."

"Henderson thinks it was a burglary gone bad."

"That's because Henderson is an idiot. I'm not saying that wasn't what happened. But it's unlikely."

"Why do you say that?"

"Battering is a pretty nasty way to kill somebody. If the burglar was a little deranged, yeah, I'd go along with it. And maybe he was. But this looks like something else to me. Whoever killed Laura Williams was one pissed-off son of a bitch."

"I can't imagine anyone doing that to her. Laura was a really nice woman."

"How well did you know her?"

"She was just an acquaintance."

"Well, trust me. People can fool you." Fay punched a few more keys, her lips edging into a sly smile. "I also heard that Ethan Millner was with you when you found the body."

"Yes, he was."

"Now, there's a body I'd like to discover. Has he made a move on you yet?"

"Come on, Fay. Nothing happened between Ethan and me. I think his reputation with women is a little overblown."

"Aw, dish me some dirt, will you? All I can do anymore is live vicariously."

"Your husband would be pleased to hear that."

"The day my husband looks like Ethan Millner is the day I stop dreaming it and start living it." She turned around in her chair. "I'll stay on top of this and see if I can come up with anything else. And I'll run a nine-one-one call history from your area. See what kind of mayhem people have been calling in for the past couple of years. Maybe I'll see a pattern and we can pin down who might have done this. Might have been a stand-alone, though, and that'll make things a little harder."

"Have you talked to Henderson yet?"

"Nope. He was already out and about when I got here. Probably holed somewhere finishing off a sack of doughnuts. I'll talk to him as soon as he comes back."

"Thanks, Fay," Sandy said. "I appreciate it."

"You bet. I'll be in touch if I come up with anything."

Twenty minutes later, Sandy came through the back door of her shop, relieved the moment she caught the scent of flowers. It was a life-affirming aroma that always invigorated her. She needed this to be a nice, routine day so she could be sure there really was some semblance of normality in the world. Unfortunately, the first thing she saw when she went into her shop were Lyle's legs sticking out from beneath the sink.

"Lyle? Don't tell me the sink's leaking again."

"Afraid so," he said, his voice echoing from inside the cabinet. "It's time for an extreme makeover on these pipes. But I'll take care of it."

He slid out from beneath the sink, stood up, and brushed the dust off his turquoise shirt, which contrasted wildly with his cantaloupe-colored pants. His clothes looked like an explosion in a Santa Fe art gallery, but on Lyle, somehow it worked.

Just then the back door opened and Imogene came into the shop. Her steel-gray hair was pushed away from her face with a stretchy hairband, and she wore a flowered dress that hung all the way down to her plastic flip-flops. As always, she was lugging a straw purse the size of a small suitcase.

Lyle turned and gave her a look of utter delight. "My *God!* Imogene! That's an absolutely *stunning* dress you're wearing today!"

She shut the door and gave him a deadpan stare. "Thirty bucks and a trip to Wal-Mart and you can have one just like it."

"Ah. Such style. If I ever decide I need an older woman, you *will* be available, won't you?"

"If you ever decide you need a *woman,*" Imogene said, "I'll faint dead away."

As Imogene headed to the coffeepot, Sandy felt a glimmer of relief. Okay. That felt good. Something nice and normal like Lyle and Imogene sniping at each other. A casual observer might think they detested each other. Sandy knew better.

Having employees who were also good friends lightened her load in more ways than one. Lyle handled all kinds of things around the shop that kept her from having to pay repairmen outrageous amounts of money, and Imogene respected her as a boss at the same time she treated her like the daughter she'd never had. And to Sandy's surprise, Josh got along well with both of them.

"Lyle?" Sandy said. "Are you sure about taking care of the pipes? I can call a plumber."

"Not necessary. I did learn a few things from my father the handyman. Sexual orientation, no. Sweating a plumbing joint, yes."

"But you do so much around here already."

Lyle gave her a sly smile. "It'll be worth it just to see Imogene swoon when I strap on a tool belt."

Imogene rolled her eyes and poured a cup of coffee.

Lyle stopped and eyed Sandy carefully. "Sandy? What's up? You look like you didn't get a wink of sleep."

"I barely did."

A smile spread across Lyle's face. "Tell me you finally had a fabulous evening with a wonderful man."

"I was with a man, yes. And we discovered the body of one of my neighbors who'd been murdered."

"What?"

Imogene set the coffeepot down with a clatter. "Is that the one I read about in the paper this morning?"

"I hope there wasn't another murder in Tolosa last night."

"And you were the one who found the body?"

"Yes. Ethan Millner and me."

"Who?"

"The lawyer who came on crime-watch patrol with me."

Lyle pulled out a chair for Sandy. "Sit down. Tell us all about it."

Imogene brought Sandy a cup of coffee. She wrapped her hands around it and took a sip, then told them how she and Ethan had happened to discover Laura's body.

"You were at the scene," Lyle said. "Did you see anybody? You know, like, running from the scene of the crime?"

"No. I didn't see anything. Neither did Ethan."

"So they have no idea who did it?"

"As far as I know right now, no. I just want them to find out who did it, and fast. Nobody in my neighborhood is going to feel safe until they do."

Ten minutes later, Sandy finished the last of her coffee and opened up the shop. She waited on a few customers, then got started on some flower arrangements for a dinner at the convention center. At ten fifteen, the phone rang. It was Josh.

Sandy checked her watch. "Hey, Josh. You're running a little late today."

"I know. I called to tell you I won't be in, and . . ."

He spoke haltingly, and Sandy could tell something was wrong.

"Josh? What's the matter?"

"I'm sorry, Sandy, but I didn't know who else to call. . . ."

"What's wrong?"

"Everything's wrong. Oh, God . . . everything . . ." His voice was so shaky he could barely get the words out, and Sandy felt a stab of apprehension.

"They asked me if I did it," he said. "Those were the exact words they used: 'Did you do it?' I thought that somehow they'd found out that I missed my curfew, so I told them that yes, I'd done it. But then all of a sudden they were arresting me, and . . ."

Sandy nearly gasped. "You've been arrested?"

"Yes. I-I'm in jail right now."

Sandy's hand slid involuntarily to her throat. "What for?"

For a long time, there was no sound on the line but Josh's labored breathing. Finally he spoke again, his voice shaking. "They think I killed Laura Williams."

chapter five

For several seconds Sandy stood there, gripping the phone with disbelief, sure she couldn't have heard Josh right.

"They think you killed Laura?"

"Yeah. Now they're telling me I confessed to it, but I didn't know they were talking about a murder!"

"I don't understand. Why would they think you did it?"

"One of the neighbors says he saw me in her backyard around the time of the murder. But I was never at her house. I swear I wasn't. I didn't kill her. You have to believe me!"

"Josh. It's okay. Of course I believe you." Sandy's mind was spinning, trying to come to grips with this. "What about your grandmother? Does she know about this?"

"She was there when they took me away. And now . . . now she won't answer the phone when I call. I know I've done some dumb things before, but I'd never kill anyone. I swear to God I'd never do that. Please help me, Sandy. If my grandmother won't even talk to me . . ." His voice choked up. "I-I haven't got anybody else."

"Josh, listen to me. I'm going to go talk to your grandmother right now. I'm going to see if we can get you out of jail, and then we'll go from there, okay?"

"Okay," Josh said, his voice filled with relief. "I knew you'd help me, Sandy. I knew you would."

Sandy hung up the phone and grabbed her purse and keys.

"Did we hear you right?" Lyle said, his eyes wide. "They think Josh killed that woman?"

"Yes. But there has to be some mistake."

"Of course there's some mistake!" Imogene said. "Josh couldn't have done something like that!"

"I have to go talk to his grandmother. Do you think you two could—"

"We'll hold down the fort," Lyle said. "You go do whatever you have to do, and don't worry about a thing."

When Sandy pulled up to the curb in front of Betty's house, she saw the woman crouched on her lawn, wearing a straw hat against the summer sun. She dug a spade into the earth, turned up a weed, and tossed it onto a nearby pile. She turned when Sandy approached and slowly rose to her feet. By the taut, wounded expression on her face, Sandy could tell that the circumstances had already taken a toll on her.

"Josh just called me," Sandy said gently. "He said he'd been arrested."

The woman blinked as if she were going to cry. "Yes."

"Betty? Are you okay?"

She shook her head slowly. "I thought he was going to be all right. I thought he was turning around. And now this."

"Tell me what happened."

"The police came early this morning. They asked him a lot of questions. I don't know what all, exactly. They tore up the house looking for evidence."

"What did they find?"

"I don't know. But they took away some things. I don't know what. And then they arrested him. I asked them what the charge was, and they told me that Laura Williams had been murdered, and that they think Josh did it. After they took him away, I thought maybe they'd get him down there and realize they had the wrong person, but when I called to see what was happening, sure enough they were holding him for murder."

"Josh said that somebody supposedly saw him in Laura's yard."

"Yes. Ralph Clemmons. I know Ralph. He's not a man who lies. If he says he saw him, he saw him."

"Maybe he was mistaken."

She let out a shaky sigh. "Maybe. I don't know."

"Does Josh have an alibi?"

"He told the police he was by himself from the time he got off work until the time he came home."

"Has bond been set?"

"Yes. Two hundred and fifty thousand dollars."

"All you have to come up with is ten percent."

"With collateral for the rest. I've been down that road with my son. I'm eighty-three years old. If I lose this house, I have nowhere else to go."

"What about Josh's mother?"

"She's just as worthless as his father."

"But that means Josh will have to stay in jail until this is resolved."

"I can't help that."

"He won't run. It'll never come to that."

"What if it does? What if he disappears and I lose my house? What then?"

"What about an attorney?" Sandy asked.

"The court has appointed somebody."

"Do you remember his name?"

"Howard somebody or other."

"Linz?"

"Yes. I think so."

Sandy tried to keep her face impassive. She knew Howard Linz. He was certainly competent to handle lesser cases, but murder?

"Betty," she said. "Do you love Josh?"

Tears filled the old woman's eyes, but she didn't respond.

"I know you do. So you have to help him."

"I can't. Not if he committed murder."

"Are you telling me you really believe that Josh killed Laura Williams?"

The woman ran her finger along the spade she held, knocking off a clump of dirt. "You have to understand something, Sandy. I dealt with Josh's father for years. When he was a teenager, and later, too. Even now he has a hard time staying inside the law. But I had hope for Josh. Even after he got into trouble, still I had hope for him. If he was going to try to make something of himself, I told myself I'd help. But now that he's been accused of this . . ."

"Betty," Sandy said softly. "He's your grandson."

Betty stared at Sandy a long time, the emotion on her face slowly turning into a mask of indifference. "No, Sandy. That's where you're wrong."

"What?"

"I don't have a grandson."

Betty knelt to the lawn again and pulled up one more weed, tossing it onto the pile. Sandy stared down at her, knowing what she must be feeling, but still she couldn't imagine any scenario in which she'd give up on a member of her family or anyone else she loved.

And now she didn't know which way to turn.

Betty had been the only lifeline Josh had, and that had just snapped. For a crime like this, he could very well be tried as an adult, and if he were found guilty, he would spend the rest of his life in prison. Or . . .

Texas was a death-penalty state.

There were questions to be asked. Motions to be filed. Evidence to be examined. And all of those things could have an outcome on the verdict a jury eventually reached. A good attorney could make the most of those things from day one. A mediocre one could hurt more than he helped.

I don't have anyone else.

As Josh's words played through her mind again, Sandy was filled with a burning need to help him. It wasn't right that he be convicted of a crime he didn't commit, and as long as she had breath left in her body, it wasn't going to happen.

Josh needed a sharp attorney. Somebody who knew how to play the game. Somebody who, no matter how the odds were stacked against him, would come out on top because losing wasn't an option.

He needed Ethan Millner.

Thirty minutes later, Sandy rode the elevator to the seventh floor of the Cauthron Building. The doors opened and she was met with a pair of glass-and-brass doors that led to the reception area of Millner, Millner, Monroe, and Dade.

She opened one of the doors and stepped inside. The silence in the office was broken only by her own footsteps on the hardwood floor and the soft clacking of a keyboard behind a polished cherry-wood counter. Artwork lined the walls, each piece spotlighted with such respect that she knew it had to be expensive stuff. The floors were adorned with rugs that it would be a crime to walk on, and she could actually smell the leather furniture.

The receptionist looked up. The nameplate on the counter said her name was Sasha. She was almost painfully beautiful, with ice-blue eyes, blond hair, and flawless features to go with her size-zero body. Then again, Sandy couldn't imagine anything less than perfect in a place like this. It occurred to her that Sasha was just the kind of woman she'd expect to find with Ethan, and for a split second she wondered if anything had ever gone on between them outside the confines of this office.

Then she wondered why she was wondering.

Sandy asked to see Ethan, and Sasha directed her to his secretary. Sandy walked around a corner to find a woman sitting at a desk, maybe fifty years old, wearing wire-rimmed glasses and a pristine linen suit, perfect in her own excruciatingly professional way. But unlike Sasha, this was a woman who radiated substance over symbolism.

"May I help you?" she asked.

"Yes. My name is Sandy DeMarco. I'm here to see Ethan Millner."

"Do you have an appointment?"

"No. I was hoping I could slip in to see him for just a few minutes."

"That would be impossible right now. He's due in court within the hour. Now, if you'd like to make an appointment—"

"I need just a few minutes. Where is his office?"

"That's irrelevant, since you don't have an appointment."

"But it's extremely important that I see him."

"It's all right, Gina. I'll see Ms. DeMarco."

Sandy looked up to see Ethan standing in a nearby doorway. Her heart skipped a few beats, just as it had when she'd met him for the first time last night.

In opulent surroundings like these, she'd expected him to be wearing a designer suit that dripped with money and prestige. Instead, he wore a navy-blue sport coat and a powder-blue shirt that looked as if they were right off the rack, beige slacks that seemed a touch too casual, and a tic that might have been silk and might have been synthetic. She wondered why. But still it was Ethan underneath—a man comfortable in his own element and in total control.

"Come this way," he said.

He led her into his office, which was even more lavish than the reception area. Massive furniture. Leather executive chair and sofa. A palatial bathroom she could see a sliver of through an open door. A striking seventh-floor view of the city. And as her gaze moved around the room, she spied a closet with its door partially open. Inside it hung a few of the kind of suits she would have expected him to be wearing in lieu of what he had on right now. A second later, she realized why.

His secretary had said it. He was on his way to court.

Within the hour he'd be playing to twelve jurors who by odds would be middle-class, so he'd chosen a professional yet accessible look that said, *You can trust me. If I tell you my client is innocent, you can take it to the bank.*

He motioned her to the sofa. She sat down, perched on the edge with her purse in her lap. He sat down next to her, casually draping his arm along the sofa behind her.

"How are you doing?" he asked. "You were pretty shaken up last night."

"I'm fine. But . . ."

"What's wrong?"

She took a deep, calming breath. "Something's happened concerning the murder."

"What's that?"

"They've arrested a suspect."

"That's good news. Maybe Henderson is on the ball for a switch."

"No. It's not good." She closed her eyes with a sigh, then opened them again. "They've arrested Josh Newman."

Ethan raised his eyebrows. "The kid on probation?"

"Yes. But he didn't do it. The only reason they think he might have is because of Ralph Clemmons."

"Who is Ralph Clemmons?"

"Laura's next-door neighbor. We must have already left the scene last night when he came over. He told the police that he saw Josh in Laura's backyard near the time of the murder. By this morning they had a warrant, and they came to Betty's house to arrest him."

"What's the kid's story?"

"He says he was never near the place."

"Does he have an alibi?"

"He says he was by himself at the time of the murder."

"Nowhere near Laura Williams's house, of course."

"That's right."

"And you believe him."

"Yes, I do."

"In light of the kid's past, maybe you should reconsider that loyalty."

"I don't care what he's done in the past. I know Josh. He couldn't possibly . . ." She took a breath. "You saw the body. He couldn't possibly have done something like that."

"Why are you telling me all this?"

Sandy hesitated, wanting him to understand more about Josh before she told him why she was there. But evidently that wasn't going to be an option.

"Because I want you to defend him."

For the count of three, Ethan just stared at her. "Defend him?"

"Josh is innocent."

"His guilt or innocence isn't the issue."

"Then what is the issue? I know it'll be a tough case, but—"

"I don't turn down tough cases. But my retainer is ten thousand dollars."

Sandy felt a surge of hopelessness. She'd had no idea. She knew Ethan was good, so he had to command a lot of money. But now she knew just how big a favor she was getting ready to ask.

"Josh doesn't have that kind of money," she explained. "And he has no way of getting it. I talked to his grandmother this morning. Because of this, she's writing him off. Turning her back on him."

"If his own grandmother won't help him, maybe that should tell you something."

"She's eighty-three years old. Her son, Josh's father, was always in trouble with the law, and she can't deal with it again. I know she really loves Josh, but she just can't face this."

"So if the kid hasn't got the money for representation, why are you here?"

Sandy took a deep, silent breath. "Because I was hoping you'd consider taking the case pro bono."

Ethan's expression never changed. Even so, the moment the words were out of her mouth she could almost feel the air quivering between them.

"Pro bono," he repeated.

"Yes. I know it's a lot to ask. But I also know the state bar requires you to do thirty hours of pro bono work every year. Would you consider taking this case to fulfill that?"

"Thirty hours wouldn't even put a dent in the number of hours required for a murder case. I'm afraid I'm going to have to say no." He rose and went to his desk where he closed two files and stuck them into the side pocket of his briefcase. "I have to go. I'm due in court."

"The cops misled Josh when they went to his house to arrest him. They asked him if he did it. That's all. They said, 'Did you do it?' And he said he did."

"He confessed to the murder?"

"No! He thought he was confessing to missing his curfew!"

"Yeah, the cops can be pretty slick sometimes."

"He was trying to tell the truth!"

"Sandy, contrary to popular belief, the truth doesn't always set you free."

"That's why he needs help, Ethan. Your help."

"There are other attorneys who might be willing to take the case. I can have my secretary put you in touch with a few of them."

"Josh is almost eighteen. For a crime like this, he'll be tried as an adult. Texas is a death-penalty state. There's too much at stake here to settle for second best."

"I told you I can't do it."

"Because he can't put ten thousand dollars in your pocket?"

"You're a florist. Do you give your services away?"

"My services won't keep somebody from spending the rest of his life in prison. Yours will."

"All the more reason for me to be well paid for what I do."

"I agree with you. You should be well paid. But in this case—"

"It's not as if he won't have representation. The court will appoint an attorney for him."

"Do you know Howard Linz?"

Ethan put a pen in the breast pocket of his coat. "Yes. I know him. He's perfectly competent."

"Competent, maybe. But not nearly as competent as you are."

"I have to go."

He closed his briefcase and strode to the door. Sandy felt a surge of desperation. She rose and followed him. "Ethan, wait. Please."

He turned back, looking so much like the powerful, experienced, capable attorney he was that one thought kept circling through her mind.

You get what you pay for.

Ethan commanded a ten-thousand-dollar retainer because he was worth it. Her brothers characterized him as devious and underhanded, but only because they had to go head-to-head with him in the courtroom and all three of them hated like hell to lose. The truth was that Ethan was the very best at what he did, and that meant he was worth every penny of the ten thousand dollars it took to retain his services.

She pulled a checkbook and a pen from her purse.

Ethan looked at her warily. "What are you doing?"

She didn't respond. She merely wrote the check, ripped it

out, and laid it on his desk. "I'd appreciate it if you'd hold that until tomorrow. It'll be good by then."

She returned the pen and checkbook to her purse. "We have crime-watch patrol at eight o'clock this evening. We can talk about the case then."

With that, she turned and left his office.

Ethan watched Sandy walk out of his office, then strode to his desk and stared down at the check.

Ten thousand dollars. *Damn it.*

He couldn't believe this. She'd just handed him money she probably didn't have to defend a kid who was probably guilty as sin. And that irritated the hell out of him, because Sandy had just shoved him right between a rock and a hard place, and he wasn't sure which way to turn now.

Feeling a surge of frustration, he flung his briefcase onto the sofa, where it fell on its side, spilling the two files from the side pocket. He raked his hands through his hair, then exhaled sharply.

"What the hell is the matter with you?"

Ethan whipped around to see Gina standing at his office door. He turned away again. "Nothing's the matter with me."

"Don't lie. I see 'pissed off' written all over your face." Gina glanced over to his briefcase and its former contents sprawled across the sofa. "You know, fits of temper really aren't your style. I assume this has something to do with Ms. DeMarco?"

Ethan picked up the loose files and stuffed them into his briefcase, feeling stupid for the outburst, and even stupider that he'd done it in front of Gina.

"She's sure got you in a snit," Gina said.

"You know, Gina, most of the time I welcome your point of view. This is not one of those times."

"You'll tell me all about it sooner or later. Why don't we save a lot of energy this time and make it sooner?"

LIGHT MY FIRE   75

"Fine. If you must know, a teenage kid who works for her has been accused of the murder that happened in her neighborhood last night. She wants me to defend him."

"Oh, yeah?"

"But she wanted me to do it pro bono. I can't work for nothing. Not on a case of that magnitude."

Gina spied the check on his desk and picked it up. "Well, apparently you made that very clear to her."

"The kid has a juvenile record, no alibi, and an eyewitness has placed him at the scene of the crime. She has no business throwing away that kind of money on a kid who's probably guilty as sin."

"A lot of your clients are guilty. Since when has that stopped you from collecting your fees?"

"Ten grand is clearly a lot of money to her, and she's undoubtedly going to have to scrape to come up with it. She shouldn't be doing that."

"Really? Why not?"

"It's just a stupid thing to do. That's all."

Gina's eyes narrowed. "Hmm."

Oh, God. He *hated* it when she got that look on her face. "What?"

"Why are you second-guessing her motives when she's handing you ten thousand dollars? That's really not your style, either."

That was a very good question. One he should probably be asking himself. Sandy DeMarco was an intelligent adult. If she wanted to pour ten thousand dollars down the drain, what difference should it make to him?

"I'm making observations, Gina. Not second-guessing."

"Then I guess that means you want me to deposit the check."

Ethan paused just long enough that Gina raised an eyebrow, waiting for his reply.

"Of course I want you to deposit it," he told her, suddenly

hating the sound of his own voice. "Hold it until tomorrow, though. She told me she needs a day to get the money together." He looked at his watch. "Damn it. I'm due in court."

Gina pulled a comb out of his desk drawer. "Fix your hair."

He glanced in the mirror to find his hair sticking straight up from where he'd run his hands through it earlier. He was lucky he hadn't yanked himself bald. He took the comb from Gina and passed it through his hair a few times.

"Love the outfit," Gina said, eying him up and down. "Was Sears having a sale?"

"Fraud case. Blue-collar jury. Closing arguments today."

She held up the check. "You're sure you want me to deposit this?"

He tossed the comb onto his desk and grabbed his briefcase. "Did you not hear me the first time?"

"Oh, yeah. You said a lot of things. Some of them were even out loud."

He frowned. "I said only one thing, Gina, and that was *deposit the check.*"

She shrugged offhandedly. "Sure, boss. Whatever you say."

"I won't be coming back to the office today."

"No problem. I'll hold down the fort."

"I'll see you in the morning."

Ethan strode out of his office, down the hall, and past the reception desk, frustration still eating away at him. What the hell did Sandy think she was doing, anyway? How much could a florist make? Surely not enough that she could throw away ten grand without batting an eye. He'd seen her house. Nice enough, but hardly a palace, so money wasn't something she had buckets of. Handing him that check was just about the stupidest thing she could possibly have done.

It's not your problem. She wants you to defend the kid? So take the money and defend him. It's a no-brainer.

But as Ethan walked, his frustration grew. His definitive strides shortened and slowed, and by the time he reached the doors leading to the elevator lobby he'd stopped altogether.

He stood there for a good ten seconds, thinking about Sandy's dark, pleading eyes. Her determination as she'd written that check. Her misguided attempt to do something good for a kid who was probably bad to the bone.

The fact that he'd refused to help her because of a few thousand dollars he'd never miss.

He walked back to his office where he found Gina still standing in front of his desk, flicking the check back and forth across her fingertips. She held it up.

"Looking for this?"

Ethan snatched the check from her hand and stuffed it into his pocket. "The kid's name is Josh Newman. He's sitting in lockup on the murder charge. Get me his arrest record and anything else about him you can find."

"You got it." She eyed him carefully. "So what are you going to do with that check? Depositing it appears to be out."

"That's none of your business."

"Is something going on between you and Sandy DeMarco?"

"That's also none of your business."

"Just say yes, Ethan. It wastes fewer words."

He closed his eyes. "Gina? Have I ever told you you're a pain in the ass?"

"More times than I can count. I'll phone you later with the info you need."

Ethan got a call from Gina five minutes after he left the courtroom late that afternoon. As it turned out, Josh Newman had a substantial juvenile record, beginning with joyriding, shoplifting, and public intoxication, moving on to two arrests for assault, and culminating in a conviction for burglary for which he was currently on probation.

No, that record didn't automatically translate to murder.

But if Josh had been burglarizing Laura's house and she'd come home and surprised him, panic certainly could have driven him to react first and think later. His two arrests for assault were evidence of a quick temper. Put all that together with an eyewitness placing him at the scene of the crime around the time of the murder, and the prosecution's job just got a whole lot easier.

Yet Sandy swore he was innocent.

By the time Ethan hit the gym for an hour, then showered and ate a quick dinner, it was nearly time for him to go to Sandy's for crime-watch patrol. And through it all, he kept telling himself that the smart thing to do was to deposit the check and move on.

So why, when he knocked on her door just before eight that night, was the damned thing still in his pocket?

Sandy opened the door, giving him a cursory nod and telling him she'd be ready to go in a moment. She was all business, which was what he'd expected. The ten thousand dollars she'd given him to retain his services had shed an entirely new light on their relationship, one he wasn't sure he liked in the least.

He followed her into the kitchen, watching as she opened her dishwasher door, then deposited soap in the little cup before closing it again and turning it on. When she turned back around, he pulled out the check and held it up. "We need to talk about this."

She flicked her gaze to the check. "I don't know what there is to talk about."

"I want to know why you're so determined to help Josh Newman."

"He's innocent."

"Like it or not, the jury's still out on that."

"That's why I'm hiring you."

"Look, Sandy. I've never been one to try to save people from themselves. I figure it's a free country full of people with free will, and if somebody wants to throw money away, it's no problem of mine. But in this case . . ."

He tore up the check and tossed the pieces down on the counter.

Sandy recoiled. "What the hell are you doing?"

"I just don't want to see you lose that kind of money trying to help a kid who's not worth it."

"Not worth it?" Anger burned on her face. "Look, I know you think he's just one more bad-to-the-bone kid nobody should be losing sleep over, but you're dead wrong. And if I do nothing and he's convicted, I couldn't look at that ten thousand dollars knowing I'd had the capability to help him and didn't."

To Ethan's surprise, she grabbed her purse, pulled out her checkbook and a pen, and began to write.

"Sandy, stop it."

When she kept writing, Ethan grabbed her wrist, stilling her. "Damn it, will you *stop*? I'm not taking your money!"

She tried to pull her wrist away, but he didn't let go. After a moment, he softened his grip to a gentler one and pressed her hand down to the countertop. The room fell silent, without so much as the faint creak of an eighty-year-old rafter to break the tension.

"I'm not taking your money," he repeated, his voice only a decibel above a whisper. "But I am taking the case."

chapter six

Sandy blinked with surprise. "What did you say?"

Ethan released her wrist, then took the checkbook she still held, eased it from between her fingers, and laid it on the counter. "Josh will have to tell the court that he wants me as his attorney. I'll file a motion to substitute, and Linz will have to file a motion to withdraw. I'll make sure that happens."

"I told you that Josh can't pay you."

"I'm not asking him to."

"I can't believe you're doing this."

"It's what you want, isn't it?"

"Yes, of course it is, but—"

"Fine. I'll go see Josh Monday morning and put the wheels in motion." He checked his watch. "Now let's get moving or we're going to be patrolling until midnight."

He started to walk out of the kitchen. Sandy grabbed his arm and pulled him to a halt. "Wait a minute. I don't understand. What made you change your mind?"

For some reason, Ethan's heart beat faster. Her hand against his arm—just that simple touch—muddled his thoughts to the point that he had a hard time thinking straight. And he couldn't remember a time in his life when straight thinking had ever been a problem.

He eased away from her. "I like a challenge."

"All your cases are challenging. You wouldn't be commanding big money if they weren't."

"Howard Linz has very little experience defending murder cases."

"But he's competent. You told me that yourself."

"A rule to live by, Sandy: When you get what you want, stop asking questions."

"Only one more."

"What?"

"You could have had everything you just said and pocketed ten thousand dollars, too. Why did you tear up my check?"

As Sandy stared at him, waiting for his answer, Ethan thought about how he'd seen men do foolish things for women—acts of stupidity that brought down their careers, their marriages, their lives. He didn't think a woman had been born who could influence him to make a decision he didn't want to make.

And then she'd written that check.

At that moment, something inside him had shifted, given way, and all at once he was taking what was probably going to be a hopeless case for zero compensation.

"The truth?" he said. "I've clearly lost my mind. Consider yourself lucky that you're getting the benefit of that."

She smiled. "If I thought you'd lost your mind, I wouldn't want you defending Josh."

"I still don't see why you care so much about this kid."

"Because I see the goodness in him as clearly as you see the color of his eyes."

"Goodness?"

"Yesterday evening before he left the shop, he thanked me for giving him a job. For giving him a second chance when nobody else would. Can you imagine anyone saying those things and then committing murder not three hours later?"

"Sociopathic behavior comes in all shapes and sizes."

"But it doesn't come in Josh Newman. Trust me on that, will you?"

"Still, who is he to you but an employee?"

She looked at him without blinking. "Somebody who has nobody else."

He didn't know Josh Newman. No matter how Sandy felt about him, when Ethan saw him on Monday, he didn't expect him to be any different from a hundred other juvenile offenders who may or may not have committed a crime. But that didn't matter to Ethan, because his belief wasn't the issue here. Sandy's was. And for some reason, that had more power over him than he could possibly have imagined.

The temperature that night was one for the Texas record books—ninety-eight degrees at eight o'clock in the evening. The air conditioner in Sandy's car was blasting at full speed, but still it felt uncomfortably warm inside the car.

Sandy swung around a corner, moving from Oak Tree Place onto Cottonwood Street. They approached Laura Williams's house, which was still cordoned off by crime-scene tape. Sandy slowed the car, then stopped in front of the house. Night was falling, casting long shadows across the front yard.

"So tell me where we go from here," Sandy said.

"Hard to say at this point," Ethan said. "I need to hear from Josh tomorrow."

"This is still so unreal. I can't believe Laura is dead."

"Have any other murders ever happened in this neighborhood?"

"No. No murders. This neighborhood has one of the lowest crime rates in the city. Several heart attacks, though. There are still quite a few senior citizens who live here." She thought for a moment. "And there have been a couple of accidental deaths that I know of. A man was painting the second-story trim on his house, fell off a ladder, and broke his neck. And two men who lived in a house on Cypress Street died in a fire shortly after I moved here."

Ethan looked at the houses on either side of the victim's. One was a smaller prairie-style home much like Laura's, and the other was a two-story Victorian. An older couple sat on the front porch.

"I don't suppose he's our eyewitness, is he?" he asked.

"Yes," Sandy said. "Ralph Clemmons."

"Do you know him?"

"Yes."

"How well?"

"He and his wife are active in the neighborhood association and crime-watch patrol. And they're animal lovers, so sometimes they feed my cat for me when I'm out of town."

"Would you say they're reliable people?"

"Yes. Very much so."

"Pull over. I want to talk to them."

"Right now?"

"Yes."

"But Ralph's going to be a witness for the prosecution. Once he realizes you're defending Josh, he might not want to talk."

"I'll identify myself. It's up to him if he wants to answer my questions or not."

"What are you going to say to him?"

"It won't be confrontational. That's counterproductive at this stage. I just want to hear his side of the story if he chooses to tell it. If not, we leave."

Sandy pulled the car to the curb and killed the engine. Together they walked up the sidewalk to the porch. Ralph stood up as he saw them approach.

He was a tall, thickly built man with neatly trimmed gray hair and a pair of wire-rimmed glasses. He was probably in his early sixties, but he looked somewhat younger, still possessing a sharp, upright posture and the bearing of a man who was used to giving orders. Ethan would guess that he'd been a manager wherever he'd worked. Possibly even the big boss.

Ida, on the other hand, was a petite woman, probably in her sixties, too. Her salt-and-pepper hair was carefully styled, and she wore a long, loose skirt and a tailored shirt. A small calico cat lay in her lap, sleeping with the kind of lazy abandon that told Ethan that Ida's lap was his bed of choice.

Sandy stepped up onto the porch, greeting the Clemmonses with a friendly smile, and they returned the gesture.

"Ralph, Ida, this is Ethan Millner. He's the attorney who's going to be representing Josh Newman. If you don't mind, he'd like to ask you a few questions about what you saw last night."

As Ralph eyed Ethan carefully, Ethan instantly sensed a man who had no intention of getting caught off-guard, and for a moment it seemed as if he were going to say no. Then he motioned to the bench across from the lawn chairs where he and Ida sat, and Ethan and Sandy took a seat.

Ralph stared at Ethan. "Have we met before?"

"No. I don't believe we have."

"You look familiar." His eyes narrowed. "Can't say why, though."

Ethan leaned forward. "You say you saw Josh Newman on Laura's property around the time of the murder."

"Yes. I was standing at our patio door. It faces the backyard. I'd stepped out for a cigar, and Ida was upstairs getting ready for bed. All at once I saw him climbing the fence between our two yards about midway down. Then he headed for the grove of trees at the back of our properties and disappeared."

"You're sure it was him?" Sandy asked.

"It wasn't that far away, and there's a good floodlight out there. I may be sixty-three years old, but my eyesight's still twenty/twenty. It was Josh Newman. I know the boy well enough."

"What time was it when you saw this person?"

"It was right around ten o'clock. I step out every night for a cigar right before we go to bed."

"The crime scene was pretty bloody. It would have been hard for a murderer to escape the scene without getting some of it on him. Did you see any blood on this person?"

"I couldn't tell you that. I just saw him running away."

"You could see his face clearly, but you couldn't tell if there was blood on that face?"

"There was no blood on his face. But his clothes—that's what I wouldn't be able to tell you about."

Ethan nodded. "What was this man wearing?"

"Jeans. Black T-shirt. Some big, bold image on the front of it in a bright color, like yellow or gold. Don't know what it was."

"How well did you know the victim?"

"She was a good neighbor," Ralph said. "She was quiet, and she kept her property up. That's important, you know, when somebody lives right next door to you."

"What did you know about Laura's personal life?" Ethan asked. "Did you ever see anyone coming or going from her house?"

"There was one friend of hers who came over sometimes," Ida said. "We saw her car in the driveway occasionally, but we never met her."

"Ralph," Sandy said. "Please think. It had to have been somebody else besides Josh. I saw the body. It was a horrible crime. Josh just couldn't have done it."

"I'm not saying he did it. I wouldn't know about that. I'm just saying that it's a fact that he hopped the fence from Laura's backyard last night around the time she was killed, then ran to the grove of trees in the back of our property. I didn't see him again. I assume he climbed the back fence and crossed the creek to go home, but I can't say that for sure, either. I'll only testify to what I know to be a fact."

"But that's going to implicate him in a murder he didn't commit," Sandy said.

"Maybe, but it's a fact just the same."

Ida shifted uncomfortably, looking at her husband with a plaintive expression. "Is it possible you're mistaken, Ralph? Is it possible that it was somebody else?"

"I can only tell you what I saw."

"I hate being in the middle of this," Ida said. "This is going to kill Betty." She turned to Sandy. "Have you seen her since this happened? With Ralph being an eyewitness and all, I don't know if she'd take kindly to us paying a visit."

"Yes. I've seen her. She's pretty shaken up. It might be best just to leave her alone for a few days. She's been through a lot."

"Her son, and now her grandson," Ralph said. "What are things coming to?"

"Ralph and I have lived here for thirty-seven years," Ida said. "It's a good neighborhood where good people live. We want it to stay that way. If that boy did something like this . . ."

"I don't believe he did," Sandy said. "I just don't believe that Josh could have killed Laura."

"I hate it that I'm the one to do this," Ralph said, "because I know how you feel about the boy. But what's right is right. When I go to my maker, I'm gonna have to answer for the things I've done. If I don't tell what I know about this, what's the good Lord gonna think of me?"

Ethan didn't know what else there was to say. This was going to be a real uphill battle. Ralph Clemmons was a dream witness for the prosecution: intelligent, consistent, and beyond reproach. And how many sixty-three-year-old men still had twenty/twenty vision? Ethan would have to find a way to check that out, but he had a feeling the man was telling the truth.

"Sandy," Ethan said, rising from the bench. "We'd better be going."

"Wait just a minute." Ralph reached into his shirt pocket. Ethan heard metallic clinking, and then Ralph pulled something out and handed it to Sandy.

"What's this?"

"I want you to give it to the boy."

Ethan glanced over and saw a small silver medallion the size of a quarter with a cross on one side. Sandy flipped it over, and he saw an image of Jesus on the other.

"I don't understand," she said.

"If he really did commit that murder, it'll be a reminder for him."

"A reminder?"

"That all he has to do is repent and accept Jesus, and he'll be forgiven."

Ethan couldn't believe this. The chief witness for the prosecution was worried about the defendant's eternal soul?

"Thank you, Ralph. That's nice." She handed it to Ethan. "Will you give it to him when you see him?"

Ethan took the medallion and stuck it in his pocket. Yeah, he'd give it to the kid. And chances were good that he'd give it right back.

He and Sandy started down the porch steps.

"Wait a minute," Ralph said, coming to his feet.

Ethan turned back.

"I thought I'd seen you before. Now I know where. On the news. That rape case with the executive from Bryan Industries." Ralph's eyes narrowed. "You were the one who defended him."

"Yes, I was."

"Walked away a free man, didn't he?"

"Yes. He did."

Ralph nodded thoughtfully. "Are you a religious man, Mr. Millner?"

"No. I'm not."

"Didn't think so." Ralph stared at Ethan a long time. Then he pulled another silver medallion out of his shirt pocket and held it out. "Doesn't matter, though. You don't have to believe in God, because God believes in you."

Ethan stared down at the medallion, then met Ralph's eyes again. "You might want to give that to somebody who'd appreciate it more than I would."

Ralph returned the medallion to his shirt pocket, then turned to Sandy. "You be sure to tell that boy we'll be praying for him."

"Even when you think it's possible that he killed Laura?"

"Hate the sin, love the sinner," Ralph said.

Ethan sighed inwardly. He was praying for the kid? This was too much. No doubt about it—where Ralph Clemmons was concerned, Ethan had an uphill battle ahead of him.

Sandy and Ethan got back into her car. She put the key in the ignition, then sat back in the seat with a miserable sigh. "He's going to be a good witness for the prosecution, isn't he?"

"They don't come any better," Ethan said. "And that means I'll be looking for dirt."

"What?"

"Senior citizens are generally easier to discredit. Bad eyesight. Fear. Paranoia. Bias against teenagers. But in this guy's case, it's not going to be so easy. What profession did he retire from?"

"He was an engineer."

"A professional. The jury's more likely to buy his testimony. That'll make things tougher. But it certainly won't be insurmountable. I'll find a way around him."

"I don't want you trashing Ralph Clemmons."

"You can't have it both ways. If you want Josh acquitted, I'll have to play hardball. I'll be looking for some agenda on Ralph's part. Some ulterior motive, even if it's the fact that he had a second cousin twice removed who was murdered and now he'd do anything to solve this one."

Sandy sighed. "I still don't like this."

"You swear Josh is telling the truth. If he is, that means Ralph is wrong about what he saw. If he's mistaken, don't you want me to bring that to the attention of the jurors?"

"Well, yes, of course, but—"

"Then you're going to have to let me do my job."

Sandy gave him a reluctant nod. "So what now?"

"I'll go see Josh tomorrow. Hear his side of the story. Then we'll wait for the forensic evidence to come back to see exactly what we're up against."

"How long before that happens?"

"Impossible to say. A few days to a few weeks."

Sandy sighed. "Josh is just a boy. I can't imagine him locked up in jail. He must be so scared."

"He's been there before."

"Not on a murder charge."

"That's right. And the wheels grind slower on a case of this magnitude, so he could be in there for some time before he finally goes to trial."

"That's not making me feel any better."

"I'm just preparing you for what's coming."

"What if there's nothing tying Josh or anyone else to the crime?"

"Even if the forensic evidence doesn't clearly implicate Josh, he's still in trouble. Ralph Clemmons's eyewitness testimony is strong enough to build a heavy circumstantial case. You say Josh has no alibi. If the prosecution finds a way to work in his past arrests and conviction, sometimes that's all it takes to convict. You never know what a jury's going to do."

"You have a lot of control over that," Sandy said.

"Not nearly as much as I'd like to have."

"But a whole lot more than most attorneys."

"You seem to have a lot of faith in me."

"Why shouldn't I? Word has it that you're the best there is."

A smile edged across his lips. "All related to my competence as an attorney, of course."

Just the sound of his voice, low and sensually charged, made Sandy's skin quiver.

"Of course," she said.

Liar. She'd heard all kinds of stories related to his competence that had nothing to do with his performance in the courtroom.

"For now," Ethan said, "about all we can do is wait until the investigation is complete and the forensic evidence has been compiled. Then we'll know what we're up against."

"The waiting is going to kill me."

"I know. But it's not going to do you any good to worry about it. For now, just know that I've got a handle on things and try to put it out of your mind."

She started the car, and they began to patrol the neighborhood. She had no idea how she'd feel right now if Ethan hadn't decided to take the case, and if he hadn't been there to tell her that everything was under control. Because of him, the situation that had seemed so dark and dire suddenly seemed manageable, and Sandy actually felt herself relax.

But as they drove, that relaxation was replaced by tension of a different kind. Slowly she became aware of Ethan watching her. Sometimes she felt it rather than saw it, but still she knew he was doing it.

The question was, *why* was he watching her?

Not a damned thing about her should have appealed to a man like him. And if she was the nice girl the whole world thought she was, not a damned thing about him should have appealed to her.

But there wasn't much about him that *didn't* appeal to her. He was clearly intelligent. He had a way with words that fascinated her. And he was quick-witted, thank God, because dull men made her want to scream. That he was reputed to play dirty in the courtroom and sleep with any woman with a pulse didn't bother her in the least, because she knew that a lot of that was probably just rumor and speculation by people he clashed with on the job.

And the truth was that the older she got, the more she flew in the face of her own reputation. With every passing year, she found herself more and more attracted to men who stepped off the straight and narrow, who colored outside the lines, who were just a little bit bigger than life. And the fact that he was handsome enough to turn the head of just about any woman on the planet was merely icing on the cake.

She picked up the Coke she'd brought with her and took a big gulp, then set it back in the beverage holder. It was cold. She wasn't. Not when Ethan's eyes were on her far more than they were on her neighborhood. Self-consciousness overtook her for a moment, and she reached up to tuck a loose strand of hair that had fallen from her ponytail behind her ear.

"Your hair is beautiful," he said.

It was the first time he'd spoken in several minutes, and it startled her.

"Thank you."

"But I think I'd like it even better loose around your shoulders."

"Oh, you would?"

"Yes. Why don't you wear it down?"

"Because it just gets in the way."

"I'll give you twenty bucks."

"What?"

"I'll give you twenty bucks to take your hair down."

"Ethan—"

"Make it forty."

Her eyes widened. "Are you insane?"

"Do you care? It's an easy forty bucks." He leaned closer. "So do we have a deal?"

"No, I think I'll pass."

"Okay. My final offer. A hundred-dollar donation to the Tolosa SPCA."

She looked at him skeptically. "How did you know that's one of my favorite charities?"

"Lucky guess."

She reached up and pulled out the rubber band, tossed it to the dashboard, then stroked her hand through her hair.

"Yes," he said, "that's much better."

"I want to see some proof of that donation," she told him.

"Not a problem."

He spoke in a low, provocative drawl that seemed to shoot her body temperature up ten degrees. This man could recite the alphabet and give her hot flashes.

"Tell me, Ethan," she said. "Do you always get what you want?"

"Absolutely," he murmured. "As long as I want it badly enough."

Then tell me what else you want.

That thought popped into Sandy's head out of nowhere, and she chased it away just as quickly. Driving in circles in her neighborhood, while a worthwhile activity from a crime prevention standpoint, had to be boring as hell for somebody who had no real stake in the process. His verbal jousting was simply his way of entertaining himself, and she'd be crazy to think it was anything else.

For the next hour or so, they made small talk about insignificant things, but eventually Sandy turned the conversation more personal. Where Ethan was concerned, there was a lot more she wanted to know.

"It's Millner, Millner, Monroe, and Dade," she said. "Which family member are you in partnership with?"

"My father."

"So how do you like that?"

"Our firm is very successful."

"Obviously. But that wasn't what I was asking."

"We're having a nice conversation, Sandy. If I'm forced to talk about my father, I'm afraid it'll cease being so nice."

"Okay. Then what about your mother?"

"She and my father divorced when I was eight. I haven't seen her since."

Sandy blinked with surprise. "You haven't seen your own mother in all this time?"

"That's right."

His voice held an edge of irritation, and Sandy decided to let that subject drop. "How about the rest of your family?"

"There isn't one. Not much of one, anyway. I have two aunts who live overseas."

"No brothers or sisters?"

"I'm an only child. My family isn't a terribly interesting subject. Why don't we talk about yours instead?"

Sandy smiled. "It's a big one. Aunts, uncles, cousins, grand-parents. Most of them are into law enforcement in one way or another."

"Your father was a cop, too."

"Yes. Shot in the line of duty."

"I remember that."

"Most everybody does. He was a real icon in the Tolosa PD."

"What about your mother?" Ethan asked.

"She died when I was fourteen. Cancer. I'm the oldest, and I practically raised my brothers. I think it's the reason we're as close as we are today."

"So what's it like having a big family like that? Sounds as if it would be very . . . busy."

Sandy laughed. "It is. Holidays are nuts. And I swear, we must celebrate somebody's birthday at least once a week."

Ethan was silent for a moment. She glanced over to see his brows drawn together.

"What's the matter?" she asked.

"What's the date today?"

"The twenty-second." She paused. "Why do you ask?"

"Because today's my birthday."

"Your birthday? Then what are you doing on crime patrol? I certainly would have let you off the hook for tonight."

He shrugged. "I've never been one to celebrate birthdays."

"Not at *all?*"

"No. Not at all."

Sandy couldn't believe it. Where she came from, birthdays were big business. Okay, so it wasn't always nice to be reminded every time she turned a year older, but it made her feel good to know that somebody cared enough to recognize the day. She couldn't believe that Ethan had no family, no connections, no celebrations. What kind of life must that be?

She turned right onto Cottonwood Street. "Are you telling me that even at your office nobody did anything for your birthday?"

"Nobody knows when my birthday is."

"But your father—"

"My father," he said, "is not inclined to throw a party."

"But he's your *father,*" Sandy said. "At least he could acknowledge—"

Ethan suddenly sat up straight. "Sandy—stop."

"What?"

"Pull over to the curb. Right now."

She wheeled the car to the curb and brought it to a quick halt.

"Kill the headlights," he said.

She flicked them out. "What's going on?"

Ethan pointed. "There's a car parked at the curb in front of Laura's house. Somebody's getting into it."

Sandy looked down the block to see a late model Nissan, and a tall, dark-haired man was unlocking its door.

"The plate is Texas NJD three-eight-four," Ethan said.

Sandy repeated the letters and numbers to herself until she could pull a piece of paper and a pen out of her purse and write it down.

"Who do you suppose it is?" she asked.

"I don't know. You don't recognize the car?"

"No."

Taillights lit up, and the car pulled away from the curb.

"He's leaving," Sandy said. "Should we call the cops?"

"No point. Whoever it is, there's no probable cause to stop him. A person can park on any public street he wants to."

Sandy grabbed her cell phone. "I'll call Dave. He can run the plate for us and tell us who owns the car."

A few minutes later, she hung up the phone and turned to Ethan. "It belongs to A-1 Rental. But Dave said there's no way to find out who's renting it. It's a private company and their records are confidential."

"That's right. The cops would need a court order to find out that information, and there's certainly no probable cause for that."

"Probable cause," Sandy muttered. "That damned constitution gets in the way every time, doesn't it?"

"Depends on which side of the law you're on."

Sandy turned to stare at Laura's house. "Who do you suppose it was?"

"Truthfully? Nobody who has anything to do with Laura's murder. I just thought it was worth checking out."

"Could it be a relative of Laura's from out of town?"

"Possibly, if Henderson actually went out of his way to track somebody down."

"In other words, probably not."

Sandy slid the piece of paper into the side pocket of her purse, then pulled away from the curb again, driving slowly past Laura's house. The crime-scene tape was still there, which meant that the investigation hadn't yet been completed.

She continued down the street. Soon it was nearly ten, and they'd made the last round of her neighborhood. She turned into the alley behind her house, pulled her car into her driveway, and killed the engine.

"Oh, wait," she said. "Your car's in front of my house. Would you like me to drive around?"

"I'll just go through the house."

Sandy nodded. They got out of the car and walked through the gate. Once Ethan closed it behind them, Sandy realized how dark her backyard was.

"Sorry," she said. "I forgot to flip on the porch light before we left."

Ethan slipped his hand around her elbow. "Walk carefully, then. The moon's not even out tonight."

Her heart skipped a little when he touched her, her skin hypersensitive where the heat of his hand met her arm.

He's just being nice, she told herself. *Nothing more.*

They climbed the steps to the porch. She flipped through her keys, looking for the one that opened her back door, but there were so many on her ring that it was nearly impossible to make out one from the other in the dark.

"Sorry," she said. "I can't seem to find the right key."

"I'm in no hurry."

His soft, smooth voice washed over her, sending a warm shiver right down her spine. A small gust of summer breeze sang through the wind chimes that hung from the eave above her kitchen window, contrasting with the wild beating of her own heart.

Finally she managed to find the key. She opened the kitchen door and flipped on the light. Ethan followed her inside, clicking the door shut behind them, and the sound of it echoed through the silence of her kitchen.

"Well," she said, setting her purse down on the counter, "I guess that's two more hours out of the way. We're scheduled again for the day after tomorrow."

"That's fine." He paused. "Actually, better than fine."

"So you've decided that crime-watch patrol is a worthwhile activity?"

"It all depends on the company I get to keep while I do it."

Sandy told herself that he merely thrived on saying things that knocked her off balance. But the look on his face as he spoke them seemed to say something else entirely. And now she was alone with him. In her house. Just the two of them. Every moment that passed seemed intense and singular, and all at once her brain was buzzing, awakening her to possibilities that she shouldn't even be considering.

At this point in her life, she knew what kind of man was good for her: a stable, even-tempered, responsible man who would fit comfortably and seamlessly into the life she'd built for herself. But the truth was that all the men she'd dated in recent memory—the ones relatives and friends and neighbors swore were perfect for her—had bored her to tears. They took her to nice restaurants, made nice conversation, then asked if they could give her a nice little good-night kiss at the door.

They were perfectly nice. Perfectly good. Perfect, perfect, perfect, and *God,* she'd had enough of it.

Ethan was unpredictable. Different from any man she'd ever known. His mind moved like lightning, leaving her breathless in her attempt to keep up. He challenged her with every word that came out of his mouth. In this life she'd probably never walk a tightrope, or scale the sheer side of a cliff, or jump out of an airplane, but just once she wanted to have her heart beat with that kind of exhilaration—the exhilaration she'd feel in the hands of a man who was dangerous for a woman like her in a hundred different ways. A man who would meet her in the middle and not back down, who knew his own mind, who had a reputation that would send nice women screaming into the night.

"Well," Ethan said, looking at his watch. "I guess I'd better be going."

As he turned to leave the kitchen, Sandy felt an unaccustomed surge of boldness. Yes, it was crazy. It was the wrong time. He was the wrong man. And if she pursued this in any way, she'd probably end up getting hurt, because leopards didn't change their spots, and if she was to believe anything she'd heard about him, Ethan just might be as predatory as they came. But that didn't stop her from wanting to take a walk on the wild side.

Maybe even tonight.

"Ethan?"

He turned back.

"In two hours, it won't be your birthday anymore," she said.

"That's right."

"Do you usually stay up late?"

"Yes. Until midnight on most nights."

"Do you have any plans when you leave here?"

"No. Why?"

She reached into a cabinet, pulled out a mixing bowl and put it on the counter, then opened the fridge door and grabbed a carton of eggs.

"What are you doing?" he asked.

"Everyone should have a cake on his birthday," she said, tossing a smile over her shoulder. "If you'd like to stay around for a while, I'll make you one."

The instant she saw the deadpan look of disbelief on his face, she knew she'd said the wrong thing. A birthday cake? That must sound positively ridiculous to a man like him. *Damn it.* Why couldn't she have come up with something a little more enticing to him than an evening with Betty Crocker?

"Never mind," she said quickly, putting the eggs back in the fridge. "Dumb idea. You told me you don't celebrate birthdays. I just thought . . . see, I'm on this diet and I'm dying for something sweet, so really, any excuse at all . . ."

As her voice faded away, she sneaked a peek at him. A faint smile crossed his lips. Slowly he came back across the kitchen, pulled out one of the stools at her counter, and sat down.

"A birthday cake," he said, "sounds wonderful."

chapter seven

Women had offered to do some incredible things for Ethan over the years, most of them involving sexual favors guaranteed to take him straight to the stratosphere. With any other woman he'd have taken Sandy's offer to mean, *Hey, baby, let's get cooking together.* But here she was, putting on an apron, getting a bowl from a cabinet, measuring spoons from a drawer . . . .

Good God. She really was making him a birthday cake.

His amusement at that, though, went on hold when Sandy opened the pantry door and bent over, evidently looking for something that it was taking her a *long* time to find. And as she moved those things around, her backside followed suit, shifting around in a provocative little dance that had him mesmerized. And the fact that she didn't even know she was doing it made it that much more enticing.

Finally she rose with a box of cake mix in her hand. "You do like chocolate, don't you?"

"Yeah. Chocolate's good."

She dumped the mix into the bowl. "I'd make one from scratch, but we're short on time."

Make a cake from scratch? He didn't think he'd ever dated a woman who would even be inclined to try that. In fact, the women he dated generally ate cake one day, then went to the gym the next day to punish themselves for it.

"Need some help?" Ethan asked.

"Of course not. You're not allowed to help with your own birthday cake." She cracked a few eggs into the mix, then added water. She started to reach into a lower cabinet, then stopped short. "Oh. I forgot. My mixer's on the fritz." She gave him a smile. "Well. I guess I'll have to do it the old fashioned way."

She pulled out a wooden spoon. She began to mix and beat and smack that batter into submission, her dark, lustrous hair fluttering back and forth. Sequestering it in a ponytail had been a crime against nature. If Ethan had wondered if the sight of it loose and long and spilling over her shoulders was worth a hundred bucks, he wasn't wondering now.

But no matter how much he'd been thinking about her tonight with lust in his heart, Ethan knew he could *not* take advantage of this situation. Just looking around her kitchen gave him yet one more good reason why he needed to keep his distance. Everything surrounding her screamed *permanence,* from the kids' drawings on her fridge, to her ruffled curtains, to the dozens of cookbooks lining her counters. He wasn't a man who stuck around for the long haul, and women like Sandy didn't take kindly to being loved and left. In fact, given the large family she was from and the house she lived in, he found it hard to believe that she didn't already have a husband and three kids.

"Have you ever been married?" he asked.

She looked up. "No. I haven't."

"Why not?"

She shrugged. "I've come close a time or two."

"What stopped you?"

"I don't know, really. Maybe just the feeling that I was fine without them. No value added. I've got a lot of good people in my life already, so getting married just to be getting married didn't seem like the right thing to do."

"So you just haven't found the right man."

"I guess not. Have you ever been married?"

"No."

"Ever come close?"

"No. Not even close."

"I imagine there have been a few women over the years who would have liked it if you had."

"Maybe. But even though I have very few good people in my life, getting married just to be getting married still didn't seem like the right thing to do."

She tilted her head. "Why do you have so few good people in your life?"

"Maybe because it takes one to know one."

"You are a good person."

"What brings you to that conclusion?"

"Because you're taking Josh's case and not asking for anything in return."

"Don't think it's such a big sacrifice, Sandy. A ten-thousand-dollar retainer isn't much for me to forgo. I'm thinking of raising it to fifteen just to keep out the riffraff."

"You're giving up your time, then."

"One case is pretty much the same as another."

"Then why *are* you doing it?"

That question knocked him off balance, because he still wasn't completely sure of the answer.

"Okay," he told her. "Here's the truth. As embarrassing as it is to admit, I'm afraid my tragic flaw kicked in again."

"What's that?"

"You're a beautiful woman. A single glance at one of those, and I find myself doing all kinds of inadvisable things."

She rolled her eyes a little. "Yeah. Right."

"Excuse me?"

"I haven't been around you very long, Ethan, but already I know that you're calm, you're controlled, you calculate every move you make and weigh every word you speak. The odds of a so-called pretty face making you do something 'inadvisable' are just about zero."

She was right. He'd never been a member of that pitiful class of men who had no control over their thought processes, their decision-making ability, or their hormones. He'd taken this case because of Sandy, but not because he'd been mesmerized by the sight of her pretty face. There was something else about her, something deeper, something that went beyond her obvious physical attributes. He just hadn't completely figured out yet what it was.

"Speaking of doing inadvisable things," he said, "what made you agree to spend forty hours alone in a car with a man your brothers think is the devil himself?"

She laughed a little. "Actually, Alex did have a word with me about that."

"And?"

"And I promised him I'd keep pepper spray and a gun handy, and put my knees to good use whenever the need arose."

Ethan smiled. "So you're a dangerous woman."

"Come on, now. You don't seem to be the kind of man who'd run scared from a few toxic chemicals and a little gunfire."

"It's the knees, Sandy. Strikes fear in a man's heart every time. Maybe I'd better keep my distance."

"Now, there's no need to do that," she said, her mouth edging into a smile. "You're safe with me. I promise."

He was safe with *her*? That almost made him laugh out loud.

But now the strangest thing was happening. Sandy was just standing there staring at him without saying a word. He prided himself on his ability to translate facial expressions and every other kind of body language there was, but suddenly he couldn't read a single one of her thoughts.

She turned and pulled a teaspoon from a drawer. She dipped the tip of it in the batter, then eased up next to him and held up the spoon.

"Have a taste," she said.

Her voice was soft and lyrical, a near whisper that barely broke the silence. Ethan felt a sudden surge of intense awareness, as if the atmosphere in the room had suddenly changed from one moment to the next.

What the hell was she doing?

He opened his mouth and she eased the spoon inside. The batter melted against his tongue, but for some reason, he didn't taste a thing. With her gaze still concentrated on his, she lifted her other hand and rested it against his cheek. With the pad of her thumb, she swept away a bit of the batter from the corner of his mouth, then teased that thumb gently across his lower lip. And that was when the truth hit him like a brick to the side of the head.

Good God. She's seducing you.

That thought triggered an all-out, full-blown, brain-zapping sensation that rattled every nerve in his body. He could spot a woman coming on to him from across a crowded room, and he hadn't spotted this? He was going to keep his distance, and now she was coming on to *him?*

He sat motionless for a moment before touching his tongue to his lower lip and licking off the batter. She swallowed hard, then parted her lips slightly, her breath coming faster. He couldn't believe this. Women had stripped naked in front of him and it hadn't given him one-tenth of the reaction he was having now.

He shifted his gaze to her lips, then eased it back up to meet her eyes again. "At what point did this stop being about the cake?"

She looked at him without blinking. "It was never about the cake."

A current of sheer sexual energy shot between them like an electrical circuit gone haywire. He could feel it. Hear it. Smell it. *Taste* it. But still it shocked the holy hell out of him when she let go of the spoon and it clattered to the floor.

Then she took his face in her hands, dropped her lips against his, and kissed him.

He was so astonished that for a moment all he could do was sit on that stool and let it happen. She moved closer, her hips brushing against his inner thighs, sending lightning bolts of sensation right to his groin. She had the softest, sweetest lips he'd ever felt, yet she was kissing him with the wild abandon of a woman who was dying for a man and he was the last one on earth.

Contrast.

He shouldn't be doing this. He knew that. But suddenly his heart was pummeling his chest and his synapses were firing like machine guns, and any thoughts about dissuading her were slipping farther and farther from his mind. After all, they were just kissing, right? Was there really anything wrong with that? A few kisses, a bite or two of cake, a pleasant good-night . . .

Then she reached for his shirt buttons.

She undid three of them in record time, then reached her hand inside his shirt to stroke his chest. She continued to kiss him, moaning softly at the skin-to-skin contact, her lips humming against his mouth.

Another button bit the dust.

Then another.

Good God. She wants it right now.

He couldn't believe it. Where was she planning on doing it? On the floor? On the kitchen table? Up against the wall?

Any one of those sounded fine by him.

No. This is Sandy. Sandy DeMarco. The happy home-maker. The woman you pictured married with a bunch of kids. The woman who'll hem you in so fast you won't know what hit you. The one you vowed to stay away from.

She unfastened the last button and spread his shirt open, still kissing him, those soft but insistent hands sliding beneath his shirt to curl around his ribcage with an urgency that made stars explode inside his head.

Then he felt her hands on his belt.

He pulled away suddenly, taking her by the shoulders, his breath coming in sharp spurts. "Sandy," he said, "you don't know who you're messing with."

"Don't patronize me, Ethan. I get enough of that from my family."

Those eyes. Swimming with desire. Looking at him in that way he'd never expected—as if she were going to die if she didn't have him right now. And when she dove in to kiss him again, it was all he could do not to clear her kitchen table with a sweep of his arm and hurl her down on top of it.

Then she clamped her hands on the outsides of his upper thighs and slid them to his hips, a slow, intense, almost carnal move that had him rock hard in a matter of seconds.

Good God.

Ethan grabbed her wrists, holding her motionless for a second or two to get himself under control.

Sandy blinked with surprise. "What's wrong?"

"This isn't a good idea."

"Why not?"

Why not? Because she had a family who cared about her and hated him. Because it would be damned frosty in her car for thirty-six more hours when she wanted more from him than he was willing to give. He only slept with women who knew the score, women with whom there was no morning-after awkwardness because there was no morning after. He'd be nothing but bad for a woman like Sandy, and he'd be a real bastard if he let her think anything else.

"I'm just not the man for you," he told her. "Trust me on that."

He released her, slid off the stool, then turned and walked out of her kitchen.

"Ethan?"

He kept walking, striding through her living room to her front door and right out of her house, assaulted by ninety-degree heat even at ten thirty at night. He slid into the driver's seat of his car, slammed the door, and closed his eyes with a sigh of frustration.

Well, he'd handled that brilliantly.

For all his ability to think on his feet, to persuade and dissuade at will, to command any circumstances he found himself in, he'd extricated himself from that situation with all the finesse of a first-year law student. The look on her face as he'd backed away from her told him he'd confused her and humiliated her all at the same time, and that was the last thing he'd intended to do.

Why couldn't he have thought of something else to say? Anything?

As he started his car, sheer physical need made him think about hitting Bernie's and picking up one of those women he was so used to being with—women whose names he didn't have to remember, women for whom sex was just another form of recreation, women who wouldn't expect his face at their breakfast tables the next morning. But for some reason the thought of that left him cold, even as thoughts of Sandy burned through every molecule in his body.

This was unprecedented. He couldn't remember a time in his life when a beautiful woman had wanted sex and he'd said no.

Then again, women like Sandy never asked.

Sandy stood at the window beside her front door, watching the taillights of Ethan's car disappear into the night. He was a man who allegedly slept with any woman whose breath could fog a mirror, and he'd turned her down?

Maybe that reputation was a crock.

She squeezed her eyes closed. Or maybe, in spite of all the

compliments he'd thrown her way, he just wasn't attracted to her.

A sick feeling rose in her stomach. All at once she felt as if she were standing on the last rung of the ladder. Crawling around at the bottom of the barrel. Hugging the wall at a school dance and feeling invisible. Her house was so quiet she could hear the blood pulsing in her ears, circulating humiliation through her whole body.

You threw yourself at him, and he said no.

With those words ringing inside her head, she went upstairs to her bedroom, intending to grab a nightshirt and go to bed, hoping that by tomorrow morning the sting of his rejection would have disappeared.

She sighed. Who was she kidding? This one was going to stay with her into the next decade.

As she slipped out of her clothes, she thought back to the last time she'd slept with a man, and she felt a pang of distress when she had to think hard to remember when it was.

And even who she'd been with.

Over the years she'd wrapped herself up in other people's lives to the point that she barely had one of her own. Yes, she had family and friends, more of both of those things than most people, and she loved every one of them. She had a profitable business, worthwhile volunteer activities, and a stature in her community that she valued.

But she didn't have much of a life for herself.

She turned slowly and looked at herself in her dresser mirror. Just for a moment, it was as if a stranger were looking back. Age had crept up when she'd least expected it, etching a few wrinkles into her face and sending selected parts of her body in a southerly direction. Over the past couple of years she'd read about all kinds of new diets, but she'd never put any of them into practice. Her hips were too round, her thighs too chunky. She looked over her shoulder into the mirror at her rear end and slumped with dismay.

Oh, God. What had happened there?

She put her hands beneath her breasts and lifted them to where they'd once been before she and gravity had gone a few rounds. She had the sudden sense that the young woman she'd been had faded away, leaving a different one in her place, one who was definitely older, without a doubt wiser, and unquestionably less desirable.

Sandy had never had a self-esteem problem, but she'd always been a realist. What had happened tonight had shined a big, bright spotlight on the fact that age was sneaking up on her, life was passing her by, the hands of time were sweeping past. . . .

Oh, hell.

If this was thirty-seven, what would forty-seven be like?

She'd be ten years older, walking the same road, leading the same life, with every day duller than the one before. And that scared the hell out of her. No wonder she'd leaped on the first attractive man who'd crossed her path in a very long time, one she was sure could inject some excitement into her life.

And he'd turned her down.

She thought about how she was going to have to spend thirty-six more hours with Ethan in the close confines of her car with his rejection swirling around in her mind. That alone filled her with a sense of dread, not to mention the fact that since he was representing Josh, they'd undoubtedly have to spend time together conferring about that.

Oh, God. Josh.

Ethan hadn't wanted to represent him in the first place. And now, after this . . .

Sandy groaned out loud. In one ill-conceived seduction attempt, she'd humiliated herself beyond description at the same time she may have alienated the one man who could get Josh acquitted.

Was there any way she could have screwed up more?

She had to talk to Ethan. Somehow she had to make things right between them so every moment they spent together from now on wouldn't be excruciating.

She sighed painfully. There was only one thing more humiliating than throwing herself at a man and getting rejected. And that was having to apologize for it.

chapter eight

On Monday morning, Ethan was sitting at his desk at work, sipping a mug of coffee and reading the morning paper. More to the point, he was staring at the business page and not really reading at all. He couldn't get his mind off Sandy. He hadn't stopped thinking about what had happened between them last night for five minutes. Hell, he thought maybe he'd even dreamed about it.

He heard footsteps outside his office. Looking up, he was shocked to see Sandy standing at his door. He sat up suddenly, tossing the newspaper aside, his heart suddenly beating rapid-fire. *Good Lord.* Just the sight of her sent his brain into a tailspin.

"Sandy? What are you doing here?"

"I need to talk to you. Do you have a moment?"

"Of course." He stood up and came around his desk. "Have a seat."

As she sat down on the sofa, he walked over to close the door. "Uh . . . would you like a cup of coffee?"

"No, thank you. I won't be staying long."

He sat down beside her. Judging by the way she was fidgeting with the strap of her purse, she was nervous, so he knew what this had to be about.

"Sandy, if this is about last night—"

"Of course it is," she said, staring down at her lap. "I made a fool of myself."

"No. You didn't."

"Yes, I did. And I'm sorry. I was out of line. Believe me, I don't normally do that kind of thing. Actually, I don't *ever* do that kind of thing. I don't know what came over me. I just hope . . ." She twitched her shoulders in a helpless shrug. "I just hope you'll forgive me for it."

Forgive her for it? For giving him kisses so hot they burned him all the way down to his shoe soles? The only thing she'd done wrong last night was to be the kind of woman the average man would kill for. Unfortunately, in matters of the heart, Ethan was decidedly below average.

"I mean, you've been so generous in offering to represent Josh," she went on. "And what I did . . . well, I just hope you won't hold it against him."

"Hold it against him? Why would I do that?"

"I don't know. I thought maybe I'd made you uncomfortable enough that you wouldn't want to—"

"Sandy, what happened between us last night has no bearing on my defending Josh. In fact, I'm going by to see him in a few hours."

"Good," she said with a sigh of relief. "That's good."

But still she looked so damned miserable. He hated this. *Hated* it.

"Last night wasn't what you think," he told her. "It was just that . . ."

She looked up. "What?"

Say something. Anything. Anything so she doesn't think she's the one at fault.

"I just thought it was best to keep our relationship a professional one. You're overseeing my community service. It wouldn't do for Judge Davis to find out I was having a good time, now, would it?"

He forced a smile, coaxing a small one out of her. "No," she said. "I guess it wouldn't."

"But that's the least of it," Ethan went on. "If your brothers found out I so much as touched you, they'd put me in intensive care. And then where would Josh be?"

She smiled again briefly, but she still looked supremely uncomfortable. A long silence stretched between them. Ethan was rarely at a loss for words, but sometimes he was at a loss for the right ones.

"It was no big deal," he said. "Really."

"No. It was. But I want you to know that you don't have to worry. From now on, I'll oversee your community service, you'll defend Josh, and that'll be that. And I swear to you that what happened last night will never happen again."

This time she stared at him intently, as if driving home her point because she clearly thought she needed to, but she had no idea how much he hated the sound of those words. Because the truth was that ever since last night, all he'd been able to think about was kissing her again, and a whole lot more.

And it was all he could think about right now.

Suddenly he felt as if he were swimming in sensation, everything about her reminding him of last night. The subtle floral fragrance she wore. The guileless way she looked at him with eyes so dark her pupils got lost. Those lips that had kissed him until he was on the verge of losing control. Her glossy hair swirled around her shoulders, and he felt a rush of pleasure at the possibility that she'd worn it down because she knew he liked it that way.

He hadn't counted on this. He hadn't counted on her coming here and looking so appealing and reminding him of how close he'd come to paradise last night. And now, as he thought about how he'd pushed her away, suddenly he felt like the biggest fool alive. This smart, compassionate, beautiful woman had wanted him with an enthusiasm that could have awakened a dead man, and he'd turned her down?

"I guess I'd better go," Sandy said, coming to her feet. "Thank you for your time. I appreciate it."

She headed for the door. Ethan stood up.

"Sandy?"

She turned back. "Yes?"

Tell her you're crazy about her. Make up for the time you so stupidly lost. Just take her in your arms and kiss her, for God's sake, and let the rest take care of itself.

"I'll let you know what happens with Josh," he said.

"Thanks. I'll be waiting to hear from you."

She turned and walked out of his office, clicking the door closed behind her.

With a muttered curse, Ethan sat back down in the chair behind his desk and spent the next few minutes kicking himself for being the coward of the century. He reached for his coffee mug and took a drink.

Cold. *Damn it.*

He slammed the mug down on his desk and grimaced as the liquid made its way down his throat. That was exactly what it had felt like when Sandy walked out of his office with her new resolve to keep her distance—a great big swig of cold coffee that was nearly impossible to swallow.

But the longer he sat there, the more logic made its way back into his brain again, no matter how much he resisted it. He knew what kind of man he was and what kind of woman she was, so it didn't matter how attracted he was to her. He'd never be able to give her what she really wanted, and if he led her to believe he could, in the end it would only make both of them miserable.

And that meant he had to make sure that what had happened between them last night never happened again.

Sandy rode the elevator to the first floor of the building, then stepped out beneath a summer sun that was scorching even at nine o'clock in the morning. She got into her car, slammed the door, and tilted her head against the back of the seat.

Ethan had lied.

He didn't give a damn about what Judge Davis thought. And he hadn't said a word last night about a conflict with her brothers. He'd said, *I'm not the man for you.* In reality, that had been a nice way of telling her that *she* wasn't the woman for *him*. In spite of all the compliments he threw around, he just didn't find her attractive.

Okay. So what? Get over it, will you?

Right. As if that was going to be an easy thing to do when she had to spend thirty-six more hours in this car with him sitting an arm's length away—a man who looked good, smelled good, and, as she remembered, *tasted* good.

Stop thinking about that.

She looked at herself in the rearview mirror, at her hair she'd so carefully blown dry this morning. She'd left the conditioner in for an extra three minutes, telling herself it was because she seemed to have more split ends than usual.

What a crock.

She flipped open the console and grabbed a rubber band. She swept her hair up to the crown of her head, combed her fingers through it, then twisted the rubber band around it.

Stupid, stupid, stupid.

She needed to put Ethan out of her mind, get on with life as usual, and hope that sometime in the far, far future, she might be able to forget that last night had ever happened.

That afternoon, a guard escorted Ethan into a visitation area at the county jail, which was nothing more than a barren, windowless room with a small table and a few chairs.

After a few minutes, the guard brought Josh in. He looked as Ethan had expected him to—average height and average build for a seventeen-year-old kid, dark hair, dark eyes. His face still held the shadows of a few odd piercings. He wore the obligatory orange jumpsuit and a wary scowl. He sat down in the chair across the table from Ethan, folding his arms into the insolent pose of a kid who was in way over his head but was terrified to admit it.

"Who are you?" he asked.

"Ethan Millner. I'm an attorney."

"I've already got a lawyer."

"I'm a friend of Sandy DeMarco's."

At the mention of Sandy's name, Josh sat up, his eyes widening. "Sandy sent you?"

"Yes. She persuaded me to take your case."

The kid's eyes shifted back and forth as he assimilated this new piece of information. "So you're not one of those court-appointed guys?"

"Nope."

A glimmer of hope entered his eyes, but it faded almost immediately. "Wait a minute. If you expect me to pay you—"

"I don't.

"Hey, last I checked, *nothing's* free."

"Sometimes you just luck out. This is one of those times."

"I don't get it."

"You don't have to get it. All you have to do is tell the court you want a change of counsel. I've already talked to Linz, and he's going to file a motion to withdraw from your case. I'll file a motion to take it."

"So you're a good lawyer."

"Yeah. I'm a good lawyer."

Josh still looked at him suspiciously. "You're sure Sandy sent you?"

Ethan sighed. "Believe me, kid, I wouldn't be here if she hadn't. Now, are you going to tell the court you want me as your attorney? If you are, we'll talk. If not, I'll walk."

The kid still looked doubtful, but finally he nodded. "Yeah. Okay. If Sandy thinks I should, then I will."

Ethan took out a notebook and a pen. "Okay. I need to hear your side of the story. The murder occurred just before ten o'clock. Tell me where you were during that time."

"I was by myself. Just hanging out."

"Where?"

"In the neighborhood where I live. Down by the Pecan Street bridge."

"Why were you late for your curfew?"

"I wasn't paying attention to the time."

"What was distracting you?"

"I wasn't distracted. Just not thinking about it, you know?"

"You have a court-ordered curfew. That gives you a real good reason to think about it."

"It just got by me. That's all."

"Did anyone see you during that time?"

"Probably. Cars driving by, or something."

"I need something more than that, Josh. A credible witness who can place you somewhere besides the victim's house at the time of the murder."

"There isn't anyone."

"Did you go to a store? A movie? See some friends?"

"I told you. I was by myself all evening."

"Just hanging out."

"That's right."

"You're going to have to do better than that."

"Man, don't you think I would if I could?"

"Unless you had some reason not to."

"Why the hell would I hide something that could keep me from a murder conviction? Why would I do that?"

"You tell me."

"There's nothing to tell."

Ethan sat back with a sigh. "What time did you get home that night?"

"About ten fifteen."

"What did you do then?"

"Watched a little TV. Went to bed."

"And the cops came the next morning to arrest you."

"Yeah."

Ethan's gut instinct told him that something was wrong here, but he didn't know what.

"I understand you confessed to the crime," Ethan said.

Josh sat up straight. "I confessed to violating my probation and staying out after my curfew! That was what I thought they were there for!"

"It's not wise to talk to the cops until you've got a lawyer."

"But everybody is always saying I'm supposed to tell the truth. To face up to my mistakes. So that's what I did. Only now they've screwed it all around until I committed murder!"

"But you didn't actually sign a confession."

"Hell, no!"

"A verbal confession under those circumstances hasn't got much teeth, but it won't stop a sharp prosecutor from trying to make something out of it."

"The cop tricked me into saying that."

"Yeah, kid. They do that sometimes." Ethan thumbed through his notes. "You've got two juvenile arrests for assault. Tell me about those."

"They were no big deal."

"Let me be the judge of that."

"I got in a fight once with a guy at school. He was bugging me. Wouldn't let up. So I finally decided to shut him up. Guy ended up getting his nose broken and his parents reported it. Another time a guy rear-ended my truck. Said it wasn't his fault. We got into a fight over it. He threw the first punch, but since I'm a kid and he was a guy in a suit, I was the one who was arrested. But they didn't charge me either time."

"Those incidents still show you have a violent nature."

"I don't have a violent nature."

"You can talk all day long, kid. But people watch what you do."

"They can't bring those things up, can they?"

"Possibly. Depends on what the judge allows." Ethan leaned

away, tapping his pen on the table. "The problem here is that you've got nobody who can say you were somewhere else at the time of the murder, but Ralph Clemmons is absolutely certain you were the one in the victim's backyard."

"No." Josh shook his head adamantly. "It wasn't me."

"Are you saying he's lying?"

"Maybe it was a guy who looked like me. Hell, I don't know."

"Unfortunately, Ralph knows you well enough that it's credible that he could make a positive ID."

"Yeah. He's been to my grandmother's house. Sometimes he helps her with stuff."

"Stuff?"

"You know. He repairs stuff for her. That kind of thing. All the people in that neighborhood know each other. My grandmother knows Sandy. That was how I got the job at her flower shop."

"It's tough finding a job when you're on probation. You're lucky she gave you one."

"She's helped me a lot."

"So you like her."

Josh looked surprised. "Sure, man. What's not to like?"

Ethan had to agree with the kid. So far he'd found plenty to like himself, except maybe her astonishing persistence in getting him to take this case. A case that, right about now, was going nowhere fast.

Ethan stared at Josh evenly. "Okay. I'm buying your story for now. But let's get something straight. I'm the only thing standing between you and spending the rest of your life in prison. So you do *not* lie to me. If I get even a hint that anything but the gospel truth is passing between your lips, I walk. Do you understand?"

"Yeah," he said. "I understand."

Ethan stuffed the notebook and file folder back into his briefcase, knowing his threat was probably a waste of breath.

So many clients had lied to him over the years that he was no longer capable of believing any of them. If he required knowing the truth before he took a case, his career would be over. Still, the closer he could get to the truth, the less likely it was that he'd be faced with eleventh-hour surprises that made him look like an idiot in open court.

Ethan glanced at Josh. The kid swallowed with difficulty, as if trying to hold back tears.

"I can't believe this is happening," he said. "I told myself I was never going to end up in here again. Never. I swear I didn't kill her. I've done some stupid things before, but I'd never do something like that. They said . . ." His voice trailed off, his eyes clouding. "They said somebody beat her to death. God, I'd *never* . . ."

I see goodness, Ethan. I see it as clearly as you see the color of his eyes.

Ethan searched the kid's face, wondering where the portal was that allowed Sandy to look beneath tissue and bone into that intangible something that she'd probably call his soul. And all Ethan saw was one more fish in the sea of crap that flooded the criminal justice system, a scruffy kid with a wary attitude, his words full of bravado and his voice full of fear, not because he was being wrongly accused but because he'd gotten caught and was looking at life imprisonment or worse. Ethan could read this kid like front-page news, and he didn't much like what he saw.

But Sandy had a different read on him, and Ethan didn't understand that at all.

"You say you're a good lawyer," Josh said. "Can you get me out of this?"

"I can't promise you anything. All I can tell you is that I play to win."

Josh nodded, then leaned back in his chair, clasping the arms so tightly his fingers whitened. "Don't suppose you've got a cigarette on you."

"Don't smoke."

Josh sighed and bowed his head.

"Smoking will kill you. Think of this as a good time to quit." Ethan grabbed his briefcase and stood up. "I'll be back sometime before the preliminary hearing."

He started to walk away, then turned back. He reached into his pocket, pulled out the silver medallion, and handed it to the kid.

"What's this?"

"It's from Ralph Clemmons. He's praying for you."

Josh turned the medallion over, looking confused.

"I don't get it either, kid. But where you're sitting, it wouldn't hurt to do a little praying yourself."

Alex picked up what was left of his bacon cheeseburger, finished it in one big bite, then shoved the plate aside and fixed his gaze on Sandy.

"Okay. So tell me about Millner. Is he behaving himself?"

Sandy sighed with frustration. She'd met Alex and Val for a quick lunch, thinking it might actually be possible to get all the way through a meal without her brother bringing up Ethan's name. No such luck.

The truth, Alex, is that Ethan has been on his best behavior. I'm the one who's been misbehaving.

"Alex?" Val said, "is it just my imagination, or are you a little obsessed with that?"

"Hey, the guy has practically made an Olympic sport out of using women, and now he's spending forty hours with my sister. Yes, I'm a little obsessed."

"He's a competent attorney," Sandy said, "and he's taking Josh's case. If he can get him acquitted, I don't give a flip about his personal life."

"He's a sleazy attorney, and you'd better be sure he doesn't drag you *into* his personal life."

Sandy looked at Val. "Does he ever give up?"

"You've known him longer than I have. What do you think?"

"That's it," Alex said. "I'm out of here."

He ripped his napkin out of his lap and tossed it on the table. He stood up, threw down a few bills, then pointed at Sandy. "You need to watch it around that guy. I still don't trust him. Do you hear me?"

"Hear you?" Val said. "How could she not hear you? Everyone in the place can hear you."

Alex let out a sigh of exasperation. "Val? Why in the hell do I put up with you?"

Sandy almost laughed out loud. Since the day the two of them got married, the whole family knew quite well who was putting up with whom.

Val smiled sweetly. "Is it because I'm such a good . . . cook?"

"No, sweetheart. Trust me. That's not it." He leaned over, put one hand on the table and the other on the back of her chair, and gave her a kiss. Then he hovered a few inches away, a slow smile crossing his lips. "See if you can think of another reason by the time I get home tonight."

Val gave him a smile that said she intended to do just that. Alex rose again, trailing his hand along her cheek before walking away.

For a moment, Sandy felt a twinge of jealousy for the closeness the two of them shared. Val was probably the only woman on the planet who could keep Alex in line when the need arose, and he worshiped the ground she walked on. Not that they didn't go at it every once in a while at the top of their lungs, but their love for each other always shone through.

Yes, Alex had a wonderful marriage. So did Dave and John. So how in the hell had she ended up the odd woman out, one of those pitiful souls who couldn't even seduce a man who used sex for recreation the way other people used tennis and water sports?

Sandy and Val paid the check, then left the restaurant and started back down the sidewalk. Val's office was only a few blocks from Sandy's shop, which meant that they got to go to lunch together whenever Val wasn't on a surveillance, scouring public records, chasing down deadbeat dads, or doing whatever else it was that private investigators did.

"So now that Alex is gone," Val said, "tell me about Millner. Is he really the devil in disguise?"

"Trust me, Val. Alex doesn't have a thing to worry about."

"I don't know. I've heard a few of those stories myself."

"And they might all be true, for all I know. But where I'm concerned, Ethan Millner has been a perfect gentleman."

"Well, then. That's good."

"Good? Why is that good?"

"Uh . . . do you want him to make a pass at you?"

"I don't know." Sandy shrugged offhandedly. "Maybe I do."

"Really? A guy like him?"

"Come on, Val. You're starting to sound like Alex."

"No. It's just that . . . well, I didn't figure he'd be the kind of man you'd be interested in."

Sandy stopped. "Why is it that everyone thinks that? That I'm so dull and boring that I couldn't possibly have a hot, screaming affair with a man like Ethan Millner?"

She spun back around and kept walking.

"Wait a minute!" Val said, lengthening her strides to keep up. "I didn't mean it like that! Hey, as far as I'm concerned, you should go for it. Live it up a little, you know? After all, if all you're looking for is sex, Ethan Millner has *opportunity* written all over his face."

Actually, no. The only sign Sandy had seen on his face was *No Admittance*.

"Of course," Val said, "you understand that if your broth-

ers found out that Millner so much as laid a hand on their sister, he'd be eating asphalt in under ten minutes."

"What my brothers don't know won't hurt them."

Val grinned. "Well, then. I'd say you need to give the man
the green light." She leaned in and whispered, "Go for it,
sweetie. I promise I won't tell Alex."

Sandy felt like such a fraud. It was on the tip of her tongue
to come clean and tell Val that she *had* gone for it, and in
doing so she'd chased him right out the door. But she just
wouldn't be able to stand the look of pity that was sure to
come over Val's face. She'd feel obligated to say stuff like,
He's not good enough for you, or, *You don't want a man like
him, anyway,* or, *It's his loss.*

Nope. No way was she going there.

They stopped at the intersection where they had to part.

"Lunch tomorrow?" Sandy asked.

"Can't. I've got a lead in a missing-person case that I need
to follow up on. But keep us posted on how things go for
Josh, will you?"

"Sure."

"And keep me posted on how things go with Millner."

"I'll do that, too." *Even though there'll be absolutely nothing to tell.*

They waved good-bye, and Sandy headed back down the
street, feeling even more dejected than before. She reached
her shop, and the moment she went inside Imogene stuck her
head out of the back room.

"Sandy. I'm glad you're back. You need to see this."

"See what?"

"Come here."

Wondering what was going on, Sandy followed Imogene
to a file cabinet, where she pulled out an order.

"Tell me the murder victim's name again," Imogene said.

"Laura Williams."

"Twenty-two forty-three Cottonwood?"

"Yes."

"That's what I thought." Imogene held up the order form. "I was filing orders when I found this. She sent somebody a dozen roses the day before she was murdered."

Sandy scanned the order. Lyle had taken it over the phone, and Josh had delivered the flowers.

"Sending flowers is not so strange," Imogene said. "But read what she wanted on the card."

Sandy read the sentiment Laura had given to accompany the flowers: *I refuse to let you go. I know we can work things out. Please call me. Love, Laura.*

The flowers had been delivered to a man named Chris Satterwhite. Evidently he was Laura's boyfriend, though she'd never heard Laura talk about one. An ex-husband? Maybe, though she'd never mentioned one of those, either.

"I just thought the card she sent along was kind of interesting in light of the fact that she was murdered," Imogene said. "I mean, it probably doesn't have a thing to do with it, but still I thought you ought to see it."

"Yes," Sandy said. "Thanks."

Bells clinked against the glass door at the front of the shop, and Imogene left the back room to take care of a customer. Sandy stared at the order. Laura had sent flowers to a man with whom she'd had some kind of relationship. And clearly there had been discord between them that she wanted to repair. It was a thin thread to go on, but wasn't it wise to check into any conflict between a victim and another person only a day before her murder?

She thought about calling the police. Then Ray Henderson's face came to mind.

Call Ethan. He'll know what to do.

She felt a little uptight at the thought of seeing him again, but it had to happen sooner or later, anyway. She called his office and his secretary gave her his cell number, but she kept getting his voice mail. It wasn't until after six o'clock that evening that she got in touch with him at his house. She told him she had something to show him, something she hoped would help lead them to Laura's killer. He gave her his address and told her to come right over.

Ten minutes later, she drove into Ethan's town-house complex. It didn't surprise her that it was located in Waverly Park, the high-rent district of Tolosa. The units were composed of red brick, with black shutters, cream trim, and brass fixtures. There were double French doors leading to second-story balconies. Palladian windows. Impeccable landscaping with young, perfectly pruned trees and beds overflowing with red and white petunias. Lawns of thick-bladed Saint Augustine that looked as if a gardener had plucked out every undesirable blade of grass, leaving only the most worthy to grow there.

Sandy had expected nothing less.

She got out of the car and went to Ethan's town house, a corner unit that looked out over a shimmering lake with a fountain in the center of it, surrounded by a bevy of ducks that looked as if each one had been handpicked by a landscape designer.

She knocked. A moment later Ethan opened the door, and her heart gave a little start. It was the first time she'd seen him dressed down. He wore a pair of shorts, a T-shirt, and athletic shoes, as if she'd caught him on the way to the gym. She flicked her gaze downward, centering for a split second on a pair of firm, muscled thighs that told her that he did something at that gym besides socialize. She'd hoped that he'd made things easier for her by miraculously growing considerably less attractive in the past twenty-four hours.

No such luck.

He held open the door. "Hi, Sandy. Come in."

Sandy stepped over the threshold into a two-story entry with an Italian tile floor. She suspected it was Italian tile, anyway. Wasn't that the best a person could buy?

He led her down a single step into the living room, motioning her to sit on the sofa. The room had an understated elegance but was still intensely masculine, with leather furniture, floor-to-ceiling bookshelves, bold statuary on a massive mantelpiece, and an armoire that no doubt housed that indispensable fixture in any male-dominant household—the big-screen TV.

She sat down, and he sat down next to her, a few inches too close for her to be entirely comfortable, so close she could smell the last lingering notes of the warm, discreet cologne she'd been close enough to inhale last night.

"Nice place you've got here," she said.

"It's okay."

Yeah. Like Buckingham Palace was okay. She nodded down at his clothes. "Did I catch you on your way to the gym?"

"Actually, I've had a hell of a day, and I was looking for a reason to skip working out tonight."

"Did you see Josh today?"

"Yes. I was getting ready to give you a call when you called me."

"How is he?"

"Scared to death and trying not to show it."

"What did he tell you?"

"Very little I didn't already know. Basically, what we've got so far is a defendant with no alibi, who made a verbal confession and later withdrew it. A credible eyewitness placing the defendant at the scene. Josh's record shows a conviction for burglary, two juvenile arrests for assault, and a variety of other misdemeanor charges. Believe me, Sandy. We're starting out on the low rung of the ladder."

"He's not that kid anymore, Ethan. I swear to you he's not."

"That may be a tough sell to a jury."

"I think Ralph knows that Josh has a record, so he's seeing

what he expects to see. But Josh is innocent. You believe that, don't you?"

"I want you to understand something, Sandy. I don't know Josh. Just because I'm taking his case doesn't mean I believe he didn't do it. I've made the commitment to defend him, and that means that on the professional side, everything I say, everything I do is on the presumption that he's innocent."

"And on the personal side?"

"My personal feelings are irrelevant. Just know that I never take a case I don't intend to win." He sat up on the edge of the sofa. "You say you've got something that's going to help me do that. Let's see it."

Sandy pulled the order out of her purse. "Take a look at this."

Ethan scanned it quickly. "Laura sent flowers to someone the day before her murder?"

"Yes. One of my employees remembered the order and pulled it out."

"Tell me why this is important."

"Look at what she wanted on the card."

" 'I refuse to let you go,' " Ethan murmured. " 'I know we can work things out. Please call me. I love you, Laura.' " He sat there for a moment with a thoughtful expression. "Any idea who Chris Satterwhite is?"

"Not a clue. But Laura was clearly on the outs with him. I thought that could be significant."

"It may be. The night of the murder you told me you didn't know if she was seeing someone. Or whether she was divorced."

"That's right."

Ethan stood up. "We've got a name and an address. Let's find out more about this guy."

"How?"

"Come with me."

He led Sandy into a room off the entry that contained an oak desk, file cabinets, bookshelves, and computer equipment. He slid behind the desk and motioned Sandy to a chair nearby.

"What are you doing?" she asked.

"Accessing a Web site with searchable public records. I'll put in his name and address and see what comes up."

Ethan clicked a link on a pull-down menu. He typed for a moment, then hit the enter key and sat back, waiting.

"You'd be shocked at what you can find out about somebody," he said. "Driving record. Criminal record. Schools they've attended. Houses they've owned." He glanced at the computer screen. "Just about anything that was ever a matter of public—"

He stopped short. He leaned in and stared at the screen, then picked up the flower order again, his expression confused.

"What's the matter?" Sandy asked.

He looked up. "Was Laura gay?"

Sandy blinked with surprise. "Gay? What makes you say that?"

"Because it's not Christopher Satterwhite. It's Christine."

chapter nine

Sandy blinked in disbelief. "Chris is a woman?"

"Looks that way. Did you have any hint that Laura was gay?"

"No. None at all."

Ethan looked at the flower order again. "Judging from the card that went with the flowers, they were clearly having a relationship, and they were clearly at odds the day before Laura's murder."

Ethan punched a few more keys. "Chris was married in 1997 to Stephen Satterwhite. Her maiden name is Holcomb."

"She got married? A lesbian?"

Ethan scrolled down the page, then stopped. "Yes. Which may explain why she filed for divorce five months ago."

"And started a relationship with Laura."

"It looks that way. And if so, it's possible that she knew Laura better than anyone else and might be able to shed some light on who killed her."

"You don't think she could *be* the killer, do you?"

"Possibly. But I doubt it. As a rule, women don't commit violent murders, and certainly not as violent as that one, unless there's extreme passion of some kind involved."

"Wouldn't she have come forward if she knew something about the murder?"

"Depends on what she knows."

"What else can you find about her and her husband besides vital statistics?"

Ethan put Stephen Satterwhite's name into a regular search engine and came up with the Web site of a local construction company. He was the owner. Chris's name netted nothing.

"So do we tell the police about her?" Sandy asked.

"Not until we have a chance to talk to her and see what she knows."

"We?"

"Yes. I want you to come along. You were a friend of Laura's. Even if the two of them were on the outs, you're a personal connection. And it's a woman-to-woman thing. She's more likely to talk to me if you're there."

"I take it you're not phoning ahead."

"Nope. The element of surprise can work wonders. People will say and do things they never meant to if they don't know what's coming. No need to tip her off who we are and what we want until we're standing right in front of her."

"When do you want to go?"

"We're not scheduled for crime patrol tonight, so let's go now. Any objections?"

"No. Of course not."

Ethan shut down the computer and led Sandy into his foyer, where he grabbed a set of car keys off the table.

"You're driving?" Sandy asked.

"I was planning on it."

"Are you also planning on staying under the speed limit?"

"Why, of course. There's nothing like the sight of a late-model Porsche wrapped around a pine tree to hammer that lesson home."

"You could have been killed."

"To tell you the truth, I'm surprised I wasn't." He picked his wallet up off the table and stuck it in his pocket.

"You're not changing clothes?"

"Why? Do you think I should?"

"I don't know. Right now you don't look much like a lawyer."

"Considering how most people feel about lawyers, that's probably a good thing."

She smiled. "Good point."

"Actually, I could swap out Adidas for Armani, but I think I'll stay just as I am. Chris might be more likely to let her guard down if I look as if I came from the gym instead of the courtroom."

He looked down at his keys, jingling them a little, then raised his head again. "The accident I had was a fluke," he said quietly. "It's not going to happen again, and certainly not with you in the car."

His solemn sincerity caught her off guard. "I was just teasing you, Ethan. I'm not worried."

"After what happened, you've got good reason to be. But you're safe when you're with me, Sandy. You never have to worry about that."

Chris Satterwhite lived on the east side of town, in an area of aging storefronts and apartment buildings. Ethan pulled into the parking lot of a tired sixteen-unit structure in desperate need of a paint job. He sandwiched his Mercedes between a dust-covered SUV and a ten-year-old Toyota and killed the engine.

"So what's the plan?" Sandy asked.

"We go to the door. You introduce yourself to Chris as a friend of Laura's and ask her if she has a few minutes to talk. If she doesn't slam the door in our faces, ask her if we can come in."

"What are you going to say to her?"

"It depends on what she says."

"And what if she does slam the door in our faces?"

"Then she probably knows something she doesn't want to talk about. I'll tell the cops and let them question her."

Sandy nodded. They got out of the car and headed down the sidewalk, then turned into a breezeway and walked up the metal stairs to apartment number six. It was nearly seven o'clock, but Sandy couldn't see any lights on inside.

"Doesn't look as if she's home."

Ethan knocked on the door. Sandy listened carefully, but she heard no movement inside the apartment. Ethan knocked again, louder this time. They waited.

Nothing.

Just then a door across the breezeway opened and a woman poked her head out. She looked to be in her early thirties, with hair bleached to the point of chemical overload and enough eye makeup that the Maybelline warehouse had to be running low.

She glanced at Sandy, then spoke to Ethan. "You looking for Chris?"

"Yes."

"Are you friends of hers?"

"Not exactly," Ethan said. "And you are . . . ?"

"Amber Gallagher. I'm the assistant manager."

"Hi, Amber." Ethan strolled over to her, giving her an inviting smile. "Can you tell me where Chris might be?"

Amber stepped out into the breezeway, giving Ethan a smile of her own. "Wish I could. She's a week late with her rent, and now it looks like she's skipped out."

"She doesn't live here anymore?"

"To tell you the truth, I'm not too sure. Why'd you say you're looking for her again?"

Ethan pulled out a business card and handed it to her. "I'm a lawyer. I'm settling the estate of a relative of Chris's."

Amber eyed Ethan up and down. "You don't look like a lawyer."

"You're right. I don't. There's nothing more miserable than

wearing a noose around your neck and a suit coat in hundred-degree heat. Can you imagine how hot all that polyester gets?"

Sandy almost choked. Polyester? Since when did Armani use that as his fabric of choice?

"Yeah, I hear you there," Amber said. "I had a job once where I had to wear panty hose." Her thinly plucked eyebrows arched with interest. "So what's the deal? Has Chris got an inheritance coming or something?"

"Yeah. She does."

"Really? A big one?"

"Big enough that she can pay the back rent she owes and then some. But I have to find her first. I've been trying to call her for some time now. Are you sure you don't know where she is?"

"Sorry. Haven't got a clue. All I know is that I saw her pack a bunch of stuff into her car and leave."

"Oh, yeah? When was that?"

"Yesterday morning."

Ethan glanced at Sandy, both of them acknowledging the same thing. She'd left the morning after Laura's murder.

"Did she seem to be in a hurry?" Ethan asked.

"Now that you mention it, she kinda was."

"What did she take with her?"

"Lots of clothes and stuff. A couple of suitcases."

"Do you think she was actually moving out?"

"I don't think so. I didn't see her take any furniture with her." She turned to Sandy. "So who are you?"

"This is Ms. DeMarco," Ethan said. "She's a colleague of mine."

"So you're a lawyer, too?" Amber asked.

"Uh . . ."

"Yes, she is," Ethan said. "Graduated summa cum laude from the University of Texas law school." He leaned in and spoke confidentially. "But then there was that malpractice suit, and all that bad publicity, and, well . . . now I'm afraid she's just a schlep like the rest of us."

"Oooh, tough luck, sweetie," Amber said to Sandy. "Guess every job has its hazards, huh?"

"Yeah," Sandy said, raising an eyebrow at Ethan. "Hazards."

"Maybe if Ms. DeMarco and I went inside and looked around a little, we could find out where Chris went. Then you can collect that back rent and get your boss off your back."

"God, I'm sorry," she said with a sigh. "I can't let you do that."

Ethan held up his palm. "I understand. You've got a job to do, just like I do. And believe me, mine sucks as much as yours does." Then he rubbed the back of his neck and leaned in close again. "The managing partner at my firm really cracks that whip. All day, every day. I'm getting pretty damned sick of it."

"Hey, I hear you there, too. Every boss I've ever had was an asshole. But you're still better off than me. At least lawyers make a lot of money, right?"

"Don't believe everything you hear."

Ethan eased his usual cool, watchful expression into a little-lost-puppy-dog look. The goofy smile Amber gave him told Sandy that the woman was picturing the care and feeding of that poor lost puppy. Unfortunately, what she didn't know was that the puppy could easily morph into a full-grown, teeth-baring rottweiler.

Amber tilted her head again and shot a look over her shoulder. "Tell you what. I'll let you go in for just a few minutes. Take a quick look around. The owner would probably freak if he knew I was doing this. But if Chris gets that inheritance, he'll get his money, and that's a good thing, right?"

"You bet. Thanks, Amber. You're a real sweetheart." Ethan gave her a full-blown, knock-'em-dead smile that practically brought the woman to her knees. She was so flustered that she barely managed to get the passkey, unlock the apartment door, and let them inside.

"Need some help?" Amber said.

"No," Ethan said. "You go back to your apartment, and once we're finished, I'll let you know what we find out. How would that be?"

"Sounds good, Bob. I'll see you in a minute, okay?"

Amber went back into her apartment, and Ethan shut the door.

"Bob?" Sandy said. "Who the hell is Bob?"

"He's the guy on the business card I gave Amber."

"You gave her somebody else's business card?"

"No. It was mine. It was just phony."

"You carry phony business cards?"

"Yes. A couple of different ones, actually. But they all have the same number that goes to a voice-mail account. There are times when I need information, but it's better if my informant doesn't know who I really am."

"Such as when you have to lie about why you want to rummage through somebody's apartment?"

"Exactly. If I'd told her I was investigating a murder, she might not have been as forthcoming with the passkey."

"What do you think about the fact that Chris skipped town the morning after the murder?" Sandy asked.

"I think the odds of her knowing something about it just went sky-high."

Sandy glanced around the sparsely furnished room. A baby blanket lay crumpled on one end of the sofa, along with a few toys. Two framed photographs sat on an end table. One was of a baby, maybe a year old. Sandy picked up the other photo, a candid shot of a woman holding the same baby.

"Do you suppose this is Chris?" she asked Ethan.

He looked at the photo. "I don't know. Maybe."

"If so, it looks as if she has a child." Sandy set the photo down and looked toward the dining-room table, where she saw an arrangement of a dozen roses that had come from her shop. "Those are the flowers Laura sent her."

"Is the card with them?"

Sandy turned the vase around, looking on all sides. "No. She may have taken that with her, even if she didn't take the flowers."

Ethan circled his gaze around the room. "Okay. Just look for anything that says where Chris might have gone. An airline itinerary. An address she might have jotted down. Check the bedroom and bathroom, and be sure to look for a computer. If you find one and it's on, see if she left her e-mail open. Look for anything in the vicinity that she might have printed or notes she might have taken. I'll look through the living room and kitchen, then check out her telephone to see who she's been talking to."

Sandy glanced around, feeling suddenly self-conscious. "This is kind of creepy."

"Creepy?"

"Being in Chris's apartment and she doesn't know it. What if she happens to come home?"

"Just let me do the talking."

Sandy had no problem with that.

As Ethan went into the kitchen, Sandy headed down the hall. She peeked into the bathroom. It was relatively bare, with walls painted white, a dingy bathmat, and a blue-flowered shower curtain. The curtain was closed. Sandy had the sudden sense that if she pulled it aside, she'd find something that made *Psycho* seem like *Sesame Street*.

She stepped into the bathroom, aware of the steady *drip, drip, drip* of a leaky faucet, the sound of it magnified ten times over in the silence of the bathroom. Holding her breath, she swept the curtain away.

Soap. Shampoo. Washcloths. And not a single dead body.

She took a deep breath and let it out slowly, trying to calm her rapidly beating heart. Some people were cut out for espionage. She wasn't one of them.

She peered into the bathroom cabinet. It appeared that most toiletries were missing, and there was no toothbrush in the toothbrush holder.

Sandy left the bathroom and continued down the hall into the only bedroom in the apartment. A double bed with a velour bedspread sat on the far wall. A floor lamp sat beside it. On another wall was a baby's crib sitting next to a cheap walnut-veneer dresser. The walls were bare—no framed items, no clock, no nothing.

Walking over to the dresser, she opened all the drawers, finding nothing but a few stray items of clothing—a bra, a few pairs of panties, some mismatched socks, along with some baby clothes. Opening a jewelry box on top of the dresser, she found it empty.

She closed the lid again and headed for the closet. Once again, her heart went wild. She slowly opened the door and flipped on the light.

No dead bodies there, either. With the exception of a pair of winter boots and several sweaters and long-sleeved shirts, the closet was empty. She turned out the light and closed the door. There had to be something to tell them where Chris had gone, but she wasn't finding it in here.

She went back to the living room. Ethan sat at the dining room table, phone in hand, writing something on a piece of paper. He looked up. "What did you find?"

"Nothing. Her bedroom closet was practically empty. Her jewelry box was empty. Toiletries were gone."

"So it looks as if she intends to stay away for a while."

"Yes."

"Computer?"

"I didn't find one."

"Laptop?"

"If she had one, I'd have seen it. There wasn't much to look through. What did you find out?"

"I checked the caller ID. Laura phoned Chris the day before and the day of her murder. Seventeen times."

Sandy blinked with surprise. "Do you suppose they talked seventeen times?"

"I doubt it. Chris probably didn't answer. It seems pretty clear that she was trying to avoid Laura, which is consistent with the flowers Laura sent telling Chris she refused to let her go."

"You make it sound as if Laura was stalking her."

"She may have been."

"Come on, Ethan. Laura didn't strike me as loony."

"People can surprise you. Maybe Chris wanted to call off their relationship, and Laura refused. Maybe Laura got a little obsessive. Maybe Chris got fed up with it."

"Fed up enough to kill Laura?"

"It's not probable. But it is possible."

"We may be jumping to conclusions here," Sandy said. "Chris may simply have taken a vacation."

"She disappeared the morning after the murder. I don't buy coincidences." Ethan tore a piece of paper off the pad he'd been writing on. "I took three other names and numbers off the caller ID that we need to check out. I also hit redial and got the phone number of the last person she called. We can check an online reverse directory when we get back to my place and see who the number belongs to."

Sandy heard a sudden noise outside. The sound of feet on the metal stairs. She and Ethan both froze, listening. A moment later they heard the sound of keys rattling, opening the apartment next door. She let out the breath she'd been holding.

"Ethan? This is making me a little nervous. Can we get out of here now?"

"Yeah. Let's talk to the neighbors before we go, though, and see what they know."

Ten minutes later, they'd spoken to all the neighbors who were home, but not one of them seemed to know Chris at all. Said she was quiet. Kept to herself. They saw her coming and going now and again, but that was it.

Ethan and Sandy went back to Amber's apartment. She answered the door with a big smile for Ethan, but Sandy could have been in Guam for all the woman acknowledged her. Ethan told her they hadn't found anything to tell them where Chris had gone, but asked her if she would please call the number on his card if she happened to see her. He thanked her for her help, then gave her one last killer smile before he and Sandy headed back to his car.

"Bet you've got a message from Amber on your voice mail before you even get home," Sandy said as they got into the car. "And not because she has seen Chris."

"Oh?" Ethan said innocently. "And why is that?"

"As if you don't know."

He started the car. "Maybe because she liked me?"

"She's never met Ethan. But she's sure crazy about Bob."

"No wonder. Bob's a great guy."

"Ralph Clemmons recognized you from seeing you on the news. What if Amber had, too?"

"Amber doesn't watch the news," Ethan said. "She watches *Jerry Springer,* the Game Show Network, and MTV."

"Good point. So why did you tell her *my* real name?"

"No reason not to."

"Wrong profession, though. What was the deal with that?"

"Sometimes I do things just for fun."

"Telling her I'd been convicted of malpractice was fun?"

"Actually, yes."

Sandy just shook her head.

"You're just mad because I called you a schlep," Ethan said.

"No, Ethan. I'm mad because you called me an attorney."

His lips edged into a warm smile. "Now, there you go maligning my profession again. Didn't I have a word with you about that?"

Sandy felt a shiver of satisfaction. He was handsome as sin no matter what his expression, but that smile sent him into another realm entirely. And it made her want to shout at him: *Stop making me like you so damned much!*

If only he could be the cutthroat attorney and sleazy womanizer her brothers had described all these years, she could turn away from him without a second thought.

If only.

Once they got back to his town house, Ethan spread his notes out in front of him, then logged on again to the Web site that contained public records. He checked out the three names and numbers that had been stored in Chris's caller ID, which netted nothing. Two seemed to be sales calls, and the third was a call from a hair salon, probably to confirm an appointment. Then Ethan keyed in the number he'd gotten when he hit the redial button on Chris's phone, and a few seconds later, the screen popped up.

"Damn," Ethan muttered.

"What?"

"It's a cell phone."

"So?"

"They're not accessible through this database."

"What would happen if you just called it?"

"My phone number would show up on the caller ID. If the person on the other end sees that and is feeling at all suspicious, he won't answer and we'll be back to square one. And I certainly can't ask to speak to Chris, not when it's pretty clear that she's trying to hide."

"So there's no way to find who the number belongs to?"

"Probably. But I don't have access to sites that may have that information."

Sandy felt a shot of disappointment. Then she had a thought. "Wait a minute. I know who can find out who that cell phone number belongs to."

"Who?"

"My sister-in-law. She's a private investigator. I bet she can get the information for us. Let me give her a call."

Sandy reached for her cell phone and got Val on the line. She gave her Chris's name, told her the situation, and asked if finding who the number belonged to would be a problem.

"Nope," Val said. "No problem. Give me five minutes and I'll call you back."

"Thanks, Val."

"So you and Ethan are chasing a lead, are you?" Val asked.

"Yeah.

"Is he chasing you yet?"

She glanced at Ethan, who was sitting back in his chair, his elbows on the armrests and his fingers steepled in front of him. Every time she looked at him she noticed something about him she hadn't seen before—his well-manicured but very masculine hands, the strong slant of his jaw, the rigid outline of his shoulders beneath his shirt. He was style and strength all rolled into one breathtaking package.

I wish.

"No," Sandy said. "Not yet."

"Well, let me know when he does. I love juicy gossip."

Sandy hung up and told Ethan what Val had said, and they waited for her to call back. Sandy was dismayed when the five minutes turned into twenty-five, but the information Val gave them turned out to be better than she'd anticipated.

"The cell phone number belongs to Natalie Holcomb," Val said. "She's Chris Satterwhite's sister. She lives in Larchmont at fifty-five forty-six Hillsdale Strcct."

Sandy wrote down the name, feeling a rush of excitement. Larchmont was a small town only half an hour outside Tolosa.

"Now if we only knew if Chris was there," Sandy said.

"She is."

"How do you know?"

"That's why it took me a few minutes longer to get back to you. I've got a buddy out in Larchmont. I gave him Chris's license plate number, and he did a drive-by for me. Her car was at the house."

"Thanks, Val. You've been a big help."

"If you need anything else, just give me a call."

"I will."

Sandy hung up the phone and handed Ethan the address, telling him what Val had told her.

"It's only seven o'clock," he said. "Since we know she's there, let's go now."

Sandy wavered. "Are you sure we should be getting in the middle of a murder investigation like this?"

"We're not interfering with the police's investigation. They don't even know Chris exists. She may know something about the murder and she may not. Right now we're just talking to somebody who was a friend of the victim. That's all."

"Then we call the police?"

"Depends on what we find out."

Sandy grabbed her purse. "Okay, then. Let's go."

It was seven thirty when Ethan and Sandy entered the city limits of Larchmont. They quickly located Natalie Holcomb's house, a rambling two-story with a big front porch that sat on a street almost completely shaded by trees. A woman sat on the porch swing smoking a cigarette. Ethan pulled up to the curb and killed the engine.

"Suppose that's Chris?" Sandy asked.

"Let's find out."

As they got out of the car and approached the porch, the

woman sat up straight and eyed them warily. She looked to be in her late twenties, a plain woman with brown hair and brown eyes, wearing a pair of shorts and a tank top.

They climbed the porch steps. "Hi," Sandy said. "Are you Chris Satterwhite?"

"Who wants to know?"

"I'm Sandy DeMarco. I was a friend of Laura Williams's. I believe you were, too."

The woman froze, her eyes widening. Then she turned away. "I'm sorry. I don't know anybody by that name."

"Come on, Chris," Sandy said. "We know who you are, and we know about your relationship with Laura. We just want to ask you a few questions."

The woman took another drag off her cigarette. "I told you I don't know anybody named Laura Williams."

Ethan stepped forward. "Sure you do, Chris. She was murdered two nights ago. You know that, too, don't you?"

"Who the hell are you?"

"I'm the attorney representing the kid who's accused of killing Laura. But he didn't kill her."

"That's no concern of mine." Chris flicked her cigarette butt into the bushes and headed for the front door.

"We think you killed her," Ethan said.

She whipped around, horror spreading across her face. "Me? You think *I* killed Laura?"

"So maybe you know her after all?"

"I don't have to listen to this!"

She reached for the handle of the screen door, but Ethan pressed his hand against its frame and held it shut.

"Damn it," Chris said. "Will you let go?"

"I've got records showing that Laura sent you flowers the day before her murder. The card read, 'I refuse to let you go. I know we can work things out. Please call me. I love you, Laura.'"

Chris looked dumbfounded. "How did you know that?"

"Because Laura ordered the flowers through my flower shop," Sandy said, "and I found the order."

Chris cursed under her breath.

"She also called you seventeen times the day before her murder," Ethan went on, "and I doubt you answered the phone seventeen times. Do you know what all that tells me? It tells me you and Laura had a relationship. It tells me your relationship went south. It tells me that Laura was adamant that it not end, but you thought it should." Ethan leaned in closer. "It tells me that you were going to make it end . . . one way or the other."

"No! I would never have hurt Laura!"

"Ever go out into Laura's sunroom, Chris? You two ever slip into that hot tub together? Your fingerprints are going to be everywhere, including the room where Laura was found battered to death."

Chris stared at him, horrified.

"I've got a seventeen-year-old kid who's been accused of this murder. The way it's looking now, he's liable to be convicted. If it takes me suggesting a new scenario to ensure that doesn't happen, I'll do it in a heartbeat. And guess who's going to be right in the middle of my shiny new theory? You had opportunity all over the place and a hell of a good motive. I can sell that to a jury in the time it takes to say 'death penalty.' "

"Stop it!" Chris shouted. "Just stop it! I told you I didn't kill her!"

"Two kinds of people run, Chris. Guilty people and frightened people. You say you aren't guilty."

"I'm not!"

Ethan dropped his voice to a softer tone. "Then tell me what you're frightened of."

Her voice choked up, tears welling in her eyes. She looked

back and forth between Ethan and Sandy, and he sensed her trying to swallow the words even as they poured out of her mouth.

"I didn't kill Laura," she said. "But I think I know who did."

chapter ten

Ethan felt a surge of exhilaration, the one that always came over him when a witness finally cracked.

"Tell me," he said. "Who killed her?"

Chris opened her mouth to speak, but her words seemed to clog in her throat. "You have to know the whole story. Otherwise it won't make any sense."

"Is there someplace we can talk?" Sandy asked.

"Yes. Come inside."

She unlocked the door and they went inside the house. A staircase sat on one side of the expansive foyer, and they followed Chris beyond it into the living room. Ethan waited for her to sit down on the sofa before taking a seat in the chair directly to her left. Sandy sat on the other side of her.

Just then a woman came out of the kitchen holding a baby girl in her arms. She stopped short, looking at Sandy and Ethan with surprise.

"Natalie," Chris said, "would you please take Sarah outside for a little while?"

Natalie glanced back and forth between Ethan and Sandy, suddenly looking worried. "Are you sure? Does this have anything to do . . ." Her voice trailed off.

"Please just take Sarah outside. I'm fine. I just need to talk to these people."

Finally the woman nodded and went back into the kitchen. Ethan heard the back door open, then close again.

"Who was that?" Ethan asked.

"My sister."

"And Sarah?" Sandy asked.

"She's my daughter."

"Okay, Chris," Ethan said. "I want you to tell me everything you know about Laura Williams and who might have killed her."

"I don't know where to start."

"The beginning. And don't leave anything out."

Chris's hands were trembling, and her head was bowed with resignation. Ethan knew those were both good signs. They meant she was getting ready to tell the truth.

"I denied what I was for a lot of years," Chris said, staring down at her hands. "But finally I couldn't any longer. I left my husband five months ago." She took a deep breath and let it out slowly. "Shortly after that, Laura and I met at a bar down on Colfax Street. After we talked there a time or two, she invited me to her house. Soon we were seeing each other all the time. I loved her. You have to believe that. I never would have hurt her."

"We know," Sandy said. "Just tell us your story, okay?"

"First of all, her name wasn't really Laura Williams."

"It wasn't?"

"No. It was Pamela Barton. She had her name legally changed when she moved to Tolosa."

"Why?" Ethan asked.

"Because she wanted to disappear."

"Disappear?"

Chris paused, taking a deep breath. "The night before she was killed, Laura went out to rent a movie, and I stayed at her house. I was in the bedroom. She'd been gone about twenty minutes, when all at once I heard the front door open and a lot of commotion in the living room. Shouting. I couldn't imagine what was going on. When I came down the hall, I saw a man. He had Laura by the throat, and he'd backed her up against the wall. He was yelling at her. Threatening her."

"A burglar?" Ethan said.

"That's what I thought at the time. I knew where Laura kept a gun, so I ran to her bedroom, grabbed it, and hurried back to the living room. I pointed the gun at him and shouted at him to let Laura go. He spun around, shocked as hell to see somebody else in the house.

"Laura backed away. He started yelling at her again, telling her she'd better tell him where the tape was or he was going to kill her. I had no idea what he was talking about. Then Laura told him that she didn't have it, that it was locked up in a safe place, and that she'd left instructions that if anything happened to her, it would be turned over to the police and he'd be arrested."

"Tape?" Ethan said. "What tape?"

"It all goes back to when Laura lived in Austin six months ago." She paused. "But when I tell you what happened there, it's going to make her sound like a terrible person. But she wasn't. I swear she wasn't."

"I know," Sandy said. "I knew her, remember?"

"But you didn't know everything about her."

"Go on," Ethan said.

"The man who came to her house the night before her murder was Vince Mulroney. She met him when she worked in a bar in Austin. He was into all kinds of bad things, including drugs. He started giving Laura cocaine."

"She had a drug habit?" Ethan asked.

"Eventually, yes. And as soon as she was hooked, Vince had her right where he wanted her."

"What do you mean?"

"He made porn flicks and wanted her to participate."

Sandy's mouth fell open. "Laura was a porn actress?"

"Yes. Cocaine is an expensive habit, and as long as she did

what Vince wanted her to, he supplied her." Chris paused. "But that wasn't the worst part." Her eyes filled with tears again, and she took a few deep breaths before continuing. "Vince moved Laura into progressively darker films. Violent films. A lot of bondage and sadomasochism. One day they were filming, and there was another actress there, somebody Vince had picked up just that day. In the scene, Laura was supposed to shoot her. Vince told Laura to put the gun to her head and pull the trigger, that he'd dub in the gunshot later. She did." Chris paused. "The gun was loaded."

Sandy slid her hand to her throat. "She shot the woman?"

"Yes. The woman died instantly. Laura thought it was some kind of horrible accident. Then she realized that Vince had intended that gun to go off."

"But why?" Sandy asked.

"Snuff films," Ethan said. "Real murders on tape. There's a big underground market for that."

"He's an evil man," Chris said. "I swear I could tell just by looking at him. He's tall, with jet-black hair. And he has the strangest blue eyes, as if there were nothing behind them at all. No conscience, no soul, no nothing."

"What happened then?" Ethan asked.

"Laura told Vince she was going to the police, but he told her she wasn't going to report anything, because he had her on tape pulling the trigger, and he could easily convince the police that she'd been part of it."

"Yes," Ethan said. "A videotape of her holding a smoking gun would have been hard to refute."

"Exactly. She was terrified that she'd been recorded pulling that trigger. But somehow she managed to steal the tape and get out of Austin without Vince knowing it. She told me she knew she needed to take it to the police, that a woman had been murdered, but she was so afraid of them not believing her story that she never did. Instead, she ran."

"To Tolosa," Ethan said. "And changed her name."

"Yes. What had happened that night scared her completely straight. She assumed a new identity. She got a job. She found somebody who was willing to let her do a lease purchase on a house in that pretty neighborhood with almost no money down because it needed a lot of work. She didn't care. She loved that house. And as far as I know, she got off the coke. At least, I never saw her use it during the time I knew her. She was just so horrified by what had happened that there wasn't anything she wouldn't do to turn her life around. But still she was terrified that Vince would come after her."

"Just because she stole the tape?" Ethan said. "She was the one shown committing murder, not him."

"But when Laura pulled the trigger and realized what she'd done, she went berserk. Vince ended up on camera. The tape she stole was the unedited version, and Vince knew it." Tears filled Chris's eyes again. "I think he finally caught up with her. And he killed her."

"Wait a minute," Ethan said. "Didn't Laura tell Vince that the tape would go to the police if something happened to her? As far as we know, the police haven't received anything like that."

"She told me after Vince left that she was bluffing, but that she did have the tape, and it was somewhere safe."

"You don't know where?" Ethan said.

"No. I have no idea."

"But Vince had no way of knowing that Laura wasn't telling the truth," Sandy said. "And if that's true, why would he kill her?"

"Maybe he didn't intend to," Ethan said.

"What?"

"Maybe he just meant to intimidate her, and it got out of hand."

"He tortured her like that to get information out of her?"

"His anger probably got the better of him. This is someone who makes snuff films. I doubt he's an emotionally stable man."

"After he left that night," Chris said, "Laura tried to convince me that she was in the clear because she'd bluffed Vince. But I was so horrified by all of it that I told her I couldn't see her anymore. That's when she started calling me. I didn't want to ignore her, but I couldn't talk to her, either. I just couldn't."

"Assuming all this is true," Ethan said, "then why haven't you told the police what you know?"

"Because I can't be implicated in any of this."

"Why not?"

"I'm in the middle of a divorce right now. I left my husband under some pretty hostile circumstances. He was furious when I told him that I'd been living a lie for years. That I . . . that I was attracted to women. I think he thought it made him less of a man, and it was an embarrassment to him. He's done everything he can since then to try to discredit me and get full custody of our daughter."

"Your sexual orientation shouldn't make any difference," Ethan said.

"In a perfect world, maybe not. But if I'm a lesbian who was having an affair with a drug-addicted porn star who killed somebody and then was murdered herself? My husband has a real bastard of an attorney. He'll have a field day with that one. My relationship to Laura can't come out. It *can't*."

"Do you have representation?" Sandy asked.

"Yes. But my husband is the one with the money, not me. And if I'm connected to Laura in any way, I know his attorney will make a case for me being unfit as a parent."

"What's your custody situation right now?" Ethan asked.

"The judge granted temporary joint custody. I have my

daughter during the week, and my husband has her on the weekends."

"Which means you have to return your daughter to him by Saturday?"

"Yes."

"Do you intend to do that?"

Chris just stared at him, her indecision hovering in the air. "I'm not sure yet."

Ethan fixed a tight gaze on Chris. "If you stay gone with your daughter, that's kidnapping. Do you understand that?"

Chris paused. "Yes."

"But you're not going anywhere. You're going back to Tolosa. You're going to tell the police what you know about Vince Mulroney."

"I can't do that."

"The police could keep your identity a secret."

"Oh, please! You know as well as I do that the press has ways of finding out about things like this! My husband owns a construction company in Tolosa. He's a prominent businessman. Reporters live and breathe for stories like this, and he's not a man who likes to be embarrassed."

"But even if it comes out that you knew Laura, you can tell the judge that you had no idea what she was involved in," Sandy said. "Surely he'll see that her past is no reflection on you."

"Can you guarantee me that? Can you absolutely guarantee me that a judge won't declare me an unfit mother and take my child away?"

"Maybe there's a way around it," Sandy said. "If you say you were just a friend of Laura's—"

"No," Chris said, her voice escalating, "I can't risk any connection at all. If my husband finds out about all this, I'll never see my daughter again!"

"Ethan," Sandy said. "Can't we just tell the police that we

know Vince Mulroney is making those films? Get them to search his house, or something? If they can get him on that, then they might be able to tie him to Laura's murder."

"In order to search his house they'll need probable cause. Somebody with a direct connection has to come forward and make an accusation."

"But we could tell them. Keep Chris out of it."

"No. Chris telling us and then us telling the police is nothing but hearsay, and a judge won't issue a search warrant based on that alone." He turned to Chris. "That's why we need you to tell the police that you heard Vince threaten Laura."

"Damn it!" Chris shouted. "I told you I'm not going to do that!"

"But if Mulroney thinks you know something, he could come after you. Your life could be in danger."

"I don't know that for sure. The only thing I do know for sure is what my husband is going to do if I go to the police and all this comes out. And that's a chance I'm not going to take."

"You can't stay gone forever."

"Don't bank on that."

Ethan sat back, rubbing his hand over his mouth. This was going nowhere. This woman was running on emotion. Acting irrationally. Illogically. Unfortunately, right now she saw her husband as a bigger threat than Mulroney, and Ethan could see that he wasn't going to be able to get her to think straight about that. There was only one thing he could do now.

He had to play hardball.

He leaned forward and gave her a no-nonsense look. "Okay, Chris. Here's where we're at. If you don't tell the police what you know, a seventeen-year-old kid is liable to go down for a murder he didn't commit. I'm not going to let that happen. If I have to subpoena you to testify, I'll do it."

"You'll have to find me first."

"I can have you arrested right now as a suspect in Laura's murder. You'll be forced to tell them what you know to save yourself."

Sandy spun around. "Ethan!"

"You wouldn't do that," Chris said hotly.

He leaned in closer. "My client is accused of murder. It's my job to get him acquitted."

"So you don't mind ruining my life to make that happen?"

"I'll do whatever I have to."

Tears filled Chris's eyes. "You son of a bitch."

"Call me what you want to. But one way or the other, you're telling the police what you know."

"Like I said. You're going to have to find me first."

"Fine. Run. I'll tell your husband your last known whereabouts. You say he has deep pockets, which means he should be able to hire the best private investigator in town. He'll track you down, Chris. And when he does, you'll be arrested for kidnapping. Try getting custody after you've been convicted of that."

"Damn you!" Chris shouted. "How can you do this to me? I didn't do anything wrong, and yet I'm going to get dragged through the mud?"

"Chris," Sandy said. "Take it easy, okay? He's not going to do any of that."

Ethan whipped around. "Sandy—"

"He's not going to have you arrested. And he's not going to accuse you of the murder. I promise you that."

Ethan recoiled with shock. What the hell did she think she was doing?

He turned to Chris. "What happens here is not up to Sandy. It's up to me, and I'll do whatever I have to in order to force you to tell the police what you know."

"No, he won't," Sandy said. "I don't care what he's telling you. He's not going to do either of those things."

Ethan couldn't believe this. Did she *want* to lose this witness?

He leaned toward Chris again. "Chris, I want you to listen to me, and listen good. Sandy has a much bigger heart than I do. That's why she's trying to convince you that I won't go after your testimony any way I can. But the truth is that I've chewed up and spit out witnesses ten times more problematic than you. So do you really want to take the chance that I'm bluffing?"

Chris looked back and forth between them. She swallowed hard, her angry glare slowly melting into an expression of despair. Her face crumpled, and she bowed her head and began to cry.

There, he thought with satisfaction. He had her. Resignation. That was exactly what he was looking for. He was sure she wasn't going to give him any more trouble.

Then Sandy shot him a look of disgust and reached over and patted Chris on the shoulder.

Ethan felt a surge of anger. Damn it, this was *not* the time for sympathy. Sandy was dulling a moment that needed to stay razor-sharp.

Enough was enough.

He stood up suddenly. "Sandy. Come with me."

She glared at him.

"Now."

Sandy raised her chin in a gesture of defiance, but still she rose and followed him. They stepped out onto the front porch, Ethan's anger growing with every step he took.

He closed the door and turned to Sandy. "What the hell do you think you're doing?"

"What?"

"Telling Chris I wouldn't send somebody after her if she takes her kid and runs."

"Are you telling me you would?"

"Sweetheart, I'd have the cops on her so fast it would make her head spin."

Sandy looked aghast. "You would actually have that poor woman arrested for kidnapping?"

"I believe I made that clear."

"And you'd accuse her of killing Laura, even when you know she didn't do it?"

"It won't come to that. But I sure as hell want her to think that it will."

"But—"

"Sandy. Listen to me. You want Josh to stay out of prison. I can make that happen, but I have to do it on my own terms. So from now on, you need to shut up and stay out of my way. Do you understand?"

They remained at an impasse, a long silence stretching between them. Hell, no, she didn't like it. She didn't like the way he had to coerce and manipulate people in order to make them say and do what he needed them to. But it was what his clients paid him for, and he was damned good at it, whether it required him to pour on the charm to finesse an apartment passkey or incite a down-and-dirty confrontation to secure a witness.

After a few moments, though, Sandy's anger seemed to fade. She looked away, letting out a long breath. Then she turned back, and he was surprised to see an expression of agreement on her face.

"Okay," she said. "I see your point."

Her compliance knocked Ethan off guard, and he looked at her warily.

"I mean it," she went on. "I had no right to undermine you in there. I know you had to accuse her of the crime in the first place to shake her up enough that she'd talk to us. But then . . ." Her eyes drifted closed for a few seconds, and she let out a gentle sigh. "Look, I know I told you to pull out all the stops to help Josh. And I'm not saying that what you're doing won't get results. It's just that . . ." She glanced through the window at Chris with an expression of melancholy, then lowered her voice.

"You see her as just a witness. A means to an end. But she's more than that. She's a woman who just found out a shocking truth about someone she loved. A woman whose lover was murdered. A mother who's on the verge of losing her child. She's hurt, she's scared, and she's grieving." Sandy looked up at him, her expression pleading. "All I want you to do is just stop and *look* at her."

The plaintive tone of Sandy's voice arrested his anger, and he found himself glancing through the window to the living room. Chris sat on the sofa, her head bowed, her shoulders still shaking with sobs.

"Handle the situation however you think you need to," Sandy said. "But you're smart about these things. If there's some way to protect Chris and still get Josh out of this, will you please try to find it?"

With that, she turned and walked back into the house.

As the screen door slapped shut behind her, Ethan stood near the window, watching as she sat down next to Chris again and took the woman's hand. He didn't have the first idea what Sandy was telling her, but he did know this: Whatever it was, even if Chris was on the verge of her whole life falling apart, it was going to make her feel better.

Yeah, okay. She'd feel better. But that didn't alter the facts. She needed to tell the police what she knew. He and Sandy relating the story secondhand had no legal teeth at all. Chris was the one who had heard Vince Mulroney threaten to kill Laura, and Chris was the one who needed to talk.

What Sandy didn't understand was that being forceful could be very expedient. It had gotten to the point where no one had a prayer of verbally outmaneuvering him, and that generally got him what he wanted as quickly as possible. He used threats because threats worked.

In spite of the effectiveness of his methods, though, Sandy's words chipped away at his conscience, making him think about how he'd done similar things to people in the past in order to extract information or otherwise control a situation. But now he realized that he couldn't remember the faces of a single one of those people. His eyes had been open, but he'd never really seen them.

Just stop and look at her.

He pictured the expression on Chris's face when he'd accused her of killing someone she loved, then demanded that she do something she was sure would make her lose her child. He was a high-powered attorney coming at her with both barrels blazing, threatening to make her life hell so he could control the situation. As always, he was so centered on doing what was best for his client that he wasn't considering collateral damage.

For a few moments, he forced himself to look at the situation through Sandy's eyes. Could he have taken more time? Spelled out Chris's options? Been firm but sympathetic? Was there a way to protect her and help Josh at the same time?

He thought about it for a moment and decided that maybe there was.

He went back into the house. As he sat down on the sofa, Chris recoiled, her posture tense.

"Ethan—"

"Sandy, let me talk."

"But—"

He cut her off with a pointed stare, then turned to Chris. "Tell me again exactly what Laura told you about where she hid the tape."

Chris looked at him warily. "She told me she'd put it someplace safe."

"At her house?"

"I assume so."

"Okay. This is a long shot, but if I can tell the police that I've got a tip about that tape, that it's evidence leading to Laura's killer, maybe I can get them to search her house for it. If they can find it, it'll go a long way toward taking Mulroney down."

Chris blinked with surprise. "I wouldn't have to talk to them?"

"No. Without the tape, we need your testimony that Vince threatened to kill Laura, because we need enough for a judge to issue a warrant so the cops can arrest him. But they don't need a warrant to reinvestigate the crime scene. If I can convince them to look for the tape and they find it, that alone will give them all the probable cause they need to arrest Vince, plus provide a motive for Laura's murder. Then as long as there's some forensic evidence to tie him to the crime, he can be convicted on that and you can remain an unnamed informant."

"But how do we know Vince didn't find the tape in Laura's house the night he killed her?" Chris asked.

"We don't."

"She may not even have kept it at her house. It may be somewhere else entirely."

"Yes. That's true. I told you this was a long shot."

Chris let out a shaky sigh. "So what's going to happen if the police don't find the tape?"

"You'll have to tell them that you heard Vince threaten to kill Laura. At that point, there will be no other option."

Chris's jaw tightened, and tears filled her eyes again. Ethan looked away. He sensed Sandy watching him expectantly.

Just stop and look at her.

Slowly he turned back. A tear rolled down Chris's cheek, and she wiped it away with her fingertips. Her eyes were full of despair, and all at once it was as if a wall that had been surrounding him for years had suddenly crumbled away, and he was hit with a stunning realization. He'd never had trouble reading people when it suited his purpose, but he'd never given much thought to what suited theirs.

He knew what suited Chris's purpose now.

"Who is your husband's attorney?" he asked her.

"Russell Green."

Ethan nodded grimly. "Hotshot divorce lawyer. Tough opponent."

Chris sighed. "I know. If all this comes out, my lawyer doesn't stand a chance against him."

"Maybe he doesn't. But I do."

Chris stared at him. "What?"

"If you have to come forward to testify against Mulroney and it causes a problem in your custody battle, I'll take your case."

For several seconds, the room was silent. It was clear that neither Chris nor Sandy could believe what he was saying. Hell, he didn't believe it himself.

"You're a divorce lawyer?" Chris asked.

"That's not my specialty. But I'll bring in the best family-law attorney at my firm for consultation. Together it's a safe bet that we can take care of Mr. Green. At the very least we'll make sure you maintain shared custody."

"But that must mean you're a really good lawyer, right?" Chris said.

"Yes."

Her face fell. "If I could afford a good lawyer, I'd already have one."

"Just pay me whatever you're paying your attorney now."

"You'd let me do that?"

"Yes. As long as you hold up your end of the bargain. But I'm warning you, Chris. If the police don't find the tape and you try to run, the deal is off. I'll have to go back to plan A. I'll track you down and have a subpoena served. Everything will come out about your relationship with Laura, only you'll be fending for yourself in your custody battle. Do you understand that?"

Chris nodded.

"And one more thing. Even if they find the tape and arrest Mulroney, if it turns out that there's no forensic evidence tying him to Laura's murder, your testimony is probably the only thing that'll make him a stronger suspect than my client. If that happens, you'll also have to come forward. Do you understand?"

Chris nodded. "Yes. I understand." She wiped her eyes again, then turned to Sandy. "I don't want you to think that I don't want that man to pay for what he did to Laura. I do. And I don't want that boy convicted when he's innocent." She shrugged weakly. "I was just afraid, you know?"

"I know," Sandy said. "But you're not alone in this. Ethan is the best at what he does. Trust me on that. He'll make sure your little girl isn't taken away from you."

Ethan stood up. "Sandy, we'd better go."

Chris stood up, and Sandy gave her a hug. "Does your sister know about all this?"

"Yes. I've told her everything."

"Good. I don't want you to be alone in this. I'm so sorry about Laura. I know you loved her."

"Yes. I loved her even when she told me who she was and what she'd done. That night Vince caught up to her, she told me . . ." A tear rolled down Chris's face, and she wiped it away. "She told me that she had this idea that if she started living a good life, then maybe someday she could take the tape to the police and they'd believe her. That was why she kept it instead of destroying it. But she knew they'd never believe a porn actress with a drug habit. She said she knew deep down that eventually she had to make everything right.

She just hadn't worked up the nerve to do it yet. At heart she was a really good person."

Chris turned and held out her hand to Ethan. "Thank you, Mr. Millner. I appreciate what you're trying to do for me. And I promise you I'll hold up my end of the bargain."

Ethan shook her hand. "We'll be in touch."

chapter eleven

By the time Ethan drove into his town-house complex, evening was turning to dusk. He pulled into a parking space. He and Sandy got out of the car, and he circled around to the passenger side.

"Ethan? Do you suppose that man we saw last night getting into the car in front of Laura's house was Vince Mulroney?"

"I don't know. It was a rental car, and if he'd flown here from Austin, he could very well have been driving one. Do you remember if the guy we saw had dark hair?"

"Looked like it to me. But it was dark outside."

"As soon as the police get him in custody, we can tell them what we saw and give them the license plate number."

Sandy nodded.

"I'll talk to Henderson tomorrow," Ethan said. "I'll call you as soon as I know what's up."

"Just how big a long shot do you think this is?"

"I don't know. First I've got to convince Henderson to look for the tape. Then they've got to find it. I think we both know that in all likelihood, Chris will still end up having to talk to the police."

"But if she does, you'll be helping with her custody battle. You'll help her keep her daughter." Sandy smiled. "That was a good thing to do."

"It was just negotiation. I wanted something from her, so I had to give up something."

"I think it was more than that."

"Sandy, as much as I'd like to delude you into thinking I'm edging into sainthood, the truth is that you merely convinced me that my strategy was flawed. I changed the battle plan. That's all."

"And how about the family-law attorney at your firm whose time you so graciously offered for peanuts? Is he also fighting this battle?"

"I'll cross that bridge when I come to it."

"If you keep giving your services away, you're going to end up in the poorhouse."

He gave her an offhand shrug. "Town-house living is over-rated."

She smiled when he said that, and he wondered at what point in time he'd become such a pushover. He still didn't like this situation. It was a crazy, dead-end path to follow. He was going to have to convince a pain-in-the-ass detective to reopen a crime scene to search for a tape that might or might not be there. If it was, and they were very, very lucky, it might hold evidence that would allow them to nail a killer.

And it might not.

But for now, it didn't hurt to talk to Henderson. If they didn't find the tape, he could always fall back on Chris's testimony. If they did, maybe it could be a win-win situation after all.

"I guess I'd better be going," Sandy said.

As she turned to unlock her car door, Ethan heard a noise behind him. He turned to see a little blond girl knocking on the door to his town house.

"Looks like she's selling something," Sandy said waving at the kid. "Over here, sweetie!"

The girl turned. Sandy motioned to her, and she tentatively walked over to them.

"Do you live here?" the kid asked.

"He does," Sandy said, flicking her thumb at Ethan. "What can we do for you?"

The little girl held up a brochure. "I'm selling cookies to raise money so our softball team can go to the regional tournament. Would you like to buy a box?"

Sandy leaned over at the waist, resting her hands just above her knees. "What kinds do you have?"

The kid named off six different kinds, taking three stabs at saying "macadamia nut."

"Hmm, I can't decide," Sandy said, tapping her finger on her chin. "Oh, well. I guess that means you'd better give us one of each."

The little girl's eyes lit up. She marked the order form and handed it to Sandy to sign. With a big smile, the kid promised to deliver the cookies in a few days, then practically skipped down the sidewalk to the next town house.

Sandy turned to Ethan with a devious smile. "There you go. You're all fixed up with cookies for the next year or so."

"Great," Ethan said. "You order half a dozen boxes of cookies, and who's going to have to pay for them when she delivers them?"

"You're a rich attorney. You can afford them. Or you could just pay her for them and toss them in the trash."

"Oh, that makes a lot of sense."

"It makes perfect sense. You're buying the cookies to support something that kid is doing. You don't actually have to eat them. Didn't you ever sell cookies or candy or magazine subscriptions or something when you were a kid?"

"God, no. My father just handed over whatever money was necessary to buy the uniforms or go on the trip or whatever the hell else kids need in schools. He's very philanthropic, as long as it shows. And if they name something after him, he's particularly generous."

"And you've been particularly generous, too. After all," she said with a smile, "you did buy six boxes."

He sighed with exasperation. "And what would you suggest I do with all those?"

"Uh . . . now, this is just me, but I'd think about eating them."

"All six boxes?"

"Well, not all at once. It would take me at least a few hours to finish them off."

Ethan smiled and shook his head.

"I'm afraid that eating sweets is one of my more persistent bad habits. And it shows."

"What?"

"It's hard to stay thin when I have a close personal relationship with the Keebler elf."

Ethan's gaze slid down her body. "If that's what you look like when you eat sweets . . ." His eyes rose to meet hers again. "Keep eating."

Sandy blinked with surprise, but just as quickly she brushed away the compliment with an offhand smile. "Now, Ethan. There you go again with the phony flattery. Haven't we talked about that?"

"Nothing phony about it. Then, or now."

Seconds passed during which neither one of them moved. They just stood there, their gazes locked together, the hot night breeze tossing Sandy's hair in a soft swirl around her head. Yes, she was a beautiful woman. He certainly wasn't lying about that. But sometime tonight he'd felt something shift inside him, and right now the physical attraction he felt for her was the least of it.

Spending time with her felt strange and new to Ethan. He was slowly accepting the fact that there was nothing false about her, nothing dishonest, nothing deceptive. Her heart went out to stray animals and wayward juveniles and frightened women and cookie-selling kids. She liked people and they liked her. Every day of her life she sent flowers into the world to make it a more beautiful place; at the same time she recognized the darker side of humanity and did what she could to help her neighbors prevent crime.

On the other hand, most of the people Ethan encountered in his life were only out for number one. They thought nothing of lying, cheating, and stealing, and trusting them from one day to the next was something he did at his own peril.

And that was just his fellow attorneys.

If he hadn't been forced to spend time with Sandy because of the community service, he never would have met her, and he might never have known what he was missing. But now that he did know, he craved more of it.

More of *her*.

"I'd better go," Sandy said. "Will you call me tomorrow the minute you talk to Henderson?"

"Yeah," he said. "I will."

"I hope he agrees to search for the tape."

"Don't worry. I'll make sure he does."

Sandy nodded, but she still looked unsure.

"I'm going to take care of it," Ethan said. "Trust me on that, will you?"

"I do trust you," she said softly. "Good night."

She unlocked her car, and he held her door open as she slid inside. He watched as she drove out of the parking lot, chastising himself for what he'd just told her. He could make the best case possible for reopening the crime scene, but in the end Henderson could still refuse to do it.

So why had he made that promise?

One reason only. Because she was depending on him. Because she had faith that he could take this situation that had gone so wrong for Josh and make it right again, and he intended to do everything he could to make that happen.

* * *

It was nearly one o'clock the next day before Ethan caught up with Henderson, who was having lunch in the form of a supersized McDonald's burger and fries while he poked at his computer keyboard checking baseball statistics. Ethan sat down in the chair in front of his desk.

"What do you want, Millner?" he said, taking a sip from the giant soft-drink cup and not even bothering to take his eyes off the computer screen. "I'm a busy man."

Yeah, he was a busy man, all right. Busy wasting taxpayer money.

"I've got something for you concerning the Laura Williams murder."

"Like what?" he said.

"Like something that's going to lead you to the man who actually killed her."

"Who I take it is not your client."

"That's right. Josh Newman didn't do it."

Henderson took another bite of his burger, talking as he chewed. "Kinda surprised you're defending that kid, Millner. Does he have a rich relative somewhere, or what?"

Ethan knew he must have met a bigger asshole than Ray Henderson, but for the life of him, he couldn't remember where.

"First of all," Ethan said, "Laura Williams wasn't the victim's real name."

"Oh, yeah?"

"It was Pamela Barton."

"Her records say her name was Laura Williams."

"You'll have to dig deeper. She had her name legally changed. Six months ago, she was a porn actress in Austin."

Henderson's eyes widened. Ethan knew just the word *porn* was enough to get his attention, and not just in a professional capacity. If the Tolosa PD hadn't frowned on his surfing naked women instead of earned run averages, that would undoubtedly be his recreation of the moment.

"Okay," Henderson said, downing the last of his coffee. "This should be good. Let's hear it."

Ethan told him how they'd found an informant who told them what had happened to Laura in Austin, why she'd come to Tolosa, and the relationship she had with that informant, all the while careful not to mention Chris's name. And he told Henderson that somewhere in Laura's house, he was likely to find video evidence of another murder. And on that tape was the man who killed Laura.

Henderson leaned back in his chair. "Pretty damned far-fetched, if you ask me."

"If you can find the tape it will prove the connection between Laura Williams and Vincent Mulroney. Once you haul him in on those charges and the forensic evidence comes back, you can tie him to the murder."

"Assuming this crazy story is true, who's your informant?"

"She doesn't want to come forward right now."

"Right." Henderson turned back to his computer. "Stop wasting my time, Millner."

"If the tape exists, you don't need her."

"Unless she exists, I'm not reopening the crime scene."

"I talked to this woman. She exists, and she's credible."

"Maybe she's blowing smoke up your ass. Ever stop to think about that?"

Ethan bowed his head with frustration. This was like talking to a brick wall. A very dumb, very belligerent brick wall.

"Think about it, Henderson. Why would I send you into that house to look for a piece of evidence if I know it doesn't exist?"

"Are you kidding me? You think I don't know you're floating a trial balloon, trying to drum up a little reasonable doubt? If I reopen the crime scene, the press will come snooping around, wondering why, which means that you've got another theory playing out there, a theory that says somebody be-

sides your client did it. But I gotta say this one's a little outlandish even for you. Porn flicks? Snuff films? When the
neighborhood the victim lived in is as middle-America as it
gets? Try coming up with something I can believe."

"Then check out Laura Williams. I told you that wasn't
her real name. Check out what she did when she was in
Austin. Where she lived. Who she hung out with. Then you'll
see that the scenario isn't as outlandish as you think."

"Here's the bottom line, Millner. I don't trust you. You've
used every underhanded trick in the book over the years.
This is just one more. I've already got what I need. A solid
eyewitness, a bad-to-the-bone kid who confessed—"

"Gotta hand it to you, Henderson. It was pretty slick how
you got him to say that. But you and I both know it's dead
wrong."

"Hell it is. He said it. And believe me, the DA is very
happy about that."

Ethan felt a swell of frustration. He had to tell Henderson.
He had to tell him about Chris, what she knew, where to find
her. It was the only way to get him to go after Mulroney.

But even as the words were poised to come out of his
mouth, he saw Sandy's face in his mind. Saw her talking to
Chris, and then pleading with him not to hurt her. And that
meant that at least for now, he was keeping his mouth shut.

But he still had to get his hands on that tape.

"Tell me this much," he said to Henderson. "Have you located any relatives of Laura Williams?"

"Not yet. We're still working on that."

Ethan nodded. "How long until retirement, Henderson?"

Henderson smiled. "Two years, six months"—he leaned in
and flipped up his calendar—"and twenty-one days."

"Coasting right into it, aren't you?"

Henderson's smile vanished. "Fuck you, Millner."

"Eloquent as always, I see. It's a gift you've got. Hang on
to it."

With that, Ethan turned and left the office to the sound of Henderson muttering under his breath. As he walked out of the building, he thought about the broken window he'd seen in Laura's sun room. Since it wasn't up to the police to clean up a crime scene once the forensic team had finished, unless a relative of the victim had surfaced, that back window would still be broken. If he couldn't get the cops to search, it was time to take an unauthorized tour of Laura Williams's house.

If that tape was there, he was going to find it.

It had been a slow morning at the shop, with Sandy filling routine orders and planning ahead for two weddings and a conference banquet next week. Then Lyle took over the arranging while Imogene manned the front of the store so Sandy could get some adminstrative stuff done.

They'd both asked her if there was anything new in the murder case, but she couldn't tell them what they'd found out about Laura's past and about her relationship to Chris. The fewer people who knew about that right now, the better. Besides, Ethan was going to talk to Henderson today. With luck the police would be searching Laura's house, and pretty soon this would all be over with.

Sandy did a little bookkeeping, then sorted through her mail. In the midst of the bills and the junk mail, she was distressed to find a letter from Waymark Properties. Not only were they sending her letters at home, but now they were starting in on her at work, too. She didn't know what it was going to take to make them realize that she liked her neighborhood just the way it was, and that she had no intention of selling them her house just so they could tear it down and put up a new one.

Just then, Sandy heard bells against glass in the front of the shop. A few moments later, she looked up to see Ethan walk into the back room. He was dressed down in jeans and a casual shirt, both of which were covered with smears of dirt and dust. Then Sandy saw something on the upper arm of his shirt. Something that looked like blood.

"Ethan! What happened?"

He glanced at his arm. "It's just a little cut."

Lyle glided out from behind the worktable, his hand extended. "You're the attorney who's defending Josh. I'm Lyle Hamilton."

Ethan shook his hand. True to form, Lyle's gaze roved over him like a diner eyeing a gourmet meal.

Ethan turned to Sandy. "Is there someplace we can talk?"

"Lyle?" Sandy said. "Would you excuse us for just a moment?"

"Why, certainly. I'd be delighted to leave you two alone." He nodded toward Ethan's arm. "Better have Sandy clean that up for you."

His voice was full of suggestiveness, and as he walked out of the room, he glanced at Sandy with an expression that said, *Very, very nice. Find out if he has a gay brother.*

"So what's happening?" she asked Ethan. "Did you talk to Henderson?"

"Yes. He refused to search for the tape."

Sandy felt a rush of disappointment. "Why won't he?"

"He thinks I'm grandstanding. Putting an outrageous theory out there just to gain the attention of the media and raise reasonable doubt. He won't reexamine the crime scene. But it may not matter anyway, because I don't think the tape is there."

"But last night you thought—"

"Last night I hadn't searched the house."

Sandy recoiled with surprise. "You searched the house?"

"Yes. And I came up with nothing."

"You're sure it's not there?"

"No. There's no way to be sure of that. But I looked everywhere I could think of. Kitchen cabinets. Closets. Behind furniture. Inside the pockets of her coat. I went through a set of luggage. I opened every box I came across. I even took a tour of the attic and looked in the crawlspace." He sighed. "Nothing."

Sandy felt a shot of disappointment. She'd counted on Henderson getting up off his butt and doing the right thing just once. She'd counted on somebody finding that tape. But as Ethan said, it really didn't matter anyway. If the tape wasn't there, it wasn't there.

"Wait a minute," she said. "You didn't have a key. How did you get into the house?"

"I climbed through the broken window into the sunroom."

"So that's how you got the cut."

"Yes."

"That's a lot of blood. Did you look at it?"

"No. But it's fine."

"If you haven't looked at it, how do you know?"

"You're being logical. Lawyers hate that."

"Come with me. We need to get it cleaned up."

"Sandy—"

"Don't argue."

She led him to the bathroom, where she told him to take off his shirt. He started to pull it off over his head. The blood had dried, though, and she had to help him ease it away from the cut and pull it the rest of the way off. She tossed the bloody shirt aside, then turned back around.

Good Lord.

A full-frontal view of Ethan half-naked would be enough to bring any woman to her knees, and since Sandy had had the advantage of touching that chest, just looking at it now made the memories come tumbling back. His body was long and lean, with strong shoulders and just a light sprinkling of dark hair over his chest. By anyone's standards, he was pretty much perfection.

Staring. She was staring.

She jerked her gaze up to find him looking at her. And judging by the expression on his face, he knew she was having a hard time keeping her eyes to herself.

Stop it. You're making a fool out of yourself all over again.

She looked away, spending more time than necessary digging around in the cabinet for peroxide and cotton balls and bandages and anything else she could think of that would help her play Florence Nightingale while she got her wandering eyes under control. She piled all the stuff on the edge of the sink. She soaked a cotton ball with peroxide, then took a deep, silent breath and curled her hand around his arm so she could dab at the cut.

Act nonchalant. You touch gorgeous men every day of your life, don't you? No? Well, at least you can act like it.

"It's not too deep. I don't think it needs stitches." She tossed the cotton ball into the trash and reached for antibiotic ointment and a Band-Aid. "I guess this means we have to let Chris know that we didn't find the tape."

"No. I'm not giving up yet. I thought we could both go back and search the house again. Maybe you can think of someplace to look that I didn't. The light fixtures in two of her bedroom closets weren't working, so it's possible that I missed something. We'll take some good flashlights with us. But I will warn you that taking an unauthorized tour of her house is marginally illegal."

"Would it be safe to assume you could talk our way out of a trespassing charge?"

"Yes. That would be a safe assumption."

"Then I'm in. Maybe I'd better borrow my brothers' flak jackets so we can crawl back through the window."

"No need." Ethan reached into his pocket and tossed a set of keys onto her bathroom counter.

"What are those?"

"Laura's keys. I grabbed them just in case we decided to have another look."

"Where did you get them?"

"They were hanging on a hook in the kitchen."

"Taking those might also be marginally illegal."

"Okay, then. Trespassing *and* petty theft."

"Which I assume you can still talk our way out of?"

"Not a problem."

She dabbed the ointment on the cut, then pressed on a Band-Aid. "There you go. You'll be good as new in no time."

He grabbed his shirt from the counter and started to put it back on.

"What are you doing?" Sandy said. "That shirt's a mess."

"It's my only alternative, unless I want Lyle staring at me even more than he was before."

Sandy couldn't help but smile at that. Most men wouldn't admit they'd even noticed such a thing for fear of becoming gay by osmosis. Ethan apparently had no such hangup.

"I have it on good authority that if any handsome heterosexual male is curious," Sandy told him, "Lyle's available."

"Tell him he'll be first on my list the moment Mother Nature takes a coffee break."

Ethan pulled on the shirt, wincing again when he moved his arm. "Let's search before crime patrol tonight. I'll come to your house about six thirty, and we can go from there."

"Okay." Sandy picked up Laura's keys to hand them back to Ethan. Then something caught her eye.

"What's the matter?" Ethan asked.

She wasn't sure. Maybe nothing.

Maybe something.

She singled out one of the keys. It was small and silver, attached by a jump ring to a silver metal disc engraved with the words *Fitness World*. Beneath the name of the gym was the number sixty-four.

"It looks as if Laura had a health club membership," she said.

"Apparently so."

"This looks like a key to a gym locker. It's a real leap, I know. But . . ."

"What?"

"Is it possible she hid the tape someplace besides her house?"

For several seconds, Ethan just stared at her. She could almost feel his mind working.

"Maybe," he said.

"Have you ever heard of a gym by that name in Tolosa?"

"No. But we can check it out."

Sandy left the bathroom and pulled a phone book from a lower cabinet. She thumbed through it, shaking her head. "I don't see a Fitness World. But if there's not one here, then where did she get this key? And why was she carrying it?"

"Wonder if there's one in Austin."

"Austin?"

"Yes," Ethan said. "What if she had a membership there, and that's where she ditched the tape before she moved here?"

"Now you really are going out on a limb."

"It would explain why she still has this key."

"Maybe she just didn't bother to take it off when she moved here," Sandy said.

"Or maybe she's keeping it for a reason."

"This all assumes there's a Fitness World in Austin," Sandy said.

"Let's find out."

Ethan called directory assistance in Austin. He asked for Fitness World, and Sandy held her breath. When he grabbed a nearby pen and pad and wrote down a phone number, her heart leaped with hope. Ethan broke the connection, then dialed that number.

When somebody came on the line, he spun a story about wanting to give his girlfriend a one-year membership to the gym as a birthday gift. In short order, he'd verified that a Pam Barton did indeed have a current membership there.

He hung up the phone. "We just hit pay dirt."

"But Laura had been in Tolosa only six months. Isn't it possible that she just didn't bother to take the key off her ring and was letting her membership run out?"

"That's what I would have thought, too, if not for one more thing."

"What's that?"

"Her annual membership ran out a month ago. She renewed it for another three months, locker included."

Sandy blinked with surprise. "A month ago? But she was living in Tolosa by then."

"Exactly. Why would she renew a membership at a club in a city where she's not living and has no intention of returning to?"

Sandy felt a shiver of excitement. "If she'd left something there that she may eventually want to go back to get?"

"I think we're on to something."

"God, Ethan. Do you really think so?"

"The pieces fit."

"So what now? Do we call Henderson and get him to co-ordinate with the Austin police?"

"No. He's made it pretty clear already what he thinks of this theory. He'd probably refuse to pursue it."

"So what's the alternative?"

"We fly to Austin and see if the tape is there."

"The two of us?"

"Yes. I can make plane reservations for tomorrow. We can fly to Austin, rent a car, and go to the health club. You can get the tape from the women's locker room. We can take it to the police. I'll explain how it relates to Laura's murder in Tolosa. Then they can inform Henderson of the tape's existence rather than the other way around."

"That keeps Henderson from being a bottleneck."

"Exactly."

"The Austin cops are going to want to know where we got it."

"I'll tell them I have an informant who directed us to it. If the tape actually contains what Chris told us it does, it should speak for itself." He picked up the phone again. "Let's check the airline schedule and see what flights are available. Can you get away tomorrow?"

"Yes. I can get Imogene and Lyle to cover for me."

Ten minutes later, Ethan had them booked on a two-o'clock flight, which would put them in Austin by four. If the tape was there, they could grab it, talk to the police, and be on a return flight back to Tolosa by nine tomorrow night. As of right now, they might be only a plane flight away from getting evidence that was going to lead them to Laura's killer, and that meant it wouldn't be long before Josh was free.

Thank God. She'd spent most of the morning picturing him in that jail cell, wondering what he was doing, how he felt, and imagining just how scared he must be. With luck all this might be over with soon.

"I have a meeting at noon tomorrow that I can't miss," Ethan said, "so it'll be tight to make that flight. Can you meet me at the courthouse around one o'clock?"

"No problem. Can I phone Chris? Tell her what we know?"

"It might be best not to get her hopes up."

"If she's still thinking about running, it could keep her close by."

Ethan nodded. "Okay. That's a good point."

Sandy walked with Ethan to the front door of her shop, sensing Imogene's and Lyle's prying eyes on them the whole time.

"I'm sorry you got hurt climbing through that window," she said quietly.

"It's no big deal."

"Yes, it is. It's a very big deal. You've really gone out of your way for Josh, and for Chris, too. I think it's about time you raised that retainer to fifteen thousand dollars. You deserve every penny of it."

"Do you seriously think I do these kinds of things for all my clients?"

Sandy blinked with surprise. Now that she thought about it, of course he didn't.

"What makes Josh so special?" she asked.

"I wasn't talking about Josh."

He stared at her pointedly, his dark eyes warm and sexy and intimate, relaying a message that clashed wildly with the hands-off message he'd sent her in her kitchen a few nights ago.

She just didn't get this. Was he interested in her or wasn't he?

"I'll see you tonight for crime watch," he said, then turned and walked out of the shop.

chapter twelve

Ethan dropped by his town house, changed clothes, then went back to his office. He'd just settled in to get some work done when his father appeared at his doorway.

Charles Millner was a man of sixty-one who looked fifty-one, who preserved his appearance with intense exercise, excruciating control over every bite of food that passed his lips, and routine visits to every kind of doctor imaginable. He never spoke words he didn't intend to, and he never raised his voice. He was a tightly coiled man who held on to emotion so firmly that it simply vanished inside him like matter into a black hole.

As always, he refused to sit in the chair in front of Ethan's desk. Instead, he slid a hand into his pants pocket and strolled over to stand behind it.

"Tell me about the Josh Newman case."

"There's nothing to tell. He's a seventeen-year-old kid accused of murder. I'm representing him."

"Howard Linz told me you asked him to withdraw."

"You were talking to Howard Linz? That's hard to imagine."

"Actually, he instigated the conversation. He found it very strange that you'd ask to take a case like that. Since when are you on the court-appointed list?"

"I'm not doing it as a court appointment."

"The defendant is seventeen years old. I assume a relative managed to raise enough money to hire you?"

"No. I'm doing it pro bono."

Charles's face remained impassive. "Pro bono."

He simply repeated the words in that deadpan voice, but still it was filled with meaning. And Ethan knew just what that meaning was. The very idea that his son could take a case of this magnitude without reaping monetary gain from it was unfathomable.

"According to Linz, the boy is on probation," Charles said. "He has a juvenile record of burglary and two arrests for assault. An eyewitness placed your client at the scene, and . . . oh, yes. I believe he confessed to the crime."

"It was a verbal confession," Ethan said. "Coerced. He thought he was confessing to missing a curfew."

"Or perhaps he merely recanted the confession once he obtained counsel."

Ethan was silent.

Charles walked back toward Ethan's desk. "Taking a case like this one to trial could require a considerable amount of your time. It's the policy of this firm that we bring cases of that magnitude to the table. We should all have input as to whether they're worth defending."

"I've taken the case. It's a done deal. And I don't care to discuss it any further."

His father nodded slowly as if accepting that fact, but Ethan knew better. He hadn't watched his father in the courtroom all these years without knowing that the old man still had ammunition he hadn't yet fired.

"The boy who was arrested," Charles said. "I understand he works for the woman who's administering your community service."

Ethan held his gaze steady. "Yes."

"Sasha said she was in the office a few days ago."

"Yes."

"Sasha also said she's quite pretty."

"Yes. I'd say so."

"Did she ask you to take this case?"

"My reasons for taking this case are my own."

Charles narrowed his eyes, regarding his son with a subtle but well-drawn expression of disapproval. "I've never known you to make a fool of yourself over a woman before."

"I assure you that my record in that regard is still intact."

"You're far too valuable to this firm to be wasting your time on cases like that one. I assume you'll plead it out as quickly as you can and get on with more important matters?"

Ethan couldn't believe this. He was defending a teenage kid on the verge of losing his freedom for the rest of his life, or maybe even losing his life altogether, and his father wanted him to get on to more important matters?

"I'll pursue the course of action most advantageous to my client. I can't imagine that you'd want me to do anything less than that."

Charles raised his chin a notch. "Just keep your priorities straight, Ethan. Your first loyalty is to this firm."

"My first loyalty is to my client."

"Yes," Charles said, his expression holding a hint of derisiveness. "That is the oath we take, isn't it?"

With that, he turned and left the office. Ethan sat back in his chair with a sigh of irritation. His father never changed. Never.

Growing up, Ethan had constantly been subjected to his father's sharp tongue, and that had always been more painful to him than a sharp hand could ever have been. And he hadn't had a mother around to mitigate any of it. She'd left when Ethan was eight, and he hadn't seen her since. Charles had been insanely in love with her—*insane* being the operative word, because his brand of love came in the form of control and coercion, and even at age eight, it hadn't surprised Ethan that his mother had cheated on his father. Being married to a man like Charles Millner would drive any woman into another man's arms.

But it hadn't been just his father that she'd left behind.

The fact that his son had also lost a mother had eluded Charles, his ego allowing him to think only about what a huge embarrassment it was for him. And from then on, he'd taught his son by example to compartmentalize his life and relegate women to a distant sector, to be used when he needed them and shoved aside when he didn't.

But even though Ethan had always had a sense of his father's character when he was growing up, it wasn't until he graduated from law school and met his father eye-to-eye in the practice of law that the old man's message had come through loud and clear: *Just win. No matter what. It's what our clients are paying us for, and don't you ever forget it.*

Whatever idealism Ethan had had when he entered the practice of law had withered under the unrelenting harshness of his father's authority. Now they stood as partners on equal footing, but Ethan still felt the effects of those early years. But only recently had he started to realize just how much he'd allowed his father's bitter cynicism to become part of his own life.

It was a calm, idyllic evening for crime patrol, with kids heading home on their bicycles, old folks taking an evening stroll, and the long shadows of dusk spilling over lawns. But even though the sun had made its way toward the horizon, the heat of the day still hung on with fierce tenacity. Sandy had her car air conditioner going full blast, but she was still sweating.

She turned to Ethan. "So Henderson was a real jerk about reopening the crime scene?"

"God, yes," Ethan said. "Sometimes I've got to wonder why they keep that guy on the payroll."

"My brothers can't stand him, either."

"I'll say this much. I may have gone to war with your brothers a few times, but at least they do their jobs, and they do them right."

She smiled. "You just have a few philosophical differences?"

"Yes. They fight to put people in jail, and I fight to get them out."

Sandy swung her car around the south end of the park. With darkness almost complete, it was nearly deserted. The glow of the dashboard lights and the low hum of the deejay's voice on the radio made these moments with Ethan seem almost surreal. She was so intensely attuned to him that even with her eyes on the road, she was aware of every breath he took. And she sensed that he was just as tuned in to her as she was to him.

Do you seriously think I do these kinds of things for all my clients?

To Ethan, there was nothing special about Josh. But she had the unmistakable feeling that he thought there was something special about her. So why had he pushed her away that night in her kitchen? And why did his explanation of why he'd done it bear no resemblance to the truth?

What *was* the truth?

They drove in silence for several more minutes, and that question just wouldn't leave her mind. She wanted to know. *Needed* to know. Finally it hammered away at her to the point that she swore it was giving her a headache, and she just couldn't contain it any longer.

At the next stop sign, she brought the car to a halt and turned to face him. "Why did you walk out on me the other night?"

He glanced at her quickly, as if she'd surprised him, then turned away again. The song on the radio ended, and the deejay began to talk again. Ethan didn't.

"See, the reason I'm asking is that I'm getting some really

mixed signals from you. I kiss you, and you walk out. But tonight you haven't taken your eyes off me for five seconds. What's up?"

He sighed. "I already told you why I walked out."

"Forget what you already told me. You don't give a damn about what Judge Davis would think, and you're not afraid of my brothers. So why don't you tell me the real reason you left?"

His mouth turned down in an irritated frown. "I'm not the man for you."

"Yeah, you said that, but it's a little vague. You want to be more specific?"

Another long silence. Finally he said, "We just approach these things a little differently. That's all."

"What things?"

"Relationships."

"You mean sex."

"It's not the sex, Sandy. It's what comes afterward."

"Afterward?"

"I'm not a man who . . ."

"What?"

"Sticks around."

She looked at him blankly. "Sticks around?"

He rubbed his hand over his mouth, sighing heavily. "For some women, sex isn't just about sex. It's about a whole lot more."

For a moment that didn't compute. Then the truth hit her, and she was flabbergasted. "*That's* why you walked out on me? Because you thought I'd have you picking out china patterns the next day?"

He paused before answering, as if he hadn't expected her to get to the point quite so succinctly. "Yeah. Something like that."

"You're getting a little ahead of yourself, aren't you? Exactly how does one night of sex translate into a lifetime commitment?"

"Depends on who's doing the translating. When it's a woman looking for something permanent—"

"And you assume that I am?"

"Yes."

"What brought you to that conclusion?"

"It's not terribly hard to deduce."

"How's that?"

He sighed. "Sandy—"

"No. I want to know."

"Well, okay," he said. "Let's start with that big, traditional house of yours."

She blinked with surprise. "What has my house got to do with anything?"

"And you have a big family."

"Yeah? So what?"

"You're a florist."

"Uh . . . yeah. Last I checked."

"You're the president of your neighborhood association."

When she continued to stare at him blankly, he expelled a sharp breath. "For God's sake, Sandy! You have a cookie jar shaped like a Persian cat!"

She was having a really hard time grasping this. "Okay. Let me see if I've got this straight. Are you telling me that if I kept my cookies in a Ziploc back in the pantry, we'd have had sex the other night?"

Ethan sighed with frustration. "You're deliberately missing my point."

"All that stuff doesn't define me."

"Oh, come on! Everybody's environment defines them. And believe me, yours speaks louder than most."

"I've had opportunities to get married, Ethan. I turned them down. What does that tell you?"

"That you're selective. But that doesn't change your end goal."

"Did it ever occur to you that I might want exactly what you want?"

"Not for one moment."

She narrowed her eyes. "Well, that's about the most condescending thing anyone's ever said to me."

"Okay, Sandy," he said sharply. "Why don't I tell you what I want and you be the judge?" He leaned toward her, giving her a no-nonsense stare. "When it comes to sex, I like it hot, I like it fast, and I like it often. I don't much care where it happens, but I do it only with women who want nothing else *but* sex. Since I like variety, once with a woman is generally enough for me before I move on. And because I tend to be truthful about these things, I never tell a woman I'll call her the next day, because chances are excellent that I won't. That's what I am, Sandy. Still want to do it?"

Sandy shrugged. "Works for me."

Ethan sat back in his seat. "Liar."

Sandy's mouth fell open. She hit the gas and crossed the intersection, then drove alongside the park for half a block and pulled into a lot near the pavilion. She brought the car to a quick halt and put it in park, leaving the engine idling, and turned to face him.

"Everybody is always making assumptions about who I am and what I want," she said. "My family does it to me. My friends. Even my employees. They fix me up with men who are technically dead already, but they're waiting around for age ninety so they can stop breathing and make it official. Everybody says, 'He's *perfect* for you. You'll just *love* him. He's *stable,* he's *sweet,* he has a *good job.*' On and on and on. And then some guy shows up who bores me to tears and I'm counting the minutes until he finally goes away. And then I lie awake staring at the ceiling, wishing a man would show up in my life who's hot and exciting and unpredictable and gives me sex that makes my fingernails sweat and my hair stand on end. I swear to God if I could have just one night like that—just *one*—I wouldn't give a *damn* about tomorrow!"

He gave her a challenging stare. "Be careful what you ask for. You just might get it."

"Big talk for a man who ran out of my kitchen as if his pants had caught fire."

His eyes narrowed dangerously. "So it really is just sex you want?"

"Yes. But since you seem determined to give me the same condescending crap I get from everyone else, it's pretty clear that you're not the man for the job."

Ethan reached to the ignition, turned off the engine, and tossed the keys to the floor of the backseat. "Take off your clothes."

"What?"

"I said take off your clothes. Right now."

"Are you crazy?"

"Now you're the one with the mixed messages, Sandy. Either you want hot, mindless, no-strings-attached sex, or you don't."

"But in the *car*?"

"First lesson in Casual Sex 101. You can't discriminate on the time or place. You have to learn to be opportunistic."

"B-But I can't—"

"Ah. I see you're a little shy about taking off your clothes in a public place. But don't worry. I'll get the ball rolling."

He pulled his shirt from the waistband of his pants.

Sandy drew back with alarm. "Ethan?"

He yanked the shirt off over his head and tossed it into the backseat.

"Ethan! What are you doing?"

In seconds he had his pants unbuckled.

"Ethan—"

His pants unbuttoned.

"Ethan, stop."

His pants *unzipped*.

"Ethan!"

She grabbed his wrist, shocked that he actually meant to take his clothes off right here, right now.

"What's the matter, Sandy? A little too wild for you?"

She sucked in a deep breath and let it out slowly, trying to get her bearings. Yes, it was wild. And yes, she was shocked. But as she glanced down at that gorgeous body she'd admired only a few hours ago, then back up to meet those deep, dark eyes, her surprise turned into a hot buzz of excitement that hummed through every nerve in her body.

"God, no," she murmured. "Just give me a second to catch up."

Sandy crossed her arms, grabbed the hem of her T-shirt, and yanked it off over her head, throwing it into the backseat on top of Ethan's. His gaze fell immediately to her breasts, then rose again to stare at her with disbelief.

"What's the matter, Ethan? A little too wild for you?"

"Hell, no."

He barely got the words out before his mouth was on hers. It happened so fast that it surprised her for a moment, but then she regrouped and leaned into him, wanting everything he could give her. And did he ever give it to her. He tunneled his fingers into the hair at the back of her head, tilting her so their mouths fit together perfectly and he could kiss her deeper and harder with exactly the kind of passion she'd lain awake nights dreaming about. *Yes.* This was what she wanted. Finally it was happening. She wanted to shout with joy, but her mouth was occupied with wonderfully erotic things and she wasn't about to get in the way of that.

She had a random thought about where they were, but it was dark, and they were at least half a block from the nearest street lamp. The storm that the weatherman had promised was apparently moving in, blowing heavy clouds across the three-quarter moon and obliterating it, leaving them in almost complete darkness. But the truth was that she didn't give a damn if they were in the middle of Times Square at high noon—she wanted this man *now*.

With a flick of his fingers, he unhooked her bra and swept the cups aside. He lifted her breast and squeezed it firmly, then traced his thumb back and forth over her nipple in an intense, incessant motion that she almost couldn't bear at the same time she was sure she'd die from the pleasure of it.

Wind whistled along her car windows, and a few sprinkles of rain tapped the windshield, but Sandy barely noticed the approaching storm. Ethan continued to touch and kiss her until her mind went blurry, until she almost couldn't breathe, until sensation seemed to be flooding her from every possible angle.

The console was between them, so it was impossible to get as close to him as she wanted to, but she stroked his shoulders, his back, his neck, his chest, his biceps, his forearms, and any other part of him she could get her hands on, relishing the feel of all that heat and bone and muscle beneath her hands and feeling so much tension building up inside her she thought surely she was going to combust.

Ethan leaned away and took her face in his hands, his voice a raw, needy whisper. "Is this it, Sandy? Is this what you want?"

"Yes."

"Because I've got no self-control left. Used it all up last night."

"Thank God."

"We're overdressed."

"And the console's in the way."

"Backseat. Now."

This was reckless and crazy beyond belief, but she only wanted more of it. She turned and reached for the door handle, only to hear a flurry of hard raps on the window.

Someone was standing outside the car.

chapter thirteen

"Oh, my God!" Sandy whispered wildly, folding her arms over her breasts. "It's Ida Clemmons!"

Ida Clemmons?

Ethan slumped with frustration. This couldn't be happening.

Sandy reached into the backseat, grabbed her shirt, and held it in front of her. Ida smacked the window with three more loud raps, and Sandy physically recoiled with every one.

"Guess she wants to say hello," Ethan said.

"Your shirt! Put on your shirt!"

"I think it's a little late to pretend we're just moon watching."

"Just do it!"

He grabbed his shirt and pulled it over his head. It was like closing the barn door after the horse was long gone, but what the hell.

"What am I supposed to do now?" Sandy whispered.

"Got me."

"You talk. You're good at talking. Get me out of this."

"Sorry, Sandy. I can do only so much for a client who's caught with her hand on a smoking gun. Particularly when it was my gun that was smoking."

"Will you *stop* with the jokes?"

Three more raps. This woman wasn't going away. And boy, did she look pissed.

Sandy turned slowly and lowered her window. "Hello, Mrs. Clemmons."

Ida drew herself up into a quivering mass of outrage. "Sandy DeMarco? What are you doing?"

"Uh . . ."

"No. Don't say it. Speaking it aloud will only make it more of a disgrace."

Sandy just sat there, the sexual flush on her cheeks quickly being replaced by a rash of total mortification.

"Ida, this really isn't what it looks like—"

"Then would you mind telling me what it is?"

Sandy opened her mouth, but nothing came out.

"What about the children in this neighborhood who might have seen this? Have you given a single thought to that?"

Sandy smoothed her hair nervously. "Really, Ida, this was nothing. Nobody saw anything."

"I saw. And so did God. What else has He seen that the rest of us haven't?"

The moment she spoke the words, Ethan heard a rumble of thunder. Wow. Maybe Ida Clemmons really did have a direct line straight to the Almighty.

"You've fooled us all this time, Sandy," Ida said, her voice brimming with indignation. "Ralph and I thought you were a nice girl."

Ethan smiled to himself. Sandy *was* a nice girl. Well, except maybe for that little matter of having sex in parked cars.

"And you," Ida said, glaring at Ethan. "I have to say that you're *exactly* what we thought you were. A man with no morals whatsoever."

Ethan resisted the urge to tell her she was a Bible-beating old bat. After all, did he really want a thunderbolt zinging down from heaven?

Ida looked back and forth between them, shuddering with righteous anger. "Now, I suggest you leave this public place and go behind closed doors. And if you care in the least about the disposition of your eternal soul, I'd suggest you start asking God's forgiveness."

With that she spun around and walked away, her nose so far in the air that rain had to be falling right into it. Sandy rolled up the window, looking as if she wanted to crawl into a hole and die.

"Very well-spoken," Ethan said. "Charlton Heston couldn't have done it better."

Sandy whipped around. "Will you stop it?"

"Why? Because some shrew of an old lady thinks I should?"

She hooked her bra and yanked her shirt on. "I must have been out of my mind to do this!"

"And very nearly out of your clothes."

"Get my keys."

"Sandy—"

She turned suddenly, scrambled between the seats, and came up with her car keys. Sitting back down in the driver's seat, she jammed the key into the ignition and started the car.

"My reputation in this neighborhood just went straight to hell."

"You're making too much out of this."

"No, I'm not! I care what nice people think of me!"

"And Ida Clemmons is a nice person?"

"Yes!"

"I don't know. She seems a little judgmental to me."

The spotty rain grew heavier, and Sandy flicked the wipers on as she pulled back onto the street. "She's going to tell everyone in the neighborhood. I can just hear the ladies at their next bridge game."

"Yeah. It'll be four old bats sitting around a card table,

condemning you for having hot sex and secretly wishing they were getting some."

"They're not like that! They're nice people who are going to have heart failure at the very idea of me having sex in a public place!"

She passed by Magnolia Street, then turned the steering wheel a hard ninety degrees and swung the car into the alley parallel to it. Ethan realized it was the one that ran behind her house.

"Where are you going?" he asked.

"Home."

"We still have time left on crime patrol."

"I know. But I just . . ." She gripped the steering wheel so tightly her knuckles whitened. "I just want to go home, okay?"

She pulled into the driveway behind her house and killed the engine.

"Come on, Sandy. Don't worry about this. It'll blow over."

"No, it won't. You don't know Ida Clemmons. If it had been anyone else—"

"The woman is a religious nutcase!"

"Why? Because she goes to church on Sunday and expects people to do the right thing?"

"She pretty much damned you to hell. Don't you think that's a little over-the-top, considering the infraction?"

Sandy reached for the door handle.

"Sandy—wait."

She ignored him and got out of the car. Ethan leaped out the passenger door, raced around the car, and followed her through the gate into the backyard. He caught her arm and pulled her to a halt.

"Hold on, Sandy."

"Please, Ethan. Just let me—"

"No. Just stop for a minute, will you?"

She pulled her arm away and put her hand to her forehead,

still looking so embarrassed and ashamed that Ethan realized just how humiliated she really felt.

He sighed heavily. "I'm sorry. It was my fault. I never should have pushed you into that."

She shook her head, sprinkles of rain lighting on her hair. "No. It wasn't your fault. You have no reason to apologize. I goaded you into it."

"I was the one getting naked first."

"No. You're not to blame for this. Really. I told you what I wanted, and all you did was give it to me."

But even as she'd told him how much she craved the excitement of it, still he'd known the truth. She just wasn't cut out for casual sex in public places, no matter how much she'd tried to convince him otherwise.

All at once there was a huge crash of lightning. The sprinkles of rain grew heavier, and then the heavens opened up and rain gushed down. Ethan took Sandy's arm and they hurried across the yard and up the steps to her covered porch. It had taken them only a few seconds to get under cover, but already they were both drenched.

Sandy slung her wet hair back over her shoulders, then shook the rainwater off her hands. Lightning crashed again, thunder rumbling behind it like a freight train. She looked up at the sky, and her whole body heaved with a sigh of resignation.

"Gee, do you think somebody up there is trying to tell me something?"

Ethan smiled, but when Sandy didn't, he knew she wasn't joking. Getting caught the way she had tonight had humiliated her. Getting caught by the neighborhood morality police had only made things worse.

Sandy collapsed on the wicker sofa beside her back door and dropped her head to her hands. After a moment, Ethan sat down beside her.

"Sandy?"

"Uh-huh."

"What is it you really want?"

Slowly she looked up, raindrops shimmering on her cheeks in the dim porch light. "What do you mean?"

"I get the feeling that it's more than just a little recreational sex."

She turned away, looking at the azalea bush beside the porch, at her hands, at her sneakers, anywhere but at him. Then her body slowly melted into a posture of defeat.

"Oh, hell," she said. "I don't know what I want."

Ethan nodded. That made more sense than anything else she'd professed in the past two days.

"Things just aren't turning out the way I expected them to," she said. "Sometimes I feel as if life has dealt me a really crappy hand."

"I don't know. You seem to have a pretty nice life to me."

"It's not that I hate the things I have—friends and family and my business and everything else. But then I look at my brothers and their wives and my friends and their husbands. . . ." She sighed. "I've tried to convince myself that I've got a great life, and if this is all I ever have, I should be thankful for it. But still, I feel cheated. Why have they gotten so lucky, while I'm pushing forty and I'm still by myself?"

"So you want to get married."

She paused. "Yeah. I guess I do."

"But you've had opportunities."

"Yes. And sometimes I wonder what my life would have been like if I hadn't said no."

"They were the wrong men, or you would have said yes."

"Yeah," she said. "Maybe so."

"But if you're looking for something permanent, why have you been trying to convince me that you're only out for a good time?"

She shrugged weakly. "I guess because I've finally accepted the fact that Mr. Right may never come along, so I convinced myself that Mr. Right Now would have to do."

And that was exactly who he was. Mr. Right Now.

Even though it was all he'd ever wanted to be, Ethan felt a stab of regret. Why did the notion of being with a woman for the long haul scare the hell out of him?

"I'm thirty-seven years old," Sandy said, so quietly that he almost couldn't hear her over the rain. "I want more. But with every day that passes, I can feel that window closing just a little bit more."

He'd been right all along. A woman like Sandy needed family connections like she needed air to breathe. She needed a husband to mow the lawn, to take out the trash, to make love with, to fight with, to grow old with. She needed to do homework with the kids and take summer vacations and bake birthday cakes. She needed a family surrounding her. *Her* family. That was what she needed, what she wanted.

But fate hadn't chosen to cooperate.

"I'm sorry about all this," she told him. "I'm sorry for what happened in my kitchen, I'm sorry for goading you into this tonight. . . ." Her eyes began to glisten with tears. "And I'm sorry for dragging you down into my stupid pity party." She wiped her eyes with her fingertips. "If Judge Davis was out to punish you, he's sure getting a lot of bang for his buck with me in charge, isn't he?"

"Actually," Ethan said, "I should probably feel really guilty."

"Why is that?"

"Because the time I've spent with you has never felt like I was serving any kind of sentence at all."

She flicked her gaze toward him, smiling briefly for the first time. They sat there awhile longer in comfortable silence, listening to the rain smack the roof and gurgle out of the gutters. Soon it began to diminish, until finally it became nothing more than a light sprinkle.

"Looks as if the rain's letting up," Sandy said.

"Yeah," Ethan said. "So are we still on for Austin tomorrow?"

"Yes. Of course. I'll meet you at the courthouse at one o'clock."

"Well, then. I guess I'd better get home."

Sandy opened the back door and they walked through the house to her front door. He opened it and started to leave.

"Ethan?"

He turned back.

"Thanks for listening."

Her eyes still glistened with tears, and he hated the fact that he'd contributed to something that had ended up causing her so much misery. He slid his hand along her face, then pressed a gentle kiss to her forehead. She leaned into him with a soft sigh, and he took a few seconds to relish it. She smelled faintly of perfume and rainwater and clean, soft skin, and it was all he could do to finally pull away.

"I'll see you tomorrow," he said.

"Good night. Drive carefully."

He walked out the door and heard Sandy click it closed behind him, then flick the locks. He made his way down the rain-soaked sidewalk.

When he reached the curb, he looked back to see her standing at the window beside the front door, the curtain pulled back, watching him. He was stunned at how beautiful she looked surrounded by the glow of lamplight against the darkness outside, and he wondered what it would be like to see her face in a window waiting for him to come home rather than watching him drive away.

The next afternoon, Sandy sat on a bench in the county courthouse, surrounded by a buzz of activity. Heels clicked madly against the checkerboard marble floor as a swirl of attorneys, cops, defendants, jurors, and employees swept through the lobby.

She checked her watch. It was five after one.

"Hello, Sandy."

She turned to see a woman behind her.

"I'm Gina Palmer," the woman said. "Ethan's secretary."

"Yes. I remember you."

"I came to the courthouse to bring some documents to Ethan. He's running a little late. He asked me to find you and let you know. Just give him a few more minutes."

"Thank you. I appreciate that."

Gina started to walk away, then turned back. "Sandy? Can I ask you a question?"

"Sure."

Gina walked back to the bench and sat down beside Sandy. "What do you think of Ethan?"

The question startled her. She couldn't imagine why the woman was asking, and she didn't quite know what to say. "He's an interesting man."

"Yes, he is."

"Smart."

"Uh-huh."

"Successful."

"To say the least."

"And he's probably one of the better-looking men I've ever met."

"Oh? You noticed that?"

Sandy smiled. "Is there a woman on the planet who wouldn't notice that? Why are you asking?"

Gina shrugged. "Just curious."

Nope. There was more to her question than idle curiosity. Sandy just didn't know what it was.

"How well do you know him?" she asked.

"I've only worked for him for a year, but . . . probably better than most people."

"I imagine he's rather demanding."

"You don't know the half of it. He's a workaholic perfectionist and thinks everybody else should be, too. I was the employment agency's last-ditch effort to get him a secretary he couldn't scare off."

Sandy smiled. "Somehow that doesn't surprise me."

"Actually, legal secretaries are used to bosses who are jerks. The nature of the work means they need at least a little bit of ego, but most of them get a bigger dose than necessary. Ethan wasn't that way. He wasn't a screamer. He wasn't a ranter. In a way, though, he was worse. If he'd yelled once in a while, it probably would have been easier for a secretary to take. Instead, he was just intensely demanding. But I needed the job, and I told myself that whatever he dished out, I'd deal with it."

"So eventually you just learned to get along?"

Gina paused. "There was a little more to it than that."

"I'd like to hear about it."

Gina stared at Sandy as if she were trying to decide whether she should continue. She looked over her shoulder, then turned back and spoke softly.

"One night I came back up to the office after hours to pick up something I'd forgotten. I was surprised to see a light on in his office. When I peeked inside, I saw him sitting at his desk, his chair turned around, staring out the window into the night. Just his desk lamp was on, and there was a half-empty bottle of scotch on his desk. See, he'd won a case that day. Gotten an acquittal for a guy accused of murdering a twelve-year-old kid. I figured that was why he was drinking. Celebrating, you know." She paused. "Then he turned around."

Gina dropped her voice lower still. "He was the kind of man whom I couldn't imagine ever being out of control, but there he was four sheets to the wind. I knew if he tried to drive he was going to end up in the drunk tank, so I told him

I was taking him home. He said no way. I told him if he got in that car to drive, I was calling the cops and having him picked up. Ethan's a good judge of character even when he's dead drunk, and he knew I wasn't bluffing."

"So you drove him home."

"Yes. He didn't say a word all the way there. But right before he got out of the car, he said, 'You know I won a case today.' I told him that yeah, I'd heard. Told him congratulations, all that. Well, for at least the count of ten, there was dead silence in that car. Then he turned to me and spoke words I'm not sure he'd said in twelve years of practicing law."

"What's that?"

"He said, 'What if he really did it?' "

Sandy felt a shudder of understanding. She thought about how Ethan had told her that guilt or innocence didn't matter. Now she was beginning to see just how much it ate at him in the dark of night when he had nothing but a bottle of scotch and his conscience for company.

"Then he got out of the car and went inside. And I remember just sitting there kinda stunned that he'd said that, since he'd never struck me as the kind of guy who gave a damn."

"I bet he was grateful to you the next morning."

"Nope. He tried to fire me."

"Fire you?"

"He doesn't like being out of control, and I'd witnessed that big-time. But I had no intention of letting him fire me. I'm fifty-four years old. I'm good at what I do, but opportunities for women my age don't come along every day. So I looked him right in the eye and told him I was leaving that job over his dead body. Then I got up from my desk, told him I was going to fix the pot of coffee he looked as if he desperately needed, and I've been there ever since."

Sandy looked at Gina with surprise. She imagined that

few people in Ethan's life had ever stood up to him like that, and it amazed her that Gina was still around in spite of it.

Or maybe she was still around because of it.

Gina glanced over her shoulder again. "Now, I just overstepped my bounds telling you that story. But I don't think you're the type to use it against him."

"Don't worry. He'll never know you told me. And I promise you that no one else will, either."

Gina nodded. "He's a good man. He doesn't really know that, but he is. He went to war with his father over taking Josh Newman's case. The old man looks at the bottom line and nothing else. It wasn't pretty. But he didn't back down."

"Why not?"

"Because of you."

Sandy's heart was suddenly beating like crazy, and a tingly feeling spread through her whole body. She started to ask Gina to elaborate on that, only to hear footsteps behind her. She turned to see Ethan approaching.

He looked back and forth between them. "Care to tell me what I missed?"

Gina rose from the bench. "Just a little girl talk."

Ethan looked at her suspiciously. "Girl talk?"

"You know. Hair. Makeup. Clothes. Recipes. Soap operas. All that silly girlie stuff that would bore a man like you to tears." Gina turned to Sandy. "It was a pleasure to talk to you."

"You, too."

She turned to Ethan. "And I'll see you back in the office tomorrow?"

"Yes."

As Gina walked away, Ethan shook his head. "I swear to God, if I didn't think she'd file an age-discrimination suit I'd fire that woman tomorrow."

Sandy just smiled. "We'd better move it. Our flight leaves in less than an hour."

"Did you talk to Chris?" Ethan asked as they walked to his car.

"Yes. She was so relieved. She said to please call her the minute we know something. She's thrilled that there's a possibility that we're going to catch the man who killed Laura."

"And keep her out of it."

"Yes. She says it's still going to be a tough custody battle, but at least without her relationship with Laura coming out, she has a chance."

"She doesn't have to worry."

"What?"

"I'll take care of the situation."

Sandy turned to him with surprise. "Even if Chris doesn't have to testify in Laura's case, you'll help her?"

Ethan shrugged. "I've resolved worse problems over a coffee break."

Sandy couldn't believe this was the same man who'd stood in his office a few days ago and refused even to take Josh's case. He'd shown her a side of himself that was totally at odds with the man everyone thought he was, and something about that made her feel warm all over.

By two o'clock, they were in the sky on their way to Austin, and for the next few hours they read the in-flight magazine and talked about the articles, declined the bags of stale peanuts, and stared out the window at the bank of clouds building on the far horizon.

And Ethan lamented the lack of first-class seats on commuter flights.

"First-class?" Sandy just shrugged. "I'm afraid I wouldn't know what to do with all that room."

"You get comfortable," he said with a sigh of disgust. "That's what you do with it. And stale peanuts aren't even an issue."

"See, you notice the difference because you're used to the good life. Nice car, beautiful office, gorgeous town house, all that. Me? I don't care because I don't know what I'm missing."

"Someday I'll show you what you're missing, and you'll pray you never have to shoehorn yourself into one of these seats again."

"Has your family always been wealthy?"

"Depends on what you consider wealthy."

"I'll take that as a yes."

"It's not that big a deal."

"Money is never a big deal when you have plenty of it." She rested her elbow on the armrest between them and put her chin in her hand. "Is that what drives you? Money?"

"Money is a way of keeping score. That's about it."

Ethan was an ambitious man. Sandy could tell that from every word he spoke and every move he made, and it was pretty clear that there wasn't much he wouldn't do to get a client acquitted and earn that paycheck. Gina had confirmed that he was indeed a workaholic, though Sandy wouldn't have had any trouble coming to that conclusion all by herself. But what else did he have in his life?

"You asked me last night what I want," Sandy said. "How about you? What do you want?"

He shrugged. "My work has been my life. And I don't expect that to change anytime soon."

"With no room for a family?"

"I'm afraid that holding up my end of any kind of relationship is a skill I never acquired."

"Why not?"

"You've had that big family. Lots of interaction. And obviously a lot of good examples. I haven't."

"You told me your mother left when you were pretty young."

"Yes."

"That left you with just your father. What was he like then?"

"Just like he is now. Demanding and overbearing."

"So he was tough on you growing up?"

Ethan was silent for a long time, leaning his head against the back of the seat and staring straight ahead. "Yeah. Truthfully, though, I didn't see much of him when I was a kid. He was either at work or playing golf or otherwise entertaining clients. If he was home, he was in his study."

"Even after your mother left?"

"Especially after my mother left."

Sandy couldn't fathom it. A father who treated his son like that?

"I spent my teenage years fighting my way through a high-dollar private school," Ethan said. "Graduated top of my class. But that was expected. Then I got my law degree so I could go into practice with my father, which was likewise expected. And for years after that, I spent almost all of my time either in the courtroom or preparing for being in the courtroom, counting the minutes until I could slash my opponent to ribbons." He rolled his head around to look at her. "That's what I was taught to do, you know. Slice and dice. Leave a bloody mess behind if I had to, but walk out a winner. And that's exactly what I've done."

His words were emotionless, matter-of-fact, but there was a sadness in his eyes that surprised her.

He looked away again. "It was different in the beginning. It was such a rush. You can't even imagine what it felt like to know I was the smartest person in that courtroom. That nobody had a chance against me. That I controlled the situation and could make it come out any way I wanted it to. God, Sandy, I *thrived* on that."

"I imagine that pleased your father."

"To no end."

"What about now?"

Ethan's lips tightened, and he slowly turned to look at her

again. "I've found out that being the smartest person in the courtroom isn't all it's cracked up to be."

Sandy thought about what Gina had told her, and suddenly she imagined Ethan going home alone to that mausoleum of a town house, where he dealt with the guilt he sometimes felt about his job all by himself.

"Maybe you need something in your life besides work," she said.

His chest rose and fell with a silent sigh. "You told me that sometimes you feel as if life is passing you by. As if the window is closing." He paused. "Sometimes I feel as if my window was never open in the first place."

Just then, the pilot came over the intercom to tell them they were on their final approach to Austin, but still they stared at each other. For the first time Sandy felt as if she were actually looking through those dark eyes to the man he was inside, and that man was far more vulnerable than she ever could have imagined.

The terminal at the Austin airport was busy, and Ethan and Sandy had a prolonged wait at the rental-car counter. Fifteen minutes later they were finally on the road, and with every minute that passed, Sandy grew more tense.

"You seem to know your way around Austin," she said.

"I did my undergrad at the University of Texas."

"Austin's a nice city."

"Yes. It is." Ethan glanced down at her fingers tapping nervously against her thigh. "But you don't really care about that right now, do you?"

Sandy exhaled. "I'm going crazy here, Ethan. I just hope the tape is there."

"We'll know soon enough."

Finally the health club came into view, and Ethan pulled into the parking lot. Before they went inside, he pulled Sandy aside.

"They might ask for ID cards of members they don't recognize," he said. "If you just walk in like you belong there, they probably won't say anything, but just in case, I'll distract the person at the counter. Get the tape, tuck it inside your purse, and come right back out. If somebody knew Laura as Pam Barton and sees you in her locker, there could be questions. Let's avoid those."

"Okay. Here goes."

They went inside the two-story lobby, which was brightly lit, with neon reflecting off chrome and mirrors. In the distance, Sandy heard the clanking of weights and the whir of bicycle tires set against a background of upbeat music. Ethan went straight to talk to the girl behind the desk, and the moment she turned away, Sandy went through the door leading to the back of the club.

Following a sign, she swung open a door to find a large room filled with benches and yellow metal lockers. Three other women were in the room, talking among themselves. Sandy moved quickly down a row on the far wall until she reached locker number sixty-four.

With her heart beating wildly, she pulled out the key, slid it into the lock, and tried to give it a twist.

It wouldn't budge.

She checked the number on the locker to verify that it matched the number on the key. She stuck the key in again and twisted harder. Shook the lock a little.

It wouldn't open.

She pressed harder still, her fingers whitening with the effort, and twisted as hard as she could.

The lock clicked open.

She let out a long breath of relief, then leaned in close and opened the locker.

It was empty.

She froze for a moment, stunned. Except for a hooded sweatshirt hanging on a hook, there was nothing there. For several seconds, she just stood there staring at it, as if she could will the tape to be there if only she focused on the emptiness long enough.

Then she realized there was an oblong two-handed pocket in the front of the sweatshirt. Feeling a shot of hope again, she quickly stuck her hand inside it.

Nothing.

She shook the sweatshirt, feeling up and down the sleeves, knowing that something the size of a videotape couldn't miraculously be hiding inside it, but she felt compelled to do it anyway.

The tape just wasn't there.

Filled with disappointment, she shut the door and locked it, then left the locker room and went back out to the lobby. As she approached Ethan, he stood up with a questioning expression.

"It wasn't there," she said.

"Are you sure?"

"Positive."

"But this makes no sense," Ethan said. "Why did Laura renew her membership when she had no intention of coming back here?"

"I think maybe we just made too many assumptions."

"No. I'm not buying that. Come with me."

Sandy followed him to the front desk. A teenage girl with heavily highlighted hair and a picture-perfect body squeezed into neon-pink spandex gave them a broad, vacant smile.

"Hi, there. What can I do for you?"

He nodded toward Sandy. "She tried to retrieve something out of locker number sixty-four and found it empty. Would the management have had any reason lately to remove any items from lockers?"

"Uh . . . not that I know of."

"Had any thefts lately?"

"No. I don't think so."

"Is there anyone else besides the management who has a master key to the lockers? Cleaning staff, somebody like that?"

The girl just shrugged, staring back at them with a dim-witted expression that said the Texas public school system was in need of a serious overhaul.

"Oh, wait!" she said. "Did you say number sixty-four?"

Sandy's heart leaped. "Yes?"

"Your boyfriend was here earlier."

"What?"

"Yeah. Not twenty minutes ago. He asked me if I'd get something out of your locker for you. So I did."

Sandy felt a sinking sensation in her stomach. "You opened the locker?"

"Well . . . yeah."

Sandy could hardly form the words. "What did he ask you to bring him?"

"A videotape. Not one like a movie you'd buy or rent. But one like you'd make at home."

"And you just *gave* it to him?"

"Uh-oh," the girl said. "Did I do something wrong?"

"I don't have a boyfriend," Sandy said. "And I didn't send anybody to pick up that tape."

The girl's hand flew over her mouth. "Oh, God! I'm sorry! I mean, he knew there was a tape in there, so I assumed he really was your boyfriend." She looked over her shoulder. "Oh, wow. I could get *fired* over this."

"It's okay," Sandy said, willing herself to stay calm. "You didn't know."

"What did this man look like?" Ethan asked.

"Well, let's see. He was just normal, you know? Dark hair. Maybe forty or so." She shrugged weakly. "Decent-looking for an older guy, I guess."

"Anything else?"

"He was pretty tall."

Sandy sighed. She'd just described half the men in the city of Austin.

"Oh," the girl said. "There was one more thing."

"What?"

"His eyes. He had the weirdest blue eyes I've ever seen."

chapter fourteen

Ethan and Sandy walked back out to the parking lot and got into the rental car. This was the last thing he'd expected to have happen, and he wasn't sure what to do next.

"Looks like Mulroney beat us to the tape," he said.

"But how? How could he have known where the tape was?"

"It's possible that he got the information out of Laura before he killed her, and he's just now getting here to pick it up."

"But days have passed. Why would he have waited so long?"

"I don't know."

"And isn't it a little strange that he beat us here by only twenty minutes?"

"Yes. It is."

"We have to tell the Austin cops what happened," Sandy said. "Maybe they can pick him up."

"No point. They won't touch this."

"Why not?"

"Because we can't say with absolute certainty that it was Mulroney whom the girl gave the tape to."

"But his blue eyes. That girl described them the same way Chris did."

"Yes. I know. But try telling the police that you've never seen Mulroney, but based on that girl's description of his blue eyes, you're sure it's a positive ID. Not only that, we have to be able to give the cops firsthand information. We don't know exactly what he looks like, we don't know where he is, and we can't be a hundred percent certain what's on that tape. We only know what Chris told us, and most of that came from Laura. They'll never issue a warrant based on that."

"But he got that girl to give him the tape by fraud," Sandy said. "By saying he was Laura's boyfriend."

"Right now we can't prove to the police that he wasn't her boyfriend. And the management willingly gave him the tape, and Laura isn't exactly here to file a complaint about that against Mulroney or the health club."

"I can't believe this," Sandy said, shaking her head. "So what do we do now?"

"There's nothing we can do."

Ethan put the key in the ignition. Then he froze as a terrible thought crossed his mind. "When you told Chris we were coming here, what exactly did you say?"

"That we thought we knew where the tape was, and that we were going after it."

"In Austin?"

"Yes."

"Did you tell her the name of the health club?"

"Uh . . . yeah." Sandy looked at him blankly for a moment. Then her face flooded with apprehension. "Chris. God, Ethan. Is it possible that Mulroney got to her?"

"I don't know."

"What if he did? After what he did to Laura—"

"Take it easy," Ethan said. "I'll phone her right now and make sure she's all right."

He pulled out his cell phone and a card with Chris's phone number on it. He dialed, and after a few rings, a woman came on the line. He asked to speak to Chris.

"She's not here right now," the woman said. "Who's calling?"

"Is this Natalie?"

"Yes."

"Natalie, this is Ethan Millner, the attorney who was at your house a few nights ago. I need to get in touch with Chris right away. Can you tell me when she'll be home?"

"I don't know." There was a hint of panic in the woman's voice. "She left Sarah with me and went out to run a few short errands. She hasn't come home yet."

"How long ago was that?"

"Four hours."

Ethan felt a shot of trepidation. "Four hours?"

"Yes. I'm so worried. I don't know what could have happened to her."

"Do you have any reason to believe she's in trouble?"

"No, but she should have been home long before now. I know Chris doesn't want anybody knowing anything about this, but that man . . ." Her voice cracked. "I'm so afraid he found her."

"Does she have a cell phone?"

"Yes. She's not answering."

"Take it easy, Natalie. Remind me what kind of car Chris drives."

"A Honda Accord. Blue."

"Year?"

"I think it's a 2001, but I don't know for sure."

"Do you know the license plate number?"

"No. I don't."

"Where did she say she was going?"

"To the grocery store for diapers and a few other things. The post office. I don't know if she planned on stopping anywhere else or not. But even if she did, four hours . . ." There was a sob in Natalie's voice. "I knew I should have made her stay here until this whole thing was over with. I *knew* I should have. But she told me she'd be all right."

"Listen to me. I'm going to call the Larchmont police. I'll give them a description of her and her car and ask them to be on the lookout for her. Do you have a pen and paper?"

"Yes."

"Take down this number."

He gave Natalie his cell phone number and told her to call him if Chris came home, and told her he'd get in touch with her the moment he knew anything.

He hung up the phone and turned to Sandy. "Chris went to run a few errands and has been gone for four hours. Natalie doesn't know where she is."

"Oh, my God."

"Don't jump to conclusions. There could be another explanation as to why she didn't come home."

"Come on, Ethan. You're jumping to as many conclusions as I am. How else would Mulroney have known where the tape was? If he threatened her, she might very well have told him. And then—"

"Sandy—stop. It's not productive to talk about that. Let's just get back to Tolosa and go from there."

"But our flight isn't for three hours."

"Let's see if we can catch an earlier one. I'm going to phone the Larchmont police and get them to start looking for Chris, and then we'll head to the airport."

Twenty minutes later, Ethan and Sandy rushed through the sliding glass doors into the terminal at the Austin airport. The same clerk who'd waited on them earlier at the rental-car counter was still there, and it took a ridiculous amount of time for him to process the return of their car. Fortunately, when they got to the ticket counter, there were still seats, but the agent told them the flight was already boarding and would be departing in twenty minutes.

Ethan grabbed their boarding passes and they hurried through the airport to the security checkpoint, falling into line behind several other people. It seemed to take forever before the people in front of them moved through the metal detector. Ethan checked his watch. They had only a few minutes left to make the plane.

"We're never going to get through here," Sandy said.

"Take it easy. We'll make it."

Fortunately, the cops in Larchmont had agreed to search for Chris even though she'd been missing only four hours. Ethan had been able to convince them that a man who had reason to abduct her might finally have done that, so time was of the essence. He only hoped that before they boarded the plane, Chris's sister would call to tell him it was a false alarm.

Finally the line moved forward, and he and Sandy passed through the checkpoint without incident and hurried down the concourse. As they approached their gate, he was relieved to see that there were still people waiting to board their flight.

"We're okay," he said. "They haven't closed the doors yet."

Identification and boarding passes in hand, they got in line behind the other people. A moment later, Ethan felt a tap on his shoulder. He turned around to see a man who had fallen into line behind him.

"Do you have the time?" he asked.

Ethan flipped his wrist to check his watch, then looked up again. The instant he met the man's eyes, he froze, stabbed by a strange sense of recognition. The man was taller than average. He had jet-black hair.

And he had the oddest blue eyes Ethan had ever seen.

He told the man the time, then turned back around very slowly, using the opportunity to furtively flick his gaze to the driver's license the man held. The typed name was too small to read, but the signature wasn't.

Mulroney.

Good God. Vince Mulroney was standing right behind him? What were the odds?

Then Ethan realized the truth. If Mulroney was eager to go to Tolosa after grabbing that tape, with only a few commuter flights a day between Austin and Tolosa, the odds were excellent that he'd be on the same flight they were.

Ethan waited nonchalantly until he and Sandy came to the front of the line. After they showed their driver's licenses and boarding passes and were heading toward the plane, Ethan pulled her aside.

"What's wrong?" she asked.

"Just stand here a minute," he said quietly. "Look at me and don't say a word."

Mulroney went through the checkpoint and passed by them as he headed toward the plane. As soon as he was out of earshot, Ethan whispered to Sandy.

"That's him."

"Who?"

"Mulroney."

"What?"

"That man who was behind us in line. He asked me the time. When I turned around to tell him, I saw his driver's license."

Sandy's eyes flew open. "He's going back to Tolosa?"

"Looks that way."

"But why?"

"I don't know."

"Do you think he has the tape with him?"

"No way to tell. But I'm going to call Henderson before the flight takes off to see if I can convince him to show up on the other end to grab him. Come on. We've got to move it."

They hurried down the bridge. As soon as they walked

onto the plane, Sandy went down the aisle to find their seats and Ethan slipped into one of the bathrooms and locked the door. He hit his speed dial for Henderson's cell phone, thankful that he'd had the foresight to program it in as soon as he'd taken this case. After four rings, Henderson grunted a hello.

"Henderson, this is Ethan Millner."

"What the hell do you want? I'm right in the middle of—"

"I don't give a damn what you're in the middle of. I want you to shut up and listen. I'm deadly serious here."

"Okay," Henderson said, clearly surprised by Ethan's insistence. "I'm listening."

"I'm on flight number four-fifty-seven from Austin to Tolosa, getting ready to take off. Vince Mulroney, the man I told you about who we think killed Laura, is on this flight. He may be carrying the snuff film I told you about. I want you to meet the plane and pick him up."

"Hold on," Henderson said. "You're in Austin?"

"Yes. And the man who killed Laura Williams is on this plane right now."

"You got a positive ID?"

"Yes. I saw his driver's license when he flashed it to the gate personnel."

"And he's carrying a snuff film."

"Yes."

"You know that for sure?"

"Somebody grabbed it out of Laura Williams's locker at a health club in Austin. It had to be him."

"Health club? What are you talking about?"

"I found out the tape was there. I went after it. Mulroney beat me to it."

"You've lost me."

Ethan tightened his hand against the phone. "It doesn't matter. All that matters is that Vince Mulroney may be carrying evidence that implicates him in a murder, and it could also lead you to the fact that he killed Laura Williams. If you're not there to pick him up when he gets off this plane, it could be your last chance."

"I'd have to get an arrest warrant."

"Yes. You have two hours to get one and meet me at the airport."

"But you said you haven't even viewed this tape. It could be *Bambi,* for all you know. If I go after the guy without somebody giving me verifiable first-hand information about what he's carrying—"

"Damn it, I *told* you what he's carrying!"

"You haven't told me crap. You already admitted that you can't say for sure that he's even carrying a tape. So even if we catch him with a snuff film, his lawyer could say later that it wasn't a proper search and file a motion to suppress the evidence. You assholes do that kind of thing all the time."

Henderson was right. For once in his lazy, worthless life, he was right. Mulroney could already have destroyed the tape he'd taken from the health club. Ethan had no proof that Mulroney had caught up to Chris and hurt her in any way. For all he knew, she could be walking through her sister's front door right now, alive and well. If Henderson got an arrest warrant based on what Ethan had just told him, any reasonably competent attorney could have the tape thrown out as evidence even if it did implicate him in a murder.

He got off the phone with Henderson, left the bathroom, and went down the aisle to find Sandy, frustration eating away at him. He passed by Mulroney sitting in his aisle seat, fiddling with his stereo headphones, and it was all he could do not to take him by the throat and do the job of the judge and jury right then and there.

He moved on down the aisle, thankful that the plane was only half-full, leaving several empty seats around Sandy. He took his seat beside her.

"Well?" she asked.

"Henderson's not going to do a damned thing."

"Are you telling me that Mulroney is going to be getting off this plane in two hours, and Henderson won't do anything about it?"

"We can't say for sure he's carrying the tape. We can't say for sure he hurt Chris. We can't say for sure he killed Laura. We can't say anything for sure about him. Unfortunately, Henderson's right. If he gets a search warrant based only on what I've told him, an attorney could have the evidence thrown right out of court."

As the flight attendants went through their takeoff procedures, Ethan and Sandy sat in silence, both stunned by this turn of events. Mulroney was going to walk off this plane when it landed in Tolosa, and there wasn't a damned thing they could do about it.

Two hours later, they were making their final approach into the Tolosa airport, and Ethan was sure he'd never spent a more miserable two hours in his life. He knew just how worried Sandy was about Chris, and he was feeling plenty of that worry himself. And there was Mulroney, sitting on the aisle only six rows in front of them.

"I can't stand this," Sandy said. "He's practically close enough to touch, and we can't stop him."

"I know, Sandy. I know."

As the pilot brought the plane in for a landing, Ethan's frustration level went right off the scale. For two hours he'd been trying to come up with some way he could stop Mulroney from walking off this plane when the time came. But even if Ethan managed to accomplish that task, it wouldn't do him any good. Unless he had solid evidence pointing to Mulroney as a suspect in something—Chris's disappearance, snuff films, Laura's murder, *something*—the police wouldn't touch him.

They descended lower and lower, until finally the wheels

touched the runway. Ethan immediately grabbed his cell phone.

"What are you doing?" Sandy asked.

"Phoning the Larchmont police."

He dialed the number. An operator came on the line, and as soon as he identified himself, she said, "Please hold. I'm transferring you to Officer Bishop. He's been trying to get in touch with you."

Ethan's heart skipped. "They're putting me through to an officer," he told Sandy.

"Does he know something?"

"I don't know."

The line clicked. "Officer Bishop."

"This is Ethan Millner. You've been trying to call me?"

"Yes. For the past twenty minutes. We found Chris Satterwhite's car. It was in a wooded area behind a strip shopping center. You were right. She'd been abducted. She was tied up in the trunk."

Ethan could barely say the words. "Is she all right?"

"Yes. She's a little hysterical, but she appears to be unharmed."

Thank God. "Did she tell you who abducted her?"

"Yes. A man named Vince Mulroney. And she insisted we warn you about something. She keeps talking about some videotape. She says that Mulroney is going after it. She says he threatened her and her sister and her baby, so she was forced to tell him where it was. Do you know what she's talking about?"

"Yes. I know. But the tape doesn't matter right now. Listen carefully. I just flew in from Austin, and I'm sitting in a plane on the tarmac at the Tolosa airport, heading to the gate. Vince Mulroney is sitting six rows in front of me."

"What?"

"He's here. On this plane."

"But if he was in Austin, how could he have—"

"Six hours ago he was in Larchmont. He abducted Chris, tied her up, then came here. And now he's heading back. I need airport security to pick him up."

"Are you sure he's the one?"

"Yes. I saw his driver's license when he flashed it at check-in. I need you to call the Tolosa airport. Make sure they hold flight four-fifty-seven at the gate so nobody gets off. That's four-five-seven from Austin. Then send security in here to pick him up. He's sitting in seat seven-C. You've got maybe two minutes to make that happen."

"I'm on it."

Ethan hung up the phone and turned to Sandy. "He's going to contact airport officials to grab Mulroney. I just hope he does it in time."

"Is Chris okay?"

"Physically, yes. But she's pretty shaken up."

"Of course she is. God, she must have been terrified. How did Mulroney know where she was?"

"It wasn't hard for us to find her, was it? With the right motivation, it isn't hard to track anyone down."

Sandy looked out the window. "How far do you suppose we are from the gate?"

"I don't know. I can't see it yet."

Several seconds passed. The pilot made a ninety-degree turn onto another runway, and Sandy grabbed Ethan's arm.

"There it is."

Ethan looked out the window. The terminal was in sight about a quarter mile away.

"How much time has passed since we landed?" she asked.

Ethan looked at his watch. "About a minute and a half."

As they bumped along the runway, drawing closer and closer to the terminal, Ethan willed the pilot to go slower, but he seemed to be determined to get to that gate as quickly as possible.

"There's no way," Sandy said. "We're moving too quickly. There's no way they'll get the message in time."

"Don't give up yet."

Seconds later, the plane reached the terminal. It slowed down, and the moment it jerked to a halt, several passengers stood up.

A flight attendant came on the intercom. Ethan held his breath, hoping she'd gotten the message, hoping she'd tell the passengers to take their seats again for whatever reason somebody had cooked up to allow security officers time to get to the plane. Instead, she merely warned the passengers to check overhead bins for their belongings and thanked them for their patronage.

Ethan looked down the aisle to see Mulroney reach beneath the seat in front of him, grab the bag he'd carried on, and stand up.

"Damn it," Ethan muttered. "If the cavalry is coming, it's too damned late."

"What are we going to do?" Sandy said.

"Stay here."

"Ethan—"

"I'm not letting that bastard walk away."

He left his seat, skirted two passengers moving into the aisle, and came up right behind Mulroney. Ethan had no idea how he could stop the man from leaving the airport, but he intended to shadow him right up to the last moment and hope something came to him.

They went to the front of the plane, then stepped off into the bridge. As they veered right and walked up the slight incline toward the terminal, Mulroney lengthened his strides, moving purposefully. Ethan picked up his pace to stay right behind him.

As they emerged into the terminal, Ethan was relieved to see three uniformed officers hurrying toward the gate. When they fanned out to prevent the dozen or so departing passengers who had already walked into the terminal from leaving the area, Ethan felt a shot of hope. He moved up beside Mulroney, and he could almost feel the wheels turning in the man's head when he spotted the officers.

This is not a problem, he was undoubtedly thinking. *They couldn't be looking for me. Nobody could possibly know what I've done.*

Filled with that false sense of security, when one of the officers approached him and asked to see his driver's license, Mulroney casually complied, and Ethan took great pleasure in the look of utter shock that crossed his face when the officer turned him around, snapped on a pair of cuffs, and took him into custody.

An hour and a half later, Ethan pulled into the parking garage near the courthouse and drove to where Sandy had left her car hours earlier. It felt to him as if aeons had passed since they'd left for Austin. Nothing about this day had gone as they'd expected it to, but he certainly couldn't argue with the outcome.

They'd stayed at the airport long enough to meet the Tolosa police officers who came to take Mulroney into custody, telling them the story of his involvement with Laura Williams and Chris Satterwhite. The officers searched his bag and found a videotape, and Ethan knew that when Henderson finally viewed the tape, Mulroney would be well on his way to being prosecuted for two murders and a kidnapping.

After they left the airport, Sandy wanted to see Chris, so Ethan drove her to the small hospital in Larchmont where Chris had been taken for a physical exam and observation. She was calmer now, unhurt, and very thankful that Mulroney was in custody. After a short visit, they got back in the car to return to Tolosa.

Sandy turned to Ethan. "Thank God Mulroney kept her

alive until he could be sure she'd told him the truth about where the tape was." Then her expression became confused. "But if he got the tape, why was he coming back to Tolosa?"

"I'm betting he always intended to return," Ethan said.

"Even if he had what he wanted?"

"Chris was still a loose end he needed to tie up."

Sandy's eyes widened. "Are you saying he meant to kill her no matter what? That if you hadn't seen his ID before that flight and had security waiting for him, Chris could be dead right now?"

"Yes."

Sandy breathed a heavy sigh of relief. "Thank God we got him, then. Thank God he's going to pay for everything he's done. And once they tie him to Laura's murder, Josh is off the hook. Can we let him know?"

"Let's wait until it's a done deal," Ethan said. "It could take a little while for the charges to be dropped against him."

"You are sure that's going to happen, aren't you? Ralph Clemmons is still going to say that he saw Josh on Laura's property that night."

"Eyewitness testimony is still refutable, no matter who it comes from. If there's no forensic evidence against Josh, and no solid motive, Mulroney will look like a far better suspect, and if there's physical evidence that ties him directly to the scene of the crime, he's probably as good as convicted. But we need to let the story play out."

Sandy nodded.

"You look a little tired," Ethan said.

"Long day."

"Yes."

"Well," Sandy said. "I guess I'd better be going. Will you let me know the minute you hear anything about Mulroney?"

"Yes. Of course."

But as she was reaching for the door handle, Ethan's cell phone rang. He grabbed it from his pocket. "Ethan Millner."

"Millner. It's Henderson. I've got some good news for you."

Sandy was already halfway out of the car, and Ethan grabbed her arm. "Henderson?"

Sandy turned back, frozen in anticipation.

"Was the tape what we thought it was?" Ethan asked.

"Oh, yeah. It's a sweet little video that shows Laura Williams blowing a woman's brains out."

"And Mulroney?"

"His ID is a little more equivocal, but I think the DA can make a case against him for that murder."

Ethan felt a surge of relief. That tape, combined with Chris's testimony and the smallest bit of forensic evidence from the scene of Laura Williams's murder, and Mulroney was going down.

"That's the good news," Henderson said. "Want to hear the bad news?"

Ethan felt a shot of apprehension. "Bad news?"

"The guy may have taken part in a snuff film, but your theory that he killed Laura Williams is shot to hell."

"What do you mean?"

"Vince Mulroney has an alibi."

chapter fifteen

By the time Ethan hung up the phone, Sandy could tell by the look on his face that something was terribly wrong.

"Ethan? What happened? Did Henderson look at the tape?"

"Yes. He says that more analysis will be necessary, but Mulroney could definitely be the man on it."

"Good," Sandy said. "Now all we have to do is wait for the forensic evidence and hope he matches up to it, right?"

Ethan dropped his head and rubbed his eyes with the heels of his hands, then let out a heavy sigh.

"Ethan? What's wrong?"

"The guy may have taken part in a snuff film, but our theory that he killed Laura Williams was dead wrong."

"What do you mean?"

He turned to look at her. "Mulroney has an alibi."

Sandy slid her hand to her throat. "What?"

"The night of the murder, Mulroney was in Tolosa, all right. He was stopped at eight o'clock in the evening for driving drunk."

Sandy stared at Ethan dumbly. "But the murder was committed around ten o'clock. Couldn't he have—"

"He failed a Breathalyzer and spent the night in jail. Alibis don't come much more ironclad than that."

Sandy sat up, stunned. "That means he couldn't have killed Laura."

"No. He couldn't have."

"But he threatened to kill her. How in the world . . . " Sandy's mind was spinning, trying to come up with some scenario that would explain this. "Could he have ordered her to be killed? Murder for hire?"

"Why would he do that? He wanted the tape."

"Maybe he hired somebody to coerce it out of her, and things went too far."

"I doubt it. He came after that tape himself the night before."

"He has to be involved, Ethan. Look at the facts surrounding him. Somehow he had to have—"

"No! Mulroney had nothing to do with it! He's not—" He stopped short and took a breath, then spoke softly, his voice laced with disbelief. "He's not the one."

A long silence stretched between them. Ethan still wasn't looking at her, and she felt his shattered expectations as surely as she felt her own.

"And if Mulroney didn't do it . . ."

Ethan's voice faded away, but Sandy knew what he wasn't saying.

"Just because Mulroney didn't do it doesn't mean Josh did," she told him.

"I know."

But still she could feel the tension radiating from him. He took a deep breath and let it out slowly.

"Please don't give up on him," Sandy said.

"Is that what you think I'm going to do?"

"I know you don't believe Josh is innocent," she said. "But I know he is. So I'm asking you. Please, Ethan. *Please* help him out of this."

"Nothing's changed, Sandy. I just have to back up and regroup. It isn't as if I haven't had setbacks like this before."

"I know. It's just . . . it's just that you don't know him like I do, and since you're doing this for free—"

"I don't give a damn about the money. If there's a way to get that kid off, I'll find it."

They continued to stare at each other, and a feeling of despair overcame Sandy. She suddenly felt lost, as if she'd been on a strong, clear path that had suddenly become tangled and overgrown and impossible to navigate.

"But if Josh didn't do it," she said, "and Mulroney didn't either, then who did?"

"I haven't got a clue. Hell, it could have been a random burglary. A crime of panic, just as Henderson said."

"How the hell could this have happened?" she said, her voice shaky. "How could everything we did today end up being for nothing?"

"It wasn't for nothing. Mulroney was arrested for the murder on that tape. That's a good thing."

"But it doesn't help Josh out of the mess he's in."

"I know. But I'm going to do everything I can for him."

She nodded, but the feeling of hopelessness that overcame her was just about more than she could stand, and suddenly she couldn't bear the idea of going home alone to her big, empty house.

Not that she had a choice.

"I-I guess I'd better go," she said.

But when she reached for the door handle, Ethan reached for her.

The moment she felt his hand on her arm, she froze. He slowly slid it down to circle his fingers around her wrist, and goose bumps rose on her skin all the way down. Then he began to trace his thumb in maddening little circles along the top of her wrist.

"Ethan—"

"Don't go," he murmured, his smooth-as-silk voice turning deep and throaty. "Not yet."

Damn it, don't talk to me like that, not in that voice that sounds like every lover I've ever dreamed about.

She squeezed her eyes closed, feeling a surge of excitement followed closely by a shiver of pure desire. And she had no business feeling this way. He had no business *making* her feel this way.

"I have to go," she told him.

"Then I'll go with you."

That voice again, punctuated by his warm hand against her wrist, moving in that soft, soothing way that was slowly breaking down every wall she'd been trying to put up between them.

"Look, Ethan. I know where this is going. I've told you what I want, and it's not casual sex. And since you told me you're not a man who sticks around—"

"I was just trying to be honest with you about that."

"I know. And now I'm being honest. I'm not a woman who can watch you walk away."

"I don't make promises."

"I know. That's why I have to leave."

"At least we can have tonight."

"No, we can't."

Even as she protested, she'd be lying to herself to say she didn't want him.

But not just his body, and not just for one night.

"I might have been able to do it in the beginning when you didn't mean anything to me," she told him. "But now . . ."

"Now what?"

The words were on the tip of her tongue. She wanted to tell him how she felt about him, but what would be the point? She'd only end up humiliating herself all over again.

"Never mind," she said. "I'll see you tomorrow night for crime watch."

As she opened the car door, he said her name, reached for her again, but she slipped out of his grasp. She got out of his car and into hers, moving quickly because she knew if she stayed he could very well talk her into doing something she wanted now but would pay hell for tomorrow. She started her car, shocked at the second thoughts that were already pouring through her mind and fighting off an irrational swell of hope that he'd stop her, that he'd tell her that of course he wanted more.

He didn't.

Proof positive he doesn't care. So go. Now. And don't look back.

Moments later she'd pulled out of the parking garage and was heading for home, her heart still pounding like mad. For a whole twenty seconds or so, she fought the urge to look in her rearview mirror. When she finally did, his car was nowhere in sight.

Of course it wasn't. What had she expected him to do? Change his mind and follow her all the way to her house?

He was right, after all. He'd spelled out his motives quite clearly last night, and he wasn't denying it today. It was her fault that she'd hoped there could be something more between them.

Then out of nowhere the tears came—big, ugly tears of self-pity that she wiped on the shoulder of her shirt, but they still kept coming. *Damn it, damn it.*

She could barely see to drive for the tears that clouded her eyes. She needed Ethan tonight. She needed him to hold her close and tell her that everything with Josh was going to work out all right. She needed him to make love to her, more than she ever would have imagined.

But she also needed him to look at her the way a man looked at a woman when it wasn't just for tonight but for tomorrow, too, and that was something he couldn't give her.

Watching Sandy drive away had just about killed Ethan, and by the time he arrived home, the feeling overwhelmed him. He'd wanted to go home with her. After everything had gone wrong tonight, he could see in her eyes that she didn't want to be alone, and neither did he. But what that might lead to . . .

He'd been honest with her about that. He didn't make promises, because he knew the chances of his living up to them were just about zero, and saying so usually wiped his conscience clean. But saying it to Sandy had felt like the biggest lie he'd ever spoken.

He went to bed thinking about her, then rose the next morning with her on his mind again. And all the way to the courthouse, the same words kept pounding away at his mind.

Vince Mulroney has an alibi.

He thought he'd had this all wrapped up. He thought he'd been the knight in shining armor that Sandy had desperately needed. And now this.

How in the hell could Mulroney have attacked the victim in her own home the night before her murder, threatened to kill her, and then have an alibi that said he couldn't possibly have done it?

But that doesn't mean that Josh did.

Sandy was right. Still, the case Ethan thought he was going to be able to seal shut suddenly seemed shakier than ever, and now he was back to square one. He told himself to get his brain back into the game. It wasn't the first time in his career that he'd had a setback like this. It simply meant he had to readjust and refocus, because losing this one was not an option.

When court recessed for lunch, Ethan left the courthouse and went to his office. As he circled the reception desk, Sasha fluttered a few messages from her fingertips, which he grabbed as he headed around the corner. Then he went into his office and nearly groaned out loud.

His father was sitting on the sofa, thumbing through his planner and making a few notes. Ethan felt the same twinge of irritation he always did whenever his father made himself at home in his office as if it were merely a satellite of his own.

Charles looked up. "Ah. There you are. Gina told me you were on your way back here."

"I haven't got time to talk." Ethan circled his desk and pulled open a drawer. "I just came by to pick up a few things, and then I've got to get back to the courthouse. McIntyre case. Closing arguments."

"So how is it looking?"

"No way to tell."

"Ethan. Did you score an acquittal, or not?"

Hell, yes, he had. He could read this particular jury like a billboard on Times Square, and they had sympathy written all over their faces for the kind and benevolent family man he'd made his client out to be, the one who was getting shafted by the big corporation he was accused of embezzling from.

He looked his father squarely in the eye. "As I said, there's no way to tell. We'll know when the jury comes back." He stuffed a file folder into his briefcase and headed for his office door.

"I saw you leaving the courthouse yesterday afternoon," Charles said.

Ethan stopped. He knew that tone in his father's voice, the one that said he was tossing out bait and waiting for a bite.

"And you weren't alone. I believe Ms. DeMarco was with you?"

At the mention of Sandy's name, Ethan turned back. "Yes. She was. We had some things to discuss."

"All the way to Austin?"

Ethan held his gaze steady, quelling the desire to ask his father how the hell he was tracking his every move and why in God's name he even felt the need to.

"To answer the question you're not asking, Ethan, I know where you were yesterday because I talked to Ray Henderson this morning. I know everything that transpired, including the fact that you chased a lead all the way to Austin on a throwaway case where you're not making a dime."

"I told you before. I'm not discussing that case with you."

"I also know that in spite of his alibi concerning the Laura Williams murder, the man you managed to have arrested is still facing kidnapping and murder charges."

"And he deserves to."

Charles shrugged offhandedly. "Perhaps."

"Excuse me?"

"Apparently the tape is equivocal. Enough to charge him, but possibly not enough to convict. And were you aware that the man who abducted Chris Satterwhite was wearing a ski mask?"

"And that same man demanded she tell him where the snuff tape was that Mulroney had in his possession at the time he was—" Ethan stopped short. "Why do you suddenly know so much about Vince Mulroney?"

"Because he phoned me this morning asking for representation."

For the count of five, Ethan just stared at his father, too dumbfounded to speak.

"Vince Mulroney called you?"

"It seems he was told of our excellent track record. I assure you he's quite willing to part with an extraordinary amount of money to receive a quality defense. The pornography business must be even more profitable than I imagined."

"You're *defending* that son of a bitch?"

Charles drew back with mock surprise. "It's what we do, Ethan. Everyone is entitled to a good defense. Besides, Vince Mulroney is innocent."

"What makes you say that?"

"The ten-thousand-dollar retainer he put in my pocket."

Money. It was all about the money.

"So everyone is entitled to a good defense," Ethan said, "as long as they're able to write a big enough check?"

"This firm hasn't become the best so we can settle for pocket change." Charles's jaw tightened, an almost imperceptible indication of anger beneath his glass-smooth surface. "And you haven't become the best this firm has to offer so you can make decisions based on the direction of whatever woman you happen to be sleeping with."

Ethan felt a surge of anger. "That's not what's happening here."

"Oh, really?" He stood up from the sofa. "I know you can spot a liar at twenty paces, Ethan. Never forget that I can, too."

As Charles left his office, anger wrapped itself so tightly around Ethan that he felt as if he were going to implode.

Fifteen minutes later, when he arrived back at the courthouse, he still felt so edgy that he stopped by the men's room and slapped cold water on his face. As he wiped it dry, he stared at himself in the mirror, telling himself that he had to get it together, that he had a job to do this afternoon.

A job for which he was being extraordinarily well paid.

A few minutes later he came into the courtroom and glanced at Paul McIntyre. The paper trail was damning, but his salary was large enough that the amount he was accused of walking off with looked like a pittance. Still, greed sometimes did strange things to men.

Had it done something to this one?

Ethan stood beside his client as court was convened. His thoughts wandered, but when the time came, he gave his closing arguments. Even on autopilot, his words were gold. Still, it took the jury until five o'clock that afternoon to reach a verdict.

Not guilty.

McIntyre smiled, shook Ethan's hand, then glanced over at the managing partner of the accounting firm who had filed the complaint against him. McIntyre raised his chin a millimeter or two, his mouth settling into a subtle sneer.

In that moment, Ethan knew.

Innocent men showed relief. Thankfulness. Even anger that the charges were brought against them in the first place. But that sneer said, *I got away with it, and you couldn't stop me.*

That sudden awareness sliced through Ethan like a razor, that painfully dichotomous feeling that even though he could never know for sure, still he knew beyond all doubt. And if his father defended Mulroney and got him off, Ethan would know beyond all doubt there, too.

The very thought of it made him sick.

He left the courtroom and got into his car, and all at once he craved the feeling of a glass in his hand, the smell of secondhand smoke, and the sensation of alcohol burning its way down his throat, all precursors to that sluggish, mindless feeling that would hopefully keep his thoughts at bay.

Ten minutes later, he sat at the bar at Bernie's, staring down at the scotch he'd ordered. It was a slow night. Only half a dozen bar stools were occupied, mostly with single guys who were hoping for some eligible women to walk through the door. A few couples sat at tables, and two beer-drinking guys were playing a video game in the corner. Ethan recognized the faces of some of the regulars, people he was acquainted with, but as he looked around, he wouldn't call any of them friends. Hell, the bartender knew more about him than just about anybody else.

He took a sip of the scotch, but suddenly it felt pointless. There wasn't enough alcohol on the planet to take the edge off the way he felt tonight.

"Is this seat taken?"

Ethan glanced over to see a woman slide onto the stool beside him. She was maybe twenty-five, maybe thirty. Maybe a natural blonde, maybe not. Maybe married, maybe not.

"No. It's not taken."

She gave him a seductive smile. "Well, then. It looks like this is my lucky night."

Suddenly it struck Ethan that that was exactly the kind of man he'd been for years now. Somebody's lucky night.

"Haven't I seen you in here before?" she asked.

"Probably," he said.

A few minutes of silence passed, and when he didn't offer to buy her a drink, she flagged down the bartender and ordered a gin and tonic.

Out of the corner of his eye, Ethan could see a few of the other guys at the bar eyeing the blonde. No wonder. She was young, she was beautiful, and she gave off the kind of vibes that said she knew how to have a good time with no strings attached. The moment she'd shown up, he knew what kind of woman she was: the kind who was on the prowl, who couldn't wait to get up close and personal, who didn't need flowers and promises.

Promises. Exactly what he'd told Sandy he couldn't give her.

The blonde started talking to him, telling him she was originally from Dallas, that she was a paralegal, and that she had two roommates but they were out of town. She kept crossing and uncrossing her legs and running her cocktail straw over her lips, and all he could think the whole time was, *Why am I here?*

Because it beat going home alone.

But he didn't have to go home alone. He had a woman sitting less than an arm's length away who was telling him she'd be pleased to follow him anywhere.

And he didn't want anything to do with her.

Instead, he was hammered with thoughts about what had happened with McIntyre today, about his father, about Mulroney. Suddenly his whole career felt like an exercise in futility. Yes, he won more times than not. But at what price?

And Sandy. What price had he paid for the things he'd said to her?

I don't make promises.

The more those words passed through his mind, the more ridiculous they sounded. As if he were some big prize, or something? As if she'd be lucky if he threw her a bone? How many more times was she going to open the door before he had the good sense to walk through it?

The blonde leaned in occasionally and touched his arm as she spoke, making it clear what she wanted, so she looked a little disappointed when he flipped a few bills on the bar and turned to leave. And that disappointment lasted for about ten seconds. By the time he hit the door, she'd already moved down the bar to talk to the next guy.

Ethan shook off the effects of the one scotch he'd had, went to the gym, and worked out harder than he had in months. He went home, took a shower, and checked his watch.

Thank God it was time to go to Sandy's.

chapter sixteen

At ten o'clock that night, Ethan and Sandy were making the last round of her neighborhood. They'd spotted two suspicious cars and reported them to the police. One turned out to be an out-of-state visitor of one of the neighborhood residents, and the other a stolen car that had been abandoned. Otherwise, little had occurred, leaving Ethan too much time to reflect on what had happened today with his father. With Mulroney. With the McIntyre case.

And what had happened with Sandy last night.

They didn't talk about that at all, as if that case were closed, and he hated the thought that he might have screwed up any chance he had of opening it up again. He remembered the first time he'd gotten into this car to do crime watch with her. There was so much more involved in the way he felt about her now that he couldn't possibly hope to sort it out.

After finishing the final round of the neighborhood, Sandy swung her car into the alley and parked in her driveway.

"We're not scheduled for crime watch again until the weekend," she told him. "But I can probably go four days next week if you want to."

"That's fine."

She started to get out of the car, and Ethan felt a surge of desperation. *Say something to her. Say anything.*

"Sandy."

She turned back.

"About last night—"

She immediately held up her palm. "You know, Ethan, those words have already started one too many conversations between us. You've told me how you feel, so let's just leave it at that."

"But you never did tell me how you feel." He paused. "About me."

She turned away. "I don't want to go there, either."

"You said you might have been able to have sex with me in the beginning when I didn't mean anything to you." His heart was pounding wildly. "What do I mean to you now?"

"Come on. Ethan. I'd have to be a complete masochist to answer that question, wouldn't I?"

"Tell me."

She faced him, her expression hesitant at first. Then slowly it transformed into one that was stronger and bolder.

"Okay," she said. "You want the truth? Here's the truth. Your reputation doesn't even begin to describe the kind of man you are. You're smart, of course. And ambitious. And God knows you're attractive. But there's more to you than that. Something good and kind and compassionate that you try to hide, but it's there just the same, and every time those things come out, just being with you makes me feel good. At least, I feel good right up to the moment you throw up those walls and treat me like every other woman you've ever loved and left. Is that how you really feel about me? As if I'm just one more?"

"God, no."

"Then cut it out."

Ethan was speechless.

"In spite of the fact that you seem to have confidence all over the place, you're terribly conflicted about your work. About women. About life itself. And I just don't know why."

Suddenly she was looking at him in that sharp, intense

way she had, as if all of her senses were probing all of his, and he just didn't know what to say.

"That night you were picked up for reckless driving," she said, "why were you driving so fast?"

He felt a start of surprise. "Why are you asking about that?"

"Because you're not a man who likes to be out of control. Going ninety in a fifty-five is pretty much out of control."

Since the day he'd slammed his car into that tree, Ethan had tried to put the memory of it behind him, refusing to acknowledge it. But suddenly the heat in the car echoed the heat of that night until it seemed to surround him again. He felt the wind whipping past. Heard the voice of the woman in the seat beside him droning in his ear. Felt the same crushing need to escape.

"That was the same day the Randall verdict came back," he told Sandy. "And . . . I don't know. I guess I just wanted to get away."

"So you drove."

"Yes."

"Fast."

God, yes.

He remembered how he'd punched that accelerator, thinking that if he only went a little faster, somehow he could leave it all behind him. It had been an irrational thought, but nothing about that day had felt rational in the least.

"I left the courtroom after the verdict," he told Sandy, his voice sounding unreal, as if he were listening to somebody else relate the story. "I went to the bar across the street and had a couple of drinks. I picked up a woman, and we got in my car and headed out. I remember thinking, Just drive. Just drive until you're not thinking about it anymore."

"But you did your job. You got your client acquitted. Why was that so hard to think about?"

"Because he did it, Sandy. Thomas Randall was guilty."

There was a long silence, and then Sandy's voice, hushed with disbelief. "Did he tell you that?"

"He didn't have to. After all these years, I know. And I kept picturing that woman. Raped by that son of a bitch. He walked out of that courtroom a free man, and she's going to be living with what happened to her for the rest of her life. And it was all because I dredged up all kinds of background on her and found a way to use it, knowing I could, knowing that if I did, I'd win."

"You stayed within the law."

"To hell with the law! Damn it, I . . . " He let out a harsh breath. "Maybe I should have let it go. Maybe I should have left her past lying on the table and let the right thing happen."

"But you've said it before. It isn't your job to decide who's guilty and who isn't."

"But when I know—"

"You didn't know for sure. You still don't."

"I knew," he whispered. "I knew."

He sat there a long time, feeling the tension that knowledge brought. For so much of his career, he'd avoided thinking about it. It had been all about winning. But slowly, like a living, breathing, tangible thing that loomed larger with every day that passed, the guilt he felt had built to a critical mass that he couldn't ignore anymore.

"They always shake my hand after the trial," he said. "They thank me for keeping them out of prison, as if they're suddenly innocent just because I managed to make twelve gullible people believe they are."

All at once, he felt as if the weight of that were crushing him. He pictured the crimes of all the people over the years who he'd convinced a jury were innocent. How many times had he done his job so well that the jury got it wrong?

"You can't believe the horrific crimes I've seen," he said. "I've defended people who have done things you wouldn't believe. But I had to close my eyes to all of it. Because if I didn't . . ."

"You wouldn't have been able to defend them."

"Yes."

"They got fair trials because of you."

"They're walking around free because of me. And pretty soon, Vince Mulroney is liable to be walking around free, too."

"No. He'll get what's coming to him."

"Don't be so sure."

"Why not?"

"Because he called my father this morning looking for representation. And I think my father is actually going to take the case."

"What?"

"Yeah. Imagine that. According to my father, the porn business is quite lucrative, so he certainly has the means to pay for a quality defense."

"How do you feel about that?"

"How do I feel? The son of a bitch kidnapped a woman. He makes snuff films. But my father will very likely get him off. How do you *think* I feel?"

He made a sound of disgust and turned away again, gripping the armrest on the car door until his fingers turned white. He hated the very thought of that bastard walking free. But it was the game they played. His father played it with the best of them, and he'd taught his son to do the same.

"So why are you in practice with your father?" she asked. "Clearly you don't get along."

He thought about that for a long time. "I don't know," he whispered. "Not anymore."

"He was all you had as a kid."

"Yes."

"I imagine you grew up trying to please him."

He wanted to deny that, but he couldn't. It was the absolute truth.

"When I was younger," he said, "the only goals I had were ones that had come out of his mouth first. And then I joined his practice, learned the law according to Charles Millner, and then the years passed. . . ." He shrugged weakly. "And here I am."

"Were you lonely growing up?"

The question took him by surprise, because he'd never really thought about it. "Lonely? Not really. The live-in maids we had were usually pretty talkative."

"That's terrible."

He just shrugged. "You play the hand you're dealt."

"But with your mother gone—"

"I barely remember her."

"Which I would think would make things that much more painful. Why did she leave?"

"If you'd been married to my father, you'd have left, too."

"That's why she left him. I was asking why she left you. I mean, if there was a good reason—"

"No, actually, there wasn't. My mother married my father, cheated on him, embarrassed him, and then he paid her an exorbitant amount of money to leave town and never come back."

Sandy's mouth fell open. "And she took it?"

"Every penny. I didn't find out until years later. I confronted my father about it. He told me that yes, he'd done it, but that she had every opportunity to turn it down. He made it seem like it was a test, or something. He said since she was mercenary enough to take the money and leave her son behind, it meant that I was better off without her."

"I can't believe he offered her money to leave."

"He's a vindictive man. He did it just to get rid of her. But right or wrong, once the money was on the table, where I was concerned, she had a choice to make. She made it."

"God, Ethan . . ."

"I've got to hand it to her, though. At least that bargain with my father was one she lived up to."

Sandy sat back in her seat, staring at him with a compassion in her eyes that made him uncomfortable.

"I don't want your pity," he told her. "It's over and done with."

"Hardly."

"What?"

"No wonder you've closed yourself off. No wonder you keep people at arm's length. There are some things you never get over."

"Come on, Sandy. I'm well aware of the attachment issues that arise from early abandonment. I'm a textbook case. Throw in a father who was cold as ice, and I didn't stand much of a chance, did I?"

"No. You didn't."

"But you know what? I'm an adult now. And I'd have to be pretty damned pitiful to blame my actions on a mother who left me and a father who was never there to begin with. Who I've become is my own damned fault."

"Maybe," she said. "But when people let you down, when you think there's nobody at all you can trust, sticking around becomes a real risk, doesn't it?"

The truth was that he didn't know the first thing about relationships. He didn't know how to treat a woman like Sandy. And if he ever really opened up to her and she found out just how screwed up he really was, she could end up being the one to walk away, and he knew he'd never be able to stand that.

But for maybe the first time in his life, it was a risk he was willing to take.

"Sandy?"

"Yes?"

Suddenly his throat felt tight, and he could barely get the words out. But when looked at her beautiful face so full of understanding, he knew he couldn't stop now.

"If there's the slightest chance that I haven't blown this completely, if there's the slightest chance that someday I might get the opportunity to make love to you, when it's all over . . ."

"Yes?"

He turned to face her. "I'll stick around."

For several seconds, neither one of them said anything. Ethan was sure that it was too little, too late, that she had no intention of taking his hot-and-cold routine one more time.

"Is that a promise?" she asked.

"That's a promise."

She touched his arm, then moved her hand up to rest her palm against his face. When she leaned in and pressed her lips to his, he slid his hand beneath her cascade of sleek, dark hair, pulled her to him, and gave her a long, slow, sensual kiss, and when he finally eased away, her eyes were wide, her cheeks flushed. He couldn't remember any woman he'd held in his arms who looked at him like this, as if kissing him held meaning beyond the physical.

"Come inside with me," she whispered.

His heart went crazy with a kind of desire he'd never felt before. He honestly didn't know where this was going, but he wasn't going to presume anything. He just told himself that he was going to relish every moment he got to spend with her and let everything else take care of itself.

They got out of the car and walked through the backyard to her back porch. She unlocked the door and they went into the kitchen. She flicked the light switch.

Nothing happened.

"What's up?" Ethan said.

"I don't know. The bulb must be out."

Sandy walked carefully through the darkened room to the dining room and hit the switch there.

Still nothing.

"A lamp is still on in the living room," she said.

"Then it's probably just a breaker. Where's your breaker box?"

"In the laundry room."

They walked back through the kitchen. By the dim light coming in from the living room, Sandy grabbed a flashlight out of a drawer and they went into the laundry room. She held the flashlight while Ethan opened the breaker box.

"No breakers are thrown. There must be something wrong with the circuit. God only knows how this old place is wired. And judging from how hot it is in here, your air conditioner is probably on that same circuit."

Then Sandy flicked off the flashlight.

Before Ethan could turn around, he felt her hand against his back. She edged closer to him and slipped her arms around him, laying her cheek against his shoulder. She dragged her hands from his chest to his ribs to his waist, then lower to stroke his thighs.

"I want you," she whispered. "Right now."

Oh, God. Yes.

He turned around, and the second he did, she circled her arms around his neck and dove in for a kiss so electric that she practically lit up the darkened room all by herself. She was telling him loud and clear that she wanted it fast and hard and hot, and he couldn't wait to give it to her.

"That night in your kitchen," he said. "I wanted you so much I thought I'd go crazy."

"Whatever you wanted to do then," she said, breathing hard, "do it now."

Ethan kissed her again, consuming her with his tongue and lips in a kiss so rough and raw that he was afraid he might be bruising her, but she just moaned against his mouth and asked for more. He ran his hands down the curve of her back to her behind and dragged her up onto her toes, crushing her hard against his chest. Her abdomen met his groin, and she shimmied hard against him.

God in *heaven,* he'd never felt anything like this. Her excitement, her eagerness, her almost desperate need for him. And he felt exactly the same way about her.

Suddenly she backed away, grabbed his shirt, and yanked it off over his head. She murmured a quick apology for hurting the cut on his arm, but he didn't feel a second of pain. He countered by pulling her shirt off and unhooking her bra before her shirt even hit the floor. He swept her breasts up in a hard caress, relishing the feel of her flesh against his palms. She was beautiful. Perfect. Just as he imagined she would be.

Sandy reached for his belt. She undid it, and in record time she had his pants halfway down his thighs.

"Damn it," he muttered. "My shoes."

"Get on the washer."

He boosted himself onto the washer and Sandy quickly pulled his shoes off, then took hold of the hems of his pant legs and gave them a hard tug. She slid them off, turning them upside down as she did. He heard the metallic clack of a cell phone hitting the tile floor, mingling with the thunk of a wallet and the jingle of change, and he didn't care. He just wanted out of these clothes. Wanted to be naked against her. Wanted her *now.*

By the time he slid off the washer, she'd kicked her shoes aside and was pulling her jeans off. She'd barely shoved them away before he'd tangled his fingers in her hair and was pulling her to his lips again, loving the feel of her naked body pressed against his. Every second of the past few days when he'd thought about making love to her seemed to coalesce into this moment, until he wanted her with the desperation of a drowning man gasping for a breath of air.

"Bed," he murmured.

"Too far away."

Sandy pulled away suddenly, grabbed one of the two laundry baskets on top of the dryer, and turned it upside down, spilling the clean laundry onto the floor. She did the same with the other basket. Then she fell to her back in the middle of the pile of clothes, dragging him right down on top of her. He fumbled for his pants, grabbed a condom, and rolled it on, thankful that it was the one thing that hadn't fallen out of his pocket. A few seconds later he moved between her legs. He stopped and stared at her, brushing her hair way from her face and kissing her forehead, her cheek, her lips.

"I've wanted you from the first moment I walked into your house. I swear to God. From the very first moment."

"Then take me."

He slid inside her, and just that first thrust was enough to bring him near the edge. He stopped and took a deep breath, staring down at her.

"I want to take this slow, but . . ." He dropped his forehead against her shoulder and exhaled. "God, Sandy . . . I just don't know if I can—"

"Just do it, Ethan. Do it now. *Please.*"

She curled her legs around his hips, her arms around his neck, and encouraged him to continue. He began to move inside her again, slowly at first, then building speed and intensity. She tightened her inner muscles as he drove hard against her, and the room spun around him, tunneling down to a single vortex of feeling centered where his body joined with hers. She pulled him deep inside her, meeting every one of his thrusts with an upward thrust of her own.

Soon he felt her tense beneath him. Heard her sharp, ragged breathing. She held her breath and gripped his shoulders, and in the next instant she cried out with pleasure. And as she rocked her hips up to meet every stroke, she ripped a climax from so deep inside him he felt as if it were tearing him wide open.

"Sandy . . . oh, *God* . . ."

He didn't recognize his own voice. It sounded ragged and breathless, the voice of a man whose words weren't chosen but dragged right out of him. For several seconds he felt totally out of control, battered endlessly by a tidal surge of sensation so intense it was indescribable.

As the feeling began to dissolve, he moved slower, then slower yet, before finally stopping altogether. He fell against her, gasping for air, a shudder of utter satisfaction rolling through every muscle in his body. Sandy moved her palms over his back in soothing strokes as he slowly eased back to reality.

He slumped against her, breathing hard, the scent of a lemony fabric softener filling his nostrils. For a long time he couldn't speak. He just lay on top of her, needing to be close to her like this, needing to assure himself that she was flesh and blood and not some apparition created by his own wishful thinking.

Finally he shifted over, landing heavily on the pile of laundry beside her with a sigh of satisfaction. And as he lay there, he waited for that feeling he always got after he was with a woman, the slow dissociation he always experienced that was his mind's way of pushing her away so he could distance himself and leave.

It never came.

He felt no impatience to be gone. No fear eating away at him that if he stayed, he'd be up to his neck in somebody else's problems he didn't want to deal with.

Only complete and total contentment.

He turned and whispered in Sandy's ear, "Let's go upstairs."

She reached for the flashlight and they picked up everything that had fallen out of his pants in the heat of the moment, along with an unfortunate amount of dryer lint to go along with it. He stuffed everything back inside his pockets and followed Sandy up the stairs.

The entire second floor was enveloped in darkness, but Sandy lit the bedroom and bathroom with candles and they took a shower. Twenty minutes later they were back in her bedroom, opening the windows wide to let in whatever breeze might press its way through the hot summer night. Then they collapsed in bed in each other's arms.

"Do you mind the heat?" Sandy asked.

"No. The windows are open. It'll cool off."

"This is August," she said. "Probably not."

"I don't care," he said. "This is exactly where I want to be."

A comfortable silence stretched between them. A soft night breeze drifted through the window, billowing the curtains for a moment before they settled back to the window again.

"I think you were too hard on yourself earlier," Sandy said.

"About what?"

"Some of your not-guilty verdicts. The ones where you thought maybe they did it. Just think about all the innocent people who looked guilty whom you helped stay out of prison. That's a good thing. Something to be proud of."

But all he could think about was Thomas Randall. Paul McIntyre. Others, too. Those guilty people who were going to walk because he'd done his job too well. And it made him sick to his stomach.

"You also defended Alicia Simmons, didn't you?" Sandy asked.

"Yes."

"That was a horrible crime. A mother accused of killing her own child. Everyone was ready to send her straight to the electric chair. But you got her acquitted."

"Yes."

"What happened three years later?"

"Her husband confessed to the murder."

"That woman might have been executed if not for you. And there have been other innocent people. So many innocent people who have you to thank for giving them their lives back."

"And dozens more walking the street who are guilty."

"It's our judicial system, Ethan. You have nothing to apologize for. But if you hate what you're doing, then do something else."

"It's not that easy."

"Then just stop throwing away your talent on guilty people with deep pockets. It's a rare situation where you'd be forced to take a case you didn't want to. Unless I miss my guess, you've got all the money you'll ever need. Take only the cases you believe in."

"I don't know how to do that."

"What?"

"Believe."

"Do you believe Josh is innocent?"

"Yes."

"But you said you don't know how to do that."

"I don't. *You* believe in him." He paused, then slowly turned to face her. "And I believe in you."

She slid her hand into his and gave it a squeeze. "He's innocent, Ethan. You can believe that."

"God in heaven, I hope you're right."

There was another long silence, and for a moment he thought she might have fallen asleep. Then he heard her voice in the darkness.

"Ethan?"

"Yes?"

"You don't know your neighbors. You don't get along with your father. You have no brothers or sisters. Who do you turn to when things get rough?"

"In the past, no one."

"And in the present?"

"You."

He couldn't believe he'd said it, and by the way she tensed in his arms, he had a terrible sense that he'd said the wrong thing.

"I just meant that lately some things have been eating at me," he said, "and we've spent a lot of time together, so naturally—"

"It's all right." She rose on one elbow and looked down at him, her dark eyes deep and endless in the dim candlelight. "Believe it or not, you're not the only one who's lonely."

"But you've got friends and family. Lots of them."

"Yeah, but it's nothing like . . ."

When her voice trailed off, he reached for her hand. "Like what?"

"Like this," she whispered.

A bittersweet longing entered her eyes, one that he knew came from having so much good in her life and feeling guilty for wanting more.

"Most of the time it's easy not to think about it," she said. "I get so busy with other things. But then I come home alone to this big, empty house. Okay, technically it's not empty, but furniture and rugs and lamps and a cat . . ." She sighed. "They're really lousy substitutes."

"For what?"

"For a man like you."

Sandy eased back down onto her pillow. Ethan pulled her into his arms. He sighed with relief, thinking about how good it felt to be with her, to let down his guard, to have there be no pretense between them. She understood who he really was, looking beyond the obvious and seeing something inside him that he'd never even seen in himself.

The lethargy that came from making love, mingling with the summer heat and Sandy's soft caresses, sent him drifting off to sleep. He stirred some time later, and for a moment he wasn't sure if he'd actually slept or not. Then he turned to the clock on the nightstand and saw that two hours had passed, and he realized that he must have.

At the foot of the bed, Sandy's cat was sleeping, curled into a tight ball. Sandy lay beside Ethan, her fist tucked beneath her chin, a strand of hair lying across her cheek. He brushed it away, letting his fingertips linger against her face for a moment before closing his eyes again.

Then he realized what must have awakened him.

He heard a soft crackling noise outside the open window. A little disoriented, he opened his eyes again and listened more carefully. But it wasn't until he raised his head and smelled smoke in the air that he realized what it was.

Fire.

chapter seventeen

Ethan threw back the covers and leaped out of bed, waking Sandy with a start. He raced to the window, muttered a curse, then wheeled around and shouted at her.

"Sandy! Get up! The house is on fire!" He grabbed his pants and threw his shirt to her. "Get dressed!"

Her heart beating wildly, she jumped out of bed and slid into his shirt, then grabbed a pair of panties from her dresser. Ethan yanked on his pants, then jerked open the bedroom door and looked out.

"There's some smoke, but I don't see fire," he said. "But we've got to go now!"

He ran back toward her. She'd barely put on the panties before he was grabbing her arm and pulling her toward the door.

"Wait a minute! Oscar!"

She jerked her hand loose and turned back to grab the cat off the bed. She slung him over her shoulder, and Ethan hustled her out the bedroom door. He held on to her tightly, half leading, half dragging her down the stairs.

Several steps down, smoke swelled up at them, and she felt the burn in her throat as she breathed. By the time they reached the foot of the stairs, smoke surrounded them. Ethan yanked open the front door and hurried Sandy down the steps and into the yard. And when she finally turned back around, she saw flames licking up over the top of the roof

from the back of the house and smoke billowing toward the
night sky.

Ethan pulled out his cell phone and dialed 911. She heard
him talking to the operator, and then he clicked the phone
off.

"Somebody already saw the fire and reported it," he told
her. "The fire department is on its way."

Sandy just stood there, staring at her burning house. "My
house. Oh, God, Ethan, my house . . ."

"I know, sweetheart. They'll be here any minute."

Ethan pulled her up next to him, hugging her tightly, and
all she could do was stare at the spectacle through tear-filled
eyes.

Seconds later she heard sirens, and soon a hook and ladder
made its way around the corner. It pulled to the curb and firefighters leaped into action. One of the men rushed up to
them. "Is everybody out?"

"Yes," Ethan said.

"Stay put," he said, as he hurried off to help the other men.

Sandy hugged her cat tightly and curled into Ethan's arms,
both of them watching helplessly as the firefighters rushed to
get the blaze under control.

The next twenty minutes passed in a blur. The sight of the
flames, the smell of the smoke, the faint sprinkling of ash in
the air—all of it put Sandy's stomach into turmoil. Neighbors came out of their houses and stood alongside them as
the firefighters did their job. One of her neighbors took Oscar
and said she'd keep him as long as Sandy needed her to,
while the others all offered to help any way they could once
the fire was out. But it was only Ethan standing next to her,
holding her tightly and whispering reassuring words, that
kept her from falling apart completely.

Fortunately, the firefighters had arrived quickly enough
that it didn't take long to get the fire under control, and soon
it was extinguished. One of them came over to tell Ethan and

Sandy that the damage had been minimal. But when he escorted them around to the backyard and Sandy saw the charred wood and broken windows, tears still came to her eyes.

"I know it looks bad," the firefighter said, "but there isn't much damage. It didn't get up into the attic, so it was pretty much contained to the back of the house. There's going to be more damage from smoke and water than anything else."

"One of the circuits was out earlier in the evening," Ethan said. "Could it have been an electrical fire?"

"In an old house like this, I'd say that's likely. A short circuit can set insulation on fire. It can smolder for hours before finally igniting."

"Why didn't my smoke alarms go off?" Sandy asked.

"Are they electric or battery operated?"

"Electric."

"They must have been on the circuit that was out. You're lucky you woke up. Sorry this happened, folks. I'm just glad we got it out as quickly as we did."

The firefighter joined the others as they put away their equipment. Sandy assured the neighbors still hovering around that she was fine for now, and they began to disperse, too.

"We can stay at my place tonight," Ethan told Sandy. "Then we'll come back tomorrow and go from there."

"I have insurance," she said, fighting tears. "It's fixable, right?"

"Absolutely. It'll be good as new again before you know it."

She nodded, knowing she had a lot ahead of her to deal with, but all she wanted to do right now was crawl into bed with Ethan and get some sleep.

"Sandy?"

At the sound of the familiar voice behind her, she spun around, surprised to see her brother walking across the yard.

"Dave?"

"What the hell happened?" he said.

He was in uniform, which meant he was working, so she knew how he'd heard about the fire.

"I don't know," she told him. "They think it might have been an electrical fire."

"Are you hurt?"

"No."

"Smoke inhalation?"

"No. I told you I'm fine."

Then Dave turned to Ethan. Sandy watched his gaze go to Ethan's bare chest, then pan over to the man's shirt she was wearing.

"Sandy? What the hell is going on here?"

"Dave, please—"

"Is this what I think it is?"

"Yes. It's what you think it is. And the last thing I need right now is you passing judgment on me."

He turned to glare at Ethan. "You're not the one I'm passing judgment on."

Ethan stepped forward, and Sandy clamped a hand onto his arm. "Ethan, don't."

"You're coming to stay with Lisa and me," Dave told Sandy.

"No, I'm not."

"Then where are you going?"

"I'll be staying with Ethan."

"I don't think so."

"That's up to Sandy to decide," Ethan said. "Not you."

Dave's eyes narrowed dangerously. He was the most even-tempered of her three brothers, but Sandy knew when he was on the verge of reaching the boiling point. She grabbed his arm and walked him several paces away, looking back over her shoulder to silently plead with Ethan to stay put.

She faced her brother. "Dave, let it go."

"I will. As soon as you explain what the hell is going on between you two."

"I think that should be obvious," she said, unable to keep the quaver out of her voice. "And it should be equally obvious that it's late and my house is in a shambles and I'm not in any mood to watch you fight with him."

Dave's angry gaze faltered.

"It should also be obvious that there are plenty of things you don't understand about Ethan or I wouldn't be seeing him."

"Like what?"

"I'm not going to stand here and explain that to you!"

Dave expelled a harsh breath.

"Dave? Have you ever known me to make a truly stupid decision where a man is concerned?"

He looked away. "No."

"And I'm not making one now. Please let the family know what happened and tell them I'll talk to them tomorrow."

She started to walk away but he pulled her back. "Should I also tell them where you're staying?"

She couldn't stand this. She didn't take any crap from her brothers, but she didn't like fighting with them, either. Especially at a time like this.

"Look," she said, "I know you don't understand, and I can't explain it to you right now. But please trust me when I tell you that what we have together is a good thing, will you?"

Dave stared at her a long time, his lips tight with worry. Finally he rubbed the back of his neck and sighed with resignation. "Actually, Sandy, I haven't got any choice but to trust you."

"No choice?"

"None at all. See, I'm not really the sensible one of the family. You are."

Sandy took a step back and gave her brother a hug, and

she breathed a sigh of relief when he closed his arms around her.

"Thanks, Dave. I can always count on you to be reasonable."

"You mean a pushover. But don't think Alex is going to be."

"I know. I'll deal with him when the time comes."

"What can I do to help you?"

"Nothing tonight. I'll give you a call tomorrow, okay?"

"Yeah. And I'll check with the fire department tomorrow. They should have some word on what caused this."

She nodded.

Dave glanced across the yard, letting out a sigh of exasperation. "Ethan Millner? Are you *sure* about that?"

"We'll have a long talk someday soon."

"I'm going to insist on that. Call me if you need anything."

"Thanks, Dave."

Sandy walked back to Ethan. He slipped his arm around her shoulders and led her to his car.

A few minutes later, they arrived at his town house, and Sandy felt as if an entire lifetime had passed in one night. They walked up the stairs to his bedroom. Ethan pulled the change from his pockets and tossed it in the ceramic jar on top of his dresser, laying his cell phone and wallet down beside it. Then he turned around and took Sandy in his arms, holding her close, running his hands in long, comforting strokes up and down her back.

"I'm glad you came home with me," he said.

"Why would you think I wouldn't?"

"Would I sound insecure if I told you that I was afraid your brother was going to change your mind about that?"

"I'm sorry about Dave," she said. "I'm sorry he treated you that way."

"I'm used to it."

"Please don't say that."

"I have an adversarial relationship with a lot of cops. Your brothers are no exception."

"I'm sorry to say that Dave's the reasonable one of the three."

"I'll accept a certain amount of animosity, because to tell you the truth, a lot of it is probably well-founded. But there's a line I won't let them cross."

"What's that?"

"I won't let them come between us."

Suddenly the events of the past several days seemed to coalesce into the most amazing feeling inside Sandy, and she realized just how important their relationship had become to him.

Maybe as important as it had become to her.

As soon as Ethan arrived at his office the next morning, he picked up the phone and arranged for carpenters to board up the broken windows in Sandy's house. Then he made appointments with contractors to assess the damage and make the repairs. And those repairs were going to include rewiring the entire house so something like this would never happen again.

Even though he'd encouraged Sandy to stay at his town house today, she told him she was going to call Val and ask her to bring over some clothes for her so she could go to work. In the end, he knew she was right. After a disaster like this, Sandy needed to be with people, to take comfort from the web of relationships she'd built throughout her life—her friends, her neighbors, her family. By the time he left home that morning to go to work, she'd already received a dozen calls on her cell phone from people who had heard what happened and were eager to help her any way they could.

Ethan sat back in his chair, thinking about that, trying to comprehend what it must be like. As he imagined what would happen if his own home caught fire and burned, he realized that he could name the people who would give a damn on the fingers of one hand.

All at once, he heard a commotion outside his office. The door swung open and Alex DeMarco strode into the room. Gina was hot on his heels. Ethan came to his feet immediately.

"Are you deaf?" Gina said. "I told you he's not seeing anyone!"

Alex came to a halt in front of Ethan's desk. "I need to have a word with you, Millner."

"Hey, you," Gina said. "If you don't get out of here, I'm calling the cops!"

Alex turned and glared at her. "I *am* a cop."

"It's okay, Gina," Ethan said, his eyes never leaving Alex. "Just leave us alone."

She eyed Alex up and down. "Are you sure about that?"

"Yes. Everything's fine. Just close the door behind you when you leave."

Gina gave Alex one last wary look and slipped out the door.

Ethan turned to Alex. "What do you want?"

"I heard what's going on. I want you to stay away from Sandy."

"Come on, DeMarco. 'Don't touch my sister'? What century are you living in?"

Alex gave him a look of sheer contempt. "Don't mess with me, Millner. I could take you down, and you know it."

"Maybe, but you'd lose a few teeth before I hit the ground. Is it worth it?"

Alex circled Ethan's desk, but Ethan met him halfway, forcing him to stop in his tracks or run right over him. Alex had a good two inches in height and thirty pounds on him, but he'd be damned if he was going to let him throw his weight around like this.

"Have you thought to ask her what *she* wants?" Ethan said.

"Sandy's naïve. She always assumes people's motives are on the up-and-up. She doesn't know how to deal with a guy like you."

"You patronizing son of a bitch. Is that what you really think of her? That she's a helpless little fool who doesn't know what's right for her?"

"She sees good in people, Millner. Apparently even in you. Sometimes it blinds her to the bad. I want you to stay away from her."

"I'll do what I want with Sandy, when I want to. You can't stop me, and you damn well know it."

"I swear, if you hurt her in any way, I'm going to be all *over* you!"

"I have no intention of hurting her!"

"Oh, yeah? If you play her like you do other women, that's exactly what's going to happen."

"Forget other women. We're talking about Sandy."

"And that's a distinction to you?"

"Hell, yes, it is!"

"I love my sister, Millner—"

"Damn it, *so do I*!"

Alex recoiled, and for several seconds neither man spoke. The office was deathly quiet, tension hanging thickly in the air between them.

"For the record, Alex, everything you've ever said about me is the absolute truth. I'd do anything to win a case. Lie, cheat . . . it didn't matter. As long as it was marginally within the law, and as long as it helped me win."

He inched closer to Alex, meeting him eye-to-eye.

"But let me tell you something. I'm in love with Sandy. I don't deserve her, and chances are that you're going to get exactly what you want in the end, because she'll figure that out soon enough and she'll be gone. But until then, don't you ever again suggest that I'd do anything to hurt her. If it came down to it, I'd protect her with my *life*. Do you understand?"

"Love?" Alex said. "I don't think a guy like you knows the meaning of the word. Consider yourself warned, Millner. Hurt her, and you'll have to deal with me."

Alex turned and strode to the door, yanked it open, and left the office. Ethan sat down in his chair, stunned by the power of his own words.

He was in love with Sandy. He'd said it loud and clear and meant every word. And who had he said it to? Alex, of all people.

"Hey."

Ethan looked up to see Gina at his door. "Not now, Gina."

As usual, she ignored him, coming into his office and closing the door behind her.

"Gina?" he said wearily. "There's a concept that seems to have escaped you. I'm the boss, and you're the employee. If I tell you to go away, you're supposed to go away."

"Only if my paycheck is in jeopardy. Is it?"

"Don't tempt me."

"Interesting conversation you had with Sandy's brother."

"You heard."

"Yes."

He looked up at her. "All of it?"

"All of it."

Gina sat down in the chair in front of his desk, tilting her head with a knowing smile.

"She's the one, isn't she?"

The one. Ethan knew what she meant by that, and no matter what he'd told Alex, he automatically started to deny it.

Then he realized how foolish that was.

He shook his head helplessly. "I don't understand it, Gina. It's been so short a time, but somehow I *know.* I didn't even think she was out there. I didn't think she existed. Then I turned around, and there she was."

"You told her brother you love her. Do you?"

"I think Alex was right. I'm not even sure I know the meaning of the word. I haven't got a clue what it's supposed to feel like."

"Like the sun rises and sets with every word she speaks? Like just looking at her leaves you breathless? Like you're going to die every minute that you're away from her?"

Ethan sighed. "Must you be so dramatic?"

"I asked you if that's what it feels like."

Someday he was going to fire this woman. He swore he was going to boot her right out the door on the grounds of gross insubordination, blatant disobedience, and total disregard for authority. And after he did that, he was going to smash that mirror she insisted on holding up in front of him, the one that forced him to look at himself.

Or maybe he'd simply thank her.

"Yes," he said with a sigh of resignation. "That's exactly what it feels like. And it makes me sound like some kind of lovestruck idiot. Does that make you happy?"

Gina smiled. "No, but it makes you happy, and I wasn't sure I'd ever see that." Her smile faded. "Now I'm being serious, Ethan. Most of us wait our entire lives to feel the way you do right now. Please don't take it lightly."

She had no idea how pointless that warning was. Ethan had never been more serious about anything—or anyone—in his entire life.

The phone rang. Gina leaned over his desk and picked it up. "Ethan Millner's office." She smiled. "Yeah, Sandy. He's here. Just a minute."

Gina handed Ethan the phone, and to his surprise, she didn't even wait for him to tell her three times to leave before she exited his office with a knowing look and a little wave of her fingertips.

"Hi, Sandy," Ethan said. "How are you?"

"I'm fine. But I'm not so sure about Josh."

"What do you mean?"

"He just called me. He wants to see us. Both of us."

"What does he want?"

"He wouldn't say, but he sounded upset. Can you get away right now?"

Ethan checked his watch. "I'll meet you at the jail in twenty minutes."

chapter eighteen

As a guard escorted Ethan and Sandy into the small visitation room, Ethan could sense her anxiety. He'd refused to speculate about what the kid might want, because he couldn't imagine what might be going through his mind. But if Sandy said he sounded upset, chances were that whatever he had to tell them wasn't going to be good news.

Then the door opened and the guard escorted Josh into the room. His face was tight and drawn, and he refused to look at either of them.

The moment he sat down, Sandy leaned across the table and took his hand. "Josh? Are you all right?"

Still he stared down at the table. "Yeah. I'm—" He stopped short, took a deep, shaky breath, then shook his head. "No. I'm not."

"Josh," Ethan said, "If you've got something to say, you'd better say it."

The kid finally looked up, glancing nervously between Ethan and Sandy.

"Go ahead, Josh," Sandy said. "You can tell us."

He turned to Ethan. "The first day you came here . . ."

"Yes?"

"I lied."

Ethan felt a stab of foreboding. "About what?"

"Mr. Clemmons was right. He did see me in Laura Williams's backyard the night of the murder."

Sandy leaned away from him, her eyes flying open wide. "You were there?"

"Yes. But Sandy, you've got to believe me. I swear to God I didn't murder her. I was in her yard, but I never got anywhere near her house that night!"

"You lied to me," Ethan said.

"I was afraid if I didn't then everyone would think I killed her for sure!"

"What the hell were you doing there?"

"Just . . . just hanging out."

Ethan leaned in, anger rumbling inside him. "Define 'hanging out.'"

"I was sitting with a guy I know in the barn at the back of Laura's property."

Ethan blinked. "What did you say?"

"I said a friend of mine and I were hanging out that night in Laura Williams's barn."

"Wait a minute," Ethan said. "You were with somebody before the murder?"

"Yeah. The barn is kind of hidden away. This guy showed it to me, and we went there a couple of times."

"Who is this guy?"

"His name is Aaron."

"Last name?"

"I don't know."

"So you don't know him well?"

"He's just somebody I run into every once in a while."

"Keep talking."

"We were sitting out in the barn. Aaron kept trying to get me to stay a little longer, so I did. And then . . . then he decided that he wanted to go down the hill."

"What do you mean?"

Josh stared down at his hands. "He wanted to . . ." He exhaled. "Three or four days before the murder, Aaron talked me into going down by Laura's house. The blinds were open in her back room. She has a hot tub in there, and . . ."

"And what?" Ethan said.

"We peeked in at her and her girlfriend."

Ethan stared at him in disbelief. "You *what*?"

"I know it was stupid. I never should have let him talk me into it."

"Kid, that alone will get you thrown in jail. What the *hell* were you thinking?"

"We only did it once. And he wanted to do it again that night. He started down there, but I ran after him and talked him out of it."

"So the night of the murder, you weren't anywhere near the house."

"No. When I looked at my watch, it was almost ten o'clock. I knew I needed to get home fast, so I left the barn and started walking along the fence on the west side of Laura's property. I'd planned to walk out to the street in front of her house. I knew I could get home faster if I went that way rather than going all the way back across the creek and around. About halfway there, though, I saw headlights shining through to the backyard from the driveway."

Sandy turned to Ethan. "It was nearly ten when we stopped to catch the cat. That was probably my car when I pulled into Laura's driveway."

"I knew I was violating my curfew," Josh went on, "so when I saw the headlights, I was afraid somebody was going to see me. So instead of going out to the street in front of the house, I jumped the side fence into the Clemmons's yard next door, ran back into the woods, and climbed over the back fence. But it took me longer to get home that way, so I didn't make it until ten fifteen. But I swear I never went anywhere near the house that night."

"What happened to Aaron?" Ethan asked.

"He went over the fence behind Laura's barn and back to his truck parked by the Pecan Street bridge."

"So neither one of you ever got near Laura's house that night."

"That's right."

"What time did you first see Aaron?"

"About eight thirty."

"And you went straight to the barn?"

"Yes."

"And stayed there until almost ten o'clock."

"Yes."

"Why didn't you tell me this earlier?"

"Because I thought if I admitted to being anywhere near there that night, I didn't stand a chance. I guess I thought that since Mr. Clemmons is an old guy, then maybe somebody would think his eyesight was messed up, or something. Hell, I don't know what I thought."

Ethan sat back in his chair. "Well, you really screwed up, kid."

Josh stared down at the table.

"If you'd told me the truth in the beginning, I may have seen a way out of this sooner."

Josh jerked his head up. "What?"

"That other kid is your alibi."

For the count of five, dead silence fell over the room.

"But if he tells somebody I was there—"

"In the barn an acre away," Ethan said, "not in the house."

"But Aaron's got a record, too. Who's going to believe him?"

"All we need is reasonable doubt. If we can find Aaron and he can verify that he was with you during the hour and a half preceding the murder, a jury will be forced to take that into consideration."

"I barely know the guy," Josh said. "Why would he put his neck on the line for me?"

"Because I'm going to persuade him to."

"But they'll just try to say that I murdered her earlier and then met Aaron."

"I saw the body, kid. The blood was fresh. The forensic evidence is going to place the time of death well within that hour and a half window when you say you were with Aaron."

Josh swallowed hard, hope edging into his eyes.

"Ethan?" Sandy said. "If the other kid backs up his story, will it be enough to get Josh acquitted?"

"It's possible. Now, if that looks like a winning strategy, the DA will likely propose the theory that Josh and Aaron were both burglarizing the house that night. That they both committed the murder, and now they're covering for each other. But the minute the prosecution goes there, I'll know I have them on the run."

He took out a pen and paper, then turned to Josh. "Tell me everything you know about Aaron."

Josh gave him a physical description, then told Ethan he was nineteen years old and he lived somewhere near Sandy's neighborhood in an apartment complex that he thought had "Oak" somewhere in its name. He also knew Aaron had been arrested at least once for breaking and entering.

Ethan jotted down the information. "Is that all you can tell me?"

"That's it."

"Are you sure?"

"Yeah. I told you I don't know the guy very well. He may even try to pretend that he doesn't know me so he doesn't have to get involved."

"Let's worry about that when the time comes." Ethan finished jotting down a few more notes, then looked up at Josh. "Okay. You haven't given me much to go on, but it's something. With luck, we'll be able to find this kid and go from there."

Josh nodded, but he still looked scared.

"Josh," Sandy said, "this is good news."

"I know. But until I'm walking out of here . . . I just don't want to get my hopes up, you know?"

Sandy reached across the table and patted him on the hand. "Ethan's the best. He's going to help you. You just hang in there, okay?"

He nodded.

"Come on, Sandy," Ethan said. "We'd better go."

As they rose to leave, Ethan thought of one more question he wanted an answer to.

"Josh?"

"Yeah?"

"What finally made you come clean?"

"Sandy."

Sandy looked surprised. "What?"

"You told me once to always tell the truth and nothing bad would happen to me. And I got to thinking about how I'd lied, and about how much you'd done for me, and finally . . ." The kid's eyes filled with tears. "Finally I just couldn't take it anymore."

Sandy gave Josh a hug, and she and Ethan left the building, walking to where Sandy had parked her car in a lot adjacent to the jail.

"I can't believe it," Sandy said as they walked. "Ralph Clemmons was right after all. He really did see Josh in Laura's backyard that night."

"Looks that way."

"What about the fact that he was down by Laura's house a few nights before the murder?"

"It has nothing to do with where he was on the night of the murder itself. And since I won't be putting him on the stand, even if the DA wants to ask if he's ever been near Laura's house, he won't get the chance. But this isn't over by a long shot, Sandy. We've still got to find that other kid and get him to testify."

"You can do that."

"Then a jury has to believe that he's credible."

"You can make them believe it."

"And they also have to believe that his testimony adds up to reasonable doubt."

"You can make that happen, too."

"You seem to have a lot of faith in me."

They reached her car, and Sandy turned and smiled up at him. "Why shouldn't I? After all, rumor has it that you're the very best there is."

That smile was enough to make Ethan wish they could go back to his town house right now and hide out in his bedroom for the rest of the day.

"I have to be in court in thirty minutes," he told her, "but I'm going to phone Gina with this and see what she can find out for me. She's a regular bloodhound when I need information. Maybe I'll have something by tomorrow."

"If she comes up empty, let me know and I'll see if Val can help."

Ethan nodded. "When will you be home tonight?"

"By six thirty or so."

"I'll be home earlier, so I'll pick up some dinner on my way."

He leaned in and gave her a good-bye kiss, intending it to be a short, sweet one, but suddenly he couldn't stop himself from making it long and spicy. Then he opened her car door and she slipped inside. He watched as she drove away, and he didn't stop watching until her car had disappeared from sight.

He turned around to walk back to his car, only to see a man standing across the parking lot beside a late-model Lexus, watching him.

Charles Millner.

Ethan stopped short. He could read that expression even at

this distance, and it told him that his father had been standing there for quite some time.

Long enough, anyway.

Ethan walked to his car, got inside, and drove out of the parking lot, knowing for a fact that where Sandy was concerned, his father wasn't through chastising him yet. But he also knew he was long past caring about anything the old man had to say.

As Sandy was driving along Briarwood Boulevard to return to her shop, her cell phone rang. She dug through her purse, grabbed her phone, and looked at the caller ID. Fay Moreno. In her capacity as a crime analyst, she'd never called just to chat, and Sandy wondered what was going on.

"Hello?"

"Hey, Sandy. It's Fay."

"Hi, Fay. What's up?"

"Heard about the fire at your house last night. Any idea yet what caused it?"

"No. I haven't heard. But right before the fire, one of the electrical circuits in my house went dead, so the firefighters think it might have been an electrical problem."

"Oh. That's good."

"Good?"

"Yeah. I mean, this is probably nothing, but I wanted to let you know anyway."

"Let me know what?"

"As soon as I heard about your fire, I checked some statistics. There have been three fires in your neighborhood in the last five years that were suspicious in origin. One of those was actually ruled arson, but no arrest was made."

Sandy blinked with surprise. "Are you telling me you think somebody torched my house?"

"Nope. Not at all. I'm just telling you there's a pattern. For a neighborhood your size, not a substantial one, but a pattern nonetheless. It's just something that warrants looking into."

"I heard about two men who were killed in a fire right after I moved into the neighborhood three years ago," Sandy said.

"Yep. That was one of the suspicious ones."

"But I haven't heard about the others."

"They happened before you moved there."

"Can you give me the three addresses?"

Fay gave them to her, and Sandy jotted them down on the back of a receipt she pulled out of her purse.

"You know your neighborhood," Fay said, "so if you think there's any kind of connection among the houses, will you let me know?"

"Sure. Thanks, Fay."

Sandy hung up and started to return the receipt to her purse. Then she stopped and stared at the addresses. Nothing came to mind as far as a connection, but still she wondered. What had happened to those fire-damaged houses?

She started her car, pulled out of the parking lot, and headed to her neighborhood. She drove past the first house. It had been rebuilt to its original period look. Then she drove by the next two, and a sick feeling rose in her stomach. They'd both been torn down, with brand-new houses built in their places. And Sandy recognized the builder of both of them.

Waymark Properties.

chapter nineteen

Sandy pulled to the curb, grabbed her cell phone, and dialed Fay's office.

"Okay, Fay. This is weird. Waymark Properties has been going after houses in my neighborhood for years now. They want to tear down old houses and put up brand-new ones. Several people have sold to them, but most of us wouldn't even consider it. Waymark built houses at two of the three addresses where there were suspicious fires. I know it sounds a little crazy, but do you think they could have had anything to do with those fires?"

"Hmm." Fay was silent for a moment. "I don't know. Seems like a stretch. They could just be opportunists. If they're actively canvassing that neighborhood looking for houses to buy and demolish, they'd be the first to jump on a fire-damaged house."

Fay was right. That made sense.

"Have you been approached by Waymark to sell your house?" Fay asked.

"Just with flyers on my door and mailings like everybody else. That's all."

"To tell you the truth, Sandy, I wouldn't give it a second thought, particularly if the firefighters thought your fire was an accident. But I'll do some checking into it for you on the off chance that there's a pattern in any other neighborhoods. It may take me a day or two, but I'll get back to you."

"Thanks, Fay. I appreciate it."

Even though it was probably meaningless, Sandy phoned Ethan and let him know what Fay had told her. He came to attention immediately, telling her not to go back to her house for any reason until they could determine for sure that the fire had been accidental. She knew his concern was unfounded, but still she loved hearing it in his voice.

It was nearly six thirty before she pulled into the parking lot next to Ethan's town house. Just the prospect of seeing him again tonight had kept her spirits up all day and pushed thoughts of her damaged house to the back of her mind. He had arranged for insurance estimates and a cleanup crew to come by tomorrow, which meant it wouldn't be long before it was as good as new again. And now that it looked as if they might be able to find a kid who could provide Josh's alibi, it wouldn't be long before he'd be out of jail and everything would be back to normal there, too.

She used the key Ethan had given her and opened the front door. Once inside she put her purse down on the entry table. When she turned around, she looked at the staircase and was surprised to see something on the bottom step.

A single bird-of-paradise.

She set her purse down and picked up the flower, then noticed that there were more—one on every third step.

Intrigued, she moved slowly up the stairs, following the trail of flowers, picking them up one by one. When she reached the second floor, they led her down the hall, into Ethan's bedroom, and finally to his bathroom. She heard the whir of a motor, and as she stepped inside, she realized the Jacuzzi tub was going. Half a dozen candles rested on the counter, their warm glow mingling with the steam drifting up from the tub, making the room look soft and dreamy.

Then she felt hands on her shoulders.

She gave a little start of surprise, only to realize they were Ethan's hands, strong but gentle, moving down her arms and back up again. He edged closer, wrapping his arms around her waist from behind and kissing her neck. She clutched the flowers, her heart beating madly with anticipation.

"I didn't hear you come up behind me," she said.

"I didn't intend for you to."

"The flowers are beautiful."

"Sorry I gave your competition the business. But I wanted it to be a surprise."

His voice was low and sensually charged, his breath hot against her ear. She dropped her head back against his shoulder, her eyes drifting closed. "I had no idea you were such a romantic."

"I want to give you the best of everything. Flowers and candlelight are only the beginning."

He kissed his way along her neck, ending with a tiny nip at her earlobe. "I brought home dinner," he went on, "but I was hoping you wouldn't mind waiting."

"Of course not."

He took the flowers from her and deposited them in a vase full of water that he already had sitting on the counter. When he turned back around, she saw that he'd removed his tie, but he was still wearing slacks and a dress shirt.

She walked over to stand in front of him, then reached up to unbutton his shirt. The cotton fabric felt smooth and crisp beneath her fingers, and as she bared his chest one button at a time, he stood stock-still, his tension revealed only by the rise and fall of his chest with deep, silent breaths. She unbuttoned one of his cuffs, then the other, and slid the shirt off his shoulders, stunned once again by his beautiful body beneath it.

As his shirt dropped to the floor, she touched her fingertips to his upper chest, dragged them down a few inches, then placed her palms flat against him. Slowly she leaned in and kissed a spot just beneath his collarbone.

He exhaled. "God, Sandy . . ."

Tucking his hand beneath her chin, he tilted her head up and kissed her warmly and leisurely, as if he had all night to do it. Then he backed away and unbuttoned her shirt. He slid his palms beneath it near her neck, then moved them outward, pushing the garment off her shoulders. She closed her eyes, her heart beating wildly, as he traced his palms along her arms, following the descent of the shirt. When his hands reached her elbows, she straightened her arms and let the shirt fall to the floor behind her. She took off her bra, and he slid her jeans off just as deliberately as he had her shirt.

When she kicked them aside and stood naked in front of him, he stared down at her, not moving a muscle. He just stared. Last night they'd made love in the dark, and she'd still been in bed when he left this morning. By the light of half a dozen candles, he could see her body more clearly, and suddenly she felt very self-conscious.

"Ah," she said, "I see you've noticed that 'supermodel' wasn't one of my possible career choices."

"I've noticed," he said, "that I can't seem to take my eyes off you."

"I'm thinking I should blow out a few of the candles."

He looked at her with an expression of astonishment. "God, Sandy, don't you know you're absolutely beautiful? I can't believe that men aren't lining up around the block to tell you that."

"I bet you say that to all the girls."

"No," he said, his voice low and sincere. "Never."

He kissed her gently, then backed away from her, but only to get as naked as she was. Then he took her by the hand and they got into the tub. To her surprise, though, Ethan settled into the opposite end from where she sat. Then he surprised her again by reaching beneath the water and finding her foot. He pulled it up to the surface and began to rub it, pressing deep strokes of his thumb against the arch. She settled back against the side of the tub with a blissful moan as the water bubbled up around them. Never in her life had a man rubbed her feet, and it shocked her just how good it felt.

After a while, he lowered that foot into the water and picked up her other one. The water sloshed as he lifted it to the surface and worked the same kind of magic on it, too. She stared at him through heavy-lidded eyes, watching steam rise from the hot water to adhere dark locks of hair to his forehead, and in the dim candlelight, water droplets shimmered on his shoulders.

He lowered her foot to the water and held out his hand. She put her hand in his, and he pulled her toward him, turning her around as she floated through the water until her back was to his chest. He settled her between his legs, wrapping one arm around her waist and using his other hand to sweep her hair away from her neck. She felt his erection pressing hard against the small of her back, proof positive that he was anything but relaxed himself.

His lips brushed her ear. "I couldn't wait to get home. Just the thought that you were going to be here tonight . . ."

He kissed her just below her right ear, making the nerves along her spine quiver. He stroked her arm, up and down. The total relaxation she felt was compounded by her buoyancy in the warm water, and she felt as if she were floating.

He found the soap with one hand, dipped it in the water, then brought his hands together in front of her and lathered them. He set the bar down, then placed his palms against her chest.

"Lean against me," he told her. "Close your eyes and relax."

She tilted her head back against his shoulder, and he began to move his hands over her breasts, his slick, sudsy fingers tripping across her nipples. At the same time, he leaned in and kissed her neck, sending hot shivers racing down her spine. Beneath the water she placed her hands against his thighs, stroking them back and forth. The candles on the counter flickered softly, casting a golden glow around the room.

"This wasn't supposed to happen," she murmured.

"What?"

"The two of us together like this."

"We did a pretty good job of avoiding it for a while, didn't we?"

"Come on, Ethan. We did a lousy job of avoiding it."

He laughed softly. "Maybe there's a reason for that."

"Which is?"

"Opposites attract?"

"Makes sense."

"Or maybe," he said, his voice becoming a solemn whisper, "this was just meant to be."

Meant to be.

It seemed impossible, but little else explained why something inside her seemed to recognize something inside of him. Why they seemed to be drawn to each other in spite of everything that said they shouldn't be.

Why they couldn't seem to keep their hands off each other.

Ethan moved one of his hands beneath the water. As he leaned in and kissed her neck again, he eased his hand between her legs. She gave an involuntary start of surprise, but he held her firmly and continued to touch her there as he caressed her breasts with his other hand. With every tiny shift of her body, every sigh of satisfaction, he changed direction, changed intensity, until a hot, tingly sensation began to build inside her. She tightened her fingers against his thighs, her breath coming faster, and he maintained the rhythm he'd found right up to the point where she knew she was only moments away.

"Ethan, not yet—"

When he continued, she twisted away from him, but he slid his hand from her breasts to her abdomen, holding her steady as he continued to stroke her with his other hand. "Take it easy, sweetheart."

"But I want . . . both of us . . ."

"In good time."

"But—"

"Maybe I'm moving too fast. I'll slow down."

Suddenly his fingers that had been stroking her so intensely were featherlight against her, providing just a whisper of feeling. She arched up slightly in the water, but he pulled away just enough that the touch was there but the pressure wasn't. When she groaned softly with frustration, he pressed his hand to her and resumed the maddening movement of his fingers, but as she regained the sensation and tightened her hands against his thighs, he eased away again.

"Ethan," she whispered hotly, "you don't know what you're doing to me."

"I don't?"

Yes, he did. He knew exactly what he was doing to her. He made his living reading people—their thoughts, their emotions, their intentions and he was pouring every bit of that talent into discovering exactly what made her breathless with desire.

"What they say . . . about you . . . is true . . ." she said, barely able to catch her breath.

"What's that?"

"You're an evil, *evil* man."

He laughed softly and kissed her neck, finally touching her between her legs in the way she responded to the most, caressing her breasts at the same time, and she was sure she was going to die from the pleasure of it. Only seconds passed before she felt herself on the brink again.

She sat up suddenly and floated around to face him. Kissing him again, she reached beneath the water to wrap her hand around his erection, stroking it up and down.

"Do you have a condom?" she whispered.

He reached to a ledge beside the tub and grabbed one. He opened it and tossed the package aside, then reached below the water to roll it on.

"I've never done this in water before," she told him.

He smiled and held out his hand. "I'll show you how."

He pulled her toward him, and she put her legs on either side of his thighs and her hands on his shoulders. He grasped her hips, and as she slid over him, he let out a soft groan of satisfaction. She rose above him and then lowered herself again, the water in the tub sloshing gently. She did it again and again, trying to move faster, but he put his hands against her thighs and slowed her down, concentrating her movements into slow, deep strokes that just about made her crazy.

"Ethan . . . please . . ."

"Easy, baby," he said. "We've got all night."

"No," she said breathlessly, "dinner's downstairs."

"In the fridge."

"Don't want it cold."

"That's what microwaves are for."

She moaned with pleasure, then groaned with frustration. After a moment, though, his breathing quickened and he finally began to guide her faster and harder, his body growing more tense beneath her.

"Do it now, baby," he said in a strangled voice, and she complied. "Yeah, just like that . . ."

For a few moments she continued. Then she thought better of it.

She slowed down, taking long, leisurely strokes instead of the hard, fast ones he was begging her for. He clamped his hands down on her hips, his fingers digging in as he tried to control her pace, but still she continued to move so slowly that she was driving them *both* crazy.

She leaned closer and whispered, "You want more, baby?"

"Hell, yes."

She continued to move up and down with excruciating slowness. "I'll take that under consideration."

"Look who's evil now."

She laughed softly and moved faster, clamping down hard on him, then shifting her hips to take him to the hilt with every stroke. He moved his hands to her breasts, squeezing them gently, then grasped them and ran his thumbs over her nipples. Soon the all-over tension she felt seemed to tunnel down to a single focus of energy, growing smaller but burning so hot she was sure she couldn't take it one more second, overloading her senses so much that soon she was moving by instinct alone.

Ethan's breathing suddenly escalated, becoming tight and raspy, and then all at once he clamped his hands onto her hips. He took a deep, gasping breath, then groaned her name through gritted teeth, convulsing beneath her and driving her right to the edge herself. She drove hard against him, edging closer and closer, blood pulsing wildly in her ears and her nerves coiled so tightly that she was on the verge of coming apart.

And then she did.

When the first shock wave struck her, she clutched Ethan's shoulders to steady herself, but the sensations came in such rapid succession that she felt as if she no longer had control of her own body. She gasped again and again because she couldn't breathe, and soon her head started to spin, but Ethan held her steady, arching up to meet her and grinding against her with every stroke, forcing every bit of pleasure out of the moment that he possibly could.

Finally she slowed down. Stopped. She dropped her forehead against his shoulder for a moment, trying to breathe, then turned and kissed along his neck, his jaw, before finding his mouth and kissing him hard and deep. Then she fell against him, and he closed his arms around her and hugged her tightly to his chest. It took a long time for the sensations to subside, for her muscles to relax, for her breathing to become something more than a succession of needy gasps.

After a moment, Ethan eased her off of him and turned her around until she floated into his arms. He cradled her there, kissing her forehead and letting her float back to earth again. The hum of the Jacuzzi mingled with her delicious feeling of exhaustion, and Sandy didn't think she'd ever felt more wonderful in her life.

Ethan felt the same way.

Later, as they lay in bed together, he tried to recall the last time he'd taken a woman to his bed in his house and held her in his arms like this. He couldn't remember, so he knew for a fact that the span of time could be counted in years, not months. But this woman . . .

He felt as if he wanted to keep her here forever.

And he likewise couldn't remember the last time he'd bought a woman flowers, much less laid a trail of them in order to seduce her. He'd felt a little silly doing it, but he just hadn't seemed to be able to stop himself. It was the act of a man who was infatuated. Lovestruck. So crazy about a woman that he'd do anything to please her.

In spite of the fact that her family wholeheartedly disapproved.

"I suppose I should tell you that your brother came to see me today," Ethan told her.

Sandy lifted her head. "Which one?"

"Alex."

She dropped her head back down again with an anguished groan. "Oh, *God*. At your office?"

"Yes."

"Did he make a scene?"

"Only a small one. He seems to think I need to stay away from his sister."

"I knew he'd do something stupid like that. I just *knew* it."

"It's okay, Sandy. It was nothing I couldn't handle."

"What did you tell him?"

Ethan swallowed hard at the memory, because it thrilled him and scared him to death all at the same time. *I told him I was in love with you.*

"I told him what you and I did together was none of his business."

"And then he left?"

"Pretty much."

Sandy lay back down again. She let out a sigh of frustration, tapping her fingertips against his chest. He took her hand in his, kissed her fingertips, then laid it back down again, covering it with his and stroking it softly.

"I'm sorry, Ethan. I'm so sorry."

"You have nothing to apologize for."

"He had no right to treat you that way. He may be a whole lot bigger than me, but I can still back him up against a wall and knock some sense into him. And if he messes with you again, that's exactly what I'm going to do."

Ethan smiled at the mental image that created. "No need to get into a fistfight with your brother. I just wanted you to know what happened."

"He'll come around, Ethan. They all will. It'll just take time."

Ethan wasn't completely sure about that. Her brothers loved her fiercely, and if they thought he was out to hurt her, they'd come after him with fists flying. But the truth was that if he thought somebody was out to hurt her, he'd do exactly the same thing.

Because he loved her, too.

God, how insane was that? It had been such a short time, and only airheaded idiots fell in love so quickly. Up until a week ago, he'd have said that only airheaded idiots fell in love, *period*. But now he felt his own heart ruling his head, and it confused the hell out of him.

Even though he knew just how incompatible they were at

the very core, still he was falling hard for her and he had no idea how to catch himself. He never spent much time thinking about the future, because he assumed that the days ahead would be pretty much like the ones he'd left behind. But just for a moment, he felt his mind jump ahead five spaces in the game of life, wondering what the future might hold. Wondering if Sandy could ever fit into his life.

Or, more to the point, if he could ever fit into hers.

Ethan was in court most of the next day, so it was four thirty before he got back to his office. Gina met him with good news.

"I think I've got a possibility for you," she said. "Aaron Dempsey. He lives on the outskirts of Sandy's neighborhood in the Oakwood Village Apartments. He's the right age, but I have no idea whether he fits the general description or not."

"A conviction for breaking and entering?"

"Two, actually."

"Sounds as if he's worth checking out."

Gina handed him a photocopied sheet. "Here's the information for you."

He folded the paper and stuck into his pocket. "I'm going to pay this kid a visit."

"Now?"

"No time like the present. If he's going to be Josh Newman's alibi, I'd like to get him on board." He grabbed his briefcase. "Thanks for the lead, Gina." He headed for the door. "I'll see you tomorrow."

Ethan left his office, feeling a shot of optimism. He knew the real reason he was heading over to talk to that kid right now. If he pinned him down as Josh's alibi, it meant that when Sandy got home tonight, he'd have good news to share. Just imagining the smile it would put on her face put a smile on his.

He circled around to the reception area and was almost out the door when he heard his father's voice.

"Ethan?"

He didn't even slow down. "I'm on my way out. We can talk tomorrow."

"Actually, I think this is something you're going to want to see right now."

Ethan stopped at the glass doors and turned back. "What is it?"

"Come with me."

With a silent breath of frustration, Ethan followed his father down the hall into his office. Charles went behind his desk and picked up a file.

"This arrived from the police department by courier an hour ago," he said. "I think you'll be interested in what it contains."

Ethan picked up the file, and his heart skipped when he realized what it was.

The forensic report for the Laura Williams murder.

For several seconds he just stared at it. He'd never been hesitant to open one of these before. Whatever they contained he merely made the best of. But this wasn't just any client he was defending.

He opened it slowly. As he scanned one page, then another, a sense of dread began to overtake him. With every word he read, his throat became tighter, his muscles weaker. And by the time he reached the last page, the most horrendous feeling of shock had practically knocked him to his knees.

Slowly he turned his gaze up to meet his father's. The barest hint of a smug smile crossed the man's lips, just enough to let his son know what a misguided fool he was.

Ethan slapped the file shut, tossed it down on the desk, and left his father's office. Gina was standing at the reception desk. She said something to him, but he passed by her, ripping open one of the glass doors and striding toward the elevators. A set of doors was already open. He got on, punched a button, and the elevator descended.

Seconds later he left the building and strode through the parking lot, his shock quickly being replaced by anger. Once inside his car, he called Sandy and told her to meet him at the county jail, then tossed the phone back down to the seat.

His father thought he was a misguided fool, and now it looked as if the old man was absolutely right.

chapter twenty

From the moment Sandy talked to Ethan she'd felt a heavy sense of foreboding, and now, as the guard escorted her to a visitation room, the feeling only grew stronger. Something had clearly happened, but Ethan wouldn't say what. In a tight, clipped voice, he'd merely told her to drop everything and meet him at the county jail.

When the guard let her into the room, Ethan and Josh were already there. They weren't speaking.

The guard closed the door behind her. Sandy looked back and forth between the two of them.

"What's going on?"

"Sit down," Ethan said.

She could hear the anger in his voice—hard, restrained anger bubbling just beneath the surface, and just the sound of it chilled her. She sat down.

Ethan reached into his briefcase, pulled out a file folder, and slapped it down on the table.

"What's that?" Sandy asked.

"The forensic report on the Laura Williams murder."

Sandy's heart nearly stopped. "And?"

Ethan turned to Josh. "Explain to me how your finger-prints were found on the back window of Laura's house."

Sandy froze with disbelief.

"My fingerprints?" Josh said, his eyes widening. "On the window?"

"That's right."

"I-I don't know. Maybe . . . maybe I touched it when Aaron and I went down there. That night we looked through the window."

"Try again, kid."

"No, Ethan," Sandy said. "He's right. He told you he'd been down there. He could very well have touched that window. If that's all the police have—"

"Oh, no. That's not all. You'll never guess what they found on the wood fence between the two properties."

Sandy held her breath. "What?"

"Laura Williams's blood. Near the place where Josh now admits he climbed the fence."

"Wait a minute," Josh said. "Are they saying that blood got there when I went over the fence?"

"Yes."

"No! No way! I climbed the fence. I admitted that. But I was nowhere near her house that night! How could I have gotten her blood on me for it to rub off on the fence?"

"Are you saying the crime-scene investigators got it wrong?"

"No! But that blood didn't come from me!"

"Tell the truth. You were burglarizing Laura's house. You panicked when she came home. The report says there were three rocks with Laura's blood on them. What happened, Josh? One didn't do the trick, so you picked up two more?"

"No!"

"Wait a minute, Ethan," Sandy said. "Did they find any blood on Josh's clothes?"

"No, but what does that prove? He had from ten o'clock that night until the next morning to get rid of the clothes he wore."

"Did they find his fingerprints on the murder weapon?"

"The granite was too rough. They couldn't lift any prints."

"But if Josh is guilty, then why did he call us in here to admit to being at her house on another night?"

"Because he thought he'd better admit to what he knew he was caught at, or what he was likely to get caught at. He admitted to being at the back window of Laura's house on another night, just in case he left any fingerprints. And he knew Ralph was a strong witness who was going to testify that he saw him going over that fence, so he thought he'd better come up with a story about that, too."

"But what about his alibi?" Sandy said.

"Another lie."

"You think he made that guy up?"

"Doesn't really matter. The cops have physical evidence. That beats an alibi any day." He turned back to Josh. "I told you if you lied to me, I was going to walk."

"No! I'm not lying! Not this time!"

"You little *bastard*," Ethan said. "You haven't told me the truth yet. And I'm not giving you the opportunity to lie anymore." He stood up suddenly and grabbed his briefcase.

"Ethan?" Sandy said. "Where are you going?"

He strode to the door. "We've got nothing else to discuss."

"What about Josh?"

He turned back, looking at Josh, then at Sandy, his expression cold and bitter. "He's on his own."

Ethan yanked open the door and left the room. Sandy sat there, stunned. This had to be some kind of terrible mistake. It had to be.

"Sandy," Josh said. "I swear to God I don't know how the blood got there. I didn't kill her. I swear I didn't."

"I know, Josh. I know."

"He's the only chance I had of getting out of this, and now he thinks I'm lying!"

"Please don't worry. Everything's going to be fine. Just let me go talk to him, okay?"

She rose from her chair and ran after Ethan, catching up to him just as he was leaving the building.

"Ethan! Stop!"

When he kept walking, she followed him out the door and caught his arm.

"Ethan, *please!*"

He spun around and glared at her. "I'm through, Sandy. I'm through with the lies."

"He didn't do it! I don't know how that blood got on the fence, but he didn't do it!"

"Are you kidding? The kid is a liar! He was burglarizing Laura's house and then panicked when she came home. He killed her!"

"No! It still could have been Mulroney. Murder for hire. Or maybe just a random killing—"

"Will you stop being so damned naïve?"

"Do you actually believe that Josh committed that horrible crime?"

"Who would have believed that a man like Thomas Randall would rape some poor innocent woman? But he did it. The son of a bitch was guilty."

"But Josh isn't!"

"Good *God,* Sandy! How many more times does that kid have to lie before you give *up* on him?"

Sandy flinched at his outburst, but she held her ground. "I don't give up on people."

"Then you're a goddamned fool."

He turned and strode away again, and she hurried after him. As he approached his car, he flicked the locks with his remote. When he reached for the door handle, she grabbed his wrist.

"Ethan," she said, breathing hard, "I remember what you told me about Thomas Randall. About the day you won that case. About how you were driving so fast because you wanted to get away, about how the fact that he was guilty ate at you to the point where you couldn't stand it any longer. So I know how you feel right now. You desperately need Josh to be innocent."

He jerked his wrist from her grasp. "I don't need your amateur psychoanalysis."

"After all the crap you've been through, you need to believe that you're defending somebody who deserves to be defended. And now that it looks as if he might be guilty, you can't take it. But instead of facing those feelings, you're letting Josh go to jail for something he didn't do when you have the power to make sure that doesn't happen."

"I don't give a damn how good an attorney I am. That kid is going down for this, and there's no way I can stop that."

"But you can't just abandon him. You're still his best hope!"

Ethan looked away, anger and frustration running wild on his face. For a moment she thought he was going to relent, but when he finally turned back, his expression was cold.

"You know what, Sandy? You're right. What's the point of walking away from this case? One lying client is as good as another. And you know what? I bet you're right about something else. I bet you anything I can get him off. See, I'm very, very good at helping guilty men go free. In fact," he said, his voice harsh and bitter, "I believe it's what I do best."

He yanked open his car door and got inside. He started the engine, then drove out of the parking lot and sped away.

Ten minutes later, Ethan was sitting at the bar at Bernie's, one hand wrapped around a highball glass, the other hand clenched beside it, feeling as if his mind were swimming in darkness. No matter how much he drank, he had the feeling he would still feel perfectly lucid, perfectly coherent, perfectly able to discern the truth: Josh Newman killed Laura Williams, and Sandy was a fool for believing he hadn't.

He loosened his tie and took a deep breath, then rubbed the back of his neck. Even with the cool air in the bar, he still felt hot.

He hated this feeling. It was the same one that had eaten away at him every day for the past several years, the feeling that there was nothing to trust, nothing to hold on to, nothing to believe in.

Then he'd met Sandy, and for the first time in his life, he'd wanted a woman beyond all reason, stripped himself bare for her. He'd found a tiny bit of hope for people because of the goodness he saw in her. But this was too much. Just too damned much. Even in the face of such convincing evidence that no attorney on the planet would be able to save that kid, she still believed in him.

She looked at Josh and saw an innocent man. He looked at him and saw Thomas Randall. He saw Paul McIntyre. He saw every other guilty son of a bitch he'd defended over the years for some of the most terrible crimes imaginable, men who walked away without so much as a slap on the wrist. That was reality as he knew it. Then Sandy had come into his life, and suddenly he was living in a dreamworld.

Tonight he'd woken up.

Sandy had no idea where she was going. She just drove.

Her stomach was still in turmoil, her mind reeling from the terrible things Ethan had said to her. Even though she knew his hurtful words had come from someplace inside him so raw and painful that he just couldn't face it, they had still felt like a slap across her face.

He was a man who lived for his profession, only to have it turn on him in a way he'd never anticipated. He had no family to fall back on. More enemies than friends. He had no sanctuary at all, including the place he lived. She sensed his detachment from it every time he walked through the door. Yes, it was beautiful. But it was also showy and pretentious, the kind of place people poured money into because they had nothing else. He didn't even know his neighbors.

He was a man who was connected to nothing, not even the place he called home.

Tears clouded her eyes. She blinked, trying to clear her vision, but then the road became blurry in front of her. She pulled into a convenience-store parking lot and brought her car to a halt. Putting it in park, she let it idle, tears streaming down her face.

She'd never felt so lost and alone in her life. She was thirty-seven years old and starving for the kinds of qualities in a man she'd found in Ethan. But now she wondered if that was a window that had opened for only a few moments in time, and now was slammed shut again even tighter than before.

She unzipped her purse and grabbed a packet of tissues. She wiped her eyes, willing the tears to go away. With this turn of events, Josh could very well be convicted, and it broke her heart to think about it. But even if he wasn't, Ethan would still believe he was guilty, and that gave her the most ominous feeling that nothing was ever going to be the same between them again.

She sniffed a little and took a deep, calming breath, then wiped her eyes one last time. She tossed the tissues back into her purse and started to zip it, only to see the keys to Laura's house.

Suddenly she knew what she had to do.

She put her car in gear again. She wanted to see that blood on the fence. She wanted to see it through the eyes of a person who knew Josh was innocent and was looking for another explanation. Even though it seemed hopeless that she'd find any answers, she knew his only chance might be for somebody to find something that the investigators had missed that might possibly help clear his name.

And when it was all over, maybe Ethan would believe that the tenuous trust he'd found in the past several days was worth holding on to.

* * *

"I thought I'd find you here."

Ethan turned on his bar stool to see his father standing beside him.

God, no. Not him. Not now.

Charles slid onto the stool beside Ethan. "You left the office rather abruptly this afternoon. Care to tell me why?"

"You damn well know why."

"Yes," Charles said, "I suppose I do. So does this new development mean that you're going to reconsider handing that kid thousands of dollars' worth of your services for nothing?"

Ethan was silent.

"I'll take that as a yes."

Ethan didn't want to deal with this. He just didn't. All he wanted right now was for his father and everyone else on the planet to go away and leave him the hell alone.

"Taking that case showed considerable bad judgment," Charles went on, "but rest assured that neither I nor the other partners have any intention of holding it against you. In fact, I'm going to need your help on the Mulroney case."

"The Mulroney case?" Ethan looked at him incredulously. "Have you forgotten that I was the one who was instrumental in his being arrested in the first place?"

"Of course not. But in light of the fact that he's facing murder charges, he's going to want the best team behind him he can possibly buy, so I'm sure he wouldn't hold that against you."

Ethan blinked in disbelief. Mulroney? Hold something against *him*? The absurdity of that flabbergasted Ethan so much that for a moment he was speechless.

So it had all come down to this. His father expected him to dump Josh Newman and work on Mulroney's case, which would mean that he was accepting his father's judgment and coming back into the fold.

In that moment, something shifted inside Ethan, and he had a sudden flash-forward of the man he'd be ten years from now. He'd still be in the courtroom, grinding his opponents into dust, earning his paycheck and then some, honing his already razor-sharp skills and making far more enemies than friends. And he'd be living in his town house, with its expensive furniture and stunning art and a Jacuzzi tub that would still be available for periodic one-night seductions.

There had been a time, not very long ago, when he'd thought all of that was enough.

He faced his father. "If you think I want anything to do with the Mulroney case, think again."

"Big mistake, Ethan. He's a client with very deep pockets."

"I don't give a damn if he has the key to Fort Knox. I don't want anything to do with him."

His father's stoic expression never wavered. He merely shook his head slowly, as if he were talking to an obstinate five-year-old. "This is still about that woman, isn't it?"

That woman. As if Sandy were an inanimate object of no importance at all. As if she meant nothing at all to him.

As if he weren't in love with her.

At that moment, understanding began to unfurl inside him. Sandy wasn't misguided, and she wasn't a fool. She was merely a woman who had the capacity to trust without reservation and love without expectation. She was full of positive thoughts and heartfelt encouragement, a warm, sexy woman whom he needed to hold on to with his last breath.

As every terrible word he'd spoken to her played back inside his head, Ethan felt as if he'd been kicked in the stomach. He turned his gaze to meet his father's.

"Yes. It's about Sandy. And to answer the question you asked me earlier, no, I won't reconsider representing Josh Newman. I'm staying on his case for as long as it takes to get an acquittal."

Charles sighed. "She really does have you wrapped around her finger, doesn't she?"

"Call it what you want to. I don't give a damn."

"Well. I've always known there was such a place as a fool's paradise. I just never imagined that my own son would take up residence in one."

"A fool's paradise?" Ethan said. "Maybe. But I'd rather be a fool in her world than a bitter old man in yours."

Surprise flickered across Charles's face, and he raised his chin in a warning gesture. "Watch yourself, Ethan. I don't think you have any idea what you're doing."

"Yes, I do. I know exactly what I'm doing."

With that, he stood up, tossed a few bills on the bar, and walked out. He sensed his father's angry gaze boring into his back, and he didn't give a damn. All he cared about right now was Sandy.

The moment he got into his car, he dialed his home number and got no answer. He called her cell phone, and it immediately kicked to voice mail. He tried several more times, but it wasn't until he got home that he saw why he couldn't get in touch with her.

She'd left her cell phone on the table beside the sofa.

Damn.

He had no idea where she'd gone, but eventually she'd probably end up at one of her brother's houses. And if she said anything to them about the things he'd said to her, he'd have to go through three big, brawny men with murder on their minds before he'd even get a chance to talk to her.

He had to find her *now.*

Just as he'd picked up his phone to call her flower shop on the off chance of finding her there, he heard a knock at his door. He opened it, surprised to see a little blond girl holding half a dozen boxes of cookies.

Cookies. Sandy had ordered cookies.

He remembered back to that evening. It had been such a

small, insignificant event, but still he remembered watching her talk to this kid and thinking what an incredible woman she was. And suddenly physical attraction had been the least of what he felt for her. That had been his first inkling that she just might hold the key to the things he was missing in his own life.

He'd been right about that. So damned right.

"What do I owe you?" Ethan asked.

"Eighteen dollars."

He reached for his wallet, only to realize that he'd used up most of his cash at Bernie's earlier and was a dollar short. He asked the girl to wait, then hurried up his stairs to his bedroom, where he grabbed a handful of change from the ceramic jar on his dresser.

He trotted back down the stairs. Opening his palm, he picked out four quarters. Then he realized that one of the coins in his hand wasn't a quarter at all. He held it up to examine it.

It was a small silver medallion with a cross on one side and an engraving of Jesus on the other.

Ethan stared at it with surprise. He'd given the only one of these he'd ever had to Josh. So where had he gotten this one?

He gave the girl four quarters, then shut the door behind her. He put the cookies on the entry table, then looked at the medallion again. Turning it over in his fingers, he tried to imagine where it could have come from.

Just then his phone rang. Hoping it might be Sandy, he shoved the change into his pocket and grabbed his cell phone.

"Ethan Millner."

"This is Alex. Let me talk to Sandy."

The alarm in Alex's voice brought Ethan to attention. "She's not here."

"Where is she?"

"I don't know."

"Listen to me, Millner. I just talked to Dave. He heard from the fire inspector. That fire at Sandy's house last night was no accident. There were accelerant flame patterns. Subtle but definite. Somebody set that fire on purpose."

"What?"

"The fire inspector said that the wires on the dead electrical circuit were cut. The same circuit her smoke alarms were on."

Ethan felt a shot of apprehension. "Are you telling me it's possible that somebody's trying to kill Sandy?"

"I don't know, but we need to find her. She's not answering her cell phone."

"That's because she left it here."

"I tried her shop. She's not there, either. Did she tell you when she's coming home?"

"No. Could she be at a relative's house?"

"Maybe. I'll make some calls."

"I'll go to her house," Ethan said. "It's possible that she stopped by there to pick up a few things."

"Stay in touch," Alex said. "If you find her, give me a call."

"I will. You do the same."

Ethan hung up the phone, grabbed his keys, and headed out the door.

chapter twenty-one

Sandy pulled her car into Laura's driveway and turned off the engine, stopping for a moment to stare at the house. The yellow-and-black crime-scene tape had been removed, but in her mind she would always see it. Once a murder had taken place in a home, she couldn't imagine anyone wanting to live there.

She got out of her car, walked through the gate, and circled around to the back of the house. Laura had a pretty backyard, with a brick patio, wrought-iron furniture, and pink azalea bushes clustered in beds near the house. A shovel and a few other gardening tools lay on the patio, along with two clay pots filled with soil and a pair of wilted petunia plants still in their white plastic containers. The evening sun hung low on the horizon, a huge pecan tree shading the patio from its orange-red glow.

Sandy crossed the patio, then headed to the fence between Laura's property and the Clemmons's. She didn't know exactly where Josh had climbed over it that night, so she started near the house and worked her way down, looking for the blood the forensic report said was there. But she saw nothing that looked the least bit like blood. She walked slowly, following the fence all the way to the trees at the back of the property, eyeing the weathered boards carefully.

Nothing.

She didn't understand this. If she couldn't see it, then how had the crime-scene investigators?

She turned around to start back up the fence line. Thinking she must have missed something, she looked closer this time.

Then all at once she remembered.

The rainstorm. That fierce rainstorm only a few nights ago could very well have washed away any blood remaining on the fence. She felt a rush of disappointment. She'd wanted to see for herself what the investigators had found, but the only evidence of it now was the documented samples in the crime lab. Her faint hope that she might see something they hadn't had just withered up and blown away.

As Sandy walked back to the patio, she glanced at the window that Ethan had crawled through, one of several that looked into the sunroom, broken by whatever burglar or other perpetrator had entered the house. She'd been so shocked and disoriented the night of the murder that she couldn't remember many details, only an overturned table, books and magazines scattered everywhere, and blood. Everywhere there had been blood.

In spite of the carnage she was sure to see, still she found herself drawn compulsively toward that window. Taking a deep, steadying breath, she inched forward and looked in. Even in the dim evening light, she could tell it was just as she remembered it. The table. The books and magazines.

And the blood.

It had darkened almost to black in some places, but still it was smeared everywhere.

Since the murder, she'd played over and over in her mind the scenario that must have taken place that night. She'd seen a man picking up one of the rocks in the indoor garden and striking Laura—not once, but several times—then tossing down that rock and leaving the scene. But now she remembered that the forensic report mentioned three bloody rocks.

Suddenly that seemed odd. One person had used three rocks?

Of course it was possible, but she couldn't shake the feeling that something wasn't right about that.

She dug through her purse and pulled out Laura's keys, then unlocked the door and went into the sunroom. A musty smell met her nostrils. She knew part of that was the odor of dried blood, and for a moment she felt sick. She pushed the door open wide to allow as much fresh air to enter the house as possible. Swallowing hard, she flicked on the light and gazed around the room.

It was still a horrifying sight.

The police thought Josh did this. And right now, so did Ethan. But as she looked at the carnage, the very idea of Josh destroying the room this way, crushing Laura's skull with a rock, splattering her blood, was so unfathomable that Sandy's belief in his innocence only grew stronger. Josh hadn't done this.

But somebody had.

"Sandy?"

Startled, Sandy spun around to find Ralph and Ida Clemmons standing at the back door.

Ethan drove along Briarwood Boulevard toward Sandy's house, praying that she was there. He had to find her. Protect her. Keep her safe from whomever it was who was trying to hurt her. As unfathomable as it was that someone might be trying to kill her, if that person had set fire to her house last night he must know by now that he failed. And that meant that somebody could be stalking her at this very moment.

Ethan didn't buy coincidences. A cluster of violence like this could mean only one thing. This had something to do with Laura's murder, or Vince Mulroney's arrest, or something associated with one or the other. He just didn't have a clue what it could be.

Ahead of him, the light at the intersection turned yellow. He floored the accelerator, then realized in the next instant that he was never going to make it through on the yellow light and slammed on the brake instead. He made a fishtailing stop at the cross street, cursing the red light, his foot poised over the accelerator to hit it again the moment the light turned green.

He gripped the steering wheel and closed his eyes, thinking about Sandy, images floating through his mind of how they'd made love that first night. It had been such a welcome surprise to feel her arms around him, to have her pull off his clothes with such eagerness, to dump those baskets of clothes onto the floor and drag him right down on top of her. Surrounded by darkness, they'd made love with the kind of intense desire he'd never felt with a woman before.

Darkness.

Now that he knew somebody had taken out that circuit deliberately, just that word sent apprehension flooding through him. Somebody wanted Sandy dead. And that somebody must have been in her laundry room only a few hours earlier, opening up that breaker box and . . .

And then he remembered something.

He quickly reached into his pocket and pulled out his change along with the silver medallion. And there it was. Mixed in with the coins.

Dryer lint.

He stared at it dumbly for a moment. Then all at once, understanding swept through him like a gale-force wind.

He threw the change down and grabbed his cell phone. He hit the caller ID to capture Alex's number, then pressed the talk button. It flipped to voice mail. He was on the phone.

Damn it.

Ethan hit the redial again and again, and repeatedly he was met with voice mail. When the light turned green, he floored the accelerator, heading for Sandy's neighborhood. A few minutes later, he made a right onto Oak Tree Place, then a left onto Cottonwood and sped up the block.

He punched the redial one more time. Finally Alex's phone began to ring. Once. Twice.

"Damn it, Alex," Ethan muttered, "pick up the phone!"

Two more rings. Then a click.

"Alex DeMarco."

"Alex! Have you found Sandy?"

"Not yet. I take it you haven't either?"

"No," Ethan said. "But I think I know who's out to kill her."

"We saw you in Laura's backyard," Ralph said. "What are you doing here?"

Sandy looked back and forth between Ralph and Ida, and her first thought was about how Ida had seen her and Ethan together that night in the park. She felt a surge of embarrassment.

Don't think about that now.

"You were right, Ralph," she said. "Josh did climb that fence the night of the murder. He was just too scared to say so in the beginning. But now the police are saying they found Laura's blood on the fence." She exhaled. "I know it's probably pointless, but I just wanted to come by to have another look. To see if there's something the investigators might have missed."

"So have you found anything?"

"Not yet. But I know Josh couldn't possibly have been the one who left the blood on that fence."

"You're right," Ralph said. "He couldn't have."

Sandy's heart skipped. "What?"

"That boy climbed the fence. That part's a fact. But he wasn't anywhere near the house that night."

Sandy blinked in surprise. "But you said that the only

thing you knew for sure was that Josh climbed the fence around the time of the murder."

"I lied," Ralph said.

"Lied? But why?"

"Because I didn't see him jump the fence from my patio. I saw it from here."

Sandy stared at him, confused. "The night of the murder? You were here?"

"Yes," Ida said. "Both of us. We were having a word with Laura."

A feeling of nervousness crept through Sandy. "A word? I . . . I don't understand."

"If she'd had the sense to keep her blinds shut, we might never have known," Ida said sharply. "But then we looked out the window, and there she was in this hot tub with her homosexual lover."

Sandy drew back with surprise. "You saw Laura and Chris together?"

"Yes," Ida said. "Committing unspeakable acts of abomination."

"And the fact that she seemed like a nice girl tells us just how devious the devil can be," Ralph said. "But this is our neighborhood. A place where decent people live. We don't tolerate her kind here. Laura had to go."

Sandy felt a jolt of apprehension. *Had to go?*

All at once the truth hit her. Her knees went weak, and she gripped the edge of the hot tub to steady herself, only to realize that she'd rubbed her hand across a patch of dried blood. She gasped and yanked her hand back, staring in horror at the brick-red blotch on her palm, then snapped her gaze up to meet Ralph's.

"Are you telling me you did this? *You* killed Laura?"

"The devil comes in all forms. It's up to us to battle him wherever we find him."

Oh, God. They're the ones. They did it.

Suddenly the faces that had seemed like friends before had transformed into something ugly and wicked and full of anger—harsh, righteous, judgmental anger. Fay's words swept through Sandy's mind: *Whoever killed Laura Williams was one pissed-off son of a bitch.*

"And you, Sandy." Ida shook her head. "You seemed like a nice girl, too. Right up to the moment that I saw you fornicating with that man in a public place. Even in the darkness, I saw the light in your eyes. I saw you *reveling* in that behavior."

"We tried to punish both of you last night," Ralph said. "Unfortunately, the devil woke you in time."

Sandy's head swam with shock. "My house? The fire? You started the fire?"

"Yes."

"There have been other fires—"

"Yes. Evil is everywhere. But that doesn't mean we have to tolerate it. And if you and that lawyer hadn't shown up that night, this house would be nothing but a pile of ashes, too."

Sandy felt a shudder of cold, clammy fear. They weren't rational. They weren't even sane.

They were murderers.

"The devil himself is inside you," Ralph said. "And there's only one way to deal with that."

This couldn't be happening. It couldn't. The carnage in this room . . . Ralph and Ida . . . she tried to tell herself that it just couldn't be.

Then Ralph reached for a rock.

Sandy froze, horror slithering along every nerve. "Ralph? What are you doing?"

"Sending you to the devil where you belong. Just as we sent Laura."

"Ralph Clemmons?" Alex said. "No way. I've met that guy. There's no way—"

"Damn it, Alex, I'm telling you it's him!" Ethan pulled to the curb in front of the Clemmons's house.

"What's his motive?"

"I don't know. But he clipped the wires to Sandy's fuse box. He and his wife feed her cat when she's out of town, so I'm betting he had a key to her house. I know it was him because he accidentally left something behind."

"What?"

"I can't go into it now. Just meet me at the Clemmons's house and I'll explain everything. And send a couple of patrol cops for good measure. You've got to grab him before he has a chance to—"

Ethan stopped short. He'd just happened to glance at Laura's house next door, and he couldn't believe what he saw in the driveway.

Sandy's car.

"Hold on, Alex. I found Sandy."

"What? Where is she?"

"At Laura Williams's house." He hit the gas again, continuing down the street.

"What the hell is she doing there?" Alex asked.

Ethan reached Laura's driveway, pulled his car in behind Sandy's, and killed the engine. "I don't know, but I'm going to find out." He got out of the car and strode to the front porch.

That was when he heard the scream.

"Alex!" he shouted into the phone. "I hear Sandy! She's in trouble! Twenty-two forty-three Cottonwood. Get the cops over there *now!*"

Ethan tossed his phone down and raced up the front steps. He tried to open the door. It was locked. He banged on it.

"Sandy!" he shouted. "Are you in there?"

"Ethan! Help me! *Please!*"

Every cry shocked Ethan's nervous system like a thunderbolt. He backed away and smacked his shoulder against the door once, twice. It wouldn't budge.

He picked up a flowerpot from the front porch, stepped back, and hurled it through the front window. The glass shattered, and he climbed through the broken window, oblivious to the shards of glass slicing along his back and arms. He fell to the floor in the living room, but in the next instant he was on his feet again.

"Sandy! Where are you?"

"Ethan! Help!"

Her voice sounded weaker. He raced toward the sound of her cries, into the dining room and through the kitchen.

The sunroom. She was in the sunroom.

He came around the doorway, stunned to see Sandy on the floor, curled into a tight ball, lying in the middle of the carnage that had never been cleaned up. Her arms were thrown up over her head. And there was blood.

Not Laura's blood.

Sandy's.

He started toward her, only to hear movement behind him. He spun around just in time to see a stone leave Ralph Clemmons's hand. It struck him in the head, and as he fell to the floor beside Sandy in a haze of near-unconsciousness, he heard the shrill, judgmental voice of Ida Clemmons damning him to hell.

chapter twenty-two

Ethan lay on the floor of the sunroom, his head stabbed by pain, his muscles refusing to move. Somewhere in the far distance, he heard sirens. Or was he imagining them?

With a painful groan, he rolled to one side. Through blurry eyes, he saw Sandy lying beside him, blood seeping from a wound on her forehead. She wasn't moving.

"Sandy?"

His throat felt tight, his voice almost inaudible. He coughed, took a deep breath, then coughed again. He blinked to clear his sight, and what he saw stunned him.

Fire.

To his right, flames had consumed the doorway into the kitchen. His head pounding, he sat up and turned around to look at the back of the room. Fire was licking at the walls, encroaching on the door leading out to the patio. Fighting dizziness, he rose to his knees.

"Sandy! Wake up! *Sandy!*"

Still she lay motionless.

Ethan's head pounded wickedly, but from somewhere deep inside he gathered the strength to rise to his feet. Smoke surrounded him, searing his lungs with every breath.

They had to get out of there *now*.

He gathered Sandy in his arms, holding her tightly as he stumbled toward the door. It stood ajar, and he shoved it open with his shoulder, gritting his teeth against the unbearable heat of the fire whipping at his legs. He lurched through the doorway, then staggered across the patio. He carried Sandy as far as he could into the yard before dizziness overtook him and he fell to his knees.

He laid her on the lawn. Her face was streaked with blood, and she had bruises on her forehead and cheek. For a few terrible moments, he wasn't sure she was breathing. Then he saw her chest rise and fall with shallow respirations.

"Sandy?" he said, coughing. "Are you all right? Come on, baby. Talk to me."

When she still didn't move, panic swelled inside him. Then he heard sirens wailing in the distance. *Thank God.* Somebody had seen the fire and had called the fire department, which meant an ambulance wouldn't be far behind.

Then all at once, Ethan felt something cold and wet slosh across his back. Startled, he spun around. Even without the fiery feeling of the liquid penetrating the cuts on his arms and back, one whiff would have told him what it was.

Gasoline.

Several feet away, he saw Ralph toss a can to the ground. Ida stood beside him.

She held a box of matches.

For the next several seconds, everything seemed to move in slow motion. Ida pulling out a match. Scratching it across the box. The match bursting into flame.

There was only one thing Ethan could do.

With a surge of anger, he rose to his feet and dove at Ralph, knocking him to his back. Ralph flipped over and tried to crawl away, but Ethan grabbed him by his shirt and dragged him back. With a surge of energy fueled by sheer fury, Ethan pulled him to his knees and clamped his arm around his neck. Ralph gasped for air, but Ethan dragged him around in a half circle and glared up at Ida.

"Go ahead, you old bat," he said, breathing hard. "Throw that match. Ralph can go right up in flames with me."

The woman's jaw tightened with anger, and her hand began to quiver. The glow of the fire formed an eerie halo around her head, adding a surreal component to her expression of sheer hatred. She dropped the match. It hit the lawn and fizzled out.

Ethan tightened his grip on Ralph until the man coughed and gagged. "Toss the matches away," he told Ida, "or I swear to God I'll break his neck."

As she threw the matches several feet away, Ethan saw a pair of patrol cops racing toward them, their weapons drawn. As one held a gun on Ralph, the other one yanked him up and snapped on a pair of handcuffs. Ethan told them that Ida was part of it, too, and one of the cops took her arm, pulled her hands behind her back, and bound them in cuffs.

For a moment, Ida stared at the cop as if there had been some hideous mistake, as if the wrong perpetrator were being taken into custody. Then, as her fate settled over her, she turned and glared at Ethan in one last gesture of defiance, her face twisted into a mask of anger.

"I hope you burn in hell."

As the cop tugged on her arm and led her away, Ethan knew for a fact that somebody was going to be burning in hell very soon, but it wasn't going to be him.

Coughing hard to clear his lungs of smoke, he crawled back to Sandy's side. Still doused in gasoline, he didn't dare touch her, but he edged close enough to see that she still wasn't moving. He wasn't even sure she was breathing. Panic surged through him. He swung around to see a pair of paramedics racing toward them.

"Hurry!" he shouted. "Get over here *now*!"

They knelt at Sandy's side. Felt for a pulse. Checked her pupils.

"Is she okay?" Ethan asked.

The paramedic snapped his gaze up to look at Ethan. "Do I smell gasoline?"

"Yes."

"There's a fire burning. Sparks. You need to get the hell away from this house!"

Sandy stirred, slowly blinking her eyes open. "Ethan?"

Hope surged through him. "Sandy? I'm right here."

"They killed Laura," she murmured. "Tried to kill me."

"I know, sweetheart. I know. But you're going to be okay. They're taking you to the hospital."

The paramedic turned to a cop who'd just come into the backyard. "Hey! Somebody get this guy out of here! He's covered in gasoline!"

"Ethan?" Sandy said, coughing a little. "Don't leave me."

"I'm right here."

"Ethan?" She spoke so softly he could barely hear her. He leaned closer.

"What?"

"I love you."

Ethan heard the words, but it took a second or two for them to sink in. And the moment they did, it was as if the earth stopped spinning. Even in the midst of all the turmoil, for a moment he could think of nothing else.

I love you.

Then her eyes slowly drifted closed again.

"Sandy?"

All at once a cop grabbed Ethan's arm and pulled him to his feet.

No. He couldn't leave her. Not now.

He yanked his arm loose and started back toward Sandy. The cop grabbed him again. Ethan tried to pull away again, but the man held him tightly.

"Damn it!" Ethan shouted. "Will you let me *go*?"

"Man, you need to get out of here! You're covered in gasoline, and that fire's going crazy. In a minute the sparks are gonna really start flying!"

"But she's unconscious again. I have to make sure she's all right!"

"Do you want her going up in flames right along with you? Now, come on!"

Finally Ethan relented and allowed the cop to pull him away from Sandy, only to see the paramedic put his fingers to her wrist and check her pupils again. His brows pulled together with worry, and he shouted at the men bringing the stretcher to hurry.

"They'll take care of her," the cop said, pulling him along. "There's nothing you can do for her. Let them handle it."

He was right. It was out of his hands. He'd gotten to the house to save her, but the thought that he might have been only seconds too late was almost more than he could bear.

The cop quickly led him along the side of the house that wasn't burning, and when they emerged into the front yard, Ethan looked back to see flames rapidly consuming the house, the fire lighting the evening sky and smoke billowing toward the heavens. Sirens wailed as more emergency vehicles arrived at the scene and police officers and firefighters poured out. He waited on the sidewalk in front of the house, filled with fear for Sandy's life and hatred for Ralph and Ida Clemmons, for their Bible-beating, holier-than-thou righteousness that had driven them to hurt a woman like her. He only wished he'd had the opportunity to tear them apart with his bare hands.

I love you.

He didn't allow himself to think that Sandy had actually meant that. It had to have been a product of her delirium, or maybe his own wishful thinking. But still the words kept echoing through his mind, giving him a glimpse of the tomorrow that might be waiting for them if only they could pull through tonight.

Finally the paramedics came around the house. As they loaded Sandy into the ambulance, she still wasn't moving, and Ethan felt another surge of panic. As the ambulance took off, he leaped into his car to follow it, thankful that the emergency vehicles hadn't blocked him in. He knew the cops would want him to stay at the scene for questioning, but he didn't give a damn about that.

He tailed the ambulance successfully for a few miles, but then they hit an intersection where the ambulance made it through the light and he didn't. Cursing, he brought his car to a halt, gripping the steering wheel impatiently until the light changed and he hit the gas again. Every mile he drove across town seemed like a hundred, and by the time he reached the emergency room he could barely breathe for the anxiety he felt.

He parked his car and rushed inside, his stomach in knots. When he went to the window and asked about Sandy, the clerk told him she'd send a doctor out to talk to him.

Ethan gave her his name, then took a seat in the sparsely populated waiting room. Fortunately the gasoline on his clothes was nearly dry, so the smell wasn't as strong as before. He didn't want anyone telling him he had to leave.

His mind drifted to what had happened this afternoon, filling him with shame and regret. If only he'd listened to Sandy when that forensic report came back. If only he'd let her be the voice of reason, they'd have gone home together, come to grips with what had happened, and searched for a way to deal with it. Instead, he'd gone back to being the man he never should have been in the first place, the one who trusted no one, who believed only in the dark side of life.

Then he'd called her a fool and left her behind.

Right now his head was pounding and the cuts on his back and arms stung like hell, but he didn't give a damn about any of that. He just wanted somebody to tell him that Sandy was safe. He wanted to tell her how sorry he was for the things he'd said to her and beg her forgiveness. He wanted to know that the words she'd spoken to him a few minutes ago weren't the last ones he'd ever hear her say.

He wanted to tell her he loved her, too.

He couldn't believe this. Until a few days ago, he couldn't have fathomed even thinking those words, much less saying them, but now they seemed as much a part of his thought process as Sandy was part of his life.

The desperation he felt was almost incapacitating. He dropped his elbows to his knees, put his head in his hands, and prayed to a God he wasn't even sure existed that she was going to be all right.

"Mr. Millner?"

Ethan jerked his head up to see a man in green scrubs. "Yes?"

"Are you a relative of Ms. DeMarco's?"

He stood up. "No. I'm a friend. How is she?"

"She's going to be just fine. And she's asking for you."

A flood of emotion hit Ethan all at once, so much so that his knees actually buckled and he had to put his hand on the back of his chair to steady himself. All the tension he'd felt for the past half hour seemed to drain right out of him, leaving him weak with relief.

Sandy was alive. She was going to be okay.

"She regained consciousness on the way to the hospital," the doctor said. "Her neurological signs are good, but we took her up for a CT scan just to make sure there's no internal bleeding."

"Thank God she's okay. When can I see her?"

"Imaging is a little backed up. It could be an hour or so before they put her in a room. She'll need to stay overnight for observation." The doctor eyed him up and down. "Looks like you could use a little medical attention yourself."

"Yeah," Ethan said. "I guess I could."

"Anything but bruises and lacerations?"

"No, I don't think so."

"Is that gasoline I smell?"

"Yeah. There's kind of a strange story behind that."

"I work in the ER. I've heard 'em all."

Ethan sincerely doubted the doctor had heard this one.

"Come on back," the doctor said. "You can get a shower, and then I'll take a look at you. Once I'm finished, you can go see Ms. DeMarco."

Sandy lay in a hospital bed, her head pounding unmercifully and every muscle in her body aching. After the CT scan, they'd told her that her injuries weren't severe and that she could go home after a night of observation in the hospital.

She closed her eyes, trying to remember everything that had happened tonight. She remembered the rocks striking her. Falling. Then Ethan's voice, calling to her from the front porch.

The next thing she remembered was lying on the grass in the backyard, the house burning in the distance, and Ethan staring down at her, talking to her, his face so full of worry. Even though her head had been pounding and her mind blurry, she knew that somehow he'd gotten her out of the house and they were safe.

"Sandy?"

She looked up to see Ethan standing at the door, and her heart melted at the sight. He wore hospital scrubs, and his hair was damp and sticking straight up, as if he'd just gotten out of the shower and hadn't bothered to comb it. There were two stitched cuts on his right arm and one across his left cheek, and a purplish-blue bruise spanned one side of his forehead. But even with all that, he'd never looked better to her than he did right now.

She held out her hand. He came into the room, sat down on her bed, and took her hand in his.

"You're hurt," she said, her voice a little groggy. "Where did the cuts come from?"

"I broke Laura's living room window and climbed through it. Guess I got a little hung up along the way. How are you doing?"

"Fine now. Little bit of a headache."

"So it really was Ralph and Ida who killed Laura?"

"Yes. God, Ethan, I couldn't believe it was them. I was so scared, but then you were there, and you got me out of that burning house. . . ." She closed her eyes. "They were going to kill us both."

"Yes."

"They've killed other people in the neighborhood. Set fire to other houses. And they had intended to set fire to Laura's house, too—"

"It's over now. They're in custody."

"You knew I was in trouble. How did you know that?"

"I'll tell you all about that later." He squeezed her hand. "Why did you go to Laura's house tonight?"

"I don't know. I was just so worried about Josh. I guess I just thought maybe I'd see something that the crime-scene investigators hadn't. I know it was stupid, but . . ."

"But you were desperate. Because I threatened to give up the case."

She sighed. "Yes. I guess I was."

Ethan's eyes drifted closed. "I'm sorry, Sandy. So sorry. If I hadn't said all those things to you this afternoon—"

"I don't want to talk about that. It doesn't matter now."

"But I want to tell you why I did it. It doesn't excuse it, but I want to tell you why."

Finally Sandy nodded.

"I was in my father's office this afternoon. He handed me the forensic report. And when I opened it . . . God, Sandy." He shook his head helplessly. "You were right. I needed Josh to be innocent. For once in my life, I needed to feel as if I were defending somebody who deserved it. And when it looked as if he might be guilty . . ."

His voice trailed off. He sat there as if searching for words to explain what he felt at that moment and was coming up short.

"It was the last straw," Sandy said quietly. "You felt as if there was no hope for anything anymore."

He met her gaze for a moment, then nodded slowly. "Yes. I just hope you can forgive me for everything that's happened."

Sandy stroked his hand. "Ethan? Do you remember what I said to you when I was lying in the backyard?"

He swallowed hard. "Uh . . . maybe you'd better tell me again."

"I told you I loved you."

He looked away. "This is an emotional situation. It's easy to say things you don't mean."

"I meant it. I know it doesn't seem possible, but . . . " She stopped, searching for words. "I was just going through the motions of my life. It was a good life, but I knew there had to be more. And then I met you." She closed her hand over his and squeezed it softly. "You make me think. You make me laugh. You make me feel sexier than any woman within shouting distance of age forty has a right to. You make me feel things I've never felt before." She paused again, tears coming to her eyes. "You're the man I've been looking for all my life."

For a moment, he looked stunned, staring at her as if he didn't know what to say.

"I'm not sure you know what you're getting yourself into," he said.

"What do you mean by that?"

"I've been known to be opinionated."

"Uh-huh."

"And egotistical."

"On occasion."

"I've got more baggage than a seven-forty-seven en route to China. And you know very well that I don't know the first thing about relationships."

"So you've said."

"But let me tell you something."

He stroked her hand gently, then bowed his head. When he lifted it again, she was surprised to see his eyes glistening.

"You might find another man who's a lot quicker on the uptake when it comes to being the kind of man a woman like you deserves. But you will never find one who loves you as much as I do. *Never.*"

Sandy sat up suddenly and slid her arms around his neck. He pulled her right up next to him and hugged her tightly.

Ethan couldn't believe this was happening. He'd known what it felt like to want a woman's body, but he'd had no clue what it felt like to want her mind, her heart, her soul.

Until he met Sandy.

Maybe it was the fact that every word she spoke came straight from her heart without stopping along the way to collect an ulterior motive. Maybe it was her unremitting belief in another human being even in the face of damning evidence against him.

Or maybe it was the feeling he got that if she ever loved a man, she'd never let him go.

"Thank God you're safe," he whispered. "If anything had happened to you . . ."

He rocked her gently, wanting her to feel warm and contented and very, very loved.

"So does this mean you're going to stick around for a little while?" she asked.

He smiled. "Yeah. But don't be surprised if the time comes when you wish to God that you'd never said a word about tomorrows. I'm going to be just like one of those pitiful stray cats you feed once and he won't go away, so don't count on being able to get rid of me."

"Is that a promise?"

He leaned in and touched his lips to hers. "Yes. That's a promise."

"Millner."

Ethan spun around. Alex was standing at the door.

"I need to talk to you."

Damn. Ethan didn't want to deal with this right now, but he would if he had to. He was ready for anything the man intended to throw at him. Whatever it was, though, it wouldn't change a thing, because no one was coming between him and Sandy.

He stood up slowly, meeting Alex's gaze. "Don't even think about messing with me, Alex. I told you before that what happens between me and Sandy is none of your business, and I damn well meant it."

"You're right. It's none of my business."

"What?"

"Alex has already been by," Sandy said. "We've talked. I told him everything that happened tonight. And a lot of other things."

Alex walked into the room. "You saved Sandy's life." He stuck out his hand. "Thank you."

Ethan stared at his hand for a moment, then slowly reached out and shook it.

"When you told me you'd protect her with your life," Alex said, "it looks as if you meant it."

"I did. Every word."

"And it also looks as if she's in good hands in the future."

"Bank on it."

"It seems she's in love with you."

He glanced at Sandy, and her smile told him that her conversation with Alex had indeed been a detailed one. "It seems so."

"You told me you were in love with her. Did you mean it?"

"Every word."

Alex nodded. "I'm gonna tell you the truth here, Millner. Sandy could probably talk to me until the end of time and I still wouldn't understand what the two of you have together. But I don't have to understand. If she says she loves you, that's good enough for me."

In that moment, Ethan understood. This wasn't a matter of Alex being controlling because he could and making life miserable for Sandy because he enjoyed throwing his weight around. It was that he loved her so much that he'd stand squarely in the way of anyone who he thought was trying to hurt her.

Ethan knew exactly how he felt.

"I know we've had a few battles in the past," Ethan said. "And some of them haven't been pretty. But I'm hoping that's where all of that can stay. In the past."

Alex sighed with exasperation. "You know, Millner, you're making it pretty damned hard for me to keep on hating you."

"For reasons I can't quite fathom," Ethan said, "you seem to be causing me the same problem."

Alex nodded. "We can deal with that crisis later." He turned to Sandy. "The rest of the family is on their way over. But don't worry. I'll run interference. Let everybody know what happened tonight. And what's going on with you two."

As Alex turned to leave, Ethan leaned in to give Sandy another kiss. Alex stopped at the door. He stared at them, shaking his head.

"Alex?" Sandy said. "What's wrong?"

"It's okay, Sandy. I'm accepting this. I really am. But . . ." He looked back and forth between her and Ethan, then expelled a sigh of frustration. "There's still something so freakin' *wrong* with this picture."

"Get used to it," Ethan said. "You're going to be seeing a lot of it."

"I know. It's just that I just never . . . I mean, not in my wildest *dreams* did I ever think . . ."

"I know," Ethan said. "But you'll be pleased to know that I checked the weather report tonight, and contrary to what you might think, hell did *not* freeze over."

Alex stared dumbly at Ethan for a moment, then turned his gaze to Sandy. "He's gonna be a real smart-ass, isn't he?"

"I'm afraid so."

"Well, that's something to look forward to." He sighed with resignation. "I'll be outside if you need me."

He walked out of the room, and Ethan gave Sandy a smile. "Think he'll ever get over it?"

"Don't worry about Alex. Believe it or not, his bark really is worse than his bite."

"If you don't mind, I think I'll keep looking over my shoulder for a little while longer."

Sandy leaned back against her pillow. "You know, I was thinking . . ."

"What?"

"When I get out of this hospital, maybe it's still not too late for that birthday cake."

He smiled. "Sounds great. Can I also have the dessert that comes after the dessert?"

"Just say the word."

He took Sandy in his arms again, wondering if the day would ever come when he wasn't dying to touch her.

He knew the answer was no.

As much as he wanted to stay with her, though, in just a few minutes he was going to leave her in the care of her family, because there was something he needed to take care of. Josh deserved to get out of jail as quickly as possible, to go home to his grandmother and move toward making that relationship whole again, and Ethan was going to do everything he could to make sure that happened. Then tomorrow he was going to phone Chris to see what was going on with her custody battle. If that hotshot divorce lawyer Russell Green tried to mess with her, he wasn't going to know what hit him.

And soon Ethan intended to leave his father's firm. Where he was going, he didn't have a clue. The destination didn't matter as much as the departure did. And he'd bring Gina with him. Gina, who'd been a friend to him beyond the call of duty. Now more than ever he knew that having a person like her in his life was a rare and valuable thing, and he had no intention of letting her go.

And somewhere down the line, he was going to sell that ostentatious town house of his and move someplace else. And he intended for that someplace else to be a big, rambling, drafty house on Magnolia Street, which he'd repair, rewire, and rework to any specification Sandy wanted, then stay there with her for the rest of their lives.

Okay, so he was getting a little ahead of himself. They'd barely said "I love you," and already he had them growing old together, but he just couldn't help it. Sandy had given him the kind of hope for the future that he never thought he'd have in this lifetime.

He leaned in and touched his lips to hers, unable to believe that he'd found someone to trust. Someone to love. Someone who was immersed in the kind of warm, wonderful life that had eluded him all of his, who would reach out a hand to draw him into it. He needed a woman like that as much as he needed air to breathe, and he hadn't even realized it.

And Sandy was the one.